A Cowboy Proposal

Christian Contemporary Western Romance

Brush Creek Cowboys Romance

Book Three

Liz Isaacson

ISBN-13: 978-1638760832

"Therefore I say unto you, Take no thought for your life, what
ye shall eat, or what ye shall drink; nor yet for your body,
what ye shall put on. Is not the life more than meat, and the
body than raiment?
Behold the fowls of the air: for they sow not, neither do they
reap, nor gather into barns; yet your heavenly Father feedeth
them. Are ye not much better than they?
Which of you by taking thought can add one cubit unto his
stature?
And why take ye thought for raiment? Consider the lilies of
the field, how they grow; they toil not, neither do they spin:
And yet I say unto you, That even Solomon in all his glory
was not arrayed like one of these.
Wherefore, if God so clothe the grass of the field, which to day
is, and to morrow is cast into the oven, shall he not much
more clothe you, O ye of little faith?
Therefore take no thought, saying, What shall we eat? or,
What shall we drink? or, Wherewithal shall we be clothed?
(For after all these things do the Gentiles seek:) for your
heavenly Father knoweth that ye have need of all these things.
But seek ye first the kingdom of God, and his righteousness;
and all these things shall be added unto you."

Matthew 6: 25-33

Chapter 1

Ted Caldwell whistled as he put the horse he'd worked with all morning in his stall. "You'll get it tomorrow, Yellowstone." The horse had a long way to go, but Ted just gave the animal a grin and turned toward the tack room. Yellowstone was a natural bucker, and he'd be a fantastic bronco for the rodeo if Ted could get him trained up right.

He hung up the saddle, his stomach growling for something to eat. He hadn't heard from Landon or any of the other cowboys, but Megan usually had something laid out for lunch at the homestead, especially in the summertime.

His cowboy boots made clomping noises on the packed dirt as he made his way past the exercise circle and the huge, covered horse arena. He was one of six cowboys that lived full-time at Brush Creek Horse Ranch, working and training horses for the rodeo circuit. Each of the cowboys had a different specialty, and Ted's was getting the broncos set to win championships. It could take him a couple of years to get a single horse ready, and he never worked with more than three at a time.

Right now he only had two, which gave him a bit more time to help with regular ranch duties like working in the fields and making sure the pastures stayed fenced. His spirit warmed when he thought about the weekend before him. Tomorrow afternoon, he'd take his two broncs out to the pastures by the red rock buttes, where they'd stay for a couple of days. He'd been working the horses hard lately, and everyone—himself included—needed a break.

"Landon?" he called as he entered the homestead through the sliding glass door off the pool. "Megan?" The owners of the ranch, Landon and Megan had just had their third child. Megan had only been home from the hospital for about a week, and their four-year-old twins could usually be heard from anywhere on the ranch.

But Ted couldn't hear anything right now. Neither Megan nor Landon seemed to be around, but all the sandwich stuff spread across the kitchen counter meant lunch was on at the homestead. Other cowboys had obviously been through the line, as the meat and cheese was out of the bags and the lids on the mayo and mustard had been popped.

Ted picked up his whistling again as he bustled around the kitchen, slathering mayo on white bread and then layering turkey, roast beef, and provolone on top of that. Instead of taking just a handful of chips from one of the bags, he snagged the whole, crinkly container and headed toward the front door.

The backyard baked in the Utah sun, so Megan had put

a table and enough chairs for all the cowboys to eat lunch on the front patio, where the shade kept everyone cool. As Ted exited the house, with its blessed air conditioning, he remembered how little the shade actually did in mid-July.

He sighed and took a seat at the table beside Blake, the newest member of the cowboy team at Brush Creek. "How's everyone?" He tucked a napkin into the front of his shirt and exhaled happily.

Blake chuckled. "You and that ridiculous napkin." He swiped at it, but Ted dodged him and dug into his sandwich.

"This napkin keeps my clothes pristine." He used it to wipe his beard and mustache. "And my beautiful beard lookin' great."

"For who?" Blake challenged. "Us? All the women out here are already married." He glanced across the lane to the row of cowboy cabins, two of which now housed families and not just men. Ted hadn't given much thought to expanding the residents in his cabin; he hadn't dated in the five years since he'd arrived at the ranch, since he'd left the rodeo circuit after breaking six ribs and a leg. He didn't walk with a limp, and he had enough money in the bank that he didn't have to work at all. He counted his lucky stars everyday that he'd landed at Brush Creek and could still feel the calming influence of the horses.

Walker mentioned there were lots of available women down in town, and lunch concluded. Ted stayed at the table, having only been there for a few minutes. He stretched out and put both his hands behind his head. The blue sky with those puffy white clouds made him smile.

Something crashed in the house, and Ted got to his feet, curiosity burning through him. He wanted another sandwich anyway, so he re-entered the house, expecting to see Megan carrying her newborn and trying to keep the twins away from whatever she'd broken.

He didn't see her, but another brunette, whose hair color obviously came from a bottle, along with the numerous lighter brown and blonde streaks that fell across her shoulders.

This woman crouched low to the ground, picking up pieces of a glass bowl that had broken. She muttered under her breath and didn't seem to notice Ted as he approached —a real feat considering the size of his cowboy boots and the echoing tile floor.

"Do you need some help?" he said in his gentlest voice, the one he used on the wild horses when they first arrived at the ranch.

She jumped away from him, straightening and covering her heart with her palm. "You don't have to yell."

Ted blinked at her and looked around the house, as if someone would appear and confirm that he hadn't yelled. "I'll get the broom."

"Never mind." She looked annoyed, but surely she couldn't have a problem with him. "I'll just use a wet paper towel." Her eyes didn't land directly on his as she moved to the sink and ran the water over a half dozen paper towels. She wrung them out and then swiped the makeshift pad across the floor where the break had happened. "It gets all the tiniest pieces." She threw the paper towels in the trash and finally faced him.

Her frown deepened and she wrinkled her nose as if he smelled like horse manure. Maybe he did. "Who are you?"

"Ted Caldwell. I work with the broncos." He grinned at her, pleased when she allowed her lips to curl up slightly. "Who are you?" He allowed his eyes to travel down the length of her body, drinking in her tight jeans and billowy blouse. It was the color of shamrocks and covered with flowers.

She folded her arms. "April." Her voice indicated that he'd just used the only question she'd allow. "Excuse me." She started toward the steps that led to the basement, but her hip bumped into the sideboard and a vase teetered, tipped, toppled to the ground.

April froze as more glass, this time with real wildflowers and water, spilled across the floor. She turned back to Ted with a smile with the wattage of the sun. "Could you get the broom now?"

Ted thought he'd do whatever this woman asked, and he stepped over to the pantry like an obedient dog. He shook his head as he realized what track his thoughts had gone down. Confusion riddled through him. Ted Caldwell didn't date. Hadn't dated. Wasn't interested.

But as he turned back to April, broom in hand, he wondered if maybe it was time to *get* interested. "What's your last name, April?" he asked as he wielded the broom with precision to get all the bigger pieces of glass.

"Nox."

"Where are you from?" He threw the broken glass in the trashcan and reached for the roll of paper towels.

April leaned against the back of the couch that

bordered the living room and folded her arms again. As Ted wrung out the paper towels, he noticed a distinct bump beneath her arms. His fingers stuttered and he flat-out stared.

"Wyoming," she said, her voice as sour as chokecherries. "And yes, I'm pregnant."

Chapter 2

April couldn't help the disdain, the disgust, the danger in her voice. The cowboy was staring at her. Blinking every few seconds, but staring, like a pregnant woman in Brush Creek was an anomaly.

She saw him search for a wedding ring, but he wouldn't find one. At least not today, as she kept her left hand buried beneath her right arm. But he'd find out soon enough. Everyone would, which was why she'd left Jackson Hole for this hole-in-the-wall town. Angry tears pressed against her eyes, but she wouldn't release them, not in front of Ted.

"Oh, well, congratulations." A giant of a man, Ted tore his eyes from hers, bent, and cleaned up the shards the way she had the first time. "There we go." Every word he spoke seemed too loud, but that could've just been a side-effect of April's foul mood and constant headache since she'd found out she was pregnant.

If she were looking to date in Brush Creek, Ted probably would have landed near the top of her list. Tall, broad, dark-haired. And that delicious full beard…. April turned away from him to keep her spiraling emotions in check.

The fact was, she wasn't looking to date. Not now, and not for a while. And certainly not anyone in Brush Creek. She'd only be here for five months—just long enough to have the baby, give it up for adoption, and move to a big city where no one knew her. Where she didn't have to explain anything to anyone.

"Congratulations aren't in order," she said, facing the stairs again. She needed to get out of there before she said something she couldn't take back. She'd said too much already.

"Oh, well, I'm sorry then."

"Nothing to be sorry about," she said over her shoulder, her eyes catching on Ted's for just a moment. Long enough to make her pause and add, "Thanks for your help."

He nodded, one hand going to the top of his cowboy hat. "Anything for a pretty lady."

She flashed a tight smile and escaped back to the basement. She'd come upstairs looking for something to eat, but the sight of that slimy mayo had made her stomach revolt. She'd become clumsier and clumsier in the past four months, and dropping a glass and then knocking a vase off a table were almost commonplace events these days.

Let me know when you get home and I'll come help with the kids. She sent the text to Megan and settled down on the queen bed she'd been given. She had a nice bedroom, equipped with a flat-screen TV, excellent WiFi, and a private bathroom, a living area, and a kitchenette. She could exist down here without anyone ever knowing, but that wasn't part of the deal.

Oh, no. April was to help Megan with the baby and the twins. Not only that, but she was to become a cowgirl herself, working with horses and moving pipes and whatever else she needed to do to earn her keep on this ranch.

She curled around her stomach and closed her eyes, the need to cry pressing hotly against the back of her throat. Not a single tear fell, because she'd already cried herself dry. First when she found out she was pregnant, then when the father of the baby told her he wasn't interested in marrying her, then when she had to tell her parents about it all.

Her mother's words still rang in her ears. You're thirty years old, April. You should know better.

And her father's: I'm so disappointed in you, April.

She'd left Jackson Hole to get away from their disappointment, and maybe to run away. In her most honest moments, she admitted that she'd left Jackson just to get away from everyone and everything she'd ever known.

No one would find her here, she knew that. The friends she'd left behind knew she disliked cowboys almost as much as used car salesmen.

Her phone woke her sometime later. The sun still cascaded through the window, so she hadn't lost too much time. She sat up and found a text from Megan. *Home in twenty minutes. Would love some help making dinner.*

Sure. April scooted to the edge of the bed and ran her hands over her face, noting the absence of her eyelash extensions. Her makeup. Everything she used to do to make herself presentable to the public.

Lord, she prayed. Help me fix the mistakes I've made.

She'd lost her way several years ago, made some bad choices, some more obvious than others. She rested her hands on her belly, small as it was, and imagined herself raising the child she was carrying. She couldn't quite do it. Couldn't see herself looking into the child's green eyes— Liam's eyes—and not feeling something negative. Cheated. Betrayed. Abandoned.

She went upstairs, glad when Megan returned with her family. The homestead was too big to be comfortable. Megan brought noise and excitement with her, and April stepped right in to help with the twins.

"Where did you guys go?" she asked, kneeling down to their height.

Rachel held her hand out. "The park. Look at the rocks I found!"

Ruby muscled her way into the conversation. "And look at the leaves *I* found!"

April smiled and told the girls that they must be very good treasure hunters and they ran into the backyard. Megan settled into the chair in the living room to nurse, and Landon banged around the kitchen as he unpacked the groceries and put them away.

"Leave the turkey steaks out," Megan said. "And the brown rice."

April joined Landon in the kitchen and hunted through the lower cabinets until she found the pressure cooker. She put the rice on and gave Landon a smile.

"How was your day, April?"

"Just fine, sir," she said.

He chuckled. "I told you yesterday, April. You don't need to call me sir."

She couldn't help it. Though Landon was only a few years older than her, he felt miles more mature.

"Settling in okay?" he asked.

"Yes. Everything's great."

"Megan kept your groceries separate. I think we got everything you asked for." He nodded toward the dining room table, where several brown paper bags waited.

"Thanks. How much do I owe you?"

"Nope," Megan said from the living room. "Part of the deal is you get room and board. You'll help around the house, with the kids, and on the ranch."

April nodded once. That *was* the deal. She lifted her chin. "When do you think I'll start around the ranch?" She knew the difference between a horse and a cow, barely. She'd never worked on a farm or a ranch, never even owned a dog.

"I'll assign you to one of my cowboys," Landon said. "He'll help you get started, give you tasks, that kind of stuff."

Tasks ran through her mind. She had no idea what tasks might need to be done on a horse ranch.

"In fact, I've invited him to dinner," Landon continued. "Want me to help with these groceries?"

"Sure." April collected two bags and took them downstairs, Landon following her with the rest. She unbagged them and put them away before returning to the kitchen upstairs. She heated a pan and began making dinner. Landon disappeared out the back door, and Megan seemed to be napping in the recliner with the baby.

When Landon returned, he had the girls with him.

And Ted Caldwell.

"April," he said. "This is Ted. You'll be working with him."

Part of her heart skyrocketed and the other part sank,

creating a discombobulating sensation in her chest. She only breathed because it was an involuntary reaction.

"Ted, this is April Nox. She's, well, she's...."

"She's as close to my god-daughter as she can get," Megan said from the recliner. "Her mother was one of my best friends when I lived in Jackson Hole."

Ted's coal-colored eyes seemed to look past all of April's anger, and a faint smile appeared on his lips. "Have you worked on a horse farm before, April?"

"No." She had no inclination to call him sir though he couldn't be older than Landon.

Those eyes flashed, and April could lose herself to a gorgeous pair of eyes like that. "Oh, well, this should be fun then." He gave Landon a look that clearly said it would *not* be fun, and he was *not* happy with being saddled with her.

"Thanks for the dinner invite, but I'm not hungry." He left through the front door, and Landon waited until it closed before he sighed.

"Not hungry?" Megan rose from the recliner and set the sleeping infant in his playpen. "I don't think Ted has ever been *not hungry*." She peered at the front door and turned back to Landon. "Has he?"

"I'll talk to him tomorrow." Landon sounded tired, and he scooped up both girls. "Time to eat. Let's get washed up."

April finished the turkey steaks while Megan opened a few cans of green beans. No one said anything, but April hadn't been born yesterday. She knew Ted had left because he didn't want to eat dinner with her.

CHAPTER 3

"Lolly," Ted called when he entered the house and only one of his Pomeranians greeted him. He reached down and scooped Stormy into his arms. "Where's little Lollipop, huh?"

The black and white dog licked his face, which caused a chuckle to erupt from his mouth. He set the dog down and moved to the back door. He collected the dogs' food and water bowls and cleaned them out and filled them up.

Lolly came through the doggy door just as he set the food on the floor, as usual. "There you are." He gave the dog an affectionate pat and pulled open the refrigerator. He hadn't realized April would be taking on work around the ranch, and he'd made sure Landon knew he wasn't happy about being the one assigned to babysit her. He didn't mind women on a ranch, but anyone with one good eye could tell April had never actually worked with horses, farm equipment, or hay before. Heck, if Ted's excellent people-reading skills could be trusted, she usually wore heels and short skirts to work and had a different man taking her to dinner each evening.

Not fair, he chastised himself as he pulled out a carton of eggs. *You don't even know her.*

And he didn't. But he'd found himself obsessing over her for the entire afternoon. Was she married? Engaged? Why did he care so much?

He didn't know, but he *did* care. He hadn't seen a wedding band or any indication of one during their brief encounter in the kitchen. As he chopped an onion and pulled out some leftover ham to make an omelet, he wondered how she'd come to Brush Creek, and why, and how long she'd be here.

He whistled, but the tune was sad and discordant. He hadn't dated since his retirement from the rodeo circuit. He wasn't sure why, other than he was content with his bachelor life, satisfied though his career had ended sooner than he'd have liked, happy that he hadn't had a wife or family to burden with his medical care.

Or at least he had been. Now, though, he could see and feel a hole that hadn't existed before, and he wondered how long it had been there and how he could possibly fill it.

———

THE NEXT AFTERNOON, April stood a couple of steps behind Landon in the barn. She wore jeans that made her legs seem ten miles long, and a long sleeved shirt in the exact shade of violet that reminded Ted of the lilac bushes his mother had cultivated.

A strong sting of missing hit him, but he smiled

through it. His mother had died when he was nine, and now, twenty-five years later, he still ached to see her again. He thought he better call his father as soon as possible. When he missed his mother, it usually meant his father was struggling too.

Bring him peace, he was able to send toward heaven before Landon started talking. "So April's gonna help with the broncos," he said. "Not training them, but when you take them out to pasture, which I know is happening today." He glanced at her, and though she'd plaited her hair and slicked on makeup, she also wore a look of pure fury. For some reason, Ted enjoyed the sight of her frowny face.

"So show her how to get saddled up, and bring her back in one piece." With that, Landon headed for the exit.

"And you'll be sure to go feed Lolly and Stormy tonight, right?" Ted called after him.

"The girls went and got them this morning. I wouldn't be surprised if they've already dressed them up and put bows on their ears." Landon grinned and left the barn, left Ted with that horrible image of his poor poms being treated like dolls, left him standing there with a woman who clearly didn't want to be there any more than Ted wanted her there.

"All right," he drawled. "You can ride a horse in your... condition?"

"What condition is that?" she asked.

"You know, pregnant." Ted actually knew very little about a pregnant woman, as he was the youngest of only two kids. His older brother had never married either. Had never even left home, and still lived only a mile from their father in Austin.

"I'm fine," she said, turning in a full circle. "So where are these horses we need to take out to pasture?"

"Down this way." Ted moved away from the corrals that opened into the training arena and headed down the aisle lined with box stalls. "I'm trainin' two geldings right now to be the best broncos in the rodeo circuit. One's already spoken for." He paused outside Yellowstone's stall. "But Yellowstone still has another, oh I don't know. Six months of training to complete. He's a good bucker, this one."

He ran his hand affectionately down the horse's nose. "You're gonna throw a lot of cowboys, aren't you?" The smile on his face had appeared without Ted's knowledge, and he straightened his lips when he felt the weight of April's gaze on his face.

Clearing his throat, he continued down the aisle. "You'll ride Sugar 'N Spice." He gestured toward a tall, red-coated horse that had just started training a couple of months ago. "He came to us from two of the best rodeo horses in the circuit. His mom won barrel racing for three years, and his dad is a four-time champion in both bareback and saddle bronc riding." He beamed at the horse and couldn't erase his expression before turning to April.

"You talk about these horses like they're people." She studied him, her stomach pushing against her shirt the littlest bit.

"I work with them all day," he said, his voice on the edge of defensive. "I talk to them like they're people, because I spend more time with them than I do with people." He pointed down the aisle. "Saddles in there. Let's find you one that will work."

"Aren't saddles just saddles?" She followed him at his brisk pace.

"No," he said, entering the tack room. "Sugar is a mild horse right now. Since he's not trained up, he'll just meander around if you don't ride him. And to do that, you need a good saddle." He pushed one saddle aside and chose another. He lifted it off the counter and held it up. "This one looks like it'll work."

"How can you tell?"

Heat rushed to his face. "Well, you're a little slimmer, so you need a narrower cut. And, uh, this one is one of the deluxe models, with extra padding." He ducked his head and got out of the tack room quick.

His heart seemed intent on pounding in time with his feet, and he practically ran back to Sugar's stall. He turned, almost colliding with April. Instinctively, he reached out and grabbed her shoulders so she wouldn't fall. "Sorry."

Their eyes met, and something that felt a lot like sugar and spice coursed between them. She stepped away, her cheeks the color of poppies, her chocolate-brown eyes alight with a fire Ted felt burning in his abdomen.

"I forgot the blanket and the bridle," he said stupidly, stepping past her and retracing his steps. She was the one who didn't fit on the ranch. She was the one who had no idea how to saddle a horse. He couldn't believe his brain had tried to betray him just because April smelled like cotton candy and looked like a model from one of his rodeo magazines.

A pregnant model, he reminded himself as he pulled the equipment from the hooks on the wall. He returned to the horse, and talked his way through saddling it. "You hold these while I get Yellowstone ready to go."

"Who names the horses?" she asked.

"It depends." He needed to get away from her, and he didn't even know why. He saddled Yellowstone and opened both stalls. He led the horses and April outside and took a long, deep breath of air that wasn't tainted by her fragrance. His head cleared, and he marveled at the blue sky and puffy clouds once more.

A cry of surprise and hurt sounded behind him, and he spun to find April sprawled out on the ground, the reins still in her hand. He couldn't help it—a laugh burst from his mouth. He quieted it quickly, and rushed to her aid, but she daggered him with those sharp eyes.

Chapter 4

"I don't need your help," April said through clenched teeth. No matter how much padding that "deluxe model" saddle had, the ache in her tailbone would last the rest of the day. So much for trying to mount the horse by herself. The alternative—touching Ted—had seemed so much worse than falling.

But now he was touching her anyway. Grabbing her hand to pull her up, despite her protest. Dusting her off with those large-as-frying-pan hands. Everything he touched, though clothed, sparked a buzz in her skin.

"You okay?" He gazed down at her, not an ounce of malice in his face.

"Fine." On one hand, she liked his jovial nature. Felt comfortable around him. It was the horse that had her spooked. She didn't like how the animal's eyes seemed wild, didn't like that horses were associated with trampling, didn't like that she had no idea how to control it.

She'd lost control of a lot of things over the years, and as she tried to regain some measure of freedom in her life, she was acutely aware of the distance she still had to go.

He put his hand on the saddle horn. "Your left hand goes here. Left foot in the stirrup. Give yourself a big push, swing the leg over, and done." He demonstrated, and someone as tall and muscular as him shouldn't be able to move with so much grace and power.

He dismounted and stepped back, that ridiculous grin stuck in place. "Give it a try. I'll be right here so you don't fall."

She put her hand and foot where he'd indicated, and though she had always been on the thin side, she couldn't propel her body more than a couple of inches off the ground. Her baby bump, small as it was, threw everything off balance.

"All right," Ted said after her third try. He put one hand on her hip and added, "One more time."

But she couldn't move. She breathed in the scent of him and identified horses, sunshine, chocolate. Her craving for something dark, and rich, and creamy shot toward the sky. She glanced at Ted, sure the attraction between them was only flowing from her. Of course it was. He wouldn't be interested in a surly, pregnant woman who'd disrupted his work life.

"Push off now," he coached in a gentle voice, one he probably used on his horses. One that worked, obviously, as April pushed with all her might. Ted did too, his other hand finding her thigh and lifting her leg over the horse. The next thing she knew, she sat in the saddle on the tallest horse in the world, the burn of Ted's touch racing through her system.

She panted like she'd run a marathon and tried to give him a smile. "Is getting off this hard?"

He chuckled and shook his head. "You'll get the hang of it." He didn't get on Yellowstone, but led both horses toward the homestead. "Where's your bag?"

"My bag?"

"We're staying out in the cabin for the weekend." He paused and glanced back at her. "Didn't Landon tell you?"

Those ever-present tears pressed against her eyes. "No, he didn't mention that."

"So you're not packed." It wasn't a question, and the statement didn't sound particularly kind either.

"I didn't know," she said.

He sighed and said, "Stay here. I'll go talk to Megan." He parked the horses in the shade of one of the trees in the backyard and ate up the distance to the house with long, powerful strides. April tried not to be impressed by him, but it was altogether impossible.

She sat there, sweating, for at least fifteen minutes before Megan rushed out of the house, her face a mixture of horror and amusement. "I'm so sorry!" She stopped and held her stomach. "I shouldn't have run like that." She took a deep breath. "I packed a few things. I hope it will be okay. It's just a couple of days."

Ted exited the house carrying two saddlebags. April looked down at Megan. "You'll be okay here without me?" Part of her job was to assist Megan. She sure liked that a heck of a lot more than prancing around on this pony.

"I'll be fine. Landon's not working this weekend."

April's hopes that she could get out of this trip crashed.

She tried the smile again, but it still felt wonky on her face. "Okay."

Ted arrived and attached the bags to Yellowstone's saddle before swinging himself effortlessly into the saddle. "We ready?"

"Sure are." Megan backed up, a look on her face that April had seen a time or two. She was actually enjoying herself, and a wild thought struck her in the chest. Megan had offered the ranch to April as a refuge. Said she needed help with the kids, help around the house, and from what April had seen, Megan did.

But had she also brought her out here to match her up with a cowboy? April shot a daggered look at Megan, who waggled her fingers good-bye, and April had her answer. Yes, Megan had definitely had a secondary agenda in bringing April to the ranch.

"See you Sunday!" Megan called as the horses moved through the fence on the north side of the house. April couldn't bring herself to answer, but Ted waved and bellowed, "Save me a seat at church!"

Church, urch, urch, echoed off the sky. April sank into it, for the first time in months thinking that maybe going to church wouldn't be so bad if Ted would be there too.

———

"So tell me about your family." Ted Caldwell was a talker, April had learned in the hour they'd been riding. He'd already told her all about his family—a single older brother and a retired father in Texas. He'd detailed his rodeo career, his childhood, his two little dogs, and the death of his mother. The only thing he hadn't mentioned was his dating history or if he'd ever been married. Everything about him reminded April of a big ole teddy bear, and she wanted to wrap her arms around him and squeeze him tight.

"I'm the oldest," she said. "I have two younger brothers who still live in Wyoming."

"How old are you?" He didn't look at her when he spoke, but kept his eye on the towering red butte they kept getting closer to.

"Thirty."

"Is this your first baby?"

She sucked in a breath. "Yes." She'd expected people to be curious about her, but she'd hoped with a town the size of Brush Creek, people would mind their own business.

"Are you married?"

"No."

"Who's the father?"

"You're a nosy thing, aren't you?" She glared at him, satisfied when he turned toward her and offered an apologetic grin.

"Sorry." He didn't ask again, but the unspoken questions gnawed at April. The words swirled in her mouth. Her gut clenched and released, swooped forward and back. Her tailbone seemed to have its own heartbeat and it was saying, *Tell him. Tell-tell-him.*

"Fine," she finally said. "He was my boyfriend. We'd been together for three years. I wasn't...going to church in Wyoming. I worked in a legal office, and he's a used car salesmen that one of the lawyers represented in a lawsuit." She swallowed, her tongue and throat sticky. Her emotions had been all over the place for months, and memories with Liam surged forward and stained all the hard work she'd done to find peace.

"He doesn't want the baby," she said, her voice definitely in an upper register now. "So when Megan called and asked me to come help with the kids and the homestead, I jumped at the chance." She looked at the horizon, wishing God would pour out His forgiveness and blessings upon her. At the same time, she knew she didn't deserve them. Yet.

"I'm trying to figure out what to do."

Ted let several heartbeats of silence go by. Then he said, "This is a great place to do that." He flashed her a smile worthy of millions and fell silent.

April soon learned that silence out in the wilds of Utah wasn't all it was cracked up to be, and she wished Ted would ask her another question. As more time went by, she found a comfortable place inside her own mind and used the summer breeze, bright blue sky, and steady clopping of horse's hooves to steady herself. Evaluate what she really wanted.

By the time Ted said, "Right there. See that fence line?" April knew she wanted another chance at her happily-ever-after. She wanted a loving husband. The chance to be a mother.

She glanced to the right, where Ted was looking, but she didn't see a fence. Her hands fell protectively to her belly. Could she really give her baby up for adoption? Maybe she'd never get another opportunity to be a mother.

"Do you have any regrets?" she asked, and Ted swung his attention toward her.

"That's a huge question," he said. "I think everyone has regrets."

"Big ones, I mean. Like something you'd travel back in time to fix, if you could."

Ted shrugged, but April had worked for lawyers. She knew the signs of evasion as well as anyone, even though she'd only made copies of the briefs, and ordered lunches, and brought in coffee.

"If I could travel back in time, I'd save my mom. Make sure she didn't get in the car to come pick me up from school that day." Something crossed his face, but April couldn't identify it before his chin dropped and his cowboy hat concealed his expression. He turned away from her further and clucked his tongue at his horse.

"I'm sorry," April said, the words barely leaving her lips. Ted didn't turn, and she reasoned it was because he hadn't heard her. He dismounted and fished a set of keys from a pouch hanging from the saddlebags. He unlocked the gate and led Yellowstone into the pasture.

"What's her name?" April asked.

"Who?"

"Your mom."

"Oh. Emma." He looked uncomfortable for half a second before the emotion fled.

"How big is this thing?" April's eyes followed the fence for as far as she could see, the line finally blurring into the horizon.

"Oh, I don't know." Ted sighed as he unsaddled his horse. "Are you gonna get down?"

She peered down at him. "I was hoping you'd help me." Embarrassment flowed through her, but she figured it was better than falling flat on her back and getting the wind knocked out of her. Then she'd be embarrassed *and* hurt.

He grinned with the glee of a small child on their birthday as he extended his bear paw of a hand up toward her. She put her fingers in his but stalled. "Now what?"

"You put your weight into the stirrup here." He indicated right where he stood. "Stand up, and swing your other leg over. I'll help keep you balanced with my hand here, and you'll be down."

The horse shifted, and April nearly slid off his back right then.

"Steady, Sugar," Ted said in his cooing voice, and the horse stilled. He focused on April again, and the heat burning through her blood didn't all come from the sun. "You ready, sugar?"

She rolled her eyes. "Ha ha."

His booming laugh made her heart thump to a rhythm it hadn't for a while, and she slapped her hand in his. "I'm ready. Are you?"

He leaned closer, pressing his chest into the horse's. "Oh, I'm ready."

She tried to do what he'd said. Put her weight on her left leg, check. Stand up, half a check. Swing the leg, wild check.

"Oh, okay," Ted said, his grip on her hand tightening. "Wait, yeah, no—" He grunted as she swung her whole body and landed directly on top of him. They both tumbled to the ground while Sugar 'N Spice stood perfectly still. At least Ted was on the bottom, meeting the hard ground with his bones first. Of course, landing on his abs was almost like landing on steel, so April wasn't sure if falling on top of him was better or not.

Chapter 5

Ted chuckled as April's face turned bright red. She'd lost her cowgirl hat in the scuffle and wisps of her hair had come loose during the three-hour ride. She struggled against his body, and every spot she placed her hand seemed like the wrong one—at least to her. She finally tucked her hands to her chest and rolled off of him.

He stayed on his back, his muscles popping and his laughter streaming from his mouth. "Well, that didn't work out, did it?"

"What did I do wrong?"

"Just about everything." Ted sat up and clapped his hands together. "It's okay. I needed to get a little down and dirty today."

"I'm sure." She gained her feet and strode away, her boots kicking up dust as she went. Ted should probably call after her that the cabin was in the other direction, but he sensed that she needed a few minutes to herself. He'd realized on the ride out here that he did. That one of the reasons he'd been so bothered by Landon assigning him to bring April with him was that he wouldn't have the time out here by himself.

Which made no sense, because Ted spent a lot of time by himself. Every evening. Most weekends. There was just something magical, something cleansing, about his time out here, a solid three-hour ride from anyone else. Just him, the horses, the red rocks, and God.

He got up and dusted off his clothes, confused about the woman still stalking away from him. She'd settled down enough to talk to him, and he appreciated that the things she'd said weren't easy for her.

All at once, he understood how he felt. He admired her. Surely it hadn't been easy for her to be told by her boyfriend that he didn't want their baby. It had probably been terribly lonely those first few weeks after her three-year relationship ended. And she'd moved across state lines, to a town where she knew one person.

"April!" he called after her. She stopped walking but didn't turn around. "Cabin's this way." He unsaddled her horse too and gave both animals a playful swat on their rumps. "Go on, you two. Run free."

Sugar and Yellowstone wandered off, and Ted shouldered their equipment. The gentlemanly side of him wanted to wait for April to catch up, but his pragmatic side told him to move. She'd follow.

So he moved. He walked along the fence line to the next break. He left the pasture with only a quick glance behind him. April had closed the distance between them, and now she only lingered about a dozen paces behind him.

"You okay?"

She glared, which he took as April-speak for, "I'm fine. Leave me alone." Ted turned and continued toward the stream. This late in the summer, the trees and grasses around the stream obscured it, but Ted knew every inch of this countryside. This time, he waited for April so he could point out where to step. He didn't need her bruised, humiliated, *and* wet.

"There's water here," he said. "Most of us cowboys like to come out here and fish. The best spot is down yonder a bit." He chin nodded south, closer to the homestead.

April cocked her head and folded her arms. "Do I look like I'd enjoy fishing?"

Ted peered at her as if he was really trying to decide. A shotgun burst of laughter exploded from his mouth. "Point taken. Did Megan mention anything about the cabin?"

"No." Enough panic accompanied the word for Ted to know April wouldn't like the accommodations. "What about it?"

"There's no air conditioning," he said. "Two rooms, with a bathroom. A loft." He sighed and let his happiness infuse his words. "And a spectacular view." He glanced at April, but she wasn't impressed.

"No air conditioning?"

"No, sirree."

"Any Internet service?"

Ted tipped his face skyward and laughed again. "Did you even bring your phone?"

"Of course I did. What if I break my ankle out here? How would I get help?"

Ted looked at her to see if she was being serious. She

seemed to be. "Well, April-May, you'd have to somehow get yourself back to the homestead."

April-May. Where the nickname had come from, Ted didn't know. She didn't seem to mind, but the way her jaw worked, he thought maybe he should run all future endearments past her. *If* there were to be any future endearments.

"Which." He cleared his throat. "Is where the horses come in. We always ride one out, so we always have a way back."

She glanced over her shoulder and then over his. "We just walked probably a half a mile from that pasture. And I still don't see a cabin."

"You're terrible with distance," he said. "That was maybe a quarter of a mile, and the cabin is just behind those trees." He turned away before her lasered eyes could slice him right open. "C'mon. We're almost there." And he was suddenly tired.

———

Hours later, once darkness had started to fall, Ted returned from the stream where he'd been sitting, contemplating the incoming storm. The sky had darkened with clouds by early evening, and the breeze coming in the open windows actually felt cooler than Ted liked.

"Definitely going to rain tonight," he said when he located April curled up into the end of the couch.

She didn't even glance up from her phone. "Great."

To punctuate her sarcasm, the first crack of thunder ripped through the atmosphere. Ted worried about his dogs until he remembered that they'd already been taken over to

Megan's. His next thought concerned Yellowstone and Sugar, but the horses had trees where they could find shelter.

A better scenario was that the storm would blow this rickety cabin into sticks, and he and April would be drenched once the rain came.

The first drops of rain started only a few minutes later, and April looked at the ceiling. "I patched up the roof last spring," Ted said, casting his eyes upward too. "She should hold."

"Why do men do that? Refer to everything with a female pronoun."

Ted settled his gaze on her. "I don't know." He stepped over to the refrigerator, which held bottled water and the groceries he'd brought out three days ago. He took out a bottle of water and let his eyes linger on the chocolate he'd bought. He finally swiped it off the top shelf and faced April.

"Do you like milk chocolate or dark?"

That got her attention, and she lowered the phone. "You have chocolate?"

"I brought the food out a few days ago." He crossed the room and extended her two choices to her. "Dark chocolate with sea salt or milk chocolate hazelnut."

She reached for the milk chocolate but drew her fingers back. "I can't take your chocolate."

"Sure you can."

"You certainly didn't bring enough food for me." A look of fear danced across her face. "We're going to starve out here, aren't we?"

Ted handed her the milk chocolate bar. "Keep calm and

eat your chocolate." He nodded toward her phone. "Put that on your meme maker."

She swiped her phone from the couch cushion, where the app she'd been using waited for her with a picture of the red rock butte he hadn't noticed her taking. "Seriously, Ted. We're going to be out here for two days. How could you have known that I'd be coming with you? I wasn't even in Brush Creek a few days ago."

"I always bring tons of extra stuff," he said. "Seriously, don't worry." He settled onto the couch and took off his hat with a sigh. He rubbed his hands through his hair and down his beard before ripping open his chocolate bar. He enjoyed the treat in silence, exactly how he'd envisioned when he'd bought the candy.

"Well, I'm heading to bed."

"Good-night," April said, both syllables distracted as she kept her attention on her phone. Ted shut himself into the back room, as per their agreement. She'd sleep on one of the cots in the large main front room, and he'd sleep on one in the smaller back bunk room. He'd piled several blankets and pillows onto two cots when they'd first arrived, and he pulled a few more out of the supply closet in the bunk room.

He fell asleep almost before his head hit the pillow, and he woke sometime later to a brilliant flash of lightning and a terrific crash of thunder. He sat up as the rain pounded on the roof, and he padded over to the open window and slid it shut. It hadn't been raining too bad when he'd gone to bed, so he'd left it open, but now a substantial amount of water had come in, making the floor wet with puddles.

Ted crossed to the next window and closed that one

too, and then darted toward the door separating him and April. He knocked and pulled open the door. "April? I'm just gonna close the windows, okay?"

She didn't answer, so he moved on bare feet and got the cabin secured. His fingers were cold, and his first thought was to build a fire. But all the wood sat in the shed, and it was ten yards through heavy rain to get to it. So he ducked back into the bedroom and climbed back under his blankets.

The rest of the night passed with Ted tossing from side to side on the narrow cot. Finally, dawn arrived and Ted could give up the ruse of sleeping. He slipped into the bathroom and showered, emerging from the back bedroom ready for a day of hiking, relaxing, and maybe some fishing —if he needed a break from April. She'd probably need a break from him, in all honesty. He typically saw the silver lining in every situation, but April seemed to be the complete opposite of him.

He found her standing in the kitchen, a pot of coffee already full. She stood at the sink, looking out the window and looking absolutely glorious in the morning light. It played off her dyed streaks and when she turned toward him and smiled, he thought her positively angelic.

That's the pregnant glow, he told himself as he poured himself a cup of coffee. "I see you've found all the important things."

"I left the eggs and bacon for you."

"Good, because that's for tomorrow. I always have bacon and eggs on Saturday morning so I'm good and ready for a day of working in the pasture."

"I thought you said these two days would be relaxing."

"I said I found them relaxing. Today will be. I hike to the top of the butte, and go fishing, and usually take a nap. Tomorrow, I have to check the pasture for fence breaks and I like to observe my horses when they're out in the wild." He swallowed a mouthful of coffee and glanced down at her. "What?"

She blinked, her dark eyes soulful and scared. "Hiking to the top of the butte?"

Annoyance sang through him. Funny how he could find her so alluring one moment, what with her hair falling softly over her shoulders, and so frustrating the next. "You don't have to come. You can do whatever you want." He turned away from her and snapped a banana off the bunch. "I eat toast and a banana for breakfast on day one."

"Do you always stick to the same routine?"

"Yep." He stuck a couple of slices of bread in the toaster and opened the banana. "Eat whatever you want. I dine by the river in the morning."

"Creature of habit."

"I like routines," he said. "It's not a crime."

"I didn't say it was."

"Sounded like it."

She turned fully toward him and leaned back into the counter. "I didn't mean it to."

His toast popped up and he gave his full attention to buttering it. "It's not a problem."

"So I'll shower and come find you at the river." Her voice rose at the end, like it was a question.

"Sure." He took a bite of crunchy, buttery toast. "We'll pack lunches before we go. Sometimes I just sleep in the shade."

"Still looks wet out there." She gave him a small smile. "I've never hiked to the top of a butte before. Sounds fun." She took a couple of steps toward him and paused when she was nearly past him. She reached up and placed her palm against his chest. Something strange crossed her face, and she jerked her hand back. "I'm—I'm sorry. I don't know what that was." She bent for her bag before scampering into the bathroom. The click of the lock sounded as loud as a gunshot in the quiet cabin.

Ted stared after her, her handprint branded against his chest. He bit into his toast in slow motion, not quite sure what bubbled between him and April Nox, but very much wanting to find out.

CHAPTER 6

April stepped carefully through the prairie grass, Ted's form down by the river her goal. She'd taken a long time in the shower, glad the cabin had hot water. It eventually ran out, and she'd been forced to look into her own face in the mirror and ask herself what she was doing.

The answer: She had no idea.

No idea why she'd touched Ted Caldwell.

No idea why the idea of him sleeping under the same roof as her set her pulse pounding.

No idea why she couldn't just let him go hiking while she made up for the sleep she'd lost last night.

"Hey." She stayed on her feet because the ground looked wet.

"Hey." He lifted his coffee mug to his lips, but it had to be stone cold by now.

"Sun's out, but it sure isn't that warm." She glanced around at the remains of the storm—a few clouds still marred the sky.

"It will be soon enough." He groaned as he got to his feet. "Wow, I'm not as young as I used to be. You falling off that horse really did me in."

Her face heated. "How old are you?"

"Thirty-four."

She nodded.

"Should we go make lunches?"

She simply went with him as he maneuvered toward the cabin. "Hey, how's there electricity here? I haven't seen any power lines."

"Gas generator," he said. "It's good for about seventy-two hours of energy, and we hardly ever use it during the day. So." He held the door open for her, and she had the strangest urge to pause in his personal bubble again, stretch up on her toes, and press her lips to his.

Pure horror snaked through her, choked her. She was only four months pregnant, four months out of her relationship with Liam, four months since her world had ended and a new one had begun.

How could she even be thinking about another man? Another relationship? She still felt so scarred inside, and she had outward physical evidence of her bad decisions. Her mother had offered to have April move back in with her when the baby came. But April couldn't bear the thought of that.

She was thirty years old, for heaven's sake. She couldn't move back in with her parents and allow them to take care of her. She'd moved out at eighteen, and for her, there was never the possibility of going back.

"You know, I wanted to leave Jackson Hole," she said as he untwisted the tie on the bread bag.

"Oh yeah?"

"I didn't want all my friends to know about the baby." She bypassed the mayo—the sight and smell of it made her squeamish—and spread chunky peanut butter on both slices of her bread. "They think I left town because of the break-up with Liam."

Ted finished constructing his sandwich and slid it into a bag. "So what will you tell them when you go home with a child?" He tilted his chin toward her for a fraction of a second, long enough for her to feel the weight of his gaze. "Or are you planning on never goin' to visit your folks?"

April hadn't thought very far ahead, only that she was starting to show and she didn't want to explain anything to her girlfriends. Didn't want to say why she couldn't go out to parties with them. Didn't want to lie about why she and Liam hadn't been able to make things work. Her chest felt like someone had stretched a rubber band around her ribs and let it constrict. It felt so tight, so tight. So tight she couldn't breathe.

She didn't miss the parties. She was getting too old for them anyway, and she liked her beauty rest.

She didn't really even miss her friends. She'd left town a week ago and spent a few days in Salt Lake City before coming east to Brush Creek. None of them had called or texted.

She missed her parents. Her job, though it was meaningless. She got to wear her cute skirts and shoes, and she always got a long lunch and was home by five. And if she were being honest, being here with Ted had eased the loneliness that had been prevalent since Liam had moved out of their apartment.

That's why you touched him, she thought. It was a human connection she craved. She just hadn't expected to want it with such a handsome man, even if he was a cowboy. April watched him pack all their food in a single backpack and load up several bottles of water too. He shouldered the pack and turned toward her.

"Ready?"

"I'm not what you would call outdoorsy," she said.

"The path is easy to find and follow." He glanced at her shoes. "You're wearing good footwear. You'll be fine. We'll go slow." His eyes landed on her belly and stayed for a single breath before returning to her eyes. "Do you know if the baby is a boy or a girl?"

"No," she said. "And I'm not going to find out."

"No?"

She shook her head, a tidal wave of sadness cascading upon her unexpectedly. "No...if I decide not to keep the baby, I don't want to know what it is."

He stood so still, it was almost unnerving. "Do you really think you can give your baby up for adoption?"

She didn't like the way his eyes had captured hers, hooked them and wouldn't let go. Didn't like the compassion she found there. She didn't want his pity. Didn't deserve it.

"I don't know," she said.

He extended his hand toward her, like she'd move forward and slip her fingers through his and they'd go walking up the mountain hand-in-hand. She wanted to do that. Wanted it so badly, a lump formed in the back of her throat.

So she did, and the calloused nature of his hand also brought with it the warmth and comfort and connection she'd hoped for.

CHAPTER 7

Ted felt like he was on a roller coaster he wanted to get off. Up one moment, swooping toward the sky, the track nowhere in sight. Then plummeting toward the ground, a scream ripping from his throat.

The high was holding April's hand. He wasn't sure why he'd offered his hand to her, and he was even more surprised when she took it. He sensed her loneliness like a scent on the air, though, and he wanted to ease her suffering if he could. He squeezed her hand and nodded his cowboy hat toward the path up ahead. "See it?"

"If you mean that thin ribbon of brown dirt, yeah, I see it." She glanced up at him and brushed her hair under her hat with her free hand. "We're not going to fit on it side-by-side."

"You can go first." Ted paused and indicated she go in front of him.

She gave a brief guffaw. "I don't think so. You go."

Ted stepped in front of her, regretting the loss of her

hand in his. Something gnawed at him, and he let the thought of giving a baby up for adoption roll around in his head. It never settled down, and it started to seethe and take on a pulse of its own.

The lone tree on the path stood up ahead, offering the only shade, and he stopped in it. He fished out two bottles of water and handed one to April. "I don't think I could do it," he said.

"Do what?"

"Give my kid up for adoption."

"Well." She took a long drink of water. "It's not your kid." She glared at him, and dang, if Ted's blood didn't run a little faster because of her speared look. "And not your decision."

"I know, I know." Ted drained the rest of his water. "But what if you meet someone in the future? Someone who could love your kid, and love you?"

Her anger softened and a faraway look entered her eyes as she faced the path they'd already climbed, taking in the view before them.

"Sometimes I imagine I can see the homestead from here," Ted said, switching the subject. "But you have to go all the way to the top for that. It sits down in a little valley you can't see from here."

April shielded her eyes and continued staring at something in the beyond. Only the wind whispered between them, and a measure of peace infected Ted's soul. He offered up a quick prayer to know what to say to help April, but nothing came immediately to his mind.

"I don't know if I can do it," she finally said.

"What?" he asked.

She faced him. "Give up the baby." Her eyes seemed enormous, and Ted noticed that she wore a touch of makeup. Her soul, wounded and tired as it was, called to him, and he reached his arm around her waist and pulled her into an embrace.

"You'll know what to do," he said into her ear. "When it's time."

"Some days, I'm so angry," she whispered into his chest, her hot tears burning through the fabric of his shirt. "That I don't think I can ever love the baby. Other days, I'm already in love with him."

"Or her," Ted said. "I think women always refer to their babies with a male pronoun—at least until they know if it's a girl or a boy." He had no idea if that was true or not, though the only woman he'd known to be pregnant in the past five years—Megan—had. He chuckled, glad when April did too.

He took a big breath, filled his big chest, and said, "Let's keep going. I think you'll really like the view from the top."

It took an extra twenty minutes to reach the vista of the butte, because April's steps got slower and slower as time went on. Ted had suggested they stop and turn back, but April wouldn't have it. She wanted to make it to the top for some reason.

She stood on the edge of the butte facing away from the ranch, her arms wrapped around her middle protectively. Ted watched her more than he gazed at the horizon, a new development for him he didn't quite know how to deal with.

He thought about his family, and his desire to have a

wife and children of his own roared forward again. The past day and a half had almost been torture as this new wound had opened in his life. It felt like a round hole, and April a square peg, and yet, Ted couldn't help imagining what it would be like to hold her, kiss her, feel her unborn child kick against his hand.

Surprised at the intimate nature of his thoughts, he twisted away from her. He removed his cowboy hat and let the wind cool his sweat. He drank another bottle of water, trying to lower his internal temperature, not all of which came from the blazing sun.

He couldn't make the two halves of himself line up, and he spent several minutes trying to make his feelings align. The fact was, his life had changed the moment he'd laid eyes on April Nox. Everything he'd been content with then no longer brought him the same level of satisfaction.

"Hey, are we going to eat up here?" April appeared at his side, and Ted let his eyes slide from her toes to her eyes.

"There's no shade. We can go down the path a bit, and sit on some rocks we passed coming up." He smiled at her, unsure of how the gesture sat on his face. He hadn't flirted with a woman in a long time. "Are you ready to go?"

She grinned up at him. "Yeah, coffee only lasts so long."

He picked up the backpack and draped it over one shoulder. "Let's go then. I don't need a pregnant woman fainting on me."

She punched him lightly on the bicep and he captured her hand in his. "I like you, April-May." He kicked a quick half-smile in her direction.

Her eyes danced with amusement. "My middle name isn't May."

"No? What is it?"

"I don't have one."

"No middle name? Then April-May fits just fine."

They started down the path, and it was wide enough up here at the top for them to remain side-by-side. "I don't hate it," she said.

Ted laughed. "I'll take that as a compliment." He had to move in front of her then, leading her down and back the way they'd come until he came to the shady spot where several large boulders provided some seating. The butte itself provided the shade, but not for much longer as the sun continued its arc through the sky. When it reached its zenith, Ted wanted to be nearly back to the cabin, ready to take his midday siesta.

He passed out the food, and April took hers but didn't move to open it. "So...do you go to church every week?"

"Sure do." He bit into his sandwich, the words he'd prayed for earlier suddenly there. "You want to come with me? It's not bad. The pastor says really good things, and it's nice to get down into town." He fished an apple out of his pack. "Don't get me wrong. I love the ranch. The wide open sky."

He gazed into that sky now, overcome with gratitude for his life, this place. "But sometimes, it's good to know there are people around too." He gave her a smile and went back to his lunch, hoping she'd pick up the conversation where he'd left it.

"I'm generally trying to avoid people," she said.

"Let's just go to church then. We can sneak out during the closing hymn." He had a flash of being a teenager and telling his dad that he'd gone to church when he'd only shown up for the first ten minutes. A wry smile marred his face with the memory. He still hadn't called his father, and he told himself not to forget when he got back to the ranch.

"I guess I can go to church if we sneak out early."

Relief and excitement filled Ted in equal parts. "Great," he said cheerfully.

April pinched off a piece of her sandwich and tossed it in his direction. "Are you always this happy?"

"Yep," he said, unapologetic about that, at least.

Chapter 8

April had never been so happy to see a log cabin in all her life. But the luxury log cabins that came into view back at the ranch had Internet service. Hot water. Electricity. Air conditioning. Comfortable beds.

"I'll see you in a few minutes," Ted said, swinging off his horse to help her down. He practically lifted her into his arms this time, and she didn't blame him. He took the reins of both horses loosely in his hands and continued around the homestead.

April watched him go, once again marveling at the strength and power in him—and not just physically. Ted Caldwell possessed a lot more than muscles of iron and a very kissable mouth. And if she couldn't touch his beard soon.... The temptation to manhandle him had run through her mind a lot on the horseback ride home.

"Hey!" Megan met her just inside the front door. "There you are. How was it?" She peeked out the door and closed it, her eyes bright and her skin smelling like a perfumy beach.

"It was...fun."

"Really?" Megan peered at her like she'd just said the sun wasn't yellow.

A slow smile spread across April's face. "Really. I'm going to go shower and get ready for church." She'd taken one step when Megan's hand landed on her arm. April turned back to her. "What?"

"Church? You're going to go to church?"

April felt wicked when she leaned toward her friend and said, "Ted invited me. I said yes." She added a bounce to her step that hurt her bruised tailbone just for Megan's benefit. She tossed her a laugh when she reached the top of the stairs.

"April," Megan said, giggling.

"You got your wish, my fairy godmother. You wanted me to spend some quality time with Ted? Don't even try to deny it."

"I did not," Megan said anyway, taking the baby as Landon handed him to her. She beamed down at the infant, and April paused for real now, watching Megan with fascination. Would she look at her baby like that? Would the love just come gushing out of her the way it did Megan, even if the infant had Liam's eyes, or nose, or chin?

Her hand went to her belly, as it had more and more often lately, and she once again wondered if she could go through with her plan to give her baby away. Pushing her circular thoughts away, she went down the steps and hurried into the shower.

Forty-five minutes later, she waited in a chair on the front porch, her eyes trained on the cabins across the street. Ted hadn't specified which one he lived in, but she watched another cowboy and a blonde woman climb into a truck after two tween boys exploded out of the house and ran screaming across the lawn.

When Ted emerged from the cabin way down at the end of the line, April stood, her heart beating with the reverberations of a gong. He glanced toward the homestead, and April left the safety of the porch so he'd see her. She realized he was holding a couple of fluffy little dogs in his arms.

She stopped and stared. Sure, he'd mentioned his dogs and how much he enjoyed having them around, but she'd imagined them to be big, brutish things who slobbered on her best pair of jeans. But Ted held puff balls. Puff balls who licked his face before he set them gently back in the cabin. He turned toward the homestead and caught her eye. A smile danced across his face and he strode toward her.

April told herself not to skip and squeal like a schoolgirl. She was too old to be acting like that now. Too mature. Too pregnant.

Still, it looked like Ted might sweep her off her feet and twirl her around when they met. To save herself the humiliation of him not being able to lift her, she said, "What kind of dogs were those?" when he was still several paces away.

"Pomeranians."

April tipped her face skyward and laughed. "I so didn't peg you for a puffy dog type of guy."

Ted waited with his hand in his pockets until she quieted. He gazed at her with something she hadn't seen on a man's face in a long time. Adoration.

April had been in enough bars to recognize interest,

flirtation, lust. But she hadn't had anyone adore her—not even Liam—in years. She sobered, especially when he said, "I like the way you laugh." He turned and offered her his elbow. "Shall we?"

"You probably drive a great big truck, right?"

"Guilty."

The truck parked to the side of the last cabin was indeed great, and big, and so white it looked like it hadn't been driven before. The gray leather interior seemed freshly polished, and the scent of oranges permeated the cab.

"Do you actually drive this truck anywhere?"

"Remember how I said it was nice to get down to town every week? That's about how often I drive it." He turned on the air conditioning and started down the canyon. "Sometimes I have to go to Texas, or Colorado, or wherever, for a client. But that's not very often. They come to the ranch too."

The music filling the truck had the definitive twang of pure country, and April reached for the radio. "Mind if I change this?"

"Not a country fan?"

"I like the pop version of country."

"Ah, one of those." His fingers flexed on the wheel.

April rolled down her window and let the wind blow her hair back. The air entered her nose and lungs like a breath of heaven, and April released some of her pent-up negativity. At the same time, she felt a little bit closer to the Lord than she had in years. A smile pulled at the corners of her mouth, relieved that her mother had been right.

She hadn't done something she couldn't come back

from. She didn't expect it to be easy, but until that moment, she also hadn't thought it possible.

The feeling of forgiveness and peace fled, though, when Ted pulled into the parking lot of a red brick church. The building seemed tall and narrow and obviously old.

"They built this church brick by brick, using the post office. They mailed every brick from Salt Lake City. Almost bankrupted the postal service." Ted chuckled as he got out of the truck and gazed at the building with fondness.

"Ah, so you're a history buff too." April joined him on the sidewalk.

"Brush Creek does have some fascinating history," he said. "After you, April-May."

April wasn't sure she could get her feet to take her inside a church. She gave it a valiant effort and made it three steps before her shoes stuck to the sidewalk. She spun back to Ted, pure panic pouring through her. Wave after wave of it crashed against her lungs, and she gasped for breath. Again, and then again.

"I—can't—"

Ted swooped up to her, sliding one arm around her waist and looping the other through her elbow. "Sure you can. One step at a time." The spicy, minty smell of him did nothing to calm her pulse. "Come on now, April. It's just church. Take a deep breath with me, okay?" His chest inflated, and she forced hers to go with it.

The increased oxygen cleared her head slightly. Enough for her to get her legs moving again. She climbed the four steps, crossed the threshold from cement to wood floor, breathed in the familiar scent of old paper and candle wax.

Familiar, but a unique smell she hadn't experienced in a long while.

Ted parked her on the back row of the chapel, boxing her into the pew with his large body. He kept one arm around her shoulders, and his low voice kept a constant stream of words going into her ear. She couldn't distinguish what he said, only that it made the icy waves of panic recede.

The organ began playing, further calming her. Her favorite part of church as a child had been the music. Her father had played the organ every other week for as long as she could remember, and she'd sang in the children's choir for six years before graduating high school and moving across town.

She took a deep breath and laid her head against Ted's chest. "I'm okay," she whispered, and he fell silent. The choir sang the opening hymn, and the pastor, a man who had to be close to retirement with white hair and crinkling, kind eyes, stood at the podium. He thanked everyone for coming and then turned the time back over to the choir.

April basked in the spirit of the music, letting the notes and words and feelings of happiness and love flow through her. She hadn't felt this comfortable inside her own skin since the day she met Liam. Maybe longer. Maybe since she'd dropped out of college and taken the secretarial job at the law firm.

It didn't matter. She couldn't travel back in time and change those decisions. They weren't even the one she wanted to erase.

The preacher got up and he had a jovial voice to match his happy-happy face. April couldn't help but smile watching him and listening to him. "What a beautiful day to be alive," he said, spreading his arms wide. "Yes, there are some of us that are suffering on this beautiful day. Some ailments are physical, some mental, some emotional. None of us can escape trials and tribulations. For some, today is an easy day. For others, it was hard just to come here. No matter which camp you fall into, the Lord is there for you."

April drank in his words, believed every one. She leaned forward, hoping to catch every syllable.

"My friends, my brothers and sisters, it will all work out. Be optimistic. Be positive. Be happy, even if today feels like the darkest day of your life. Trust in God, and have faith that He knows what He's doing. It will all work itself out."

April seized onto his words and tethered them to her heart. Today wasn't the darkest day of her life. That would be the day she found out she was pregnant. She remembered the feeling of elation. She was sure she'd never felt it before, and standing in a bathroom with a pregnancy test seemed like a strange time to experience it.

But she had. She looked up from the double pink lines and searched her face, which looked so different, so vulnerable, so happy.

An hour later, those same eyes were puffy and red, and they'd cried more tears than April thought humanly possible. The complete opposite of elation—devastation—coursed through her. Liam had not shared her joy. He didn't want the baby, didn't want her.

She'd thought it the exact thing they needed to take their relationship to the next level. He'd used it as an excuse to remove her from his life. It had taken her three months to understand that he'd never planned to marry her. That knowledge didn't make the feelings of abandonment any less real, but sitting in the chapel with the preacher's words ringing in her ears, that pain and hurt lessened.

She closed her eyes and whispered, "Thank you."

Ted's arm around her tightened, and she added another silent prayer of gratitude for his presence at her side.

CHAPTER 9

T ed's chest stormed during the service. While he normally relished the hour the preacher took to remind him of God's love for him, April put off so much anxiety that Ted couldn't wait to get her out of there.

Pastor Peters quoted one of Ted's favorite scriptures about the Lord taking care of the lilies of the field, and added, "The Lord did not put us here to abandon us."

Ted felt the truth of his words all the way through him, and tears streamed down April's face. He leaned forward and said, "Hey, you wanna get out of here?"

She nodded, and Ted wasted no time standing and striding out of the chapel. The sunshine beyond the doors hit him square in the face, and he breathed in the goodness of God's creations around him.

April didn't pause, her long legs moving her away from the church quickly. She didn't stop in the parking lot though, but continued down a gentle embankment to a walking trail that bordered a stream that edged the main park in town.

Ted let her go, following at a safe distance. He heard no signs of distress from her and she eventually slowed, stopping altogether at a bend in the path. She looked between two trees before turning to Ted.

"Is that an island in the park?"

He glanced in the direction she'd been looking. "Yeah. There's a bridge that goes out to it. It's a popular place for picnics."

A ghost of a smile passed across her face.

"At the risk of getting punched...are you okay?"

The smile bloomed, growing in intensity and beauty as she let it form on her face. "I'm okay, yes. That was a really powerful sermon, and it touched my heart." She ran her hands up and down her arms as if cold, but the Utah afternoon had to be close to a hundred degrees.

"You want to head back to my cabin and get some ice cream?"

"You have ice cream at your cabin?"

"I never allow myself to run out." He tucked his hands in his pockets. "And we better hurry if you want to avoid the crowds getting out of church." He studied the sun like he could determine the time from its position. "Pastor Peters knows better than to go longer than an hour in the summer."

On the way back to the parking lot and his truck, she asked, "What kind of ice cream do you have?"

"What kind do you like?"

"Orange sherbet?"

"I hate to break it to you, but sherbet isn't ice cream."

"I'll take that as a no."

Ted enjoyed the flirting, glad he was able to somehow pull it off. He enjoyed the afternoon with April, and his evening with his Pomeranians.

The next month passed in pure enjoyment for Ted. He spent mornings with his horses, and Yellowstone was coming along nicely in his training. April helped Megan around the homestead in the mornings, and she didn't come out to the ranch until sometime in the afternoon. Ted gave her tasks like cleaning equipment and feeding animals. Though Brush Creek was a horse ranch, Landon kept chickens and goats on the property too.

April turned out to be a natural with the smaller animals, though horses still disturbed her. Ted had offered to give her horseback riding lessons, but she'd vehemently denied him. He'd chuckled, his mind wandering to kissing her. He'd been thinking about that a lot lately.

He woke up thinking about kissing her, ate lunch wondering when she'd show up out in the barn that after-noon, snuggled with his poms at night while April paraded through his mind. Her belly grew over the weeks, and Ted found her sexy and strong. She went to church with him every week, and they left early with her weeping every single time.

He still hadn't taken her out to the island, and the town's apricot festival passed with Ted heading down to the parade with the other single cowboys while April hid out in the basement. He'd eaten jalapeño poppers with homemade apricot jam, laid on his back under the stars during the concert at Oxbow Park, and donated a bunch of money to Walker and Tess Thompson's Widows and Widowers Fund.

He and Walker had come to Brush Creek at the same time, and Ted had always supported his cause. He did what he could around town, and this year, he'd also donated heavily to the church's fundraiser to repair the bell tower. They held a bake sale, and Ted had brought home three of the most expensive cakes he'd ever buy.

And April was coming over on this Labor Day to share the one he'd put in the freezer a few weeks ago. He showered quickly after his work on the ranch and set about dusting and straightening up.

"You guys have to be nice tonight," he told his dogs. "Last time April came over, you jumped on her." He gave Stormy a stern look. "She doesn't like that. So stay down."

Knocking sounded on the door and Ted opened the dishwasher and tossed in the three pairs of socks he'd just picked up off the living room floor. He barely had the appliance closed when April poked her head in the front door.

Stormy barked and Lolly gave Ted a bored look and wandered over to the food bowls, which he'd filled before his shower.

"Stormy." He rebuked the dog as he strode toward it. He swept her off the floor and leaned into April's personal bubble. "Hey there, April-May." He grinned at her, and it could've been his imagination, but she seemed to melt a little in his presence.

His heart leapt to the back of his throat, where he tried to clear the lump that had spontaneously formed. He just ended up sounding like he was choking.

The moment between them lengthened, with her gazing up at him and him staring down at her. His last words hung in the air. *April-May. April-May. April-May.*

He thought of the chocolate peanut butter cake waiting on his kitchen counter, but everything paled at the thought of kissing April.

He leaned down, only a few inches separating them now, and dropped Stormy to the floor. Every muscle in his body seized, and he whispered, "Is this okay?"

"Yes," April said in an equally breathy voice, and Ted's smile was immediate. He closed the distance between them and kissed her. Finally.

The tension drained out of him with every passing second that she kissed him back. All of Ted's fantasies over the past month had included his fingers threaded in her dark hair, the warmth of her body pressed up against his, the sweet taste of her lips on his tongue.

The real kiss was everything he'd dreamt about—and more.

April held onto Ted's strong shoulders and lost herself to the heat of his touch. He kissed her like a professional, and she didn't believe that he hadn't dated or had a girlfriend in five years.

She stroked her fingers down his face, finally touching the full beard she'd been staring at for five weeks. She smiled, breaking the connection between them. He groaned and kissed her again, clearly unwilling to end the moment too soon.

His dog must not have liked the intrusion, because the little black and white animal barked and nosed April's leg. She yelped and jumped away from the cold touch, effectively breaking the kiss.

Her skin buzzed, the introduction of his touch now infecting her bloodstream. She'd never get the taste of him —chocolate; he surely had snuck some cake already—out of her system. Never be able to breathe in the scent of wood and air freshener without thinking of him.

She laughed nervously, almost stepping on the other dog.

"Stormy." Ted sounded the littlest bit cross with the dog, but his booming laughter filled the cabin in the next moment. "I guess she's jealous." Ted slipped his hand around April's waist and pulled her close again, her belly between them. Pure heat and adoration flowed from his expression.

"I think you invited me over here for cake," April said, pushing fruitlessly against his chest.

"I did, yes." But he didn't back up, didn't look away. "I like you, April-May." He released her then, turned, and took the several steps into the kitchen. She stayed near the front door, her heart and brain battling.

She liked Ted too.

She was also five and a half months pregnant.

Over the past several weeks, she hadn't allowed herself to think past the next day. When that day ended, she'd let in another twenty-four hours. Then she didn't have to think about what her future held, if she could get a job after the baby came, if she was even going to keep the baby.

Her time with Ted had been a bright ray of sunshine in her life. She loved spending time with Megan. Even folding laundry and meal planning was better with Megan, who had an infectious personality and a way of making April feel like she was valuable.

Attending church had helped with that too. She felt closer and closer to a resolution of her past wrongs with every Sunday that passed, and she was working hard to make sure she consulted with God before she did anything.

Including kissing Ted, which made the regret infiltrating her system all the more confusing. She'd felt good about Ted. He was full of life, and love, and laughter. All the things April needed in her life.

"Hey." Ted appeared in front of her, his dark-as-night eyes searching hers. "You okay? I put the little devils in the bedroom." He gave her a grin and held up a plate that held the largest piece of chocolate cake April had ever seen.

"I was just thinking," she said, reaching for the cake.

He handed her a fork. "About what?"

She lifted one shoulder in a shrug but couldn't think of a reason not to tell him. "What to do about the baby."

Ted took his cake into the living room and settled onto the couch with a sigh. "Still haven't decided?"

She tucked her feet under her body and picked up a forkful of cake. "The baby started kicking." She put the cake into her mouth, the rich taste of chocolate, and peanut butter, and sugar exploding against her taste buds. "I'm getting attached to it."

The thought choked her, and she could barely swallow. She forced the bite of cake down and dared to glance at Ted. A tremor of fear shook her fingers, and she shrugged again. "I try not to think about it."

"Why?"

"Why what?"

"Why don't you want to think about your baby?" He put his half-eaten cake on the end table, picked up his coffee mug, and gazed at her evenly.

Frustration at his nosy questions roared through her. She rarely appreciated Ted's interference in her life, but afterward, when she reflected on the conversations, she realized how therapeutic talking to him could be.

"Because, Ted," she said, her tone full of acidity. "Then I have to think about my whole future. What will I do if I keep the baby? I can't live with Megan and Landon forever. I don't have a job here. I don't have any education. So then I think, well, I just need to give the baby up for adoption. And then...." Her hand drifted to her belly, and the peculiar sensation of movement inside her fluttered to life against her palm.

Ted's large hand covered hers, and her gaze flew to his. "I don't like thinking about the future," she said, all the fear she felt evident in her tone. "It's too wide open, you know?"

"I know." He nodded, the motion slow and precise. "But you're not alone."

"Yeah, the Lord will provide a way, I know." She tried to give him a brave smile, but it wobbled on her face. "I'm trying to have faith that everything will work out, but I can't see it. So it's easier not to think about it."

He pulled his hand back, leaving April feeling cold and alone once more. "Maybe you're looking in the wrong places," he said.

"I'm not looking at all," she said. "And it's working for me right now."

"If you say so." Ted picked up his fork and finished his cake, his eyes never hooking onto hers again.

FALL CAME to Utah a little later than it did to Jackson Hole, but it still came. The fields turned golden. The grasses brown and dry. The leaves switched to red, and yellow, and orange. April loved every moment of the cooler weather, the spectacular sunsets, the evening thunderstorms in this patch of the mountains.

Ted took the horses out to the pasture again, but she didn't go with him. Her belly was too big to make riding a horse comfortable, and she didn't want her water to break while she was a three-hour ride from civilization.

He didn't make it back in time for church, and April went by herself. She liked the feelings of peace that existed at the church, thought the preacher had a soothing soul and a powerful voice.

She still left early, and she still hadn't made any attempt to make any friends in town. She didn't need friends. She had Megan, the chickens she'd come to be fond of, and Ted. She'd even warmed up to his dogs and had ordered Halloween costumes for each of them.

As she scattered feed for the hens and roosters, she let her thoughts wander. The church was putting on a chili dinner the night of the thirty-first, and pets were welcome. The way Ted fawned over his fluffy dogs—he even took them down to the dog spa in town to get them bathed and poofed—April had thought the Minnie Mouse costumes she'd bought would be a big hit.

"You got a package," Megan said when April entered the kitchen. She indicated the box on the dining room table. "Can you grab Colby? I think I hear him fussing." Megan went back to the popping oil on the stove, where she was frying chicken.

"Sure." April eyed the package and went down the hall to the nursery. She generally worked with the twins, as baby Colby brought a keen sense of anxiety to her. Megan had seemed to know, but apparently fried chicken was more important at the moment.

"Hey." April smiled at the crying baby, and he quieted. Though he was almost three months old, April still supported the boy's head as she lifted him from the crib. "No crying now, sweetheart." She hummed as she held the baby close, took in a deep breath of his soft, powdery skin. His hair felt like goose down, and she stroked his head until he calmed all the way.

She blinked, and flashes of her future zipped behind her eyes. She could have a baby like this. Soothe him when he needed it. Love him, hold him, smile at him until he smiled back.

Indecision, her faithful friend all these months, filled her. She was so tired of the constant back and forth, and with the weight of the infant in her arms, the idea of keeping the baby was definitely winning.

"Let's go see your mama, all right?" She stepped back into the hall, Landon's low voice meeting her ears. Another male voice sounded too, and April's heart leapt. She worked with Ted every afternoon, held his hand every day, kissed him every evening.

She hadn't mentioned the relationship to Megan, though surely the matron of the ranch knew about it. She hadn't told her mother, though she called every weekend to check in. Her mother was just as nosy as Ted, asked just as many annoying questions.

April walked down the hall, the baby cradled in her arms. Sure enough, Ted lingered in the kitchen, a cucumber spear dripping with ranch dressing in his hand. His eyes landed on her, and his inquisitive eyes saw everything.

Her holding the baby.

How she felt about holding the baby.

Color rushed into his face, and he stuffed the vegetable into his mouth.

"I can take over there," April said, swaying on the edge of the living room. "You want him, Megan?"

"Sure." She stepped over and made an exchange of tongs for a baby. She glanced at Colby, and then April, and then Ted. "You're welcome to stay for dinner, Ted."

"Yes, ma'am," he said automatically.

One of the twins cheered, and Ted laughed as he scooped Ruby into his arms. "Tell me about the nest you found."

"It was an old nest," the little girl said. "April thinks it was probably for a robin."

"There were shells inside," Rachel said, making an attempt to jump up to Ted. He lifted her in one arm, and both twins squealed.

April stepped over to the golden brown chicken, trying not to notice how good Ted was with the kids. The fact was, Ted was good at everything he did. He could tame wild horses. Reach the highest shelves in the barn. Cuddle tiny dogs. Make killer omelets. Laugh about everything. Hold two four-year-olds at once. Kiss a woman like he meant it.

An idea that had been circling in April's mind finally landed. If she kept the baby, maybe she could keep Ted too. Maybe they could be a family.

She wondered if he'd thought about that too. Thought about marrying her and being a father in only two short months.

Her breath came too quick, and she turned a piece of

chicken sloppily, splattering oil all over the stove. She didn't want to marry him because it was convenient, because this ranch, the chickens, Megan and Landon and their family, and the preacher had charmed her. Though that was all true, April wanted to marry and have a family with a man she loved.

She chanced a peek at Ted over her shoulder. He sat on the couch with one little girl on each knee, a book held in front of them all as he read out loud. Did she love Ted Caldwell?

No.

Could she?

Absolutely.

She spun back to the stove, her stomach swooping from side to side. She felt sick, nauseated, and it wasn't all because of the greasy food in front of her.

"Ta-da!" April brandished a bright pink dress at him, a brilliant smile on her face. When he didn't respond, she added, "It's a Minnie Mouse costume for Lolly."

He took the slip of a dress and pulled the plastic off. It really was a Minnie Mouse party dress, the size a doll would wear—or a small dog.

"It has a petticoat and everything." She shook out a second costume. "And look! Ears." She held up a pair of mini Mickey Mouse ears with a pink bow stuck on the left side. An elastic hung down to secure the ears to the dog's head.

"Wow." Ted took the ears, laughter bubbling through his chest. He picked up Lolly and wrestled her into the dress and ears. The dog cowered on the couch, shaking, clearly not a fan of the costume. "Thanks, sweetheart." He leaned over and kissed April, a quick union of their mouths.

"You know this means we're taking them to the church chili dinner."

Ted's eyebrows cocked. "We are?"

"Pets are specifically invited." April heaved her very pregnant form from the couch and went to find Stormy. She trapped the dog in the corner of the kitchen and picked her up. "There's a costume contest and everything."

"Do we have to dress up?"

"I'm going as a pregnant woman," she said. "You can be a cowboy." She handed him the wiggling dog, who quieted in Ted's arms. She sank onto the couch again, an exhausted sigh escaping her lips.

"You doin' okay?" he asked as he put the second costume on. Stormy growled and hunkered down on the couch, one paw furiously trying to get the ears off. She finally succeeded, and Ted didn't move to redress her. "You seem tired."

She gave him a sleepy smile. "Just what every girl wants to hear." She laid her head on the back of the couch and watched him with a look in her eye he'd started to see more and more often over the past few weeks.

If he wasn't careful, he'd find himself in love with April Nox. He'd resisted the idea, mostly because everything about her was literally up in the air, and he only had two hands. He wanted to make sure he caught the most important things when it started to rain.

Because he sensed a storm coming.

"You're beautiful," he whispered, reaching out and tucking a lock of her grown-out hair behind her ear.

"And you're handsome." The smile she gave him was filled with soft emotions, and Ted had the urge to ask her dozens of questions until their future together was worked out.

Instead, he inched as close as her belly would allow, and kissed her.

———

"Oh, my—wow." Ted couldn't take in the chaos at the church fast enough. People, kids, pets, the variety and bright colors of costumes assaulted him on all sides. One dog barked, and a whole pack would join in. Lolly and Stormy quivered in his arms, and he turned to April.

"I don't think my dogs are going to fit in here."

She rolled her eyes. "You baby them. Here." She took them both and set them on the floor. A dog the size of a red wagon shot toward them, sniffing for all it was worth.

Ted scooped his dogs back up and cradled them in his arms. "I don't feel good about this. They're not very social."

"That's because you never let them play with other dogs."

"They play with Walker's dogs all the time."

She scoffed. "I haven't seen that happen once."

"Walker's been busy lately." Ted glanced around the gymnasium where long serving tables had been set up. Dozens more filled the space, and several baby gates cordoned off a section of the area where people had put their pets. Ted couldn't fathom putting Lolly and Stormy in that pen with the other dogs, the cats, even a couple of guinea pigs. And was that a...ferret?

Ted clutched his poms closer. "I'll hold them while we eat."

April laughed. "How are you going to eat chili while holding two dogs?"

He lifted his chin. "Will you get me some food?"

"So now I have to serve you?"

"I'll just take the dogs out to the truck." The weather had cooled considerably; they would be fine for an hour in the cab with the windows down. When he returned to the party, he found April engaged in conversation with Tess Thompson and Renee Jackman, the other cowboy's wives who lived out at Brush Creek. Ted wasn't sure if he should be glad she'd been fraternizing with the other women at the ranch, or worried what they'd tell her about him.

He joined her, slipping his fingers into hers to let her know he'd returned. She looked at him. "Did you get your babies secured?"

"Yes." He smiled at Tess and Renee. "Hello, ladies. Where are the guys?"

"Walker's going through the line with the boys." Tess nodded her blonde head toward the long line that wound past the pots of chili, platters of cornbread, and one giant bowl of green salad.

"Justin's a judge for the pet costume contest." Renee's thumbs flashed across her phone and she tucked it into the back pocket of her overalls. Ted couldn't decide what she was supposed to be: a hillbilly or a scarecrow.

April elbowed him, and Ted groaned as he bent over. "What?"

"We totally could've won the pet costume contest with Justin as a judge."

"I think we'll survive without the year's supply of dog food." Ted rolled his eyes. "You know, you can't just change a dog's diet like that. The hardware store doesn't even carry the brand I feed my poms."

April swung her attention to him, and he squirmed under the scrutiny. "What?"

"What brand do you feed your dogs?"

"This special lamb and chicken blend," he said. "I don't apologize for it. I buy it online at a specialty dog store."

April cracked up, her laugh high and sweet and making Ted smile too. "Specialty online dog store." She turned to Renee. "Have you ever heard of such a thing?"

"Actually, yes," Renee said. "My whole job is online, and I probably know the store. I follow a lot of businesses on twitter." She glanced at Ted, whose chest swelled with pride. "Is it Barkalicious or The Dog Spot?"

"The Dog Spot." Ted chuckled and squeezed April's hand. "Renee is a social media coordinator for the National Parks Department."

April looked at Renee like she'd personally wronged her, then smiled. "I think I remember you saying that. I just forgot."

Ted let himself believe for a few brief moments that this was his life. His wife that was pregnant. His ranch family—which at least was true. He noticed the line to get food had shortened considerably, and he stood. "Should we get something to eat?"

April batted her eyelashes at him. "Will you get me some of the non-spicy stuff?" She rubbed her belly. "I'm tired."

"Sure." Ted didn't mind at all. Him going through the line for April only added to his fantasy that this temporary situation could become permanent.

———

A WEEK LATER, Ted ducked into the homestead, almost losing the door to the howling wind. Hail the size of green peas had started pummeling the ranch about thirty seconds ago, prompting Ted to run the last hundred yards to the house.

No one else seemed to be there, and Ted remembered that Landon and Megan had gone to Vernal for the day to get their major winter shopping done. Landon went every year and bought bottled water, enough food to see the whole ranch through a month of bad weather, feed and farm supplies that filled a whole barn, and now that they had a new baby, diapers.

He crossed through the house to the front door and checked out the windows flanking it only to find the hail had intensified. April's voice came closer and then moved farther away, and Ted turned to locate her.

"It's not that, Mom. It's just that...." She appeared at the top of the stairs but didn't turn toward him. She continued into the kitchen, stopping at the sliding glass door and watching the hail as it pounded everything outside.

"I don't know what I'm going to do," she continued, one hip cocking to the right. "Ranch life isn't for me. I won't stay here, I know that."

Ted couldn't hear her mother's half of the conversation, and he didn't need to. What April had said was damaging enough. *Ranch life isn't for me.*

I won't stay here.

"No, Mom. No more small towns. I'm going to find a really big city with a really small apartment, and disappear into the crowd." Her hand slid down her back and she arched as if she was in pain. She'd complained to him that the bigger she got, the more uncomfortable everything became. She'd said she could hardly sleep, and Ted noticed that she still wore a pair of exercise pants and a sweatshirt though it was mid-afternoon.

Her words landed like bombs in his head. She didn't like small towns. Or ranches. Or cowboys.

She didn't like *him*.

He turned toward the front door, determined to leave before she saw him, before he heard anything else that would confuse and infuriate him. He had his hand on the knob when she said, "I'm not going to take the baby to the big city, Mom. I don't think I'm going to keep the baby."

Ted wrenched open the door and stomped out of the homestead. He couldn't remember the last time he'd been this angry, this hurt, this betrayed.

He didn't even feel the hail as it pelted his shoulders and back. Physical pain was certainly easier than this emotional turmoil.

April stared at the hail bouncing into the homestead. The front door swung in the wind. Her phone slipped from her fingers as she moved as fast as her eight-months-pregnant body would allow. She thought she'd seen a flash of Ted's black cowboy hat, and horror filled her as she thought about what she'd said last.

She burst out of the house and onto the front porch. Ted had already crossed the lane, his head bent against the weather as he practically ran from the homestead. She called after him, but the driving hail swallowed her voice before it even left her throat. She watched him until he disappeared into his cabin.

How much had he heard?

A chill made her blood like ice, and she stepped back into the house and closed the door. The furnace blew warm air now that the front entrance had been open for a few minutes, and she retrieved her phone from the kitchen floor where she'd dropped it. The call had been disconnected, and her screen bore a hairline crack right across the middle of it. April stared at it, feeling very much like her life had just been split wide open.

She paced in the living room, the baby kicking her and her back aching along with her head. And her heart. Sleep would help a lot of her physical problems, but that had eluded her more and more often as the baby continued to grow.

Five weeks. She had five weeks until the baby came, and she still had nothing on the horizon as a for-sure future. With every passing day, she'd fallen a little further in love with Ted, but even her relationship with him hung by a thread.

A sour taste worked its way up her throat and she filled a glass with water and gulped it. The hail petered out, and April felt trapped by the walls of the homestead. She stepped out onto the porch, the smell of wet cement greeting her. She gazed toward the red rock butte in the distance, remembering when she'd stood on the top of it, looking back this way.

She hadn't spoken the whole truth when she'd told her mother ranch life didn't suit her. She didn't particularly enjoy the ranching aspect of living on a ranch, but she did enjoy the solitude, the privacy, the stillness in the very air. She liked that there was no gossipy neighbors discussing how large she'd gotten, that she could still get her girly fix with Megan, Tess, and Renee. They apparently got together every month without their husbands, and April had attended the last get-together at Tess's place.

There had been more chocolate than April thought four women could consume. But consume it they did. Her favorite had been the chocolate dipped dill pickle potato chips—a pregnant woman's dream come true.

The sky threatened to open again, and April pressed her eyes closed. *What should I do?* she prayed. She'd put off asking God for the guidance she desperately needed, choosing instead to focus on getting back into His good graces.

Stay at the ranch? Get a job in town? Find an apartment to rent?

Tell Ted I love him?

Her eyes popped open.

Did she love Ted? Her fingers migrated to her lips as she thought about how safe she felt inside his arms. How much she liked the way he gazed at her with that edge of love and adoration in his eyes. She appreciated his humor, his faith, his work ethic. He only had two strikes against him—his endless questions and the fact that he was her opposite in almost every way. Oh, and he was a cowboy and she'd never been interested in them. Double oh, his dogs.

She swallowed, her throat dry with the thought of being in love with a man who wasn't the father of her baby. How could that even happen?

She smoothed her hair back, exhaustion making her brain slow. A better question was: how could he want her? But every time he touched her, her doubts evaporated. Every time he looked at her, she felt cherished.

She sucked in a breath. She was in love with Ted Caldwell, and not only that. He loved her too.

April snatched a jacket from the front closet and entered the angry weather. His cabin sat way down on the end, and she waddled toward it, hoping to beat the precipitation threatening to burst from the heavy-looking storm clouds.

That particular prayer didn't get answered the way she'd like, and the sky opened when she still had half the distance to go. The ground was already muddy and slick, and she slowed her steps so she wouldn't fall. She couldn't even imagine the pain and humiliation that would cause.

She finally reached the relative safety of Ted's porch. Her breath hitched in her chest, and her side ached. She knocked on the door and waited when she normally would've just gone in.

Ted took his sweet time answering the door, and when he did, he leaned against the frame and stared at her.

"Hey," she said. "Can I come in?" She reached up with both hands and slicked the water from her hair. "I'm freezing."

"I suppose." He stepped back and allowed her to enter his toasty cabin. He had a fire roaring in the hearth and she moved to stand in front of it. The welcome heat thawed her fingers and bolstered her bravery. "I was just telling my mom what she wanted to hear," she said.

"I don't know what you're talking about."

She turned and found him still standing near the front door, his arms folded. Both of his pups sat at his feet, the three of them a wall of judgment.

April swallowed. "She wants me to come back to Jackson, and I know I don't want to do that."

"What do you want, April?"

She mourned the loss of the tacked-on *May*, and her insides softened. "I want you to call me April-May." She tried on a smile, but it didn't quite fit on her face. She erased it. "I want to know how you feel about me. I want to figure out how to do what's right." She swallowed, her entire abdomen stretched so tight, she felt like a balloon that had been blown up too much.

"I heard you say you weren't going to stay in town."

"I did say that. To my mother."

"You aren't going to keep the baby?" He glanced to her belly and back to her eyes.

Tears pooled in her eyes. She'd done such a good job over the past few months at keeping them dormant. Getting to know Ted, spending time with him, falling in love with him had definitely helped her emotional state. If she was being honest, she'd say she'd been happy since arriving at Brush Creek Horse Ranch.

"I think I'm going to keep her," she said, acknowledging her true feelings for the first time. She felt raw, naked, utterly alone standing before him.

He flinched but maintained his position by the door. "You know it's a girl?"

"Maybe your overuse of the female pronoun has rubbed off on me."

His lips twitched toward a smile. "Maybe."

"Can you come hug me now?" Her chin wobbled, and she let the tears fall as Ted closed the distance between them and wrapped her in those strong arms of his. "I'm sorry," she whispered into his shoulder. "I'm trying to do what's right for me, for the baby, for you. It's all a big mess."

"There's no mess here," he whispered, his lips catching on her ear. He skated them down to her neck. "You wanted to know how I feel about you." He gazed down at her, covering her with that warm feeling of love and acceptance.

"Yeah." She half-chuckled, half-sobbed. "It would help if I knew so I could make some decisions."

"Well, I wish I could tell you." His husky voice could've lit a city on fire. "When I know, you'll know." He stepped back, swiped his hand through his hair, and started making something for lunch.

———

With only a month left in her pregnancy, it became too difficult to bend over and pick up saddles. Too tiring to paint stall doors and lead horses from the barn to the arena. The weather worsened, and April started staying at the homestead and helping there instead of going out to the ranch in the afternoons.

Her time with Ted dwindled to almost nothing, even in the evenings. She wanted to give him the space he needed to figure out how he felt, and as more and more nights went by where he didn't invite her over either, her self-confidence took a nosedive.

With only three weeks left before the baby was due, Ted finally came to see her. Right down the steps and into the basement too, where she lay curled up on the couch, a cartoon playing on the television in front of her as she babysat the twins so Megan could get some accounting work done for the ranch.

She scrambled to sit up, but as she didn't do anything quickly these days, it took her several seconds. She was sure she looked like a beached walrus trying to get back to the waves, and a burst of embarrassment bolted through her. "Hi," she said when she finally reached an upright position.

"Haven't seen you in a while."

"I've been helping more around the homestead until the baby comes."

"Then what?"

She sighed. "I don't know."

He nodded. "All right. That's what I needed to know." He turned toward the steps and took them two at a time.

April stared after him for a second, then she got to her feet and followed him. Much slower, so she caught him just as he was stepping through the front door. "Ted, wait."

He paused, ducked his head so that sexy cowboy hat concealed his face, and half-turned back to her.

"What did you need to know?"

He faced her, a perfect storm of emotion raging across his handsome features. Her fingers itched to touch that beard again, kiss those lips, fall into the warmth of his embrace. She held her ground.

"I don't think this is going to work between us."

His words knocked her backward. "What?"

"I love you, and I've been hoping you'd fall in love with me too." He glanced at her belly. "But I don't think you're in a place to do that. I don't blame you. Honest, I don't." He wiped his palm over his beard. "I just need some closure before the baby comes, and I was hoping—it doesn't matter." He put his hand on the doorknob and took another step outside. "I'm sorry, April."

He left, pulling the door softly closed behind him. April sank onto the couch, the absence of that *May* haunting her.

What had just happened? And why had it happened?

CHAPTER 13

His dogs didn't know how to handle Ted's bad mood. Stormy whined and Lolly wouldn't leave his side. He patted the puffy animal, but the same comfort he'd always taken from her didn't come.

He picked up his phone and dialed his father. Ted had told him all about April, and it had been his dad who'd made Ted realize that this unsure relationship needed a solid foundation to thrive.

"Hey, Dad."

"Ted." The level of surprise in his father's voice wasn't hard to detect.

"April still doesn't know what she wants." He exhaled. "I broke things off with her."

"Oh." That was all. No condolences. No sympathy.

"Do you think I should've done that?"

"I don't know, Teddy. All I know is what you've told me."

"She doesn't know what to do. She has a lot of big decisions to make, and I don't want to be in her way."

"Has she ever said you're in her way?"

"No."

"Why do you think that then?"

Because she'd said so. She'd said she needed to know how he felt before she could decide how she felt. And while he'd hugged her when she'd asked him to last week, he didn't like that she couldn't examine and evaluate her own feelings.

"She just has too much going on right now, what with the baby due in only a couple of weeks and all."

Someone knocked on his door, and he glanced up from the couch. It wasn't April; the knock was much too solid for that. "I have to go, Dad. I'll call you later." He hung up and headed toward the door.

Blake stood on the other side, his collar turned up against the night wind. "Hey, your headlights are still on. Truck's locked, or I'd have turned them off."

"Thanks." Ted twisted to locate his keys. He'd gone down to town before lunch, his emotions a tangled mess he'd hoped to fix with sugar and fried dough. Three of the half-dozen doughnuts he'd bought from the bakery still sat in the box, and he'd eat them for breakfast tomorrow. Or maybe for dinner tonight.

He walked out with Blake and climbed in the truck. He tried to start the truck, but the ignition only clicked. He sighed. "They've been on all day." It had been raining earlier that day when he'd driven down the canyon. "Can you give me a jump?"

Blake smiled but it held hints of weariness. Ted imagined farming in the winter was miserable business.

"Let me get my cables." Blake went next door and

returned a few minutes later. The two men made short work of the dead battery, and Ted left the truck running to get the charge back up.

"Thanks." Ted shook Blake's hand. "You wanna stay for dinner?" Ted suddenly didn't want to be alone tonight, his sad dogs his only companions. He couldn't believe he'd gone and fallen in love with a pregnant woman. Not only that, but a woman who had never committed to staying in town for longer than it took to have the baby.

How many times had she said she couldn't wait to have the baby? So many Ted had lost count. Had he ever truly seen her happy? A few nights, while she cuddled with him on the couch, he thought he'd sensed some real contentment in her.

"Hey," Blake said. "You okay?"

"Sorry." Ted shook his head, wishing the thoughts of April didn't scream so loudly. "I didn't actually make dinner. Maybe we should go over to the—" He cut off. He wasn't going back to the homestead.

"Maybe Tess has something," Blake said. "Want me to text Walker?"

"Yeah."

Blake did, and said, "Yeah, Tess has chicken and wild rice soup ready. Let's go." Ted followed him to the foreman's cabin, stepping into the cheery yellow light and blazing warmth of a fire. He smiled at the tween boys and asked them if they were ready for Thanksgiving break. They started talking at the same time, and Ted absorbed himself in it the way he did with the twins at the homestead.

Walker gave him a strange look, and Tess stared him down as she put two more soup bowls on the table. "You boys eat at the counter tonight," she said and Ted helped move the boys' bowls and silverware to the counter.

Blake tried to sit across from Tess, but she said, "You sit here, Blake. Ted." She nodded to the spot where she wanted him, and he sat obediently and tucked a napkin into his collar. He'd been out of the dating game for a while, but he knew an angry girlfriend when he saw one.

Tess waited until grace had been said and everyone had food before she said, "So you broke up with April today?"

Walker swung his head toward Ted so fast, Ted thought the foreman would have a severe kink in the morning. "You what? I thought you liked her." His soup spoon hung in midair, fully loaded and ready to be slurped.

"I do like her."

Tess clucked her tongue. "False. You're in love with her."

Ted filled his mouth with food so he wouldn't have to talk. Didn't matter. Walker and Tess had a conversation about him as if he wasn't even in the room.

"Maybe he should just tell her he'd like to raise the baby with her." Walker finally put that bite of soup in his mouth.

Tess shook her head. "No, April won't believe him. Her self-worth is really low right now. Once the baby comes—"

"Why does everything hinge on the baby?" Ted interrupted.

Blake seemed riveted by the conversation, and his eating speed didn't slow. Dinner and a show.

"Ted," Tess said. "The baby is the physical representation of everything April dislikes about her life. It's something everyone can see. Something that testifies to everyone of what she did wrong. She *can't* move on until the baby is born."

"Why can't you just wait until the baby is born?" Walker asked.

"Wait a second." Ted put his spoon down. "Didn't you two get married on the fly, mere hours before a surgery you weren't sure Tess would survive?" He nodded at Blake, who looked half surprised, half horrified. "True story. So how do you get to lecture me about *waiting*?"

"I'm just saying that April can't make a decision until the baby comes."

"And what if she doesn't pick me?" Ted asked, his real fear coming out.

Tess leaned back in her chair, a knowing look on her face. "So that's what this is about. You're scared."

"Of course I'm scared. The woman I love might give up her baby. I don't know what that will do to her, but I know it's not going to be easy. She told her mom she doesn't like the ranch life, and who am I? A cowboy who works and lives on a ranch. And let's say she keeps the baby. Then what? Can I be the father? Will she let me? I don't even know how she feels about me."

He stared at Tess, his breathing almost frantic. Walker volleyed his gaze from his wife to Ted. "He has a point. A lot of them, actually."

Ted stuffed half a piece of homemade bread in his mouth, feeling justified in his fears, his decision to protect himself by breaking up with April.

"So you broke up with her so you wouldn't get hurt." Tess wasn't asking.

"Yes," Ted said. The thought of going back to his life

before April made his throat thick, and Ted remembered why he didn't date. Then he didn't have to fall in love with a brunette who didn't reciprocate.

Tess shook her head and scoffed. "Just because you've been scorned in the past doesn't mean April's going to hurt you."

"She doesn't have any idea what she'll do." Ted removed the napkin and stood. "Thank you for dinner, Tess. It was delicious." He glanced at Walker and Blake. "See you guys at work." He left the cabin because the only thing worse than having all the thoughts contained in his head was speaking them out loud, trying to make them line up, attempting to justify that what he'd done was the right thing.

As he headed back to his cabin, he knew it was. He'd freed April so she could make the smart decisions she needed to make, without emotions clouding her reason.

THE FOLLOWING DAY, Ted sat in his truck, the engine idling and the heater blowing so he didn't freeze. He didn't want to drive down the canyon to the church by himself. He couldn't believe he'd ever done that. Ever walked into that chapel alone. Ever looked around and wondered who to sit by.

Maybe he hadn't. Maybe he'd never realized how alone he was, how he went to church with Blake and the other single cowboys like it was normal.

It didn't feel normal now. Normal now was talking with April as he navigated the roads. Holding her hand on the way inside. Parking himself on the end of the back bench and draping his arm around her. How could he go back to sitting with other men? Or worse, alone?

He backed onto the lane in front of his house and drove down to the homestead and took a deep breath. "It's thirty seconds," he told himself. "Be brave for thirty seconds." He'd told himself this mantra for a decade as he rode broncs in the rodeo. Thirty seconds. He could do anything for thirty seconds. He dialed April, a constant prayer in his throat that she'd answer.

She did.

"Hey," he said. "I was wondering if you're going to church today...." Five seconds down. Twenty-five to go.

She seemed to stay silent that long before finally saying, "I don't think so, Ted."

He nodded, his bravery gone and his pride choking him. He wouldn't beg her to go with him. "All right. Sorry to bother you." He hung up before she could respond, before he could say something else to upset her.

He drove down to town alone, but he bypassed the church. He had never realized how many families filled the pews, as he'd never really considered having a family himself. April had blown up everything in his life. Everything he thought he was okay with. Everything he thought he didn't want.

He parked near the walking path at Oxbow Park and started strolling. His feet took him out to the island that had enthralled April, and he leaned his elbows against a black iron railing, able to see all the way through the two-acre park now that the leaves had fallen.

As he stood there, alone in the icy air and snowy

scenery, he felt calm. Peaceful. He realized that he didn't want to live alone for the rest of his life, and he pulled out his phone and called his dad again.

"Why didn't you ever get remarried?" he asked.

"I wasn't alone, Teddy," his dad said. "I had you and Stephen."

"I don't have anyone," Ted said, his voice falling into a hush. He thought briefly of returning to Texas, to his family, but that made his blood curdle and he dismissed the idea.

"Well, if you don't want to be alone, do something about it."

"All right, Dad." Ted finished the conversation with news about Stephen, who'd gotten a new job at the state courthouse, and hung up. He'd always loved and admired his father. It couldn't have been easy raising two sons alone.

His thoughts started to race. He didn't want April to struggle the way his family had. If she chose to keep this baby, he couldn't let her do it by herself.

The negativity that he'd allowed to infiltrate his life lifted. He still wanted April to make her own decisions, and all he could do now was hope and pray that God put her on the same path that Ted was currently on.

Is that possible? he asked. Lord, if possible, help April choose me.

Without the birds that usually twittered in the park, only silence responded to him. "Have I done the right thing?" he asked out loud this time, a bit of unease returning. "Or should I go get April and make sure she knows I want her to choose me?"

Ted had never really had a lot of decisions to make.

Certainly not hard ones like what April faced. He grew up with horses and had always wanted to join the rodeo. So he had. He'd taken to it easily, and his natural talent and skill with horses had made him a champion. His injury had put a kink in his life plans, but the decision to stay in the rodeo or leave had been easy.

He was hurt; he had a lot of money; he was done with the rodeo. Landon had called about Brush Creek the day Ted's cast had come off. The decision had been easy. And Ted had enjoyed his work on the ranch for the past five years, never once questioning if he should be doing something else, trying to find a woman to share his life with, nothing.

"So should I go talk to her?" he wondered again, and though the earth didn't shake and he didn't feel anything especially significant, he suddenly had the urge to tell April —again—that he loved her.

He hurried back to his truck, telling himself he'd have to be brave for a lot longer than thirty seconds this time.

CHAPTER 14

April lay on the couch in the basement, the homestead around her huge and hulking. Megan and Landon had left for church twenty minutes ago, and the brief conversation with Ted had ended ten minutes ago.

April wasn't sure how to feel. She didn't feel. Just stared. She'd spent the evening with Megan stroking her hair, telling her that she could still have Ted if she wanted him. Did she want him?

April hadn't been able to answer any questions with more than "I don't know." She really just needed to know what to do, but God hadn't been very vocal when she'd asked. When she'd confessed to Megan that she didn't feel worthy of someone like Ted, Megan had scoffed.

"We all make mistakes, April. Don't let yours define you—or Ted. He's wiser than you think, and you're better than you think."

Megan's words had played through April's dreams. They stuck in her mind as she put on the same clothes she'd been wearing for the past week. She didn't have much that fit anymore, and with only a few weeks left, she didn't want to purchase anything new.

She sighed and picked up the remote control, realizing she had no idea what she was even watching. She clicked the button at the same time a flash of discomfort started in her stomach. She groaned as pain ripped through her abdomen. She'd never had a baby before, but she knew she shouldn't feel like an animal was trying to claw its way out of her stomach.

The remote forgotten, April eased herself into a sitting position, her breath coming quicker as she tried to tame the pain. It receded after only a few moments, but her muscles didn't release until they were sure the discomfort wasn't going to return.

April glanced at the clock. She hadn't spent much time thinking about the delivery of her baby. She hadn't read a single book. She'd gone to the doctor several times, and was due to go on Tuesday before Thanksgiving. She wasn't due for another three weeks. Maybe she just had a little indigestion or gas.

Nine minutes later, her baby kicked and the pain shot through her with the power and speed of a bolt of lightning.

She couldn't deny it. She was having labor pains. The next one came only seven minutes later, and after it passed, April walked into her bedroom and glanced around like a fairy godmother would appear with a bag of clothes and toiletries she could take to the hospital. Nothing poofed into existence, so she threw a few things into a bag, grabbed her toothbrush and toothpaste from the bathroom and got herself upstairs before the next contraction came.

Without a hospital in Brush Creek, April had been planning to go to Vernal to deliver the baby. She hadn't planned how she'd get there, who would drive her, or anything. In a bout of panic, she wondered if she'd even be able to make the forty-five minute drive in time.

As soon as the pain was tolerable, she moved. Got herself behind the wheel of her car—which wasn't an easy feat—and started the drive. She called her mom and said, "I think the baby's coming. I'm on my way to the hospital."

Her mom sucked in a breath. "I'll get in the car in an hour. I was planning to get packed up next week."

"I know." April's emotions quivered. "She's coming early."

"Who's driving you?"

"I'm driving myself."

"April, no." Her mom sounded scared. "Where's Megan?"

"She and Landon are at church."

"So what? Call her."

"Okay," April said. "I will as soon as I hang up with you." April regretted the fib, but she wasn't going to bother Megan. She hung up and placed her phone on her leg for easy reach.

In the back of her mind, she'd thought Ted would take her to the hospital. She'd never allowed the idea to come to the forefront of her mind, had never vocalized it. But now that the moment was here, she realized she hadn't made any plans with Megan, because she'd had Ted.

And now she didn't.

Or did she? He had called that morning and invited her to church. He had told her he loved her last night. Those feelings didn't disappear overnight just because he'd said he didn't think things would work out between them.

So why had he ended things between them, only to call her twelve hours later?

Her fingers tightened on the steering wheel as the town came into view. She knew the answer: He was as confused as she was. Bolstered by that theory, she made it past the church without searching for his truck. She wasn't sure she could drive by without stopping if she saw it.

She made it past the city limits and onto the open highway that would take her to Vernal, to the hospital, to the rest of her life. She took a deep breath, which turned out to be a good thing as another contraction descended immediately after that. She eased up on the accelerator, but managed to keep her car on the road. It helped that no one else seemed to be out this Sunday morning, but as soon as April realized that she was literally all alone on this lonely stretch of highway a tidal wave of fear crashed over her.

The minutes passed and she finally arrived at the hospital, her contractions now only about four minutes apart and lasting what felt like an eternity. She didn't know where to park or how far she'd have to walk, so she navigated herself to the emergency entrance, and collapsed into a wheelchair, panting. "I'm in labor," she said to the desk clerk, who stood and came to help her.

"Are you alone?" the woman asked.

April pressed her lips together and nodded.

"Well, let me get someone to take you up to labor and delivery."

"Thank you." April's voice sounded like she'd breathed in helium, and thankfully the next person who came to help her didn't ask her anything but her name. A contraction hit just as she arrived at the nurse's station in the labor and delivery wing. She had to wait for it to subside before she could give her doctor's name and her vital info.

A nurse wrote it all down for her and then she was wheeled into a delivery room. She was left alone again, and as she undressed and put on the gown she'd been given, April thought this would be the most uneventful birth in history.

Things happened very quickly after that. Nurses seemed to come and go every few seconds. Her blood pressure was taken. Her temperature. Questions were asked, and her doctor arrived wearing a white shirt and tie and checked her. "We're getting close," he said. An older gentleman who'd delivered Megan's babies, April had liked him. He had kind, blue eyes that locked onto April's now.

"Have you decided what to do?" he asked.

All activity in the room slowed. April had to decide if she was going to keep the baby or not. Right now.

No one was here to help her. Not her mother, who had planned to come several days early to be there for the birth. Not Megan, who April hadn't even called. Not Ted, who had always been at her side whenever she let herself think about actually having a baby.

"April?" Dr. Johns came to her side and took her hand in his. "Do I need to get the social worker so she can begin the paperwork for an adoption?" He gazed down on her the way she imagined her father would. "There are many families who would love to have a baby for Thanksgiving. You don't need to worry about that. You can even pick the fami-ly." He punctuated his words with a smile that eased some of April's fears.

The snakes and serpents that had come whenever April thought about giving her baby up for adoption came back in full force. She shook her head. "No." Her chin wobbled and her chest shook. "I'm going to keep the baby."

"All right." Dr. Johns turned back to the nurses and said, "I'll go get changed and prepped," before leaving.

April didn't know where she'd put her phone, so she couldn't call anyone now anyway. Reality sunk in: She was going to have this baby all by herself.

She took a deep breath and laid her head back against the pillows. This wouldn't be easy. But she didn't mind, because she knew it was right.

———

Two hours later, her labor had officially stalled. Dr. Johns was worried the baby would start to get distressed, but so far the heartbeat looked steady and strong. The contractions hadn't progressed though, and frustration had started to set in.

Her phone had also gone off several times, and she'd finally asked a nurse to retrieve it from her purse for her.

Megan had called twice and texted double that. April wouldn't be able to put off answering her for much longer, especially as her last text said, *I'm going to call your mom and then the police if I don't hear from you in the next ten minutes.*

It had come seven minutes ago. The first call would get

Megan the information she wanted, and in another hour, April wouldn't be alone in the delivery room. She wanted Megan there as much as she didn't. Everything was very confusing.

She thumbed out I started having contractions so I came to the hospital. It's stalled now, though. Just waiting.

Megan called, and April sighed as she swiped on the call. "I'm fine, Megan."

"You drove yourself to the hospital?" Her voice had probably alerted all the dogs on the ranch, and April imagined them all whining and lining up in the homestead's backyard.

"No one else was around."

"Then you make a phone call." Megan sounded angry now. "I'm coming down there."

"You don't need to do that, Megan."

"You're not having this baby by yourself."

"You have your own family to take care of."

"April."

"Maybe I want to do this by myself," she said. "Have you ever thought of that?"

The silence on the other end of the line said that no, Megan had never considered that April would prefer to do things alone.

"Have you talked to Ted?" she asked.

"No."

"Your mom?"

"Yes."

Megan sighed, and the indecision came through the line loud and clear. "What are you going to do about the baby?"

"I'm keeping her," April said. "And I don't know what

will happen after that, but I'll probably need to stay with you for a little while before I start looking for my own place to live."

"You can stay as long as you want." Megan's words came with choked emotions and the auditory evidence of tears.

"Thank you," April whispered as a nurse entered the room. "I have to go. Nurses and doctors and stuff."

"Love you, April," Megan said, and April felt the affection of the words all the way down deep in her soul. She *believed* that Megan loved her.

As Dr. Johns checked her progress again and looked at her chart, April felt another type of love. The love of God. She wept, finally feeling like the past she'd been working to overcome had finally been conquered.

"April, I'd like to get this show on the road. I'm going to strip your membranes and break your water. See if that doesn't encourage this little one to come." He continued the explanation of what he'd do, and what she'd feel, and what he hoped it would accomplish. April nodded and gave her consent, part of her thoughts lingering on Ted.

He said he loved her. She hadn't quite believed him. But now that she believed herself loveable, maybe he had spoken true.

Dr. Johns performed the procedure, and pain poured through April. She groaned, got more meds, and prepared herself when Dr. Johns said, "Perfect. This is exactly what we want."

Only twenty minutes later, he was telling her to push. And a few minutes after that, the tinny cry of an infant met her ears, along with the words, "Congratulations, April. It's a girl."

Tears streamed down her face as the nurses cleaned the baby and then they wrapped the tiny human in white blankets and handed her to April.

She gazed down at her daughter and thought that in this moment, everything was perfect.

CHAPTER 15

Ted shot to standing when loud, frantic pounded sounded on his front door. Both Stormy and Lolly started barking, and Ted stutter-stepped around them to open the door. Landon stood there, a dark look on his face.

"What's wrong?" Ted's heart tap danced in his chest, and he hated the sensation.

"Have you talked to April?"

"I called her this morning before church. Asked her to come with me. She said no." He'd been home for a couple of hours and hadn't expected to see another human being today. Sure, Megan would invite him to Sunday dinner, but Ted had been planning to decline. He'd make up an illness if he had to.

"She's in the hospital in Vernal. The baby is coming."

Ted blinked, breathed, and grabbed his keys. He didn't hear what else Landon said. Didn't check to see if he had enough gas to make the drive. He simply knew he had to go, and now.

Every minute fueled his anxiety, and he couldn't park straight once he arrived at the hospital. He hadn't been in this hospital before, and he had no idea where to go. He didn't know if the baby had been born yet, or what April had decided, and a sob worked its way up his throat.

Somehow, over the past five months, he'd fallen in love with April Nox—and her baby. He'd fallen in love with the idea of a life with her, a family.

He punched the button to call the elevator, glancing toward the ceiling. What if she'd already had the baby and they'd taken it away? What could he do then? He knew nothing about adopting a baby or raising a child, but the desperation coating his throat told him he'd do almost anything to have April and her baby in his life.

"April Nox?" he asked at the nurse's station, and he got a room number. "Is she awake? Has she had the baby yet?"

"Let me check."

But Ted couldn't wait. He told the nurse "Never mind," and headed down the hall. *Thirty seconds*, he told himself as he arrived at the closed door. He knocked with one knuckle as he pushed open the door.

April lay in the bed, her hair a messy knot on top of her head. She swung her tired gaze toward him, her face lighting up and showing shock when she saw him. "Ted."

His emotion escaped in the form of a choked sob. He didn't see a baby anywhere, but he crossed the room and took April's face in his hands. "I love you." He kissed her, glad when she let him. "I'm totally mad at you, but I love you." He ran his hands over her shoulders as if he could tell how she was doing just by touching. "Why didn't you call me?"

"You ended things between us."

He shook his head. "Only so you could make smart decisions. I fully expected you to come back to me once you had some idea of what your future held."

"I kept the baby," she said. "I named her Emma."

Ted's breath caught. "After my mom?"

"I don't know when I decided," April said. "To keep her. What to name her. All of it. But somewhere along the way, I decided I wanted you in my life."

Ted's confusion multiplied. "Why didn't you tell me?" He wouldn't have been so frustrated. Wouldn't have been dancing around all these months, wondering, hoping, praying he could catch all the moving pieces. Wouldn't have broken up with her to protect himself.

Her eyes shown with tears. "I didn't know. I wasn't trying to lead you on or be difficult."

Ted pressed his lips to her forehead again. "I know, April-May. I know." He stepped back, his panic gone now and leaving him exhausted. "So where's the baby?"

"The nurse took her for a bath. Told me I should sleep." She yawned, and Ted fell back a step.

"I'll go then. I'll just be in the waiting room."

"Don't go," she said, reaching one hand toward him. He returned to her side, threading his fingers through hers and taking the empty chair at her bedside.

He let a few minutes go by in silence. "We need to talk."

"I know, but Ted." She turned her head toward him. "Can we just *be* today? Please?"

Though he didn't want to *just be*, he said, "Yeah, sure."

"Thanks." She closed her eyes again, and when the nurse wheeled in the baby a few minutes later, Ted leapt to his feet. He couldn't tear his eyes from the little bundle in the clear plastic container, and he reached for it.

"Can I?"

The nurse looked at him. "Are you the father?"

"No." Ted's fingers tingled as he peered down at the tiny girl, her skin pink, her eyes closed. "But I want to be."

"He's fine," April said sleepily.

"She needs to eat," the nurse said. "I'll leave you guys alone."

Ted watched her go, sure he'd break the baby if he tried to touch her. He locked eyes with April. "Can I hold her?"

"Have you held a baby before?"

Ted couldn't think of a single time, and he shook his head, suddenly filled with fear and nerves. "Maybe I shouldn't." He licked his lips, unsure of the last time he felt this unsettled.

April giggled. "Oh, go on, cowboy. Surely you're not afraid of a baby."

He glanced at April. "I'm totally afraid of that baby." He looked at her again. "She seems so frail. How big is she?"

"Seven pounds," April said. "Felt like a lot more when she was inside, trust me."

Ted squeezed her hand. "I'm going to pick her up now."

"Just support her head."

"The head, right." Ted slipped one hand under the infant's head and lifted the baby up in a single swoop. Her head sat on his forearm, but he could hold her in one hand easily. He tucked her against his chest as she squirmed and grunted, and if Ted wasn't already in love with her, the way she relaxed and snuggled into him solidified it.

"She's wonderful," he whispered. He sat on the edge of April's bed and volleyed his gaze from Emma to April. "What are you going to do now? And don't say I don't know."

April scowled but the gesture softened. "I'm going to look for somewhere to live in town."

Ted's hopes soared toward the clouds. "Brush Creek, you mean? Or some other town?"

"There you go again," she said. "You and your endless questions."

His defenses rose. "April, remember when you came to my house and said you needed to know how I felt about you to make decisions? That's where I am. I am in love with you. I want this baby to be mine." He glanced at the sleeping baby girl, and his heart took courage. "So you'll forgive me if I'm the one who needs some answers now."

She sat up, her dark eyes sparkling. "Here's your answer. I love you too, Ted, and I want to be with you."

A smile crossed his face, her words a welcome balm to everything he'd been worried about. "So we can be a family then."

"There's a long way to go to be a family." April sighed and leaned back.

Ted frowned. "I don't think so, April. We get married and you move in with me. Boom. We're a family."

The color left her face. "Married?"

"Yeah, married." He chuckled. "That's what people do when they love each other."

She swallowed and looked away. "I know."

Ted didn't understand. "April, tell me what's goin' on in your head."

She closed her eyes. "Ted, I already asked for one day without all this talk."

Stung, Ted stood. "All right." He extended baby Emma toward her. "The nurse said you need to feed her. I'll go find the cafeteria." He didn't let himself look fully at April as he passed the infant to her. And he didn't let himself look back when he walked out.

———

HOURS LATER, Ted found himself in the small chapel in a wing of the hospital he thought he'd never be able to find again. He sat in the front row this time, the candles before him false and lit by tiny red, blue, and yellow bulbs that allowed them to stay on all the time.

Darkness had fallen seemingly all at once, and the stained glass window in front of Ted wasn't opaque the way it would be when the sun shone through it. The depiction of Mother Mary was still beautiful and it still spoke peace to Ted's soul.

He wished he wasn't so pushy, so impatient, with April. But he saw the wisdom now in what Walker and Tess had done, and he thought he'd like to marry April right here in this chapel so he could take her and Emma back to his cabin with him. The thought of her going back to the basement, or worse, another house down the canyon didn't sit right with him.

He didn't trust himself to go back to her room in the maternity ward and keep his mouth shut, and he didn't want to make her or himself any angrier than necessary.

He'd always pushed April with questions. He just

hadn't realized until that afternoon that it was a flaw, that it genuinely bothered her, that he should make an effort to change. He could do it; he could figure out how to exhibit patience with April instead of pushing her for answers.

Embarrassment flooded him, as it had been doing since he'd marched out of April's room. He'd ended things with her because of his impatience, and he didn't even know it at the time. He wondered if she did, if he could apologize for such a huge personality flaw.

He didn't know what to do, so he didn't do anything beyond asking the information desk for the number of a hotel and getting a room for the night. He'd left his cabin without a bag, a toothbrush, anything. He had his wallet and his truck, and the thought of his dogs drove him from the chapel to make another phone call.

Landon answered on the first ring, and Ted realized from the tense tone of his boss's voice that he should've called earlier. "She's doing fine," Ted said when Landon asked.

"You realize Megan's here, going crazy, right?"

"April has her phone."

"She's not using it," Landon said. "Is she keeping the baby?"

"Yes," Ted said with a sigh.

"Why aren't you happy about that?"

"I am," Ted said. "I am. I want her to marry me and take her and the baby back to my cabin. She...didn't want to talk about it." He swallowed, tired of the bitterness that he hadn't been able to rid himself of.

"She just had a baby and decided to keep it." Landon

murmured something not meant for Ted. "Give her some time."

"I don't want to give her time," Ted said. "I don't want her to go back to your basement with her baby. I—"

Landon laughed, which silenced Ted. "All she's thought about for nine months is that baby," he said. "So while she's been with you and kissin' you, and you've fallen in love with her, she needs more time to get there. So you have to decide: do you want to give her time or walk away?"

Ted wiped his free hand down his beard. "Well, I walked away once and that was a mistake...."

"Definitely premature," Landon agreed, which didn't help the humiliation that kept piling up and spilling over inside Ted's chest.

"How much time?"

"She's been through trauma, Ted. How long did it take you to recover from your accident?"

"A while," Ted confessed.

"Nine months from what I understand."

Ted was starting to regret making this phone call. "What's your point?"

"And how long did it take you to get over Barb?"

Ted sucked in a breath. He didn't discuss women with Landon. With anyone. "That was years and years ago," Ted said.

"And there's my point."

"What's that?"

"You must've forgotten that we traveled the rodeo circuit together for eight years. I was there when you dated Barb, when you were engaged, all of it. I was there when she broke your heart, and I know you haven't dated since."

"I have been perfectly content without a woman in my life," Ted said.

"Until now," Landon said, vocalizing what Ted had been thinking. "Look." He sighed. "Just think about how you'd feel, how you *did* feel, after a long-term relationship ended. It took you a long time to recover emotionally, and April has had to deal with all of that, plus the enormity of a pregnancy. If you really love her, give her time."

"Landon...did you go feed my dogs?"

"I brought them over with me when you left. I've about got Megan convinced that we need an indoor dog." He chuckled and Ted hung up, grateful for good friends and good advice.

He maneuvered down the halls until he found an elevator. He arrived back at the maternity ward, ready to give April all the time she needed.

CHAPTER 16

April thought she was tired before the baby came. But with everyone coming in and out, and learning how to nurse Emma, April didn't catch more than twenty minutes of sleep. Night came, and the nurses thinned. Ted had arrived near dinnertime, and he took a long time coming back.

When he finally poked his handsome face back into the room, he wore a gentle smile. "Hey." He advanced slowly, wiping his palms down the front of his jeans. "She's sleeping, it looks like."

April pushed herself up with her elbows, glad he'd returned. "There you are. Cafeteria must have good food." She tried to smile, but her exhaustion made it difficult.

"I found the chapel." He eased his huge frame into the chair next to her bed. He spoke in a quiet, calm voice that barely tickled her eardrums. "And I called and updated Landon and Megan. And I got a hotel for tonight." He exhaled and reached for her hand. "April, I'm sorry for being so impatient with you. I hope you can forgive me."

"Not necessary." She smiled at him, a sleepy, soft smile that made his eyes melt too. She'd never labeled him as impatient, just more the type who knew exactly what he wanted in his life, and how to get it.

He pressed a kiss to her forehead and said, "See you in the morning?"

"If you don't bring me a cup of coffee, I don't want to see you."

He chuckled. "I shall return with coffee and cream then."

April slept on and off, and not only because Emma woke every few hours needing to be fed. She couldn't stop thinking about Ted's proposal. Marrying him would solve several of her current problems. Housing problems. Job problems. Money problems.

She'd tossed, turned, gotten up and pushed a sleeping Emma around the maternity ward as her mind churned about Ted. She did love him, but she didn't want to use him just to make her life easier.

Because of her restlessness, she woke to the sound of his voice the next morning. She slitted her eyes and watched as he set two coffee to-go cups on the rolling tray in her room. He turned toward Emma's cart and bent slightly to lift the baby into his arms.

"Hey there, Emma Hope," he cooed in a voice she'd heard him use on his horses, and a couple of times on her. "Did you have a good night? Were you nice to your mama?" He swayed, shifting his weight from foot to foot, his head bent toward the little girl. He glanced at her and April slammed her eyes shut. "She seems tired. Should we let her sleep?"

The baby made a guttural noise that painted April's heart with love, and Ted took that as a yes. "All right then. Let's go." He stepped out of the room, his cowboy boots barely making any noise on the tile floor.

April's heart swelled, and with the room quiet, she finally fell into a deep sleep. She wasn't sure how long it lasted. She only knew she woke to the sound of two female voices. They spoke quietly, so she kept her eyes closed and hoped they'd check her quickly and go.

"Did you see the cowboy with the baby?" one asked.

"So precious," the other said. "And it's not even his."

"Well, he's smitten."

"Wish I could get me a cowboy like that."

Soft giggles followed, and April shifted in bed. "Shh," one of the nurses said, brushing her fingers across April's forehead. She opened her eyes and looked into the face of an older woman. "Go back to sleep for a little while. We have Emma in the nursery and your boyfriend is taking your mom to lunch."

April's adrenaline started pumping. "My mom's here?"

"Not anymore, I'm sure." The woman smiled. "Ted met her, and he introduced her to Emma. They spent some time together in the nursery, and now they're going to lunch."

"It's lunchtime?" April didn't even feel the least bit hungry.

The other nurse in the room pulled the curtains closed. "Go back to sleep while you can." They left, and April pulled her blanket higher. She wasn't going to argue if they wanted her to sleep.

EMMA RETURNED BEFORE TED DID. She was fussy, and April's urge to help her felt so natural though her heart pumped like crazy. "I'm awake," she said, scooting up and reaching for the controls that would raise the bed. "I can feed her."

"Sorry to wake you," the same nurse from earlier said. "We gave her some formula in the nursery, but she didn't take much." She passed Emma to April and busied herself checking charts. "How are you feeling?"

"Good," April said. "When can I go home?"

"Has Doctor Johns been in to see you today?"

"No." April finally got Emma nursing and covered herself with the sheets.

"I'll let him know you're ready."

"I—" The nurse left before April could say she wasn't ready. She didn't even have a crib for Emma to sleep in. Her mother was supposed to come a week before Emma did, help April get all the supplies she needed. A sudden sense of complete inadequacy choked her.

She'd just finished feeding Emma and was patting her back to get her to burp when her mom entered the room. Relief like April had never known washed over her. Tears sprang to her eyes. "Mom."

Her mom's eyes were kind and full of emotion as she crossed the room and hugged April. "Oh, lets not crush baby Emma." She beamed down at the infant and took her from April. "She looks just like you. Same straight nose, same high cheekbones." She glanced at April with a smile.

And April did have that to be grateful for. When she

looked at Emma, maybe she wouldn't be reminded of Liam quite so strongly. "I heard you went to lunch with Ted."

Her mother's jaw twitched and her eyes were sharper when she looked at April. "I sure did. You never once mentioned that you had a boyfriend in Brush Creek."

That was the second time someone had referred to Ted as her boyfriend. Hers. "I could barely keep track of what day it was, Mom. Don't take it personally."

"And he's obviously more than a boyfriend. He's here, walking around with Emma, singing her lullabies while you sleep." Her eyebrows rose suggestively. "How serious is it?"

"Pretty serious, I guess," April said, thinking of Ted's suggestion that they get married. She remembered the way he said, "I love you," and a smile sprang to her face.

"I thought you didn't like cowboys. Or small towns." She bounced Emma and patted her bottom.

"I don't," April said. "But that doesn't matter, because Ted's not a cowboy."

"We're talking about the same man, right? Big, tall, dark beard, huge black *cowboy* hat?"

"He's a bronc rider." April lifted her chin, wanting nothing more than to brush her teeth.

"And what about you finding a big city and blending in?"

"I think I blend in just fine in Brush Creek." She especially would if she married Ted and settled into his cabin on the ranch.

"Sounds like things with Ted are a lot more than 'pretty serious'."

April swung her legs over the side of the bed. "I'm

going to brush my teeth and wash my face. You okay with Emma?"

"Oh, we're just fine, aren't we?" Her voice pitched toward the rafters. "Yes, we're just so fine."

April smiled and shook her head. "Hey, where's Ted?"

"He went to make a couple of phone calls."

April picked up her toothbrush and loaded it with toothpaste, glad she'd thought to bring those two things.

"I like him," her mom continued. "Very handsome. Articulate. Charming."

April brushed her teeth and rinsed her mouth. "He asked me to marry him."

Her mom nearly dropped the baby. Not really, but the way she spasmed made April lunge forward just in case.

"He did?" Pure surprise reflected in her mom's eyes.

"He says he loves me and wants to adopt Emma."

"And how do you feel about him?"

April turned on the water in the sink and pushed the handle to hot. Her mother came over to the bathroom doorway, her eyes meeting April's in the mirror. "Oh, I see. You want to be with him, but you haven't said yes yet."

"What if I'm doing it for the wrong reasons?"

"What wrong reasons?"

"He has a lot of money. I wouldn't have to work."

April's mom held up her hand. "I don't need to know. Do you love him or not?"

"Yes." April nodded, the sincerity of her feelings pushing past her fears. "Yes, I love him."

"Then that's all you need to know."

"But—"

"April, you've always complicated things. Don't do that

here. Ted seems terribly uncomplicated, and I can't imagine he'll want to talk through—"

"Actually, Mom," April said, her frustration rising. "Ted likes to talk everything to death. Not me."

"Ouch." Ted's laugh followed his words, and April's heart took a giant leap off a towering cliff. "But I guess if that's my biggest fault, I'll take it." He stepped a little closer. "Is that my biggest fault?" His eyes burned like dark fire, and April couldn't tear her gaze away. She was very glad she'd brushed her teeth so she could kiss him hello properly.

"One of them." She put her emotions and desires in check and washed her face before joining everyone in the small hospital room. Since she wasn't dressed properly, she climbed back in bed and pulled the blankets up. "So where did you guys go to lunch?"

"A Mexican restaurant next to a giant dinosaur," her mom said.

Ted leaned down and kissed her quick on the mouth. "Did you get some rest?"

She melted under his touch, and she hoped she always would. "Yes, thank you for taking Emma."

"Anytime." The smile he gave her was as genuine as any he ever had. He moved to the counter by the door and leaned against it as her mom had taken the chair next to the bed. Silence fell between the three of them, and April's thoughts started up again.

Thinking so hard was what exhausted her.

"Ted?" she asked.

He trained his eyes on hers, and he looked tired. "Hmm?"

"I think I'm going to be able to go home tomorrow."

She swallowed and sat up straighter. "I can't move in with you before we're married, and I'm just wondering if—I mean, how long would it take for your father and brother to get up here for a wedding?"

He pushed away from the counter, his bootsteps deliberate as he approached. "What are you saying?"

"I'm saying yes."

"To what?"

"I think you asked me to marry you yesterday. Didn't you?" She glanced at her mom, who wore a surprised yet joyful expression on her face.

"I did." Ted wore a mask, not a single hint of how he felt getting through.

"Well, I'm saying yes." She swallowed her fear, but it rebounded right back up her throat. "I—I love you, and I want us to be a family. Me, you, and Emma."

He blinked; his mouth twitched. "Don't forget about Lolly and Stormy."

Happiness sang through April. "They don't sleep with you, do they?"

"They have their own beds," he said.

"Then sure. Me, you, Emma, Lolly, and Stormy."

He leaned closer, the mask cracking. "You're serious, aren't you?"

She pushed herself up, her lips coming within inches of his. "Very." She didn't look at her mom when she asked, "Mom, could we put a wedding together by Christmas?"

Ted flinched, and his breath shuddered in his chest. Her mom said, "I think we can, yes."

"Christmastime?" she asked Ted. "Does that work?"

"Of course it works." He touched his lips to hers, not

hanging on long enough to satisfy her. "I love you, April-May."

She pressed closer to him, capturing his mouth and really kissing him the way she wanted to, in a way he'd know how she felt about him.

ONE MONTH LATER:

"The flowers will be late." Megan stood in the mouth way of the hall, her anxiety bleeding into the living room, where April sat with a checklist on the coffee table in front of her and Emma rocking in an automatic swing beside her. "The trucks can't get through the storm."

April sighed. "It's okay. We don't need flowers to get married." She did want them, and a blip of disappointment stole through her. At least her parents and her two younger brothers had arrived ahead of the bad weather. "What about the cake?"

"Alison said she has what she needs and it will be ready tonight, as promised."

April scanned her list. "I suppose the island is out." She didn't need to look at Megan to know. "Pastor Peters said we could use the church in case of inclement weather." She should've expected snow in December in Utah. She'd made contingent plans just in case. They just weren't the plans she wanted.

She checked something on the list and scribbled a note in the margin.

"What else?" Megan asked.

"Ted's picking up his father at the airport right now. He

just texted to say the flight is delayed, and he thinks they'll have to stay in Salt Lake tonight."

"So the groom isn't going to be here on his wedding day?"

April jerked her eyes to Megan's. "My stars. What if he can't make it?" The thought of standing at the altar by herself brought pure, unadulterated horror to her.

Megan laughed. "He's going to make it."

April scrambled for her phone and sent a text to Ted, asking him if he was going to be able to get back to Brush Creek in time for the wedding the following afternoon.

Yes, he sent back immediately. *Nothing will keep me away.*

She knew it had been pure torture for him this past month with her and Emma sleeping in the basement while he had to go back to his cabin. He stopped by before he went out to the ranch, and he spent lunchtime with them, and he stayed as long as he felt proper in the evenings. He'd told her a hundred times that he couldn't wait to be married to her, to come home to her all the time, to be hers.

Ted knew how to say all the right things, and the best part about him, April had decided, was that he meant the things he said.

"Groom, check," Megan said. "Preacher, check. Family, check. What else do you need?"

"You're right," April said, turning toward Megan. "I'm really marrying Ted Caldwell, aren't I?" Giddiness pranced through her bloodstream.

Megan giggled. "You sure are."

CHAPTER 17

Ted's collar itched. His tie strangled him. And April still hadn't come through the doors at the back of the chapel. Her mother had come in ten minutes ago, baby Emma in her arms. Megan had slipped into the second row with Landon and their children nine minutes ago. Tess, who had been commissioned to do April's up-do for the ceremony had taken her place with her family five minutes ago.

But April was nowhere.

Ted was just about to stride down the aisle and find her when the doors opened. The organist switched to the wedding march like an old pro, and everything inside Ted released. His muscles and organs tensed right back up at the sight of his beautiful April-May.

Her dress seemed like a second skin up top, with a puffy, bubbly, billowy skirt that started at her waist and covered her feet. She stepped toward him slowly, one hand clutching her father's arm. Tess had worked magic on April's hair, swirling and pinning it into three knots on top of her head. Ted couldn't wait to get those pins out, let her hair fall around her face, push it back just before he kissed her.

He swallowed and tugged on the ends of his jacket sleeves. They weren't quite long enough, but the suit he'd taken to Vernal for tailoring was still in Vernal. The snow had put a kink in several of their wedding plans. He noticed April carried a bouquet of silk flowers, the best she could find after the fresh ones she'd ordered had gotten stuck in Salt Lake. He couldn't even go to the warehouse and get them, though he'd called and tried.

She glowed and he basked in the light and warmth of it when she stepped next to him, switching her hand from her father's arm to his. Ted breathed her in and said, "Hey, beautiful."

They stepped up to the altar and Pastor Peters began the ceremony. Ted liked the sound of his voice as he spoke of love, help, companionship, forever. He never thought he'd have a bride, certainly not one as beautiful and head-strong as April.

Vows were read and accepted, and Ted soaked in every word, every moment, until the preacher said, "I now pronounce you husband and wife."

Ted kissed April, holding her tight and murmuring, "I love you, my sweet April-May."

And when she said, "And I love you, cowboy," he grinned for all he was worth. They turned to face the crowd, and Ted lifted his and April's joined hands. People applauded and cheered as her mom stepped forward and handed her sweet baby Emma, dressed in a pretty pink dress. Landon handed Lolly and Stormy to Ted, who had authorized Landon's twins to dress the Pomeranians in similar pink party dresses.

Cameras flashed, and Ted committed this happiness to memory, sure this would be another life-changing day, just as the one where he'd met April had been. He laughed as he and April took their family down the aisle, rice raining down on them, glad God had seen fit to send him someone who could make his life better, make him better.

————

Read on for a sneak peek of the next book in the Brush Creek Cowboys series, **A NEW FAMILY FOR THE COWBOY**.

SNEAK PEEK! A NEW FAMILY FOR THE COWBOY CHAPTER ONE

Blake Gibbons picked himself up off the floor, where he'd been rolling around with a pair of dogs named Bruce and Wayne. The black lab licked his face and Blake chuckled. "You ready for me, Tess?"

A blonde-haired woman gestured him into the kitchen, setting the broom she'd been wielding against the counter. "Sit right there."

He took the stool his boss and the foreman at Brush Creek Horse Ranch had sat on. Then Tess and Walker's two boys. And now Blake.

"What do you want this time?"

"Shave it off." Blake didn't even reach up to touch his thinning hair. Only twenty-seven and already with a heinous receding hairline.

Tess's fingers swooped through his hair. "You sure?"

Blake nodded, his mind made up. "Yep. Take it off. I don't even care if you use an attachment."

"It doesn't look that bad if we keep it short."

"Yes, it does." Blake was tired of trying to make his hair

cover the balding areas. "I look like I'm trying too hard. I'm going bald. Might as well embrace it." Who he was trying to impress, and why, he wasn't sure. Just another reason to shave his head completely.

Tess switched on the clippers, the hum filling the air between them. "This isn't going to get it smooth," she said over the buzz. "You'll have to use a razor for that."

"I'm fine with a super short buzz."

"You'll look very military."

"I wear a cowboy hat almost all the time."

Tess smiled and started on his right side, just above his ear. "Yes, you men and your love affair with cowboy hats."

"They're practical," Blake said as Walker came back into the kitchen, freshly showered. His new haircut made him seem even more distinguished than he already looked. "Takin' it all off, huh?" he asked before opening the fridge and pulling out a plastic container. He popped the lid and the scent of dill wafted into the air.

"It's time," Blake said as Walker got down a box of crackers. They were headed into the summer months, and Blake didn't want to spend time he didn't have taking care of hair he didn't have. This haircut was a win-win in his mind.

Tess finished and used quick, short movements with the brush to flick the tiny hairs away. "There you go, cowboy." She unpinned the drape and started oiling the clippers.

"Thank you, ma'am." He'd been getting his hair done by Tess since he moved to Brush Creek, almost three years ago. When she'd married Walker and moved up to the ranch, Blake had cut a half an hour from his schedule.

He reached for the broom and swept up his hair with a

single pang of sadness. He wasn't going to dwell on the loss of his hair. It was just hair.

Still, he knew women fantasized about a man's hair, and the loss of his almost felt like a death sentence. With every swipe of the broom, Blake told himself it didn't matter. He wasn't dating. He'd tried, but Brush Creek didn't have a lot of selection as far as potential partners went. The few women he'd gone out with had helped him learn that he wasn't over Jessica yet. Jessica, his high school girlfriend he'd longed to reunite with.

Jessica, who'd gotten married and moved to California over a year ago.

Blake bent and swept the hair into a dustpan, wishing he could swish away his negative thoughts just as easily.

"Any chance of me taking Wayne tonight?" he asked Walker.

Walker rolled his eyes. "You and that dog."

"He loves me." The black lab trotted over as if he'd try to get Walker's permission with his big doe-eyes.

"He likes to sleep on the bed with you and that mutt of yours." Walker held out the box of crackers, but Blake waved him away.

"The girls will be here any minute," Tess said, Blake's cue to get the heck out of there. Walker's too, judging by the way he leapt to his feet.

"Is that tonight?"

"Sure is." Tess gave him an affectionate pat on the shoulder. "Don't tell me you didn't know. I told you about it this morning. And last night. And the night before that."

"No, I knew." Walker met Blake's eyes and his expression clearly said he hadn't known.

"You and the boys want to come hang at my cabin?" Blake asked. "You can come if Bruce and Wayne come."

Walker chuckled and reached for his cowboy hat hanging on the peg by the backdoor. "As soon as you open that door, Wayne will run off. You know that, right?"

"He always comes back." Blake grinned, threw the hair clippings in the trash, and washed his hands in the kitchen sink.

Tess pulled out the tallest chocolate cake Blake had ever seen and set it on the counter. "I'll get the boys." She left the kitchen and called down the hall. A few seconds later, two tween boys—one dark like Walker and one light like Tess—appeared.

"My cabin, boys," Blake said, lifting his arm and slinging it over Michael's shoulders.

"Tess, will you save me some cake?" the boy asked his step-mother.

She grinned and giggled. "I made you guys your own cake. Remember I said you could eat cake for breakfast on the last day of school?"

Graham, Tess's biological son, whooped and they ran out the back door with the dogs. Walker followed them, but Blake headed for the front door, as he'd stopped here on his way home and his truck sat out in the lane.

He opened the door and stepped out—and right into a soft body. A woman cried out, and Blake tried to reach for her, tried to grab her. His fingers scrambled over hers, and he looked into a pair of stricken brown eyes before she fell down.

He'd just knocked down a woman. "I'm so sorry," he

said, his voice filled with embarrassment. He bent down and looked at her. "Are you okay?"

She forced a laugh through her throat and allowed him to take her hand and help her stand. "I'm fine." Her voice sounded with a decidedly sexy Southern twang, and Blake's heart drummed out an extra beat—something it hadn't done in a while.

"I really am sorry. I didn't know you'd be there."

She tucked her shoulder-length brown hair behind her ear and straightened her blouse. Blake peered at her, finding her unfamiliar. "I don't know you. I'm Blake Gibbons."

"Erin Shields." She held out her hand for him to shake. "I'm a friend of Tess's and I just moved to town."

He shook her hand, wanting to hold on a lot longer than necessary. "Oh yeah? What brings you to Brush Creek?"

"My aunt owns the pie shop here, and she needed some help. I said I'd come."

He checked her left hand for a wedding ring, but it was nearly dark and he couldn't tell for sure in the split second he allowed himself to look. "That's great," he said. The dating pool in Brush Creek had just gotten a new, beautiful, intriguing fish.

"Yeah, I guess." Erin shifted her feet, and Blake realized he was blocking her way into the house. "Tess is a better cook than me. I keep telling her she should help Shirley at the bakery."

"But then I'd be too exhausted to have chocolate nights." Tess joined them on the porch and gave her friend a hug. The look of happiness in her smile as she hugged Tess made Blake grin too.

"You made it." Tess linked her arm through Erin's and stepped around Blake to enter the house. He stood there dumbly, staring at Erin. She glanced back at him too, and dang if his blood didn't start on fire.

Then the door closed between them, startling Blake and reminding him that cowboys weren't invited to Tess's chocolate nights.

Can Blake and Erin make a family for the cowboy? Find out in **A NEW FAMILY FOR THE COWBOY - available now in ebook, paperback, and audiobook!**

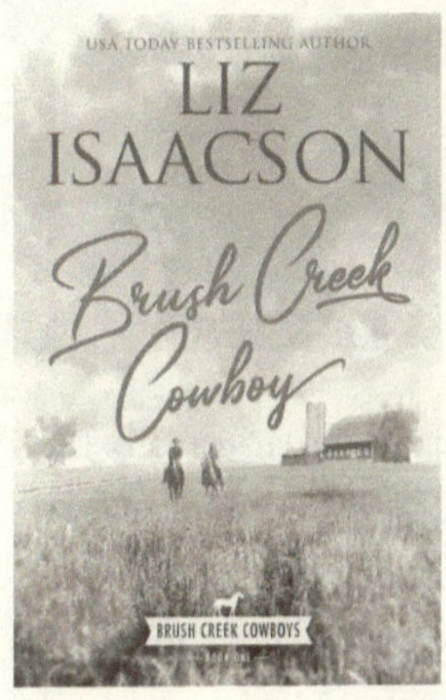

Brush Creek Cowboy (Book 1): Former rodeo champion and cowboy Walker Thompson trains horses at Brush Creek Horse Ranch, where he lives a simple life in his cabin with his ten-year-old son. A widower of six years, he's worked with Tess Wagner, a widow who came to Brush Creek to escape the turmoil of her life to give her seven-year-old son a slower pace of life. But Tess's breast cancer is back...

Walker will have to decide if he'd rather spend even a short time with Tess than not have her in his life at all. Tess wants to feel God's love and power, but can she discover and accept God's will in order to find her happy ending?

The Cowboy's Challenge (Book 2): Cowboy and profes-sional roper Justin Jackman has found solitude at Brush Creek Horse Ranch, preferring his time with the animals he trains over dating. With two failed engagements in his past, he's not really interested in getting his heart stomped on again. But when flirty and fun Renee

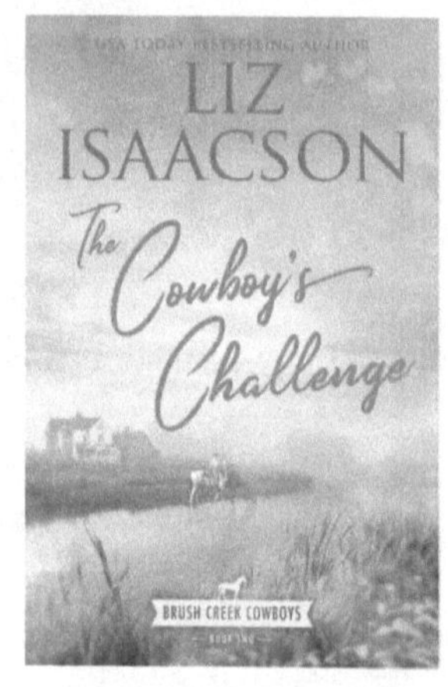

Martin picks him up at a church ice cream bar--on a bet, no less--he finds himself more than just a little interested. His Gen-X attitudes are attractive to her; her Millennial behav-iors drive him nuts. Can Justin look past their differences and take a chance on another engagement?

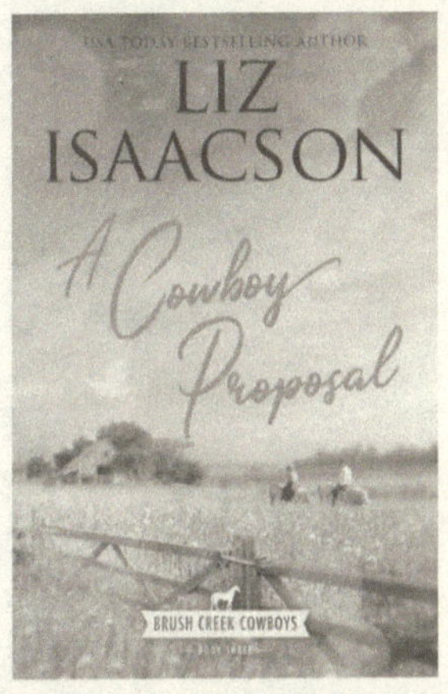

A Cowboy Proposal (Book 3): Ted Caldwell has been a retired bronc rider for years, and he thought he was perfectly happy training horses to buck at Brush Creek Ranch. He was wrong. When he meets April Nox, who comes to the ranch to hide her pregnancy from all her friends back in Jackson Hole, Ted realizes he has a huge family-shaped hole in his life. April is embarrassed, heartbroken, and trying to find her extinguished faith. She's never ridden a horse and wants nothing to do with a cowboy ever again. Can Ted and April create a family of happiness and love from a tragedy?

A New Family for the Cowboy (Book 4): Blake Gibbons oversees all the agriculture at Brush Creek Horse Ranch, sometimes moonlighting as a general contractor. When he meets Erin Shields, new in town, at her aunt's bakery, he's instantly smitten. Erin moved to Brush Creek after a divorce that left her

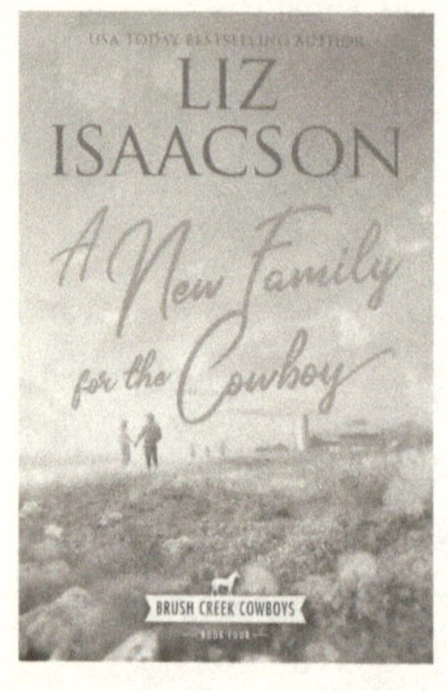

penniless, homeless, and a single mother of three children under age eight. She's nowhere near ready to start dating again, but the longer Blake hangs around the bakery, the more she starts to like him. Can Blake and Erin find a way to blend their lifestyles and become a family?

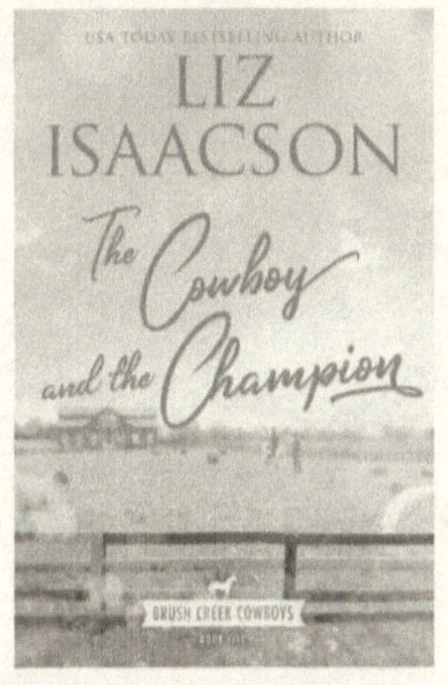

The Cowboy and the Champion (Book 5): Emmett Graves has always had a positive outlook on life. He adores training horses to become barrel racing champions during the day and cuddling with his cat at night. Fresh off her professional rodeo retirement, Molly Brady comes to Brush Creek Horse Ranch as Emmett's protege. He's not thrilled, and she's allergic to cats. Oh, and she'd like to stay cowboy-free, thank you very much. But Emmett's about as cowboy as they come.... Can Emmett and Molly work together without falling in love?

Schooled by the Cowboy (Book 6): Grant Ford spends his days training cattle—when he's not camped out at the elementary school hoping to catch a glimpse of his ex-girlfriend. When principal Shannon Sharpe confronts him and asks him to stay away from the school, the spark between them is instant and hot. Shan-

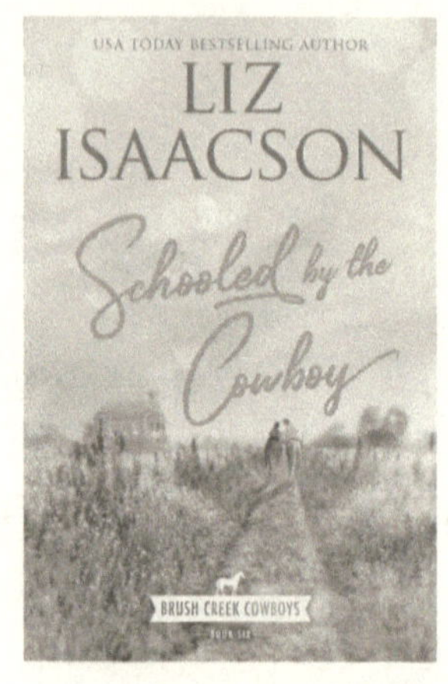

non's expecting a transfer very soon, but she also needs a summer outdoor coordinator—and Grant fits the bill. Just because he's handsome and everything Shannon's ever wanted in a cowboy husband means nothing. Will Grant and Shannon be able to survive the summer or will the Utah heat be too much for them to handle?

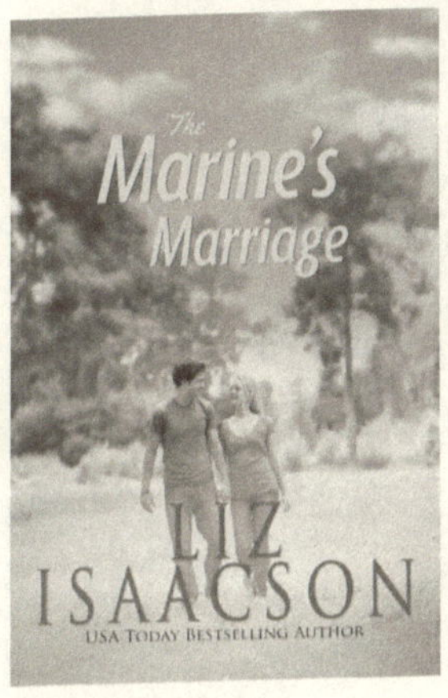

The Marine's Marriage: A Fuller Family Novel - Brush Creek Cowboys Romance (Book 1): Tate Benson can't believe he's come to Nowhere, Utah, to fix up a house that hasn't been inhabited in years. But he has. Because he's retired from the Marines and looking to start a life as a police officer in small-town Brush Creek. Wren Fuller has her hands full most days running her family's company. When Tate calls and demands a maid for that morning, she decides to have the calls forwarded to her cell and go help him out. She didn't know he was moving in next door, and she's completely unprepared for his handsomeness, his kind heart, and his wounded soul. **Can Tate and Wren weather a relationship when they're also next-door neighbors?**

The Firefighter's Fiancé: A Fuller Family Novel - Brush Creek Cowboys Romance (Book 2): Cora Wesley comes to Brush Creek, hoping to get some in-the-wild firefighting training as she prepares to put in her application to be a hotshot. When she meets Brennan Fuller, the spark between them is hot and 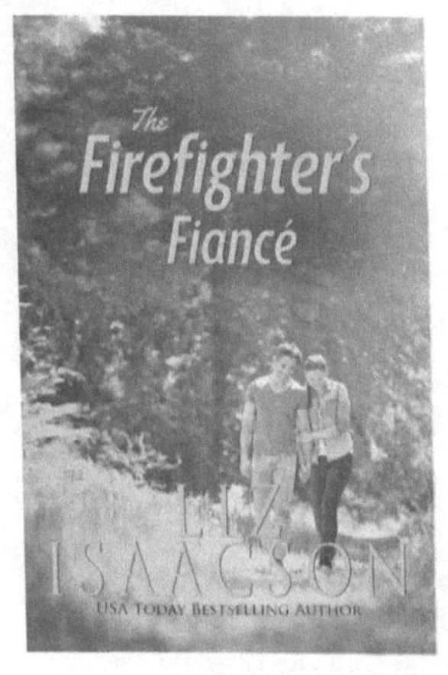 instant. As they get to know each other, her deadline is constantly looming over them, and Brennan starts to wonder if he can break ranks in the family business. He's okay mowing lawns and hanging out with his brothers, but he dreams of being able to go to college and become a landscape architect, but he's just not sure it can be done. **Will Cora and Brennan be able to endure their trials to find true love?**

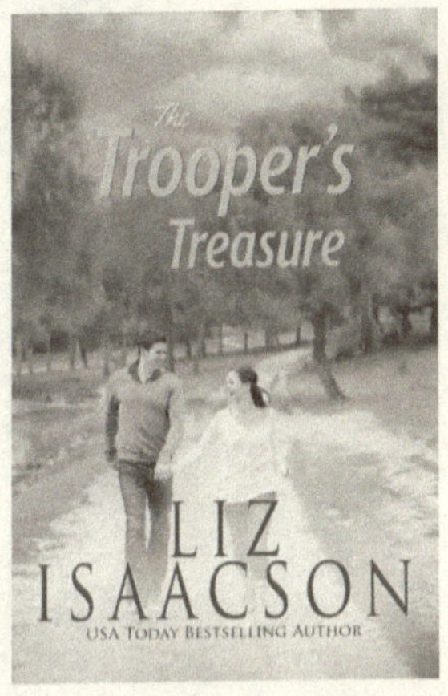

The Trooper's Treasure: A Fuller Family Novel - Brush Creek Cowboys Romance (Book 3): Dawn Fuller has made some mistakes in her life, and she's not proud of the way McDermott Boyd found her off the road one day last year. She's spent a hard year wrestling with her choices and trying to fix them, glad for McDermott's acceptance and friendship. He lost his wife years ago, done his best with his daughter, and now he's ready to move on. **Can McDermott help Dawn find a way past her former mistakes and down a path that leads to love, family, and happiness?**

The Detective's Date: A Fuller Family Novel - Brush Creek Cowboys Romance (Book 4): Dahlia Reid is one of the best detectives Brush Creek and the surrounding towns has ever had. She's given up on the idea of marriage—and pleasing her mother—and has dedicated herself fully to her job. Which is great, since one of the most

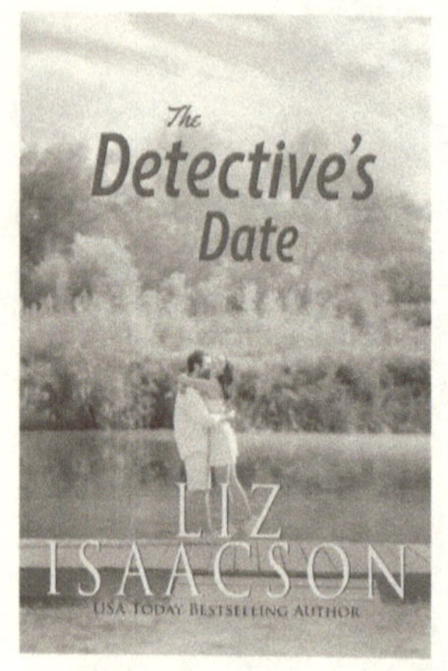

perplexing cases of her career has come to town. Kyler Fuller thinks he's finally ready to move past the woman who ghosted him years ago. He's cut his hair, and he's ready to start dating. Too bad every woman he's been out with is about as interesting as a lamppost—until Dahlia. He finds her beautiful, her quick wit a breath of fresh air, and her intelligence sexy. **Can Kyler and Dahlia use their faith to find a way through the obstacles threatening to keep them apart?**

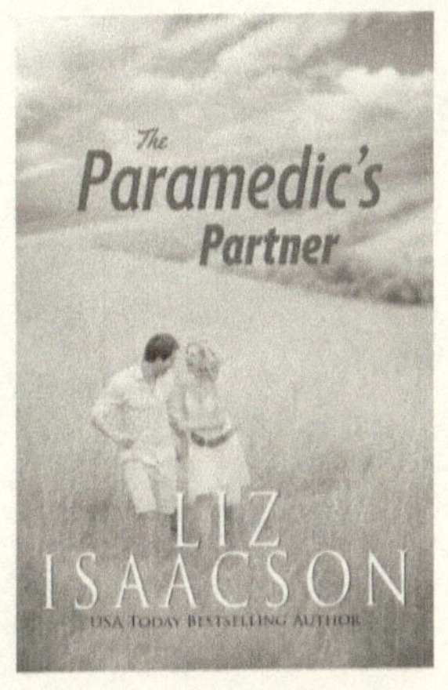

The Paramedic's Partner: A Fuller Family Novel - Brush Creek Cowboys Romance (Book 5): Jazzy Fuller has always been overshadowed by her prettier, more popular twin, Fabiana. Fabi meets paramedic Max Robinson at the park and sets a date with him only to come down with the flu. So she convinces Jazzy to cut her hair and take her place on the date. And the spark between Jazzy and Max is hot and instant...if only he knew she wasn't her sister, Fabi.

Max drives the ambulance for the town of Brush Creek with is partner Ed Moon, and neither of them have been all that lucky in love. Until Max suggests to who he thinks is Fabi that they should double with Ed and Jazzy. They do, and Fabi is smitten with the steady, strong Ed Moon. **As each twin falls further and further in love with their respective paramedic, it becomes obvious they'll need to come clean about the switcheroo sooner rather than later...or risk losing their hearts.**

The Chief's Catch: A Fuller Family Novel - Brush Creek Cowboys Romance (Book 6): Berlin Fuller has struck out with the dating scene in Brush Creek more times than she cares to admit. When she makes a deal with her friends that they can choose the next man she goes out with, she didn't dream they'd pick surly Cole Fairbanks, the new Chief of Police.

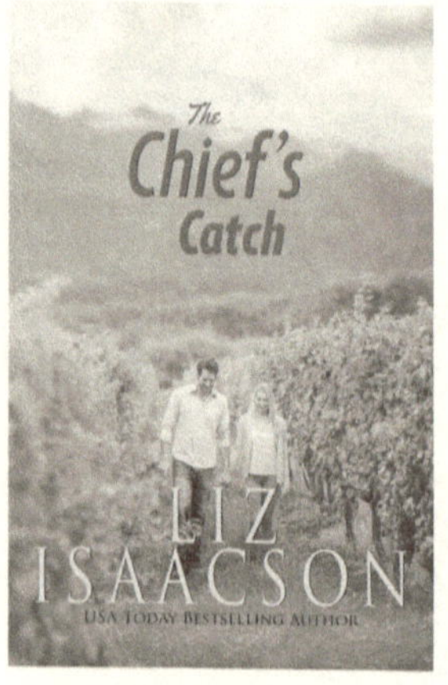

His friends call him the Beast and challenge him to complete ten dates that summer or give up his bonus check. When Berlin approaches him, stuttering about the deal with her friends and claiming they don't actually have to go out, he's intrigued. As the summer passes, Cole finds himself burning both ends of the candle to keep up with his job and his new relationship. **When he unleashes the Beast one time too many, Berlin will have to decide if she can tame him or if she should walk away.**

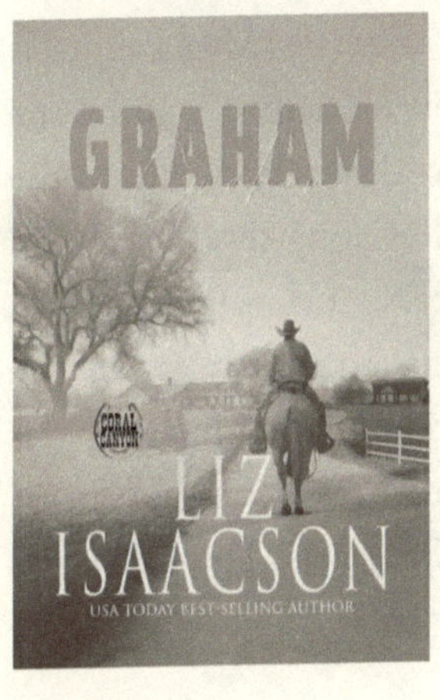

Graham (Book 1): Graham Whittaker returns to Coral Canyon a few days after Christmas—after the death of his father. He takes over the energy company his dad built from the ground up and buys a high-end lodge to live in—only a mile from the home of his once-best friend, Laney McAllister. They were best friends once, but Laney's always entertained feelings for him, and spending so much time with him while they make Christmas memories puts her heart in danger of getting broken again...

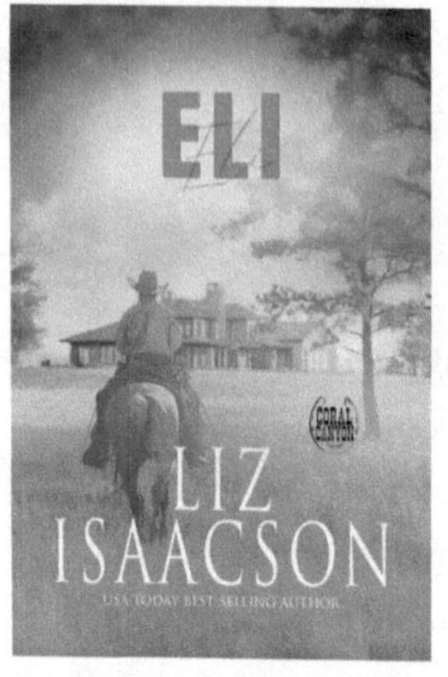

Eli (Book 2): Since the death of his wife a few years ago, Eli Whittaker has been running from one job to another, unable to find somewhere for him and his son to settle. Meg Palmer is Stockton's nanny, and she comes with her boss, Eli, to the lodge, her long-time crush on the man no different in Wyoming than it was on the beach. When she confesses her feelings for him and gets nothing in return, she's crushed, embarrassed, and unsure if she can stay in Coral Canyon for Christmas. Then Eli starts to show some feelings for her too...

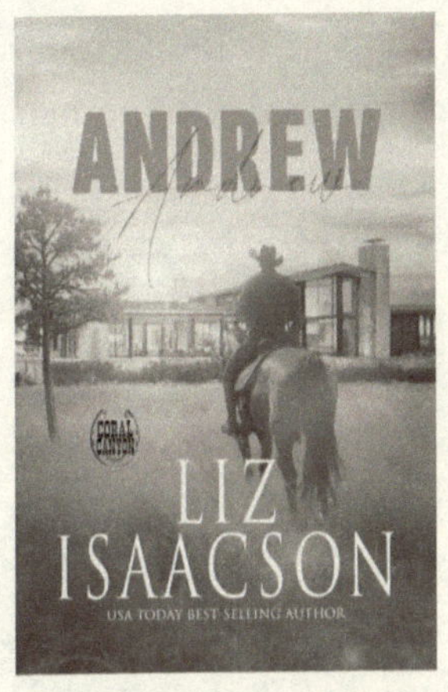

Andrew (Book 3): Andrew Whittaker is the public face for the Whittaker Brothers' family energy company, and with his older brother's robot about to be announced, he needs a press secretary to help him get everything ready and tour the state to make the announcements. When he's hit by a protest sign being carried by the company's biggest opponent, Rebecca Collings, he learns with a few clicks that she has the background they need. He offers her the job of press secretary when she thought she was going to be arrested, and not only because the spark between them in so hot Andrew can't see straight.

Can Becca and Andrew work together and keep their relationship a secret? Or will hearts break in this classic romance retelling reminiscent of *Two Weeks Notice*?

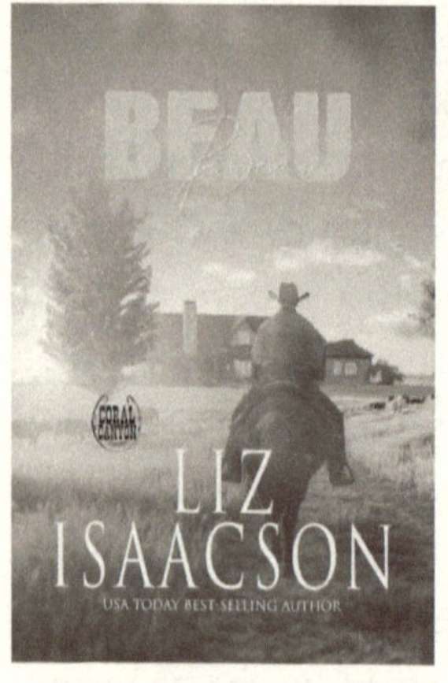

Beau (Book 4): Beau Whittaker has watched his brothers find love one by one, but every attempt he's made has ended in disaster. Lily Everett has been in the spotlight since childhood and has half a dozen platinum records with her two sisters. She's taking a break from the brutal music industry and hiding out in Wyoming while her ex-husband continues to cause trouble for her. When she hears of Beau Whittaker and what he offers his clients, she wants to meet him. Beau is instantly attracted to Lily, but he tried a relationship with his last client that left a scar that still hasn't healed...

Can Lily use the spirit of Christmas to discover what matters most? Will Beau open his heart to the possibility of love with someone so different from him?

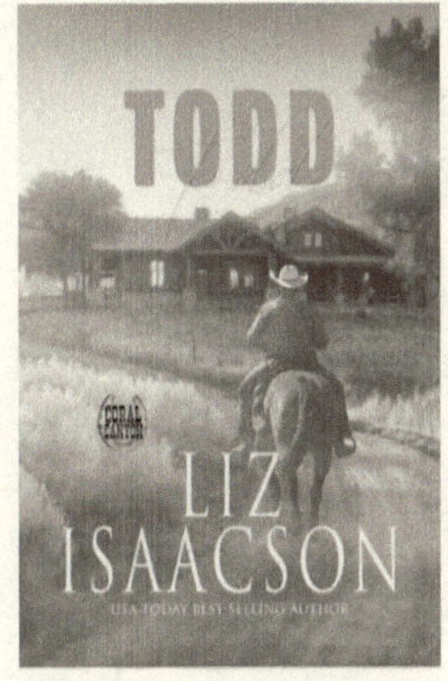

Todd (Book 5): Todd Christopherson has just retired from the professional rodeo circuit and returned to his hometown of Coral Canyon. Problem is, he's got no family there anymore, no land, and no job. Not that he needs a job--he's got plenty of money from his illustrious career riding bulls.

Then Todd gets thrown during a routine horseback ride up the canyon, and his only support as he recovers physically is the beautiful Violet Everett. She's no nurse, but she does the best she can for the handsome cowboy. **Will she lose her heart to the billionaire bull rider? Can Todd trust that God led him to Coral Canyon...and Vi?**

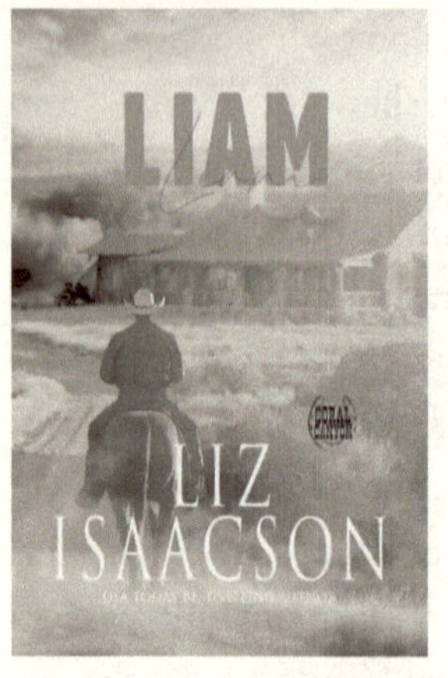

Liam (Book 6): Rose Everett isn't sure what to do with her life now that her country music career is on hold. After all, with both of her sisters in Coral Canyon, and one about to have a baby, they're not making albums anymore.

Liam Murphy has been working for Doctors Without Borders, but he's back in the US now, and looking to start a new clinic in Coral Canyon, where he spent his summers.

When Rose wins a date with Liam in a bachelor auction, their relationship blooms and grows quickly. **Can Liam and Rose find a solution to their problems that doesn't involve one of them leaving Coral Canyon with a broken heart?**

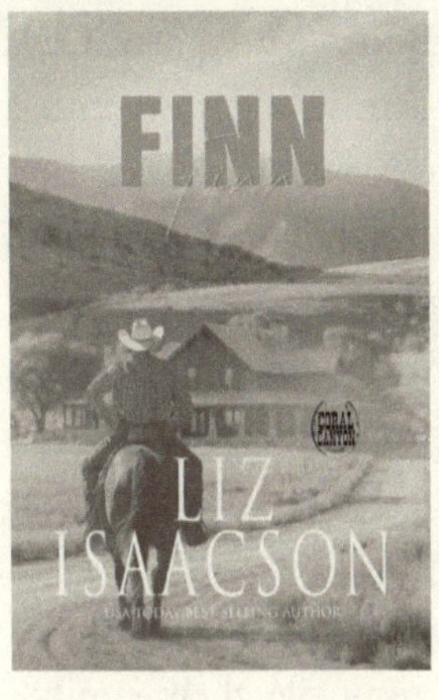

Finn (Book 7): Her sons want her to be happy, but she's too old to be set up on a blind date...isn't she?

Amanda Whittaker has been looking for a second chance at love since the death of her husband several years ago. Finley Barber is a cowboy in every sense of the word. Born and raised on a racehorse farm in Kentucky, he's since moved to Dog Valley and started his own breeding stable for champion horses. He hasn't dated in years, and everything about Amanda makes him nervous.

Will Amanda take the leap of faith required to be with Finn? Or will he become just another boyfriend who doesn't make the cut?

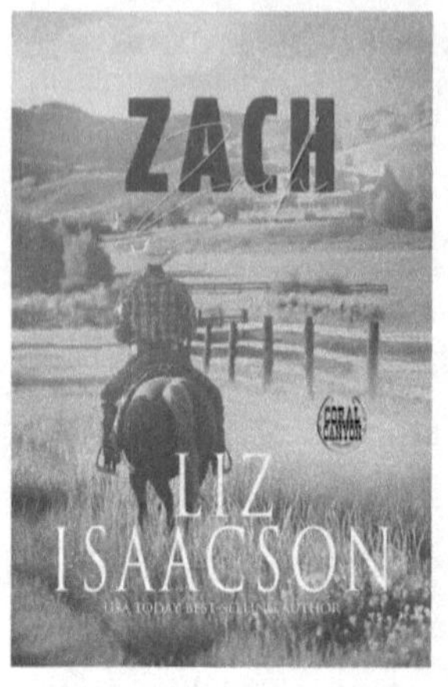

Zach (Book 8): When Celia Abbott-Armstrong runs into a gorgeous cowboy at her best friend's wedding, she decides she's ready to start dating again.

But the cowboy is Zach Zuckerman, and the Zuckermans and Abbotts have been at war for generations.

Can Zach and Celia find a way to reconcile their family's differences so they can have a future together?

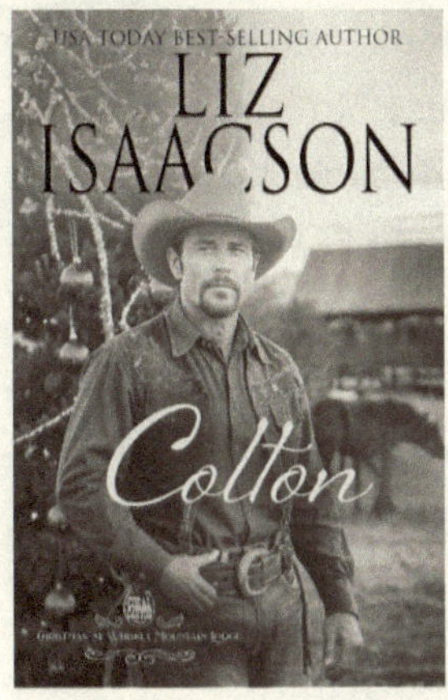

Colton (Book 1): All the maid at Whiskey Mountain Lodge wants for her birthday is a handsome cowboy billionaire. And Colton can make that wish come true—if only he hadn't escaped to Coral Canyon after being left at the altar...

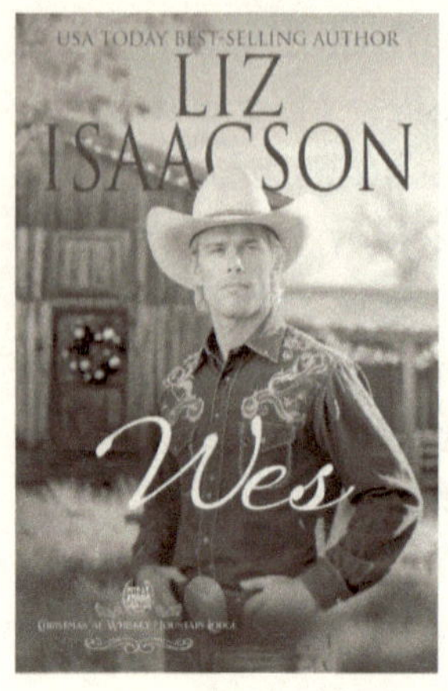

Wes (Book 2): She broke up with him to date another man...who broke her heart. He's a former CEO with nothing to do who can't get her out of his head. Can Wes and Bree find a way toward happily-ever-after at Whiskey Mountain Lodge?

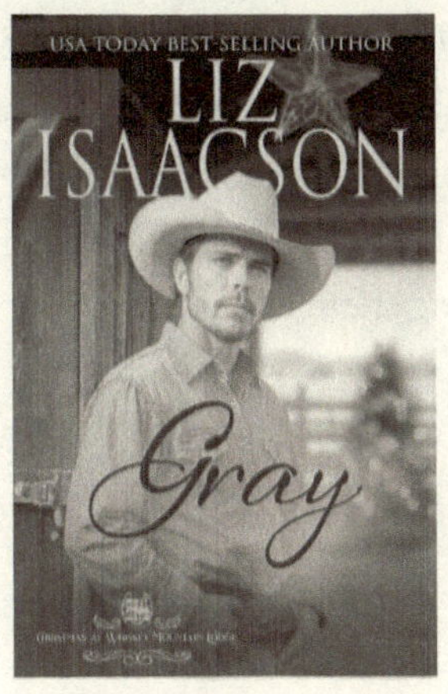

Gray (Book 3): She's best friends with the single dad cowboy's brother and has watched two friends find love with the sexy new cowboys in town. When Gray Hammond comes to Whiskey Mountain Lodge with his son, will Elise finally get her own happily-ever-after with one of the Hammond brothers?

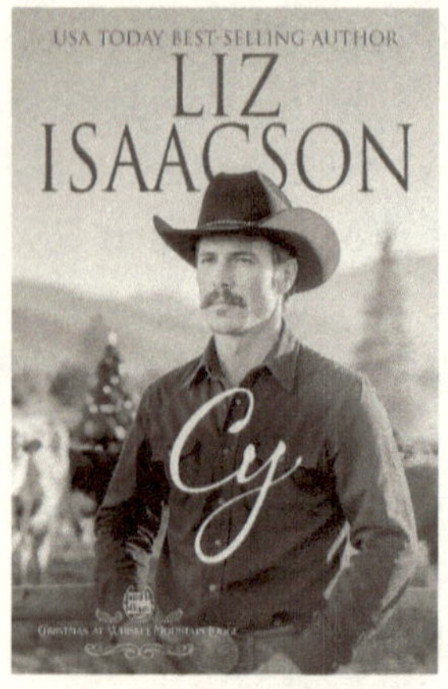 **Cy (Book 4):** A cowboy billionaire beast, his new manager, and the Christmas traditions that soften his heart and bring them together.

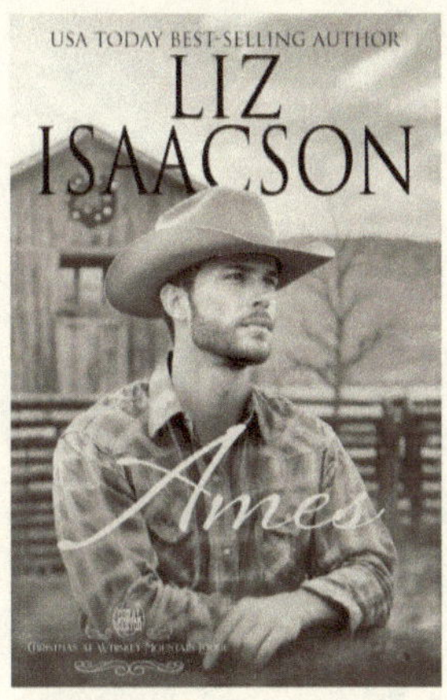

Ames (Book 5): A cowboy billionaire cop who's a stickler for rules, the woman he pulls over when he's not even on duty, and the personal mandates he has to break to keep her in his life...

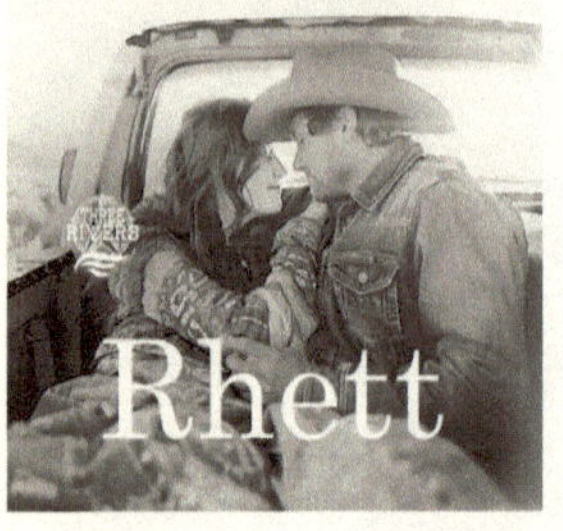

Rhett (Book 1): To save her business, she'll have to risk her heart. She needs a husband to be credible as a matchmaker. He wants to help a neighbor. **Will their fake marriage take them out of the friend zone?**

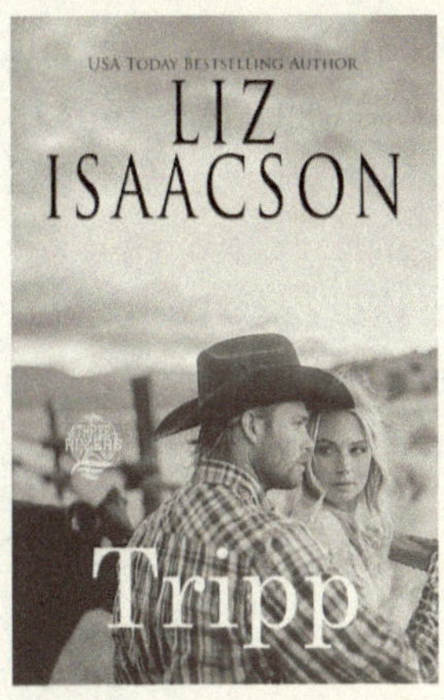

Tripp (Book 2): She needs a husband to keep her son. He's wanted to take their relationship to the next level, but she's always pushing him away. Will their trivial tie take them all the way to happily-ever-after?

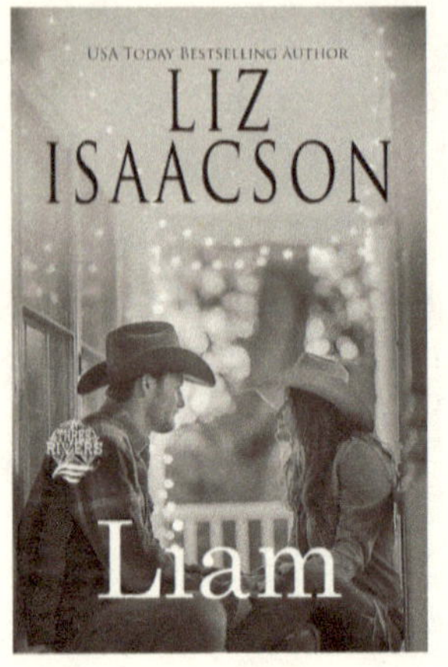

Liam (Book 3): She's desperate to save her ranch. He wants to help her any way he can. Will their invented I-Do open doors that have previously been closed and lead to a happily-ever-after for both of them?

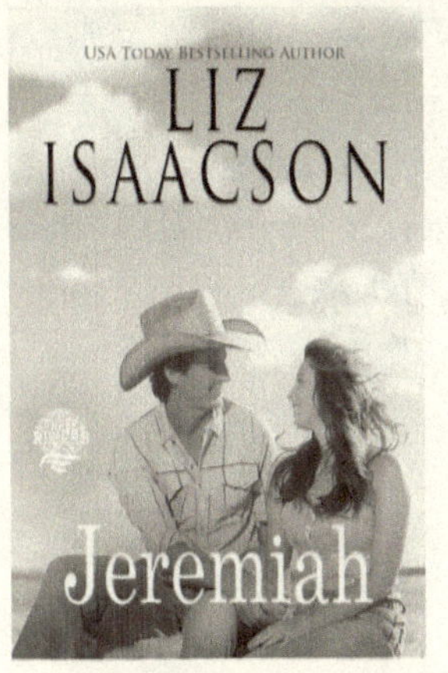

Jeremiah (Book 4): He wants to prove to his brothers that he's not broken. She just wants him. Will a fake marriage heal him or push her further away?

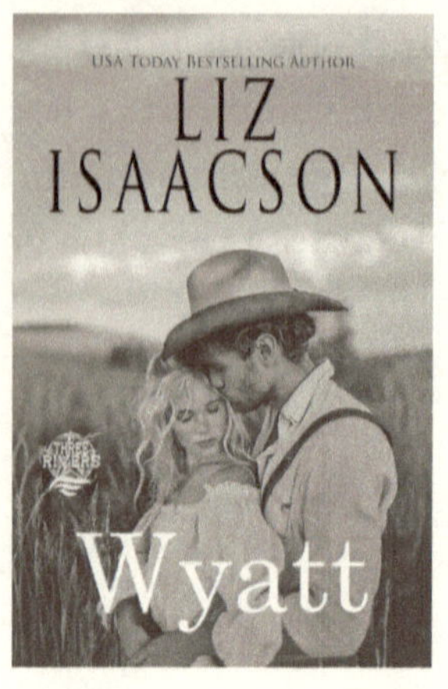

Wyatt (Book 5): To get her inheritance, she needs a husband. He's wanted to fly with her for ages. Can their pretend pledge turn into something real?

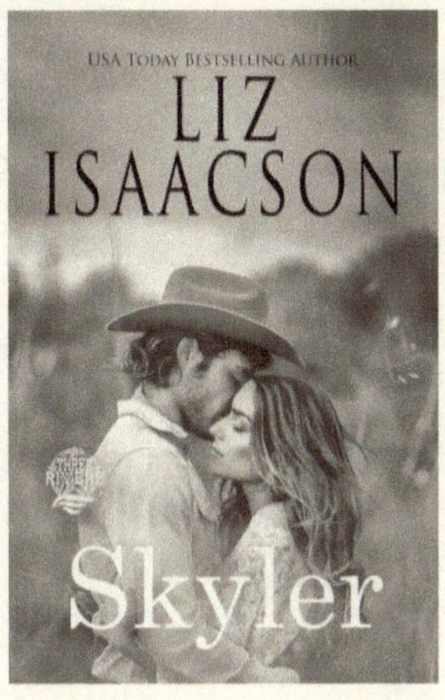

Skyler (Book 6): She needs a new last name to stay in school. He's willing to help a fellow student. Can this wanna-be wife show the playboy that some things should be taken seriously?

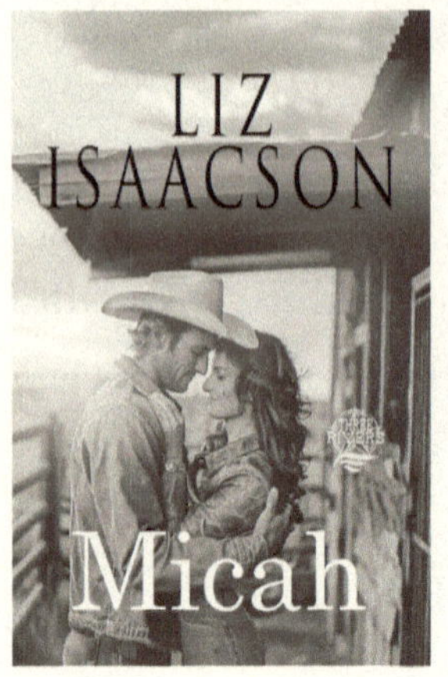

Micah (Book 7): They were just actors auditioning for a play. The marriage was just for the audition – until a clerical error results in a legal marriage. Can these two ex-lovers negotiate this new ground between them and achieve new roles in each other's lives?

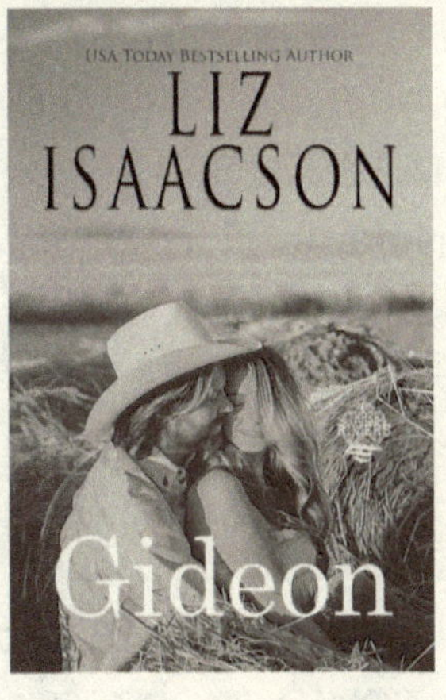

Gideon (Book 8): It's 1971, and Gideon Walker is on the cutting edge of all the technology coming out of Texas. He has big dreams and wants to make something of himself. Then he meets Penny Aarons, and everything changes. He only has eyes for her, but she's got plans and dreams of her own...

Read this origin romance for Momma and Daddy from the Seven Sons series today!

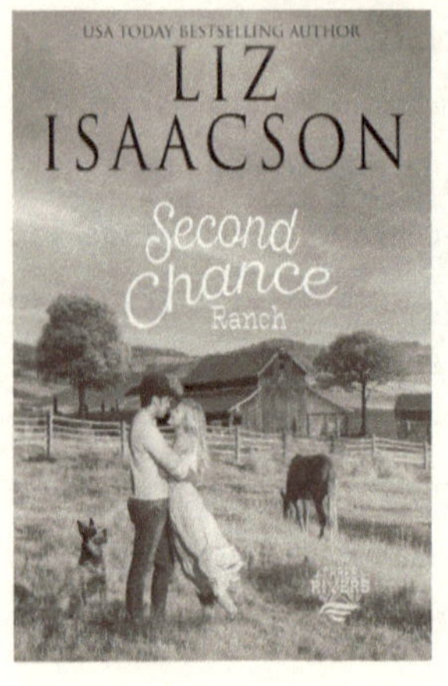

Second Chance Ranch: A Three Rivers Ranch Romance™ (Book 1): After his deployment, injured and discharged Major Squire Ackerman returns to Three Rivers Ranch, wanting to forgive Kelly for ignoring him a decade ago. He'd like to provide the stable life she needs, but with old wounds opening and a ranch on the brink of financial collapse, it will take patience and faith to make their second chance possible.

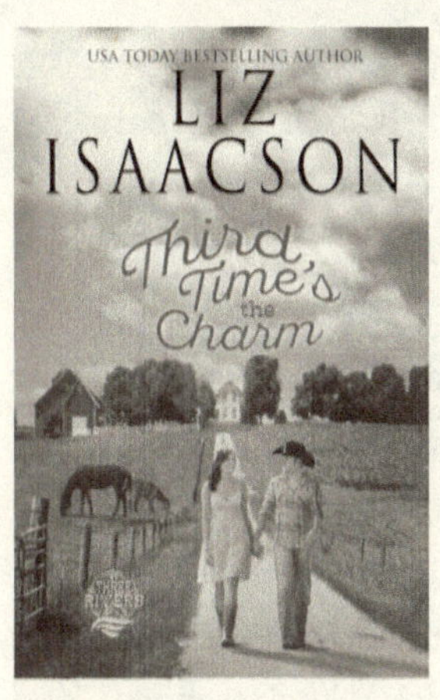

Third Time's the Charm: A Three Rivers Ranch Romance™ (Book 2): First Lieutenant Peter Marshall has a truckload of debt and no way to provide for a family, but Chelsea helps him see past all the obstacles, all the scars. With so many unknowns, can Pete and Chelsea develop the love, acceptance, and faith needed to find their happily ever after?

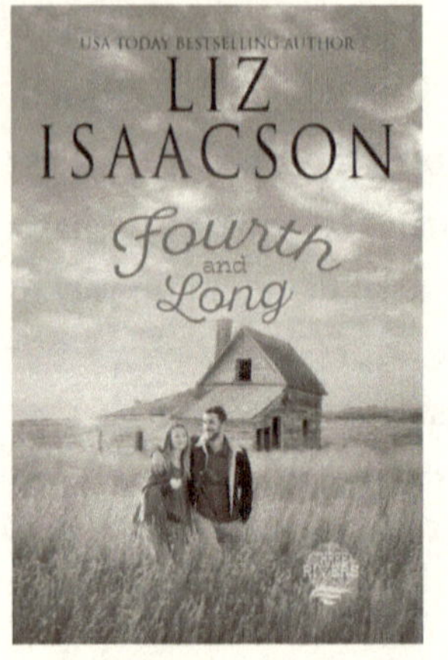

Fourth and Long: A Three Rivers Ranch Romance™ (Book 3): Commander Brett Murphy goes to Three Rivers Ranch to find some rest and relaxation with his Army buddies. Having his ex-wife show up with a seven-year-old she claims is his son is anything but the R&R he craves. Kate needs to make amends, and Brett needs to find forgiveness, but are they too late to find their happily ever after?

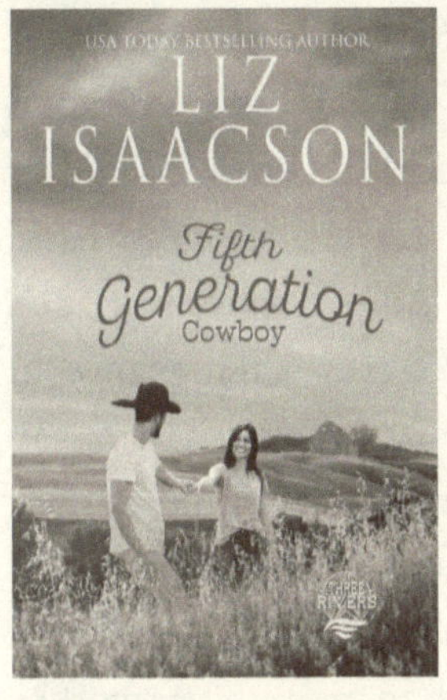

Fifth Generation Cowboy: A Three Rivers Ranch Romance™ (Book 4): Tom Lovell has watched his friends find their true happiness on Three Rivers Ranch, but everywhere he looks, he only sees friends. Rose Reyes has been bringing her daughter out to the ranch for equine therapy for months, but it doesn't seem to be working. Her challenges with Mari are just as frustrating as ever. Could Tom be exactly what Rose needs? Can he remove his friendship blinders and find love with someone who's been right in front of him all this time?

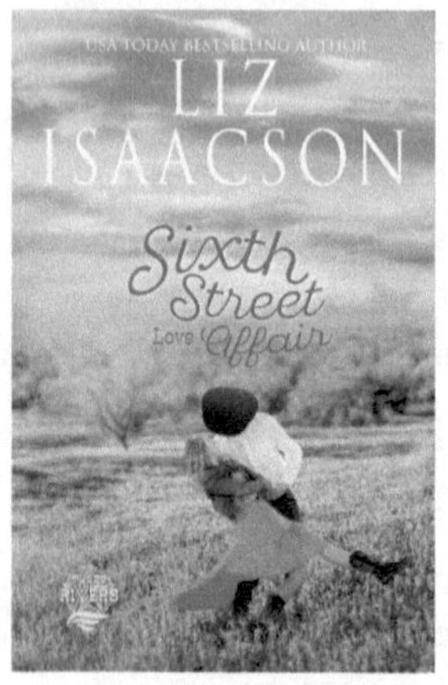

Sixth Street Love Affair: A Three Rivers Ranch Romance™ (Book 5): After losing his wife a few years back, Garth Ahlstrom thinks he's ready for a second chance at love. But Juliette Thompson has a secret that could destroy their budding relationship. Can they find the strength, patience, and faith to make things work?

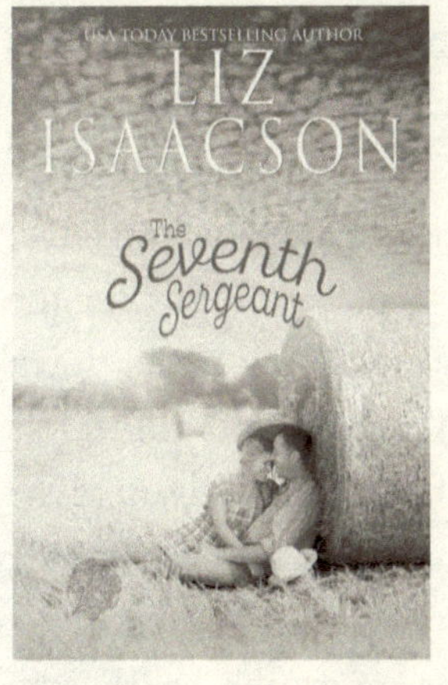

The Seventh Sergeant: A Three Rivers Ranch Romance™ (Book 6): Life has finally started to settle down for Sergeant Reese Sanders after his devastating injury overseas. Discharged from the Army and now with a good job at Courage Reins, he's finally found happiness—until a horrific fall puts him right back where he was years ago: Injured and depressed. Carly Watters, Reese's new veteran care coordinator, dislikes small towns almost as much as she loathes cowboys. But she finds herself faced with both when she gets assigned to Reese's case. Do they have the humility and faith to make their relationship more than professional?

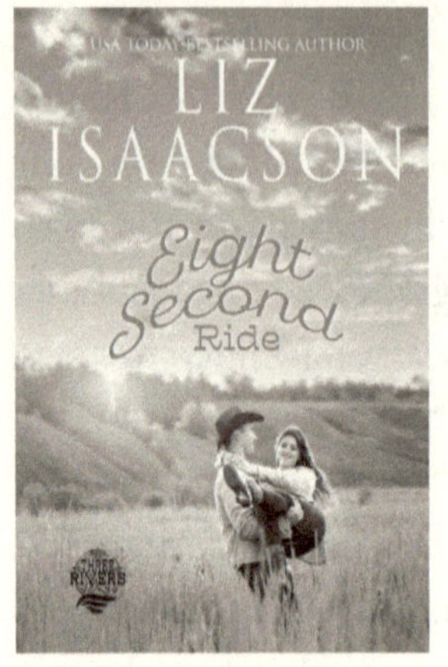

Eight Second Ride: A Three Rivers Ranch Romance™ (Book 7): Ethan Greene loves his work at Three Rivers Ranch, but he can't seem to find the right woman to settle down with. When sassy yet vulnerable Brynn Bowman shows up at the ranch to recruit him back to the rodeo circuit, he takes a different approach with the barrel racing champion. His patience and newfound faith pay off when a friendship--and more--starts with Brynn. But she wants out of the rodeo circuit right when Ethan wants to rejoin. Can they find the path God wants them to take and still stay together?

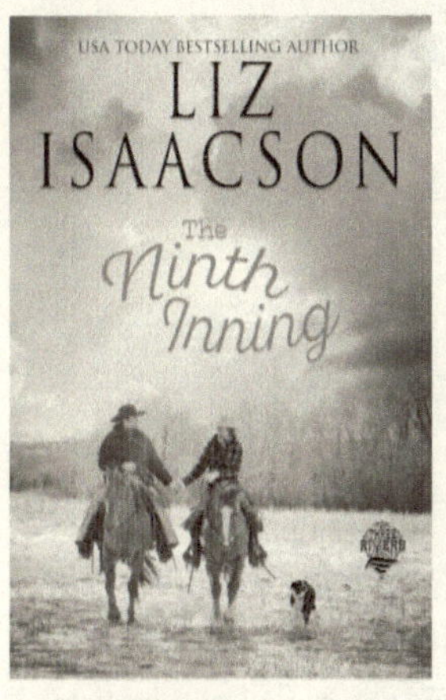

The Ninth Inning: A Three Rivers Ranch Romance™ (Book 8): The Christmas season has never felt like such a burden to boutique owner Andrea Larsen. But with Mama gone and the holidays upon her, Andy finds herself wishing she hadn't been so quick to judge her former boyfriend, cowboy Lawrence Collins. Well, Lawrence hasn't forgotten about Andy either, and he devises a plan to get her out to the ranch so they can reconnect. Do they have the faith and humility to patch things up and start a new relationship?

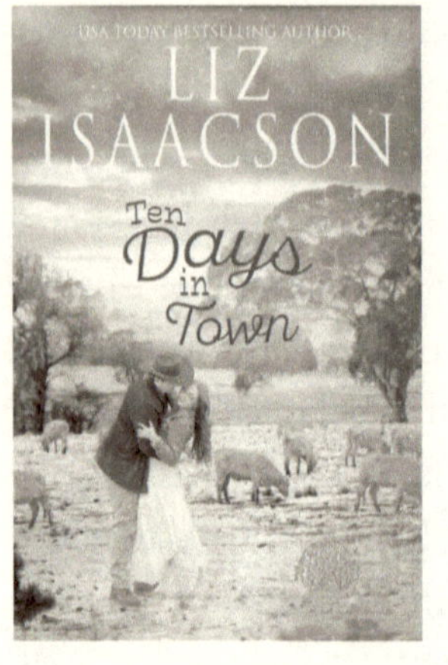

Ten Days in Town: A Three Rivers Ranch Romance™ (Book 9): Sandy Keller is tired of the dating scene in Three Rivers. Though she owns the pancake house, she's looking for a fresh start, which means an escape from the town where she grew up. When her older brother's best friend, Tad Jorgensen, comes to town for the holidays, it is a balm to his weary soul. A helicopter tour guide who experienced a near-death experience, he's looking to start over too--but in Three Rivers. Can Sandy and Tad navigate their troubles to find the path God wants them to take--and discover true love--in only ten days?

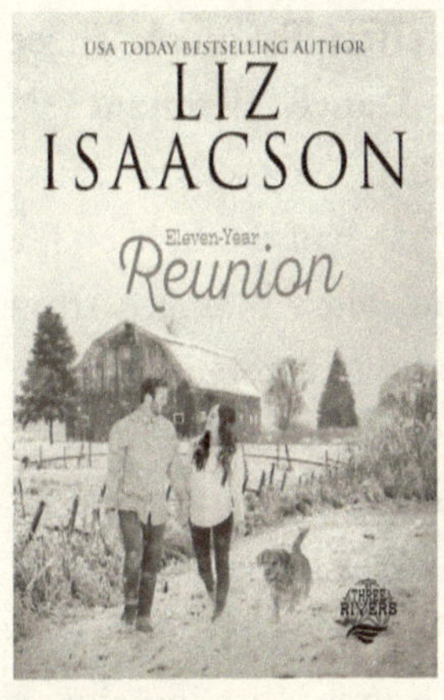

Eleven Year Reunion: A Three Rivers Ranch Romance™ (Book 10): Pastry chef extraordinaire, Grace Lewis has moved to Three Rivers to help Heidi Ackerman open a bakery in Three Rivers. Grace relishes the idea of starting over in a town where no one knows about her failed cupcakery. She doesn't expect to run into her old high school boyfriend, Jonathan Carver. A carpenter working at Three Rivers Ranch, Jon's in town against his will. But with Grace now on the scene, Jon's thinking life in Three Rivers is suddenly looking up. But with her focus on baking and his disdain for small towns, can they make their eleven year reunion stick?

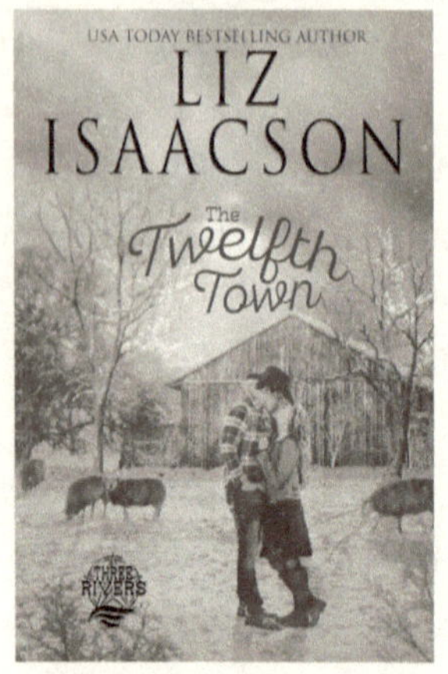

The Twelfth Town: A Three Rivers Ranch Romance™ (Book 11): Newscaster Taryn Tucker has had enough of life on-screen. She's bounced from town to town before arriving in Three Rivers, completely alone and completely anonymous-- just the way she now likes it. She takes a job cleaning at Three Rivers Ranch, hoping for a chance to figure out who she is and where God wants her. When she meets happy-go-lucky cowhand Kenny Stockton, she doesn't expect sparks to fly. Kenny's always been "the best friend" for his female friends, but the pull between him and Taryn can't be denied. Will they have the courage and faith necessary to make their opposite worlds mesh?

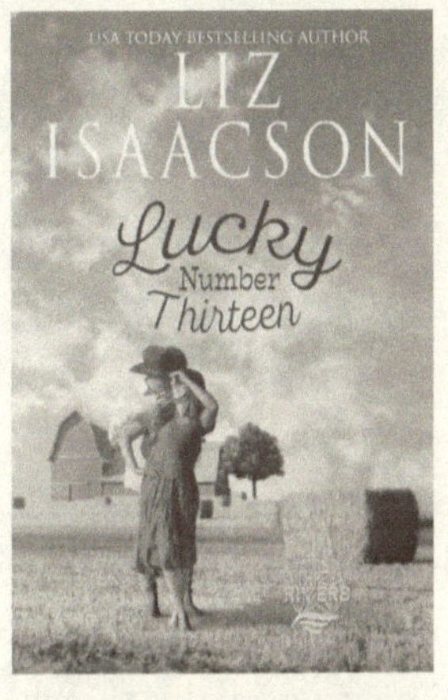

Lucky Number Thirteen: A Three Rivers Ranch Romance™ (Book 12): Tanner Wolf, a rodeo champion ten times over, is excited to be riding in Three Rivers for the first time since he left his philandering ways and found religion. Seeing his old friends Ethan and Brynn is therapuetic--until a terrible accident lands him in the hospital. With his rodeo career over, Tanner thinks maybe he'll stay in town--and it's not just because his nurse, Summer Hamblin, is the prettiest woman he's ever met. But Summer's the queen of first dates, and as she looks for a way to make a relationship with the transient rodeo star work Summer's not sure she has the fortitude to go on a second date. Can they find love among the tragedy?

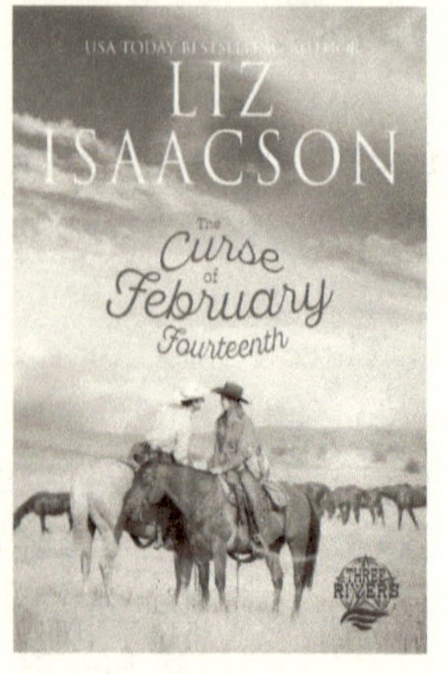

The Curse of February Fourteenth: A Three Rivers Ranch Romance™ (Book 13): Cal Hodgkins, cowboy veterinarian at Bowman's Breeds, isn't planning to meet anyone at the masked dance in small-town Three Rivers. He just wants to get his bachelor friends off his back and sit on the sidelines to drink his punch.

But when he sees a woman dressed in gorgeous butterfly wings and cowgirl boots with blue stitching, he's smitten. Too bad she runs away from the dance before he can get her name, leaving only her boot behind...

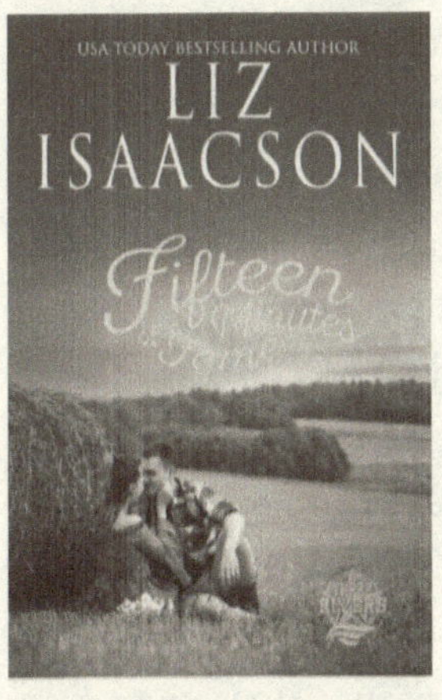

Fifteen Minutes of Fame: A Three Rivers Ranch Romance™ (Book 14): Navy Richards is thirty-five years of tired—tired of dating the same men, working a demanding job, and getting her heart broken over and over again. Her aunt has always spoken highly of the matchmaker in Three Rivers, Texas, so she takes a six-month sabbatical from her high-stress job as a pediatric nurse, hops on a bus, and meets with the matchmaker. Then she meets Gavin Redd. He's handsome, he's hardworking, and he's a cowboy. But is he an Aquarius too? Navy's not making a move until she knows for sure...

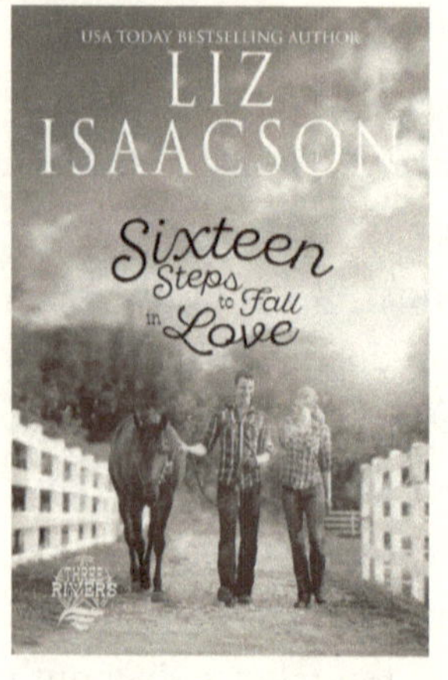

Sixteen Steps to Fall in Love: A Three Rivers Ranch Romance™ (Book 15): A chance encounter at a dog park sheds new light on the tall, talented Boone that Nicole can't ignore. As they get to know each other better and start to dig into each other's past, Nicole is the one who wants to run. This time from her growing admiration and attachment to Boone. From her aging parents. From herself.

But Boone feels the attraction between them too, and he decides he's tired of running and ready to make Three Rivers his permanent home. **Can Boone and Nicole use their faith to overcome their differences and find a happily-ever-after together?**

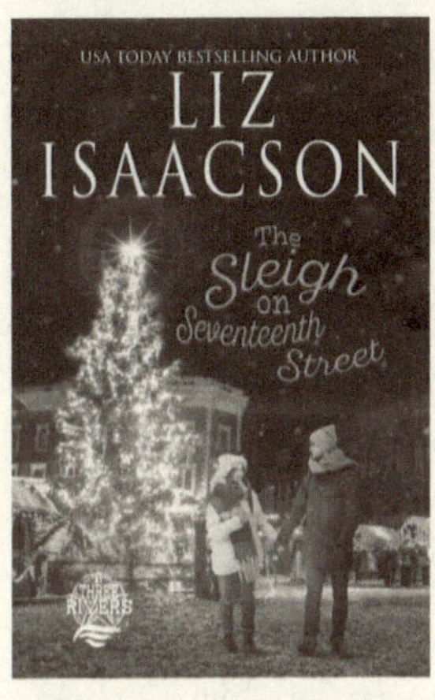

The Sleigh on Seventeenth Street: A Three Rivers Ranch Romance™ (Book 16): A cowboy with skills as an electrician tries a relationship with a down-on-her luck plumber. Can Dylan and Camila make water and electricity play nicely together this Christmas season? Or will they get shocked as they try to make their relationship work?

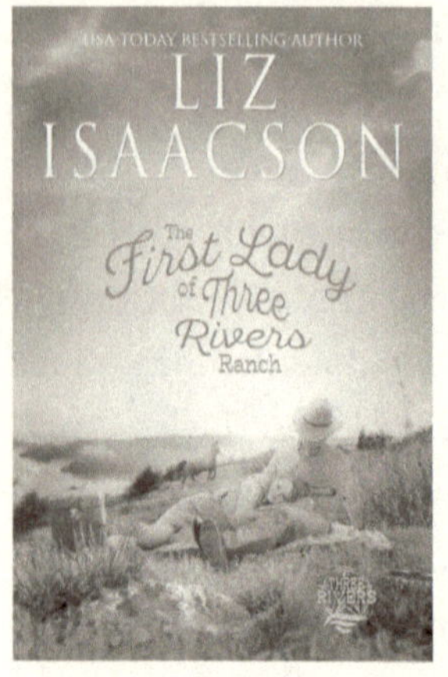

The First Lady of Three Rivers Ranch: A Three Rivers Ranch Romance™ (Book 17): Heidi Duffin has been dreaming about opening her own bakery since she was thirteen years old. She scrimped and saved for years to afford baking and pastry school in San Francisco. And now she only has one year left before she's a certified pastry chef. Frank Ackerman's father has recently retired, and he's taken over the largest cattle ranch in the Texas Panhandle. A horseman through and through, he's also nearing thirty-one and looking for someone to bring love and joy to a homestead that's been dominated by men for a decade. But when he convinces Heidi to come clean the cowboy cabins, she changes all that. But the siren's call of a bakery is still loud in Heidi's ears, even if she's also seeing a future with Frank. Can she rely on her faith in ways she's never had to before or will their relationship end when summer does?

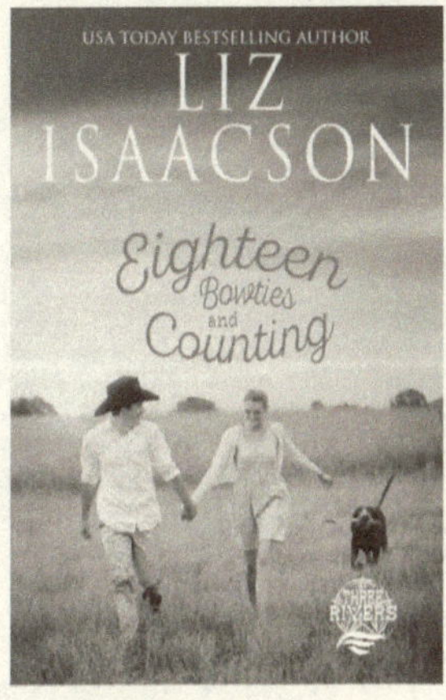

Eighteen Bowties and Counting: A Three Rivers Ranch Romance™ (Book 18): He's her older brother's best friend and completely off-limits. She's got a way with horses...and a heart condition. Can Beau and Charlotte navigate close quarters to find their happily-ever-after?

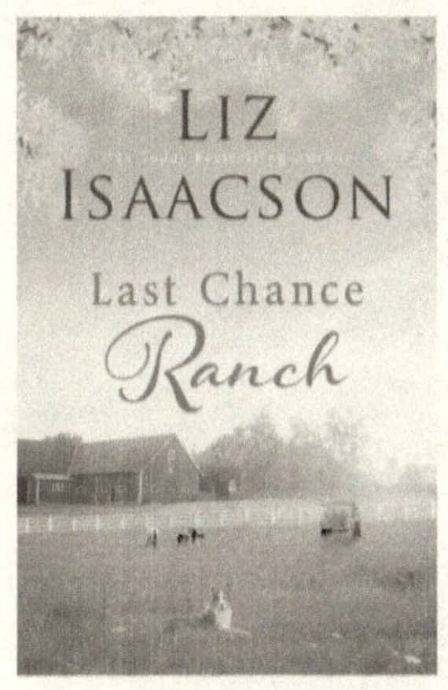

Last Chance Ranch (Book 1): A cowgirl down on her luck hires a man who's good with horses and under the hood of a car. Can Hudson fine tune Scarlett's heart as they work together? Or will things backfire and make everything worse at Last Chance Ranch?

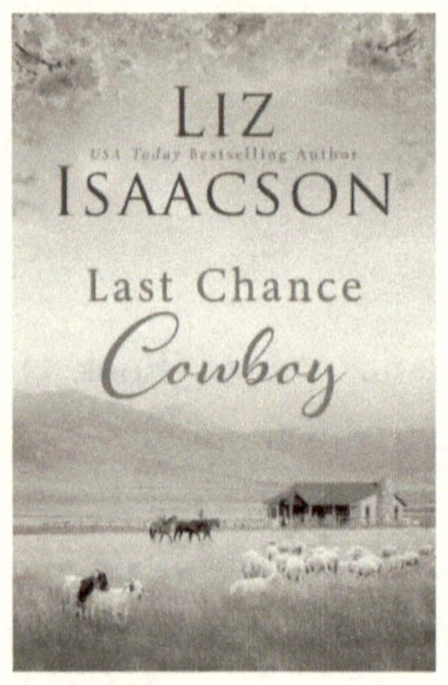

Last Chance Cowboy (Book 2): A billionaire cowboy without a home meets a woman who secretly makes food videos to pay her debts...Can Carson and Adele do more than fight in the kitchens at Last Chance Ranch?

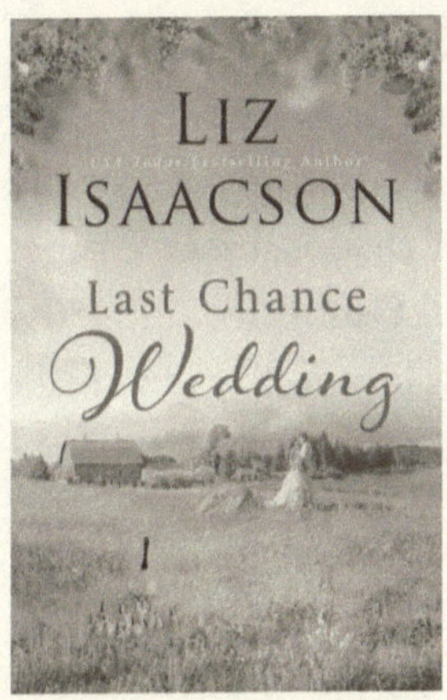

Last Chance Wedding (Book 3): A female carpenter needs a husband just for a few days... Can Jeri and Sawyer navigate the minefield of a pretend marriage before their feelings become real?

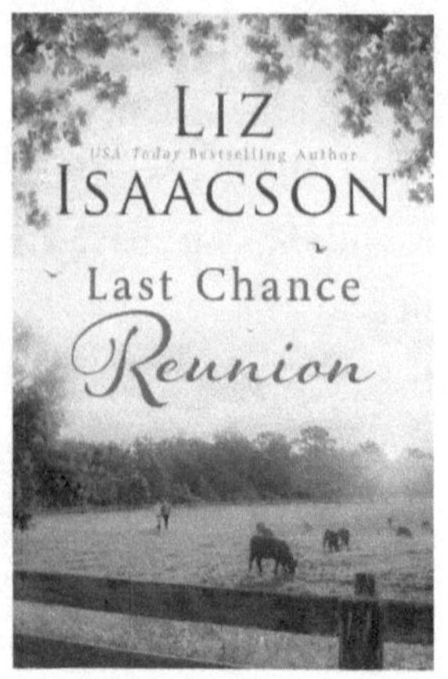

Last Chance Reunion (Book 4): An Army cowboy, the woman he dated years ago, and their last chance at Last Chance Ranch... Can Dave and Sissy put aside hurt feelings and make their second chance romance work?

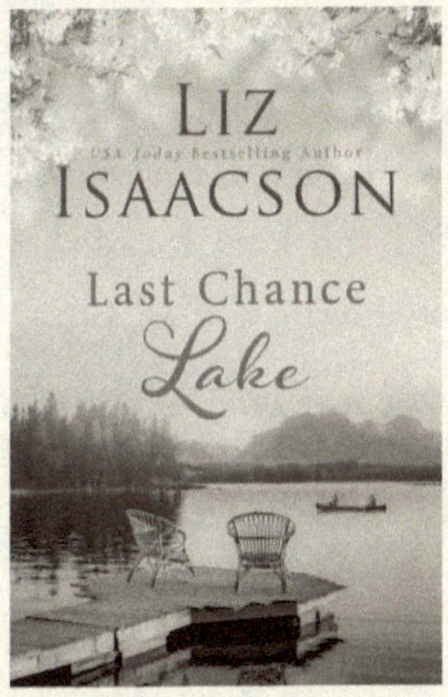

Last Chance Lake (Book 5): A former dairy farmer and the marketing director on the ranch have to work together to make the cow cuddling program a success. But can Karla let Cache into her life? Or will she keep all her secrets from him - and keep *him* a secret too?

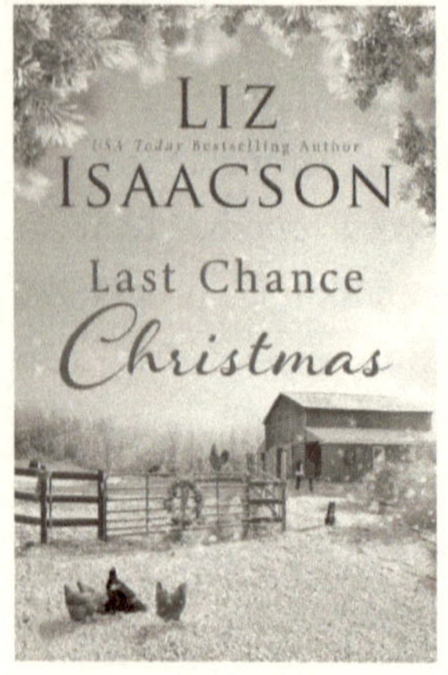

Last Chance Christmas (Book 6): She's tired of having her heart broken by cowboys. He waited too long to ask her out. Can Lance fix things quickly, or will Amber leave Last Chance Ranch before he can tell her how he feels?

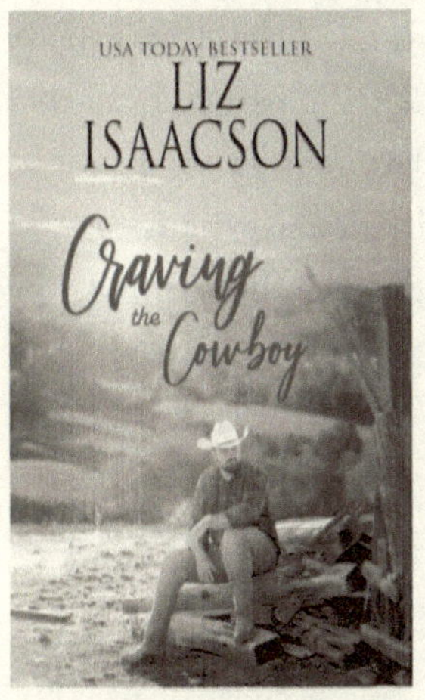

Craving the Cowboy (Book 1): Dwayne Carver is set to inherit his family's ranch in the heart of Texas Hill Country, and in order to keep up with his ranch duties and fulfill his dreams of owning a horse farm, he hires top trainer Felicity Lightburne. They get along great, and she can envision herself on this new farm—at least until her mother falls ill and she has to return to help her. Can Dwayne and Felicity work through their differences to find their happily-ever-after?

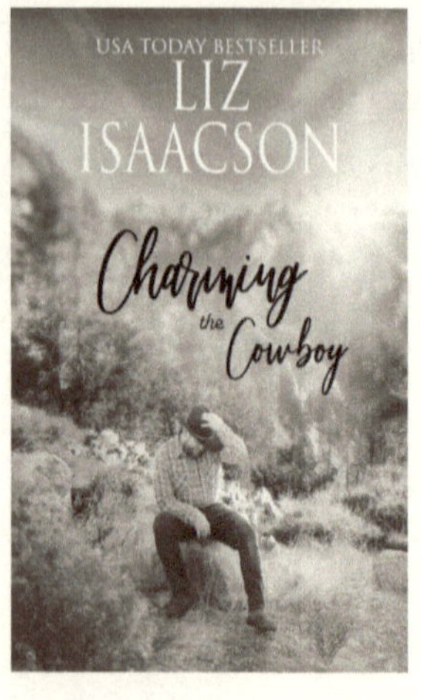

Charming the Cowboy (Book 2): Third grade teacher Heather Carver has had her eye on Levi Rhodes for a couple of years now, but he seems to be blind to her attempts to charm him. When she breaks her arm while on his horse ranch, Heather infiltrates Levi's life in ways he's never thought of, and his strict anti-female stance slips. Will Heather heal his emotional scars and he care for her physical ones so they can have a real relationship?

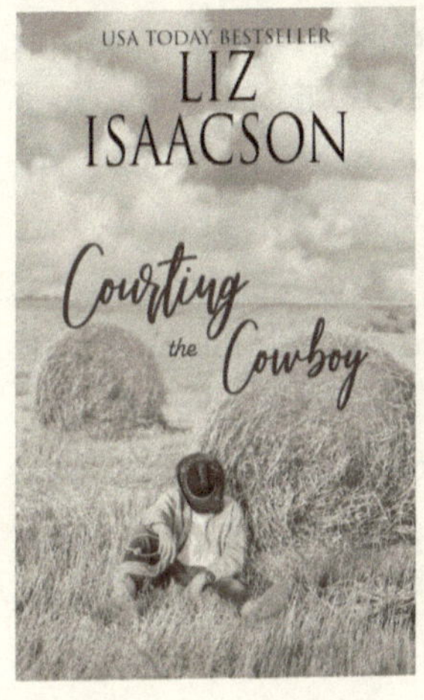

Courting the Cowboy (Book 3): Frustrated with the cowboy-only dating scene in Grape Seed Falls, May Sotheby joins Texas-Faithful.com, hoping to find her soul mate without having to relocate--or deal with cowboy hats and boots. She has no idea that Kurt Pemberton, foreman at Grape Seed Ranch, is the man she starts communicating with... Will May be able to follow her heart and get Kurt to forgive her so they can be together?

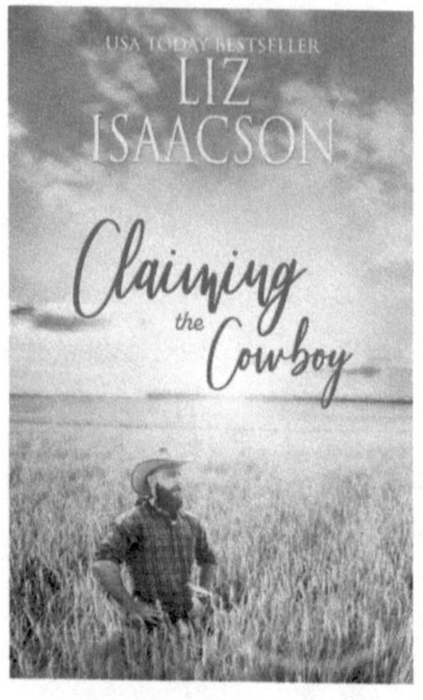

Claiming the Cowboy, Royal Brothers Book 1 (Grape Seed Falls Romance Book 4): Unwilling to be tied down, farrier Robin Cook has managed to pack her entire life into a two-hundred-and-eighty square-foot house, and that includes her Yorkie. Cowboy and co-foreman, Shane Royal has had his heart set on Robin for three years, even though she flat-out turned him down the last time he asked her to dinner. But she's back at Grape Seed Ranch for five weeks as she works her horseshoeing magic, and he's still interested, despite a bitter life lesson that left a bad taste for marriage in his mouth.

Robin's interested in him too. But can she find room for Shane in her tiny house--and can he take a chance on her with his tired heart?

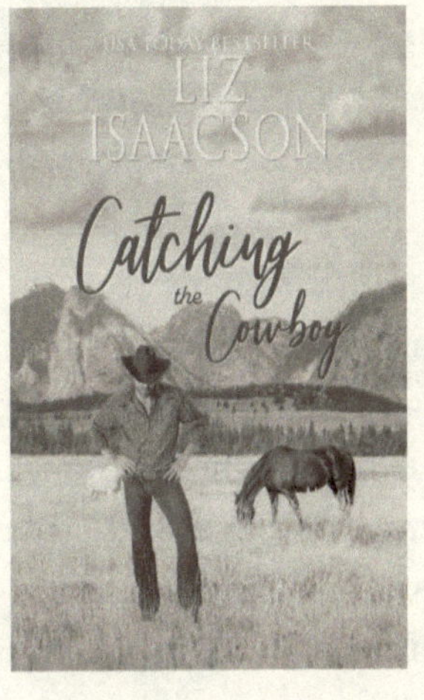

Catching the Cowboy, Royal Brothers Book 2 (Grape Seed Falls Romance Book 5): Dylan Royal is good at two things: whistling and caring for cattle. When his cows are being attacked by an unknown wild animal, he calls Texas Parks & Wildlife for help. He wasn't expecting a beautiful mammologist to show up, all flirty and fun and everything Dylan didn't know he wanted in his life.

Hazel Brewster has gone on more first dates than anyone in Grape Seed Falls, and she thinks maybe Dylan deserves a second... Can they find their way through wild animals, huge life changes, and their emotional pasts to find their forever future?

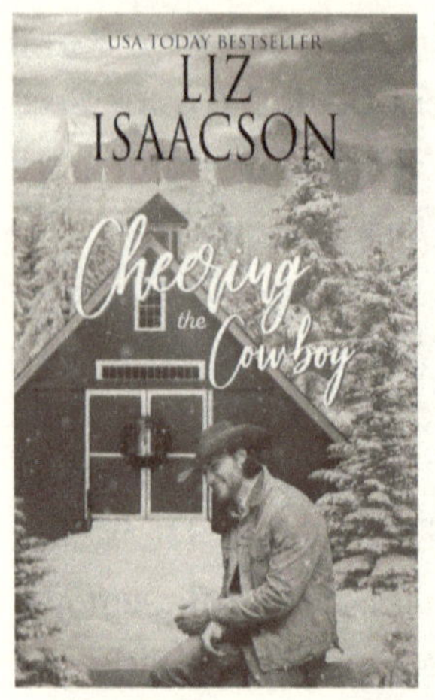

Cheering the Cowboy, Royal Brothers Book 3 (Grape Seed Falls Romance Book 6): Austin Royal loves his life on his new ranch with his brothers. But he doesn't love that Shayleigh Hatch came with the property, nor that he has to take the blame for the fact that he now owns her childhood ranch. They rarely have a conversation that doesn't leave him furious and frustrated--and yet he's still attracted to Shay in a strange, new way.

Shay inexplicably likes him too, which utterly confuses and angers her. As they work to make this Christmas the best the Triple Towers Ranch has ever seen, can they also navigate through their rocky relationship to smoother waters?

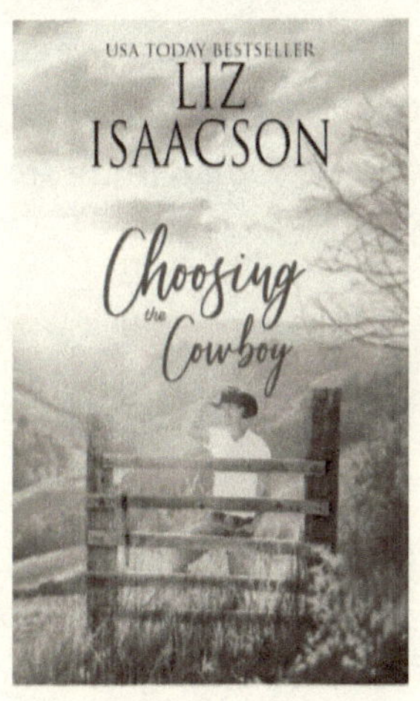

Choosing the Cowboy (Book 7): With financial trouble and personal issues around every corner, can Maggie Duffin and Chase Carver rely on their faith to find their happily-ever-after?

A spinoff from the #1 bestselling Three Rivers Ranch Romance novels, also by USA Today bestselling author Liz Isaacson.

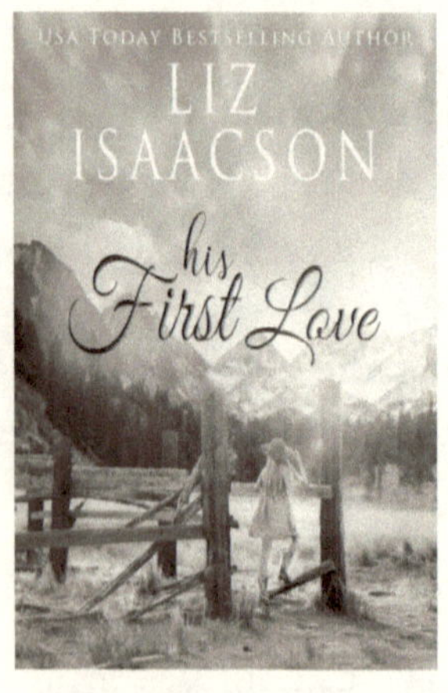

His First Love (Book 1): She broke up with him a decade ago. He's back in town after finishing a degree at MIT, ready to start his job at the family company. Can Hunter and Molly find their way through their pasts to build a future together?

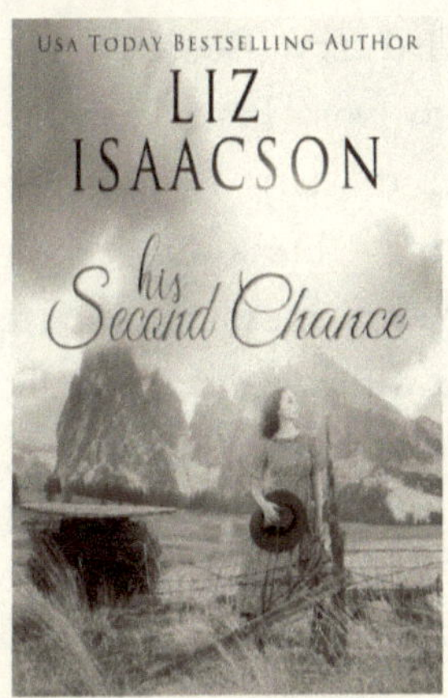

His Second Chance (Book 2): They broke up over twenty years ago. She's lost everything when she shows up at the farm in Ivory Peaks where he works. Can Matt and Gloria heal from their pasts to find a future happily-ever-after with each other?

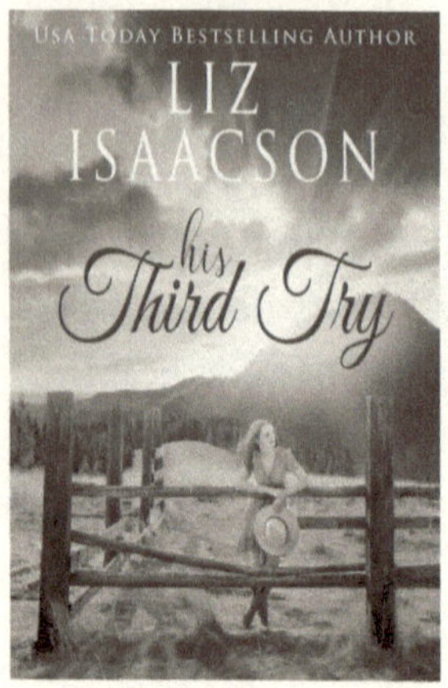

His Third Try (Book 3): He moved to Ivory Peaks with his daughter to start over after a devastating break-up. She's never had a meaningful relationship with a man, especially a cowboy. Can Boone and Cosette help each other heal enough to build a happily-ever-after...and a family?

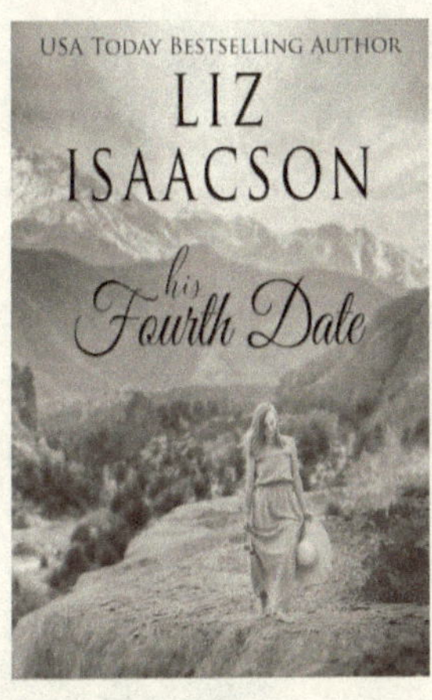

His Fourth Date (Book 4): Their relationship has been nothing but loose goats, a leaking roof, and her complete humiliation after he pays her mortgage so she won't lose her farm. Travis wants to go back in time and start over with Poppy, but he doesn't know how. Can a small town speed-dating event get their second chance off on the right foot?

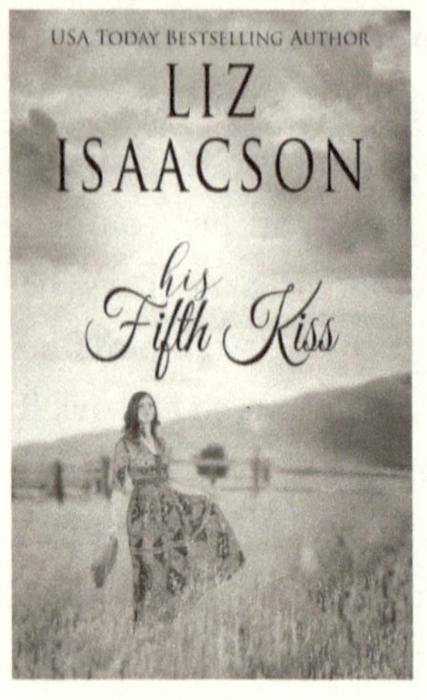

His Fifth Kiss (Book 5): They once had a few summers together. Now, Michael Hammond is back in town after a devastating injury overseas. He's looking to reset and recover...not to fall in love. But with Gertrude Whettstein also back at the farm, can Gerty and Mike make their second chance romance into a happily-ever-after?

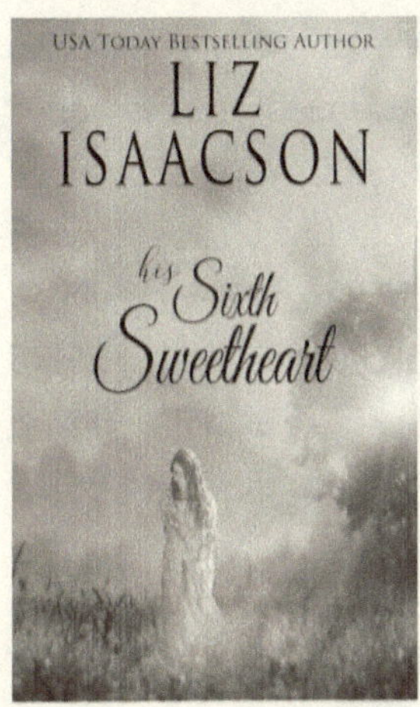

His Sixth Sweetheart (Book 6): She's had a crush on him for decades. He's finally in a place where he feels ready to date the boss's daughter. Can Cord and Jane take their relationship to the next level without getting burned?

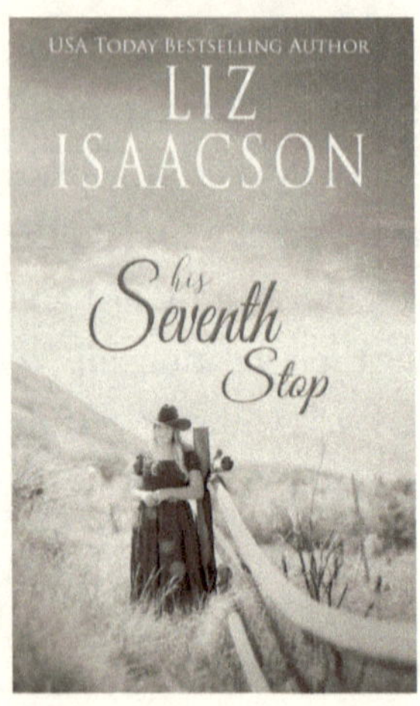

His Seventh Stop (Book 7): He's a seasoned cowboy on a delivery mission. She's a resilient hobby farm owner braving the winter storm. Can Keith and Lindsay forge a bond in the heart of a tempest and find love in the calm that follows?

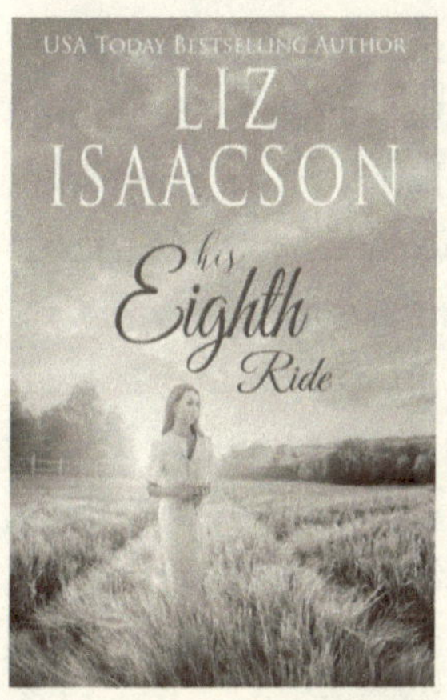

His Eighth Ride (Book 8): Tag has secretly admired Opal from afar. He even went so far as to ask her out, but the timing was all off, and now he's just awkward around his best friend's little sister. Can their unexpected reunion mend the fences between them and finally lead them to the forever love they've been waiting for?

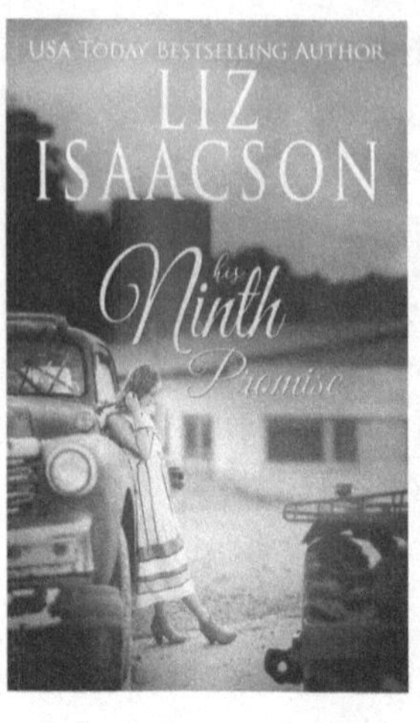

His Ninth Promise (Book 9): At home on the Hammond Family Farm, where gypsy souls and rodeo dreams collide, Tucker's heart has been beating for Bobbie Jo. But with her heart set on a distant love and Tucker searching for something more, their paths seemed destined to cross but never converge. Can he stick it out for another ride if the promise is coming home to Bobbie Jo?

About Liz

Liz Isaacson writes inspirational romance, usually set in Texas, or Wyoming, or anywhere else horses and cowboys exist. She lives in Utah, where she writes full-time, takes her two dogs to the park everyday, and eats a lot of veggies while writing. Find her on her website at feelgoodfiction-books.com

www.ingramcontent.com/pod-product-compliance
Lightning Source LLC
Chambersburg PA
CBHW050134110726
47898CB00008B/2530

Wedding Bell Blues

Something Old, Something New
Book 3

Suzanne Stengl

Publisher: Mya & Angus
Cover Design: Tammy Seidick

www.SuzanneStengl.com

MYA & ANGUS

Dedication

To the memory of my mother,
Alice

~ with love and gratitude

Chapter One

On a cool and windy Thursday evening in September, Krista MacKenzie tugged her old suitcase on its squeaky wheels through the shiny revolving doors of the Palliser Hotel, and got stuck. Three revolutions later, she hopped out, yanking on the handle of the troublesome bag. The wheels skidded, the handle twisted, and the suitcase jammed in the door.

"Happens all the time," said the young bellhop who released her bag. He smiled and shrugged.

"Thank you." Krista took hold of the suitcase handle again. It wobbled, more than usual. It had wobbled for the entire walk from the Greyhound depot. "Sorry, I should have used the side door." And if she hadn't been so tired, she would have thought of that.

"Can I carry it for you?"

"No, um, thank you," she stammered. "I've got it." She wished she had money to tip the young man, but she didn't. She didn't have money for tips, and she didn't have money to stay in a place like this.

She glanced at the high ceilings, the textured walls, the marble floors. If she'd any idea this hotel would be so . . . so *magnificent*, she would never have agreed to stay here.

"I'm meeting a friend," she told the bellhop. "I'll wait in the lobby." As she turned around, she saw Michaela, rushing toward her. Michaela—tall and elegant, wearing her long navy blue coat.

"Oh, there you are, sweetie," Michaela said, hugging her. "I'm so glad you're here."

Michaela Andrews was forty-two years old, fifteen years older than Krista. In the two months they'd known each other, they'd become close friends.

"Room 701," Michaela told the bellhop, who remained ready to serve. "I've already checked her in."

A minute later, the three of them were on the elevator, silently rising to the seventh floor. At least the elevator was silent.

"Any problems with leaving?"

Krista swallowed. "No," she said, fiddling with the buttons on her old coat.

"You got the apartment?"

"I did," Krista answered. "And the first month is paid." She'd used the last of her money. Well, almost the last. There had been that other fifty-five dollars.

"I'll take you there tomorrow," Michaela said. "And then on Monday, you have an interview with my friend Marge. She may have a job for you."

Krista tipped her head back and briefly closed her eyes. "Thank you," she said. "That was quick."

"An opening came up. I told Marge to hold it for you. It's not a lot of money, but—"

"I don't care," Krista said. As long as she got a job, soon.

They watched the numbers blink on the brass plate above the elevator doors.

"How was the bus ride?" Michaela asked.

Long and tiring. "It was fine," Krista said. "But I should probably go to bed soon."

"Not yet."

"Not yet?"

"First, I have something for you."

Ding. The doors slid open.

"This way." Michaela headed down the hall, and Krista followed. Behind her, she heard the bellhop and the squeaky wheels of her suitcase.

Michaela touched a key card to the sensor on Room 701 and opened the door.

Stepping inside, Krista stared at the draperies and the paintings and the little oak table by the windows and the red tweed of the wingback chairs and—and the large black box on the bed. In the background, she heard the bellhop say, "Thank you very much."

Of course, Michaela would have tipped him. Krista should be covering the tip. Michaela had already done enough getting her this room, even though the room was free. A prize Michaela had won for helping with the hospital lottery.

Michaela rushed over to the bed, picked up the box and, with a big smile, she presented it to Krista. "For you."

"But—" Krista held up both hands, palms out.

"A little something to welcome you to Calgary."

"It doesn't look like something little." Krista dropped her hands and took a step back. "I mean, I don't want to be ungrateful, but you can't spend money on me this way and—"

"I've told you. When I was in my early twenties, I went through the same thing you're going through now."

"Not quite."

"Well, close. And, besides, I'm not spending money." Michaela laughed, weighing the box in her hands. "I won it when I volunteered for the Collins Parade of Homes last month."

Michaela was always working on some fundraiser—and winning prizes. "I didn't need anything like this," she said, "so I asked for it in your size."

"My size?"

"Clothes." Michaela's eyes sparkled. She set the box back on the bed and clasped her palms to her heart. "Open it."

In a few moments, Krista had opened the box and scattered the contents over the bed. There was a silky dress, a beaded evening bag, and a pair of high heeled sandals. That, and some wispy lingerie. Everything was black except for the gold sandals—shiny gold, with a mesh of straps.

"I thought you'd like it," Michaela said. "For tonight."

Krista felt her stomach clench. "Tonight?"

"For the first night of your new life."

Letting go of a sigh, Krista picked up the dress, fanning the silky fabric. This dress, and the shoes, they were not the sort of clothes she wore. Ever. "I can't wear this."

"Of course you can, and it will be fun. We'll go downstairs and have one drink."

Krista dropped the dress back on the bed. "Don't you have to meet your husband at the airport?"

"Not for another hour. You can have some Baileys and cream. That'll make you drowsy. Then you'll sleep well."

If only, Krista thought. If only she could relax and finally sleep. And she should probably eat something. It had been a long day of travel, with nothing to eat. "I really don't feel like going out."

"You're not going anywhere. You've got this gorgeous hotel for one night. You might as well make the most of it." Full of energy, Michaela marched about the room, with her hands held up, as if she were orchestrating an event. "All you have to do is get dressed and get on the elevator. Seven flights down and you're at Kipling's. You'll love it. You can sip your Baileys and pretend you're Pretty Woman waiting for Edward to pick you up."

"Michaela . . ."

"I didn't say you'd actually do that. I said pretend. It will totally change your mood."

"There's nothing wrong with my mood. I'll be fine."

"You will be fine. And tonight, you'll have some fun. Now won't you at least try this on?"

Chapter Two

Logan Nicholas folded his arms and leaned on the edge of his mahogany desk, while his good friend Roger Claymore paced the large office, and reported on the train wreck of a fundraiser that was supposed to happen tonight.

Finally, Roger collapsed in one of the guest chairs. "I thought Hayden knew what he was doing."

"Hayden knew exactly what he was doing."

"He said the events planner—"

"The events planner didn't screw up. Hayden told her he wanted hookers."

Roger grimaced. "Escorts, Logan. Escorts. There's a difference." He rotated his head and rubbed the back of his neck. "We can still salvage this."

Logan moved away from his desk and sank into the other guest chair. "How is that possible?"

Scrubbing his hand over his face, Roger thought a moment. "We'll make it classy," he said. "And I'll be the master of ceremonies."

"You'll be the auctioneer. Auctioning women to the highest bidder, *for Chrissake*. How will that ever be classy?"

"I'll wear a tux."

Logan slanted him a glance. "You think that will make any difference?"

Roger stared at the floor-to-ceiling windows in front of

them. "It will set a tone," he said, "You know. A certain kind of . . . ambiance."

Right, Logan thought. *Ambiance.* It was like putting lipstick on a pig. He looked out at the view—at the reflected light of the setting sun bouncing off the glass high rises surrounding the Sun Valley Tower. He wished he'd never let Hayden Bonningham get involved.

"Think about it, Logan. It's not like anyone's having sex with them. It's drinks and dinner." Roger shrugged. "Maybe some dancing, later."

"Dancing?" Was Roger serious? "You think these guys know how to dance? In case you've forgotten, half of them are engineers."

"We'll all be in the Stephenson Lounge at the hotel. And," Roger added with a ruffled tone, "I'm an engineer and I can dance."

"That's because your big sister forced you to learn." No way was this salvageable. "What about the married guys? You think their wives want them bidding on hookers?"

"Escorts, Logan. Escorts," Roger said, again.

"I can't believe the Palliser let him do this."

"Uhhh, about that."

When Roger didn't elaborate, Logan turned to face him. "What?"

"Hayden told the hotel it was a charity auction."

Logan clenched his fists. "Of course he called it a charity." That's what Hayden would do. "It's a bunch of ex-football players raising money for a fishing lodge. It's not a charity."

"I know, I know," Roger said, still staring out the windows.

Logan pressed his fingers into his forehead. "I didn't think today could get any worse."

Roger's attention shifted. "What do you mean? Is there a problem at one of the sites?"

"No, nothing like that," Logan said. His head hurt and he wanted to be alone. Wanted to stop the world for a couple of days and hide.

They were quiet for a few beats, and then Roger figured it out. "Cheryl?"

One thing about Roger, the guy was astute. "Yeah."

"Now what's she done?"

Logan ran his hands through his hair. "I gave her a key to my condo."

"You didn't."

"She said she had something to drop off. It seemed reasonable."

"And?" Roger prompted.

"And," Logan hated to say it, hated to admit he hadn't seen it coming. "She started painting my kitchen."

Roger's head dropped and a muffled laugh followed.

"It's not funny."

"It's your own fault for giving her a key." Roger laughed out loud. "But, that's presumptuous, even for Cheryl." He sat quietly for a minute. "What did you tell her?"

"I haven't seen her yet. When I got home this afternoon, there were drop cloths on the floor and several shades of yellow on one wall."

"She's testing colors." Roger nodded.

"Yeah."

"She's moving in?"

"No! I gave her a key, that's all. We don't have that kind of relationship."

"Are you sure?"

"Yes, I'm sure."

Cheryl was beautiful and she was fun to be with. And they liked the same things. Everything from theater to parties to jogging. But, he should never have given her a key.

"We're supposed to have lunch tomorrow. I'll clear it up then." *One problem at a time.* "And tonight, we'll cancel the fundraiser."

"We can't." Roger's tone was matter-of-fact. "The deposit will set us back. Besides, it's almost seven-thirty. We don't have time. They're all going to show up."

Logan got to his feet. "I won't be there," he said, his voice flat, his decision made.

"But you have to be there." Roger stayed seated. "The fishing lodge is your brainchild."

It was. And tonight was supposed to be the final push to get the capital together. But not if it meant participating in this farce.

They heard the elevator chime, and they looked at each other.

"No idea." Roger shrugged.

A moment later Cheryl charged into his office, her blonde hair perfectly smooth, her light pink suit perfectly tailored, her high heels perfectly matched to her suit. She looked like a model right out of the pages of a magazine.

And, she looked a little . . . upset? Did she know he was unimpressed with her decorating efforts?

"I just heard," she said, with a tone full of importance.

"That I don't like what you're doing to my kitchen?"

She blinked. "Are you out of your mind?"

"No. I'm not. I don't need my kitchen painted. I don't *want* my kitchen painted. How could you do that without asking me first?"

She stared at him, gave her head a little shake, and said, "I wanted to surprise you. I am an interior designer. I know what I'm doing."

"Give me my key back." He held out his hand.

"Don't be silly!"

"You're not painting my condo. I like the color it is. Or was. Now I've got to get someone to fix that wall, and"—

he held out his hand again—"I'd like my key, please."

"That's not why I'm here."

Yeah. The day was going from bad to worse. "Okaaay. And you're here because?"

"I just heard about your ridiculous idea for a fundraiser."

He felt his mouth drop open. Cheryl was his girlfriend, not his mother.

"It wasn't actually his idea," Roger said. "Hayden Bonningham was supposed to—"

"I'm talking to Logan. This is none of your business."

As a beat of silence fell over the office, Logan studied his girlfriend. The tone of her voice, it was so different. She'd never talked to him this way before.

"Actually, it is my business," Roger said. But that's all he said. He swiveled his chair back to face the windows.

"Honestly, Logan." Cheryl crossed her arms and lifted her chin.

"Don't worry about—"

"You can't seriously think you're selling hookers to raise money for your stupid fishing lodge."

"I—" Her words clicked into place. *Stupid?* Did you call my fishing lodge, *stupid?*"

"Yes I did!"

"It's not— How did you hear about the fundraiser?"

"Everyone's talking about it." She kept her arms crossed and frowned at him. "I think it's juvenile. And I happen to know that Mark and Ryder are *not* going."

Logan let out a breath as a sudden coldness landed in his gut. Did Cheryl really think he would—

"You cannot do this." She stabbed her index finger in the air. "You cannot attend that fundraiser. I forbid it!"

For several seconds, he heard a buzzing sound in his head and he forgot where he was. He watched Cheryl's mouth moving but he didn't hear what else she was saying.

Then the fog cleared and he straightened his shoulders.
"Did you say *forbid?*"

Chapter Three

Krista hardly recognized herself as she looked in the mirror. Her auburn hair was swept up with two shiny black combs. With the makeup, her blue eyes looked dark and sultry. The combs belonged to Michaela and were probably expensive. The eye makeup was Michaela's too. Michaela seemed to specialize in makeovers. And the silky black dress . . .

"It's a little tight, don't you think? And short?"

"It's perfect."

"But . . . this isn't me. I don't look like this."

"You look beautiful, sweetie."

"I look like I want to pick up some guy in a bar."

"Try the shoes," Michaela said.

The shoes were pretty. Gold sandals, high heels, strappy. Krista slipped them on and took a few steps. She wasn't used to high heels.

"Good," Michaela said. "Here." She handed Krista the tiny beaded purse, glittering like black glass. "Now, let's go."

"But, Michaela—"

"No buts. Come on. We're going to the bar."

Krista sighed. Might as well go downstairs. Michaela would soon leave for the airport, and then Krista could come back and, hopefully, she'd be able to fall asleep.

"You really do look gorgeous," Michaela said, as they

rode down the elevator. "And you're smart and you're a hard worker. Don't worry. Everything will turn out for the best."

Krista didn't know about that. But she did know that sometimes, when she heard her friend's kind words, it was enough to make her break down and cry.

She inhaled and squared her shoulders. A few minutes later, they were at the door to Kipling's.

"When's the plane arrive?"

"In about an hour, if it's still on time."

"Then you'd better go."

"I'll leave in a half hour," Michaela said. "First we sit down. Over here."

They approached the long bar, dark polished wood. Krista climbed up on her seat, tugging the hem of the dress down.

"Can I help you ladies?" The bartender wore a burgundy jacket and a bow tie.

"I'll have a club soda. My friend will have Baileys and cream." Michaela handed the bartender a folded bill. "Thank you," she said, smiling at the man.

In the mirror behind the bar, Krista studied the rest of the room. Well-dressed customers talked quietly in small groups. Cream-colored walls, dark wood beams, wall sconce lighting. Tables of various sizes were surrounded by upholstered chairs.

Running her hand along the smooth wood of the bar, Krista looked up at the rows of sparkling stem glasses suspended from racks. Below the glasses, colorful bottles lined up, reflecting in the mirror and bouncing color everywhere. "If my sisters could see me now. They would not believe their eyes."

"Never mind your sisters," Michaela said. "Someday they'll figure out you've grown up and have your own life."

No, they wouldn't. They would always see her as a

failure. The little sister who never could.

The bartender had their drinks ready. A glass of cream over ice, golden with the Baileys, sitting on a white marble coaster like a magic potion. And a tall frosting glass for Michaela, also on a marble coaster, but that coaster was blue.

"Are you ladies here for the job fair?" the bartender asked.

Krista turned to Michaela. Was that why she wanted to come here?

"Job fair?" Michaela squinted. She didn't seem to know what the bartender was talking about.

"In the Alberta Room upstairs," the bartender answered. "There are about forty employers there tonight. Giving you info about their companies."

"Do you need to register?" Krista asked.

"Just show up," the bartender said. "It's like speed dating for people looking for jobs." He moved down the bar to help a new customer.

"What do you think?" Krista asked.

"About the job fair? Did you want to go?"

Hardly. "Not dressed like this."

Michaela nodded. "Maybe not the best choice. But, don't worry. I think you'll like Marge and I'm pretty sure she can find you a job."

They spent the next half hour talking a little bit about Marge's "Girl Friday Staffing Solutions", and a lot about Michaela's twin sons and their university courses. They also talked about where to get a bargain on apartment furniture and where to buy the best loose tea.

Not once did Michaela mention Paul—which was a good thing. Krista wanted to forget all about him, especially that fifty-five dollars.

Michaela glanced at her watch. "I need to send a quick text." It was half past eight.

"There," she said, putting her phone away. She reached out and squeezed Krista's hand. "Be home by midnight, sweetie."

And then with a whirl of her long blue coat, she winked, and was gone.

At half past eight, Logan pushed through the revolving doors of the Palliser Hotel. Roger was already here, in the ballroom, and Logan had said he'd join him.

What else could he do after Cheryl had forbidden him to attend?

His cell beeped a text notification, one he recognized. It was Mark, his friend Mark Bainbridge.

> *Meet me at Kipling's. On my way. Should be*
> *there in 10 minutes.*

Cheryl had said that Mark would not be at the fundraiser. So what was this about? Logan pocketed his cell and headed for Kipling's.

The place buzzed with activity. All the tables were occupied but there was room at the bar. A guy and a girl on the left end. A couple of empty seats. Then an old man drinking alone. One empty seat. Then two women, probably in their fifties, around his mother's age. Three more empty seats and then a young woman at the very end. A woman with brown hair, brown with reddish tints.

As Logan took the middle of the three empty seats, a familiar bartender approached. "Hi, Jason. How's business?"

"Steady. How's your business?"

"Same."

"What can I get you?"

"Big Rock Traditional."

While Jason got the drink, Logan glanced in the mirror behind the bar and got a better view of the woman on his right.

He wasn't trying to look at her, but he couldn't help it. Her hair was swept up with shiny black combs so that tendrils cascaded in pretty curls over her shoulders.

Jason set a frosting glass on a white marble coaster in front of him.

"No," Jason said, leaning close to him.

"No, what?"

"You don't want to buy her a drink."

"I wasn't going to," Logan said, keeping his voice low.

Jason nodded, like he'd heard it all before. "The last two guys that have come in have offered. And that old guy, Jason angled his head to the old man drinking alone, he's tried too. She's not interested."

"Good to know."

"I think she's waiting for someone."

"You don't know?"

"She's not talkative. But someone should buy her dinner."

The woman might not be talkative, but Jason was. "Why should someone buy her dinner?" Logan asked, still speaking quietly.

"She's eating all my cherries."

Logan shot a look in her direction, saw a pile of cherry pits and stems next to her half-full drink.

Not his problem. He angled on the barstool to scan the room. Mark would see him at the bar, but Logan checked the room anyway. Then he checked his cell again. Then he wanted to look at the woman again.

Maybe sitting on this end of the bar had not been a good idea because he had this urge to turn his head in her direction, this unsettling impulse to study the woman with the reddish brown hair and the little black dress—the short black dress, the gorgeous legs, and the gold sandals.

Wrong.

Logan finished his beer, and then risked another glance at the woman. Only to find she was looking his way. Her brilliant blue eyes flashed at him for a second, and then she opened her little purse and searched for something.

Okay, enough of waiting for Mark.

Logan got up to leave, and then he stopped and motioned for Jason, who returned to their end of the bar. "If she asks for more cherries," Logan said, "bring her a sandwich." He tossed some bills on the bar, and left.

At the other end of the hotel, Logan slipped into the wild and noisy chaos of the Crystal Ballroom. Men in business suits and women in fancy, somewhat skimpy dresses ranged about the room. The men gathered in clusters of two or four or ten. The women circulated from group to group, pausing to shake hands, laughing at jokes, smiling like they were at an old-fashioned family reunion.

Professionals.

A tuxedo-clad waiter approached with a tray of champagne flutes. Logan declined. He didn't feel celebratory, and anyway, he'd just had a beer.

Another waiter stepped up beside him. Logan did a double take. Not a waiter, but Roger—in a tux. Around the office, the guy wore jeans and polo shirts. But then he was a drilling engineer. He could wear whatever he wanted. Tonight though, he looked impressive.

"Nice tux," Logan commented.

"Thanks," Roger said, and got right to the point. "Some of the guys are not showing up. I got a few texts." He patted the phone in his pocket. "Some of them," he paused, clearing his throat. "Some of them are *pleased* with the entertainment. And some of them—mostly those from out of town—have no idea what is going on."

"Right," Logan said. And then, "What's with the champagne?"

Roger shrugged. "I told you. I'm trying to set a tone. To give this a more favorable atmosphere."

Logan must have looked doubtful.

"Ambiance, Logan. Ambiance." Roger scanned the crowd. "There's Hayden. Have you talked to him yet?"

"No, have you?"

"No time. I just finished arranging for the champagne."

Hayden had seen them and was threading his way through the crowd toward where Logan and Roger stood near the entrance to the ballroom.

"I think he's put on more weight," Logan said.

"Yeah, I think so."

"He still a sales rep?"

"Yeah. For several sporting goods stores," Roger said. "Travels a lot."

That's what Logan had heard. That Hayden traveled a lot for his job, leaving his wife and two little kids at home in Vancouver. Apparently Hayden was the model husband when he was at home, but when he was on the road, it was different.

Finally, Hayden made it to their side. "So!" He clapped his hands together, rubbing them. "Can I organize an auction or what!"

"We were hoping for something more PC," Logan said.

"Nah, this is a great idea!" Hayden snickered. His extra chins jiggled as he slapped a hand over Roger's shoulder. "And, a worthy cause. Of course."

"Not exactly," Logan said. "You told the hotel this is a charity function?"

"I told them it was a worthy cause. Loosen up, Logan." Hayden turned his attention to Roger. "I hear you wanna be the auctioneer?"

"Yes," Roger said. "I'll be the master of ceremonies."

"Great. I don't wanna do it. I wanna bid. Here." Hayden pulled a packet of white cards from his jacket and handed them to Roger.

"What's this?"

"Their names and particulars." Hayden laughed. Then he took an envelope from his other pocket. "The checks," he said. "Thanks for the checks, Logan."

"What checks?"

"Your office did the paperwork," Hayden said.

"We did?"

"Long story," Roger told him.

"They cost me five hundred each," Hayden went on. "Bidding starts at six hundred. Who you gonna bid on, Logan?"

"I'm making a donation," he said, flatly.

Hayden's eyebrows lifted, turning into folds in his forehead. "Suit yourself." He bristled. "It's drinks and dinner. Nothing wrong with that." Craning his neck, he pointed. "I'm buying the tasty little blonde over there."

Logan glanced at the young woman and thought, no, not drinks and dinner. Not Hayden. He wouldn't settle for that, even if he had to pay extra.

Hayden squinted, patting his thumb against his numerous chins as he studied the blonde woman. "I think a thousand. Yeah, she'll go for a thousand." He nudged Logan. "Loosen up, buddy. Have a little fun."

Logan felt out of place.

Someone bumped him from behind. Bruce Irving, one of the guys on the old team. Ex-linebacker. Ex-jock. Ex-husband. A financial consultant now in Winnipeg.

"Hey! Logan! Wondered when you'd show up!" Bruce lightly punched Logan's arm.

"How ya doin'?" Logan said. "Still in Winnipeg?"

"Still in Winnipeg," the old football player confirmed.

"Flew in this afternoon. Wouldn't miss this for the world. Whose idea was the auction?"

"Mine." Hayden beamed.

"Great idea. Nice merchandise. And nice hotel too. Gives it some class, you know?"

"We were hoping for some class," Logan said, but Bruce didn't seem to have any.

"We're gonna make a lot of money," Bruce said, nodding. The guy was practically drooling as two of the ladies passed by their group.

"This has got to be a good income for these girls," Hayden said, talking mostly to Roger.

"I want the redhead, over there," Bruce said, to no one in particular. "The one in the silver dress."

Roger scanned the crowd, tapping his fingers, like he was counting.

"I wonder if any of them are lap dancers." Hayden chuckled, his chins and his jowls bouncing.

Tonight, Logan didn't like Hayden Bonningham. In fact, now that he thought about it, he'd never liked the guy.

"Hey, Logan!"

Prometheus Jones had found them. Thank God, because Logan didn't think he could handle much more of Hayden and Bruce.

"Pro! Glad you could make it." Hayden was pumping Pro's hand. "How's business, boy? Hear you're rakin' in the cash."

"Can't complain," Pro said, zeroing his focus on Hayden. "Interesting fundraiser you've set up."

"It's perfectly legitimate." Hayden took a step back.

Pro tilted his head and didn't comment.

Roger glanced at his watch. "Nine o'clock. I think we're about to begin. But I only count nineteen ladies." He frowned. "There should be twenty."

"That's not enough to go around." Bruce pouted and

bit down on his bottom lip.

"That's the whole idea, my friend." Hayden's voice boomed over the noise. "The lady goes to the highest bidder!"

"Yeah, yeah," Bruce said, rocking in place. "So long as nobody outbids me for my redhead."

"Excuse me a minute, gentlemen," Roger interrupted. "I'd better check the lobby."

"I gotta get a refill." Hayden drummed his fingers on his empty glass and headed over to the bar.

And then John Speaken was there. John—insurance broker, married, no kids, nice wife. "Are they auctioning escorts?" He wrinkled his nose and his face blanched.

"Yep." Pro nodded. "Who put Hayden in charge?"

"I think it was an oversight," Logan said.

"I'm not bidding." John frowned. "But we're all going for dinner, right?"

"Yes. Stephenson Lounge," Logan told them. "Upstairs."

"Tell you what," Pro said. "I'll bid. You can join my table for the dinner. Then we can all go shoot some pool."

"The escort too?"

"Sure," Pro said. And then, when Logan looked at him, "I don't have a girlfriend. I can bid. And I will treat the lady with respect."

"I know *you* will."

Pro gave him a strained smile, then thought a moment. "Are you bidding?"

"No," Logan said. "I'll make a donation later." He had a blank check ready, probably make it out for two thousand dollars.

Pro looked around the room. "Mark and Ryder aren't here?"

"No," Logan answered. "Mark sent me a text about a half hour ago. Said he was meeting me at Kipling's, but I expect he got tied up at the hospital. Ryder is behind on construction so he can't make it. Or, that's his excuse."

"They'll be at the game tomorrow?"

"Yes," Logan said. "And they'll make donations. Everyone wants the lodge to be a go-ahead. But I don't think everyone knew about the . . . auction."

"No, I don't think so." Pro surveyed the loud room.

The waiter with the champagne interrupted them. Pro and John each took a glass. John spotted an old friend and headed off to see him, leaving Pro and Logan alone.

"You still seeing Cheryl?" Pro asked.

"Yep."

"She knows about the auction?"

"Yep." Logan pinched his lips together.

"Not a good topic?"

"Nope."

She had not intended to stay. But after Michaela left, Krista didn't feel like being alone. At least, not alone in her room. She wanted to be *near* people, but not *with* anyone.

So when the bartender had asked her if she would accept a drink from another patron, she'd of course said no, and no one had bothered her since.

There had been that last man, the one who'd sat one seat away from her. Something about him spoke of safety, and danger, at the same time. She'd glanced at him, twice. The second time, she'd found him looking right at her, so she'd quickly looked away. With Paul barely out of her life, she wasn't even going to consider new entanglements.

For the past half hour, she'd slowly sipped her Baileys and cream, feeling it smooth over her mind. She made the drink last as long as possible. Now, it was nothing more than a few rapidly melting ice cubes.

Earlier, the bartender had caught her staring at his glass

bowl of cherry garnishes. He'd grinned and set the bowl beside her. However, eight sweet cherries didn't count as a meal. She was hungry, but no money.

She could raid the mini fridge in her room, but the mini fridge would be charged to Michaela's credit card and Michaela had already done enough for her.

She could ask the bartender for more cherries, but she'd already eaten a lot of his cherries.

She could go up to her room and try to sleep with her stomach aching for food. Or, a sudden thought, what about that job fair? Maybe there would be snacks? Maybe coffee and donuts?

It was worth checking.

She waited until the bartender was near. "Is that job fair still on?"

"I can find out for you," he said, with a smile, and he left.

She should have thought of this sooner, but her head wasn't quite clear. Never a good idea to drink on an empty stomach. Oh well. If the job fair was still happening, she'd go. She'd grab a couple of donuts. And then she'd go back to her room and get some sleep.

First thing in the morning, Michaela would drive her to that apartment. It looked okay in the photos on the website. And it didn't cost too much. She'd been lucky to find a cheap place to rent.

And then on Monday morning, there was the interview with Marge at Girl Friday. Someone would want her. Someone would have an opening. Someone would—

"Hi, I'm Roger."

Someone had sat down next to her. A friendly looking man wearing a tuxedo.

"Can I buy you another drink?"

"Uh, no thanks. I'm here on business." *Right, business. I need to find a clerical job.*

"That's what I thought."

"Pardon?"

"You're here . . . on business."

"Yes, I . . . uh—" She looked around for the bartender. Had he sent this man to tell her about the job fair?

"And you're new at this."

"Yes," she said, sitting up a little straighter. "I'm new at this."

"Then don't worry. You'll be great." The man—had he said, *Roger?*—stood up. "Come with me."

Krista glanced at the bar again, saw the shiny wine glasses suspended above it, twinkling in the soft light, and she shrugged. There had to be donuts there, right?

Picking up her little black purse, she slipped off the bar stool and balanced on the unfamiliar heels. Then she saw the bartender, across the room. He was returning to the bar, and he was carrying a sandwich. He stopped when he saw her. She gave him a little wave, and he waved back.

Roger offered her his arm. She put her hand on his elbow, and held on tightly. The thought crossed her mind that she didn't know Roger. Although, she didn't care too much. He seemed friendly, and safe. Kind of bumbly. Definitely harmless. Although, considering how she'd misjudged Paul, maybe she wasn't such a good judge of people.

At any rate, they were out in the open, walking through a lobby with beautiful arched ceilings. And, yes, he was heading toward some kind of business function in—she saw the sign—in the Crystal Ballroom. Odd, because she could have sworn the bartender had said the job fair was upstairs. But he might have been mistaken.

The doors to the Crystal Ballroom stood wide open and a cacophony of voices floated on the air. From the lobby, she looked inside and caught a glimpse of several men. A lot of men. And a few women. The men in expensive suits.

The women, dressed very . . . fashionably.

She took a deep breath, and squared her shoulders. It couldn't hurt to look. Holding Roger's arm, she crossed the threshold.

Chapter Four

Logan and Pro had drifted to the middle of the room, greeting old friends and answering questions about the auction—as diplomatically as possible. Reactions covered the gamut from embarrassment to excitement. Now they were surrounded by a rowdy pandemonium.

"If we get this lodge built," Pro said, "do you think you'll use it much?"

"Sure," Logan answered.

"When's the last time you took a vacation?"

Logan closed his eyes briefly. Cheryl often asked him the same thing. "I take vacations."

"For more than a weekend."

"I'll use the lodge. Now get off my case." Logan wished this thing would get underway but Roger was still out in the lobby rounding up his last escort.

Hayden and Bruce had returned with fresh drinks.

"Your brother still living in England?" Hayden asked.

"Yeah. Still over there," Logan told him.

"Working for that North Sea company?"

"Yeah. Oil exploration. Like I do." Although, he and Will didn't talk much. Partly because his brother was five years older than he was. And partly because they still had this competition thing going on.

"I don't think I could sit at a desk all day," Hayden commented, as he ogled the room. "I like to be on the road. I like the new scenery."

Hayden would definitely go for the new scenery.

"Look at that one!" Bruce blurted. "Maybe I'll bid on two of them!"

"Would you look at the one with Roger!" Hayden's hand shook and he almost spilled his beer. "I want that one. How much do you think she'll go for?"

Logan turned around, scanned the crowd, and his body tensed. He saw Roger at the ornately arched entrance of the ballroom—with the woman from Kipling's. Blinking, Logan looked again. It really *was* the woman from Kipling's. The woman who'd been sitting next to him, slowly sipping her drink and eating cherry garnishes. The woman in the short black dress with the gorgeous legs and the face of an angel.

She was an escort? Swallowing hard, Logan shuffled back a step. Maybe she was a university student trying to make some quick money. But God, what a way to make money. Sure, these guys would probably be safe enough. They were his friends, but still.

The woman walked with Roger, holding his arm, like he was taking her to a red carpet function.

"Nice," Hayden drawled, still staring, his mouth hanging open.

"Shut up, Hayden."

"You're no fun." Hayden moved closer to the stage.

Krista gripped Roger's elbow, even though she was more used to the high heels now. She had no idea what to expect and touching Roger's arm gave her moral support. They walked to the front of the room, to a stage. The front of the stage was draped in black velvet.

A group of women followed them. In a few minutes, they were forming a line to the left side of the stage.

"Let's put you here," Roger said, taking her hand from

his arm. He guided her to stand between a tall woman with red hair, and a woman with blonde hair who was about Krista's height. Her height, but heavier.

"Don't worry about a thing," Roger said, squeezing her hand. "You'll do great."

Great? What kind of a job fair is this?

Boisterous conversations pounded over the room punctuated by loud laughing and scattered shouts. Krista fidgeted with the chain handle of her little purse. And then she stood up straight and tried to go for a relaxed, confident posture. Employers would be looking for *confident*. Something she didn't feel at the moment.

The other people in the ballroom gradually advanced toward the stage. But—that was odd—the only women in the room were here, with her, lined up along this wall. The rest of the crowd was made up of men.

They stood in groups of two or three or four, some of them holding beer glasses, some of them holding champagne flutes. No one seemed to be drinking coffee, or eating donuts.

One man, near the back of the group, stood alone. He was tall, probably six foot, maybe taller. Dark hair, neatly trimmed. A navy business suit. And, unlike the others, he wasn't holding a drink. But he was watching her.

He was the man from the bar. The man who had sat near her in Kipling's. He didn't look like he needed a job. Ah, yes. He must be an employer. In a detached sort of way, Krista knew she wasn't thinking clearly and she wished she'd eaten something more substantial than cherries and Baileys. Because she was pretty sure she was missing something.

Roger was there again, in front of her, with a stack of papers in his hands, pale blue papers. He handed her one. And then he continued down the line, handing each woman in the line one of the pieces of paper.

Krista looked at hers.

A check?

For five hundred dollars?

Her knees started to shake. She reached out to touch the arm of the redhead standing to her left. "I'm not sure I'm the right person."

Back at the front of the room, Roger took the stairs to the stage, and stood behind a podium. He was tapping on the microphone, saying, "Testing, testing, testing."

"New at this?" the redhead asked.

The blonde on Krista's other side leaned over and said, "Nothing to it, honey. All you need to do is look pretty. Some guy buys you. And you go for a drink and dinner with him."

"Don't worry about these boys," the redhead explained. "They're all going to the dining room together. You don't even leave the hotel."

"Easiest five hundred I ever made."

"And these boys are tame."

Oh. My. God. What had she stumbled into? She looked back across the room, at the doors she had come through. They were closed.

Roger had the microphone working. "Welcome to the reunion of the—"

Roger's next words were drowned out by the cheering, whistling and hooting of the men. There was a roll of laughter through the crowd and several of the men called out to Roger, all urging him to get the show on the road.

"As you know, we've raised almost half the money we need."

Roger kept talking, smiling down at the group, waving to different people. The noise in the room grew. The cheering, the laughter, the wolf whistles.

Krista saw spots of light in front of her eyes. All the air seeped from her lungs. The check was still clutched in her hand. She stared at it. How had this happened?

"Better put that in your purse, honey. Before you drop it." The redhead reached for the check and folded it once. Then she opened the little black beaded purse that hung from Krista's wrist, and slipped the check inside.

"Don't worry," the redhead told her. "You'll be fine. And," she added, "it's all for a good cause. You're helping them to raise money."

Roger motioned for the first woman to come onto the stage. She looked beautiful. Every one of these women looked beautiful.

This first woman, standing next to Roger, had black hair, shoulder length. She was wearing a pink silky dress that came to just below her knees. The top had spaghetti straps and . . . not much of a bodice.

Krista glanced down at her own little black dress, wobbled on her heels and forced herself to breathe deeply, and think. *How to get out of this? Without making a scene?*

"Do I hear six hundred," Roger was saying into the microphone.

Several of the men shouted all at once. Six hundred. Six fifty. Seven.

The pink lady spun around, smiled a huge smile, and then she flicked up the hem of her dress, exposing a lot of thigh.

"Eight hundred!"

"Eight hundred!" Roger echoed. And then, "Eight hundred once. Twice." A little pause. "Sold to Jeffery McDonald for eight hundred dollars!" Roger pounded his gavel on the podium.

A man with short light brown hair ran to the front of the room, reached up and lifted the pink lady down from the stage, taking her into the crowd with him.

"And next we have Angie. Come on up here, Angie."

Angie wore a silver sequined dress, shorter even than

what Krista was wearing. The dress dipped low and her breasts bounced as she walked toward Roger.

Roger quickly worked the bidding up to nine hundred dollars and Angie was lifted from the stage by a man with thick reddish hair and a beard.

Four more women were auctioned off, ranging in price from eight hundred to fifteen hundred dollars. They stood next to their buyers, laughing and giggling and looking like they were having the time of their life.

And still Krista was unable to move. She could hardly believe she'd walked in to this— This— Well, it was not a job fair. That much was clear. And it was clear she needed to leave, to walk away. But there was a whole crowd of laughing, shouting men between her and the big doors that led to freedom.

"Your turn, sister." The blonde next to her gave her a nudge.

But Krista stood frozen, her legs refusing to move. Roger left his podium and came down to meet her. He reached out his hand, she put her hand in his, and she trailed him onto the stage.

This was so humiliating. She was about to be auctioned off. For some good cause. For some—what had he said? *A lodge?* Her heart raced and she wobbled on her heels.

"Do I hear six hundred?" Roger was saying.

Immediately, from the back of the room, came, "One thousand."

It was a big man. A fat man.

Another man, this one closer to the front, called out, "Eleven hundred."

He was skinny. His hair was thin, long, touching his collar. He had a crooked mustache.

"Twelve hundred," the fat man called out. The fat man had . . . jowls.

"Hey Pete! Get your own. I saw her first!"

"Fifteen hundred," the skinny man with the mustache called. He'd jumped three hundred dollars, probably hoping the other guy, the fat man with the jowls would give up.

"Sixteen hundred," Jowls said.

Oh yuck. Krista took a deep breath and willed herself to be calm. It was only a drink. And dinner. And there would be lots of people at the dinner.

She wanted to close her eyes, but she didn't. She forced herself to look out at the crowd. And then she saw him again. The tall man, with the dark hair, in the navy suit. The man from the bar.

He was watching her, staring at her. She could feel the intensity of his gaze, even from this far away.

"Eighteen hundred!" It was the skinny man at the front again. He was tugging on the end of his mustache, patting it.

There was a pause in the bidding and the room quieted. Probably because no one had bid more than fifteen hundred, until now.

Then Jowls shouted, "Two thousand!"

The room grew more quiet. Almost all of the conversation had stopped. Mustache turned around to look at Jowls.

Roger said, "Two thousand going once, going twice—"

"Ten thousand."

A hush fell over the room. Complete silence. Everyone turned around and watched as the tall, dark-haired man in the navy suit walked toward the stage. The crowd parted for him.

"Ten thousand once twice sold to Logan Nicholas!" Roger blurred the words together, like he wanted to make sure no one tried to top this man's bid. Like anyone would be stupid enough to bid more than ten thousand dollars.

In the next second, the room erupted with applause. Except for Jowls. Jowls at the back of the room was frowning.

The dark-haired man—what had Roger called him? *Logan Nicholas.* He was in front of the stage, and the applause grew even louder.

"Thanks, Logan," Roger said as he leaned down, speaking only to Logan, not over the microphone. "You're better than Hayden."

And then, Roger was back on the microphone calling up the next contestant. Or whatever they were supposed to be called.

From up on the stage, Krista looked at Logan. He wasn't smiling. In fact, he looked annoyed by all the applause his bid had brought.

"Six hundred to Eddie," Roger was saying. "Do I hear six fifty?"

Logan reached up and put his hands on her waist. She slipped the chain handle of her purse over her wrist and automatically reached for his shoulders as he lifted her from the stage.

"Six fifty. Seven. Seven fifty."

As she touched the floor, she staggered and felt his strong hands at her waist, steadying her.

Then he took his hands away. She looked up at him. He raised his eyebrows and gave her a glassy stare. Then he reached for her hand and started to lead her away from the stage.

She'd thought he would go to the back of the crowd and wait for the auction to finish. Like everyone else was waiting. But he was marching toward the doors, still gripping her hand, tugging her along with him.

"Where are we going?"

"Out." He walked quickly, making it hard for her to keep up with him.

"But—"

"Just come."

Chapter Five

In the lobby outside the ballroom, Logan could hear the laughter from the auction. He still had the escort's hand gripped tightly in his as he led her toward the hotel entrance. He was getting out of here. Now. Before anyone realized he'd left.

Hayden had wanted this escort, and Hayden would not be happy that Logan had bid on her.

"Just a minute." Her voice was soft, and tentative, as she tried to get his attention.

He didn't want to talk right now, so he ignored her. And almost pulled her over when she suddenly stopped.

"What's happening now?" she asked.

He wished he knew. Now that he'd bought her, what was he supposed to do with her? He released her, put his hands on his hips, and stared at her. She seemed even more shy than she had before. Maybe even—

Afraid?

Probably worried she'd really have to put out—for ten thousand dollars.

"I thought we were supposed to stay at the hotel."

His stomach tensed. He needed to leave. "Who said that?"

"One of the ladies."

It was news to him. "No one told me," he said, and he wondered if Hayden knew. Or if Hayden would care. At any rate, he wasn't staying here. Not if he had to watch Hayden, leering at her.

She clutched her purse with both hands. "What would you like to do?" she said, looking up at him.

What would he like to do? He'd like to throttle her. That's what he'd like to do. How could she get herself involved in something like this?

He glanced toward the door of the ballroom. Any minute now, one of them would come looking for him.

"Come on," he said, reaching for her arm.

She stepped back. "First," she said, "tell me where we're going."

"Anywhere but here." This time he caught her arm before she could move back and he led her away from the ballroom. They'd almost reached the entrance when she stumbled. If he hadn't been holding on to her, she would have fallen. How come she was so unsteady? Was she drunk?

"You're walking too fast," she said.

"Okay. I'll slow down." Gripping her arm, he steered her toward the hotel entrance. Almost there. The doorman was holding the side door for them.

"Wait." She stopped again, and he let go of her.

"Wait?" he asked, studying her. She didn't look like she'd been drinking. "What do you mean, wait?"

"We're supposed to stay in the hotel," she said, again.

Probably they were supposed to stay at the hotel. They were supposed to have dinner in the Stephenson Lounge. And drinks there, or at Kipling's, he didn't know. And right now he didn't care.

He tipped the doorman and asked for a cab. Then he looked at her, closely, and took hold of her arm again, because he had a crazy idea she might run away. But why would she . . .

"Are you worried about being with *me?*" he asked. It

was as if this were her first night as an escort and she was having second thoughts. Good for her.

She shrugged away from him and stood up straighter, lifting her head high. "It's cold," she said, looking out the door. "I don't have a coat."

It wasn't cold. A little cool, maybe. A little windy. What did she expect for the middle of September.

But, in that little dress . . .

"No problem," Logan said, slipping off his suit jacket. He wrapped it around her, put his arm around her shoulders, and guided her through the side door toward the waiting cab.

He could feel her shaking, probably not from the cold. Probably from nerves. That was good too. She should be nervous about this line of work. It might make her reconsider her career options.

They'd reached the cab. As the doorman opened the back door for them, she pulled away again. Another feeble attempt to assert herself.

"I can't do this," she said.

Oh really? "You want more money?"

"No! I don't want more money. But tonight is a drink. And dinner. And you're supposed to be joining your friends for dinner."

Logan leaned against the cab, folding his arms, watching her. The doorman waited.

At least she was trying to lay down some ground rules. But how many guys were going to listen to ground rules? If Hayden had bought her, there was no way Hayden would be listening to this.

She stood there, hugging his jacket around herself, waiting for some kind of reassurance.

Logan looked back at the hotel. Then he unfolded his arms, took a deep breath, and stood up straight. "Just get in the cab, okay? We're going to the Pelican's Roost."

"The what?"

"The Pelican's Roost."

She looked puzzled. And shy. And very pretty. And he couldn't help smiling at her.

"You're not from around here, are you?"

She'd thought Jowls would be bad. But this guy wasn't a whole lot better. Except, he looked nicer than Jowls. Or Mustache. A lot nicer, actually. Especially when he'd smiled. She would not have got in the cab, except that, he'd smiled. And it had completely changed him.

But he wasn't smiling now. Now, he looked . . . *angry?* How come he was angry?

Because he'd spent ten thousand dollars to buy her for the night and he was expecting someone much different from her. Someone who would do . . . what he wanted her to do?

He was quiet, now that they were in the cab. And he wasn't touching her. Not anymore. He was sitting on his own side of the backseat, with his hands stretched out on his thighs, drumming his fingers. His hands looked strong.

And, it was a cab, after all. It wasn't like she'd got into his car. She'd heard him tell the driver where to go. To the Pelican's Roost. So if he, if this Logan tried anything, surely the cab driver would help her?

She inhaled a jerky breath, bracing herself. She was committed to this idiocy. He'd spent his money. She had her check. Her piece of paper that made her his—

His what?

They'd only gone a few blocks before they reached another hotel. And there was another doorman, opening the car from Logan's side. Logan gave some money to the driver, then stepped out of the car. Standing by the door, he offered her his hand.

She clutched his jacket around herself, slipped across the seat toward the open door, and ignored his offer of help. She got her heels firmly on the ground and stood up, tugging her dress down.

He touched the small of her back as he steered her toward the entrance. Another doorman was there, pulling back the big glass door.

Once they were inside, she felt Logan's hands on her shoulders.

"You won't need this now."

"Thank you," she said, and he took back his jacket.

As he shrugged into the garment, he watched her, letting his eyes sweep over her. All at once, she felt exposed, and vulnerable, in her little black dress.

He took her hand again, placed it on the crook of his arm, and held it there as they walked through the lobby. As though he were afraid she might run away.

Well, she had thought of that. But she wouldn't run. She'd done enough running today to last a lifetime.

A moment later, they were walking up a wide staircase. A beautiful curving staircase, carpeted in burgundy. He walked quickly, almost dragging her along.

"Could you please walk a little slower. I'm not used to these shoes."

He immediately slowed down, and he smiled. And again, she was struck by how different he looked when he smiled.

"New shoes?"

"Yes."

At the top of the staircase, he led her toward a gated entrance with a sign on it, woven in gold filigree. *The Pelican's Roost.*

"Good evening, Mr. Nicholas," the maitre d' said.

"I don't have a reservation—"

"No problem, sir. Please follow me."

The maitre d' brought them to a table tucked away in a corner, next to a bank of windows overlooking a park with fairy lights decorating the trees. A magical sight. She couldn't help staring. A perfect September night.

Logan was standing behind her, holding the chair for her. The man had manners.

He helped her into her chair, and then he sat across from her, looking cool and distant, and in charge.

And all at once, she didn't feel nervous anymore. When they'd left the ballroom, and when they'd crossed the lobby, and when they'd got into the cab, she had been nervous. Now she wasn't. She should have felt exhausted, after traveling all day. But she didn't feel exhausted either. Or even the slightest bit tired. She felt like she was on an adventure. At the beginning of an adventure.

And, she was hungry.

The maitre d' lit the candles on the table. Three small votive lights, nestled in autumn leaves and red berries. "Your server will be right with you. Enjoy your evening."

She set her purse on the table and put her hands on top of the leather-covered menu. Then she looked up at him.

He was watching her, as he leaned forward with his elbows on the table. And, yes, she wasn't imagining it, he looked angry.

She gripped the edges of the leather folder. "Why are you doing this?"

"Doing what?"

"You're being rude."

"Me?"

"Yes. You. You practically dragged me here."

"You're an escort. I thought you'd be used to that."

"I—I'm . . ." *I'm not an escort.* But tonight she'd accepted a check to be an escort. She gripped her hands together and her body felt cold, and hollow.

She'd done it again. Lived up to what her family

thought of her. Somehow, she'd bumbled her way into an escort auction of all things. Maybe her family was right. Maybe she was a screwup and always would be.

His expression changed suddenly. "I'm sorry."

Sorry? That seemed uncharacteristic of him—from what she'd seen so far anyway. And, he seemed uncomfortable.

"I had to get away from there, before—" He cut himself off, and dropped back in his chair, letting his hands fall into his lap.

"Before what?"

He paused. "I guess I'm embarrassed being seen with an escort." There was a hint of that smile. "I've never done this before."

I've never done this before either. "I'm sorry you're embarrassed to be with me."

"Not with you. With an escort."

He took a deep breath and exhaled. "Why don't we start over," he said. "I'm Logan Nicholas." He reached out his hand, across the small votive lights.

"Krista MacKenzie," she said, putting her hand in his. His hand felt warm and solid.

He gave her hand a brief business-like shake before releasing it, and then he said, "Now, about that drink."

He didn't want a drink, but that was the bargain. A drink and dinner. That's what she'd said. And then, stupid, he'd made that crack about her being used to it, to being dragged around. It was like he'd slapped her face. She'd wilted in front of him, and he felt like an ass. A first-rate jerk.

In her line of work, there was a good chance she had been mistreated and the look on her face confirmed it. Tonight would be different.

"Would you care for something from the bar?"

The waiter had appeared. Logan looked across the table at Krista MacKenzie. A pretty name. Strange, that she had given him her full name. But then, it probably wasn't her real name.

"I don't feel like a drink," she said, echoing his thoughts. "I'll have water, please."

"Certainly. And you, sir?"

"Water."

"Yes, sir."

The waiter vanished again. Logan flipped open the menu. He didn't need to. He knew what he wanted. The prime rib was always excellent. She would probably order chicken. Or fish. Women always did. Cheryl certainly did.

Krista MacKenzie, or whoever she was, studied her menu. Her eyes were blue, a deep rich blue. Or maybe there were tears in her eyes, and that was what made them so blue. She still looked shaken. In fact, she looked pale.

He closed his menu. "Do you know what you'd like?"

"I'm not sure."

"The prime rib is very good."

"Yes, it looks good."

"Then let's have that." Logan reached for her menu, folded it and placed it on top of his. Before she could change her mind.

The waiter was back, with the silver water pitcher, filling their goblets.

"Are you ready to order, sir?"

"Yes. We're both having the prime rib."

"And how would you like that done?"

"Medium rare," they said, at the same time.

"Oven roasted potatoes, rice, or baked potato?"

"Baked potato," they said. Together.

"Anything else? Appetizer?"

"How about some—" Logan paused, and looked at her.

"Mushrooms?" she answered, starting to smile, but not quite smiling.

"Mushrooms," he confirmed. She was reading his thoughts.

"Excellent," the waiter said. "Will there be anything else, sir?"

"Do you have a good Merlot?"

"Yes, sir. I can recommend the Ravenswood."

"Bring us a bottle of that."

The waiter collected the menus and disappeared again.

Krista MacKenzie looked incredibly shy. After her short outburst, when she hadn't been shy at all, she was back to her previous manner. But he'd liked it when she'd called him on his intentions. Somewhere inside that shell, the lady had some spunk.

"Where are you from?"

"How do you know I'm not from Calgary?"

She was cute. "Well, for one thing, you said Cal Gary. If you live here, you say Cal Gree."

This time she did smile. And she looked gorgeous when she smiled. He wanted to make her smile more.

"I'll remember that. Cal Gree," she repeated. And then, "I'm from Saskatoon."

"How long have you been in Calgary?"

"Not long."

She didn't want to talk about herself.

"What was your auction for?"

"Roger didn't tell you?"

"No. I guess he didn't think to."

Logan raised his water goblet. "To the Lodge."

She lifted her own glass and clinked it against his, above the candles.

"A lodge?" she asked, suspending her glass.

"A fishing lodge. That's what the auction is raising money for."

She sipped some water and set the goblet down. "Your group is buying a fishing lodge?"

"Yeah." He took a sip of his water. "And I guess I just got ten thousand shares."

"That's a lot of money. Why did you bid so much? The bid was only up to two thousand."

"Because I don't like Hayden."

"Hayden? The man with the—"

She blushed. God, she was blushing. "The what?"

A little smile again. She'd almost said something derogatory about Hayden. "Tell me. I promise I won't say anything."

A bigger smile. "The jowls."

"That's Hayden," Logan said. He steepled his hands and pressed them to his lips, glad to be here, away from Hayden and the auction.

"It's still a lot of money. Simply because you don't like him."

Yeah, it was a lot of money, but he didn't care. He had a lot of money. "It'll give me more control in the venture," he told her. "More shares. More control."

"And you like control."

"No," he said, "I like to fish."

She laughed this time. And her voice was light, and musical. And happy. For the moment, she seemed genuinely happy.

And she was right about the control. He liked control. Why not? Somebody had to be in charge. It might as well be him.

She certainly didn't have much control. What kind of a life did she have? Being bought by someone. Being used—

"Are you still worried about being seen with me?"

"No." He'd never been worried about being seen with her. She'd noticed he was angry. He had to give her some reason. Telling her he didn't approve of her career choice, that didn't make sense. Telling her he didn't want Hayden—or any other guy—winning her, that didn't make sense either. Why should he care?

"You're looking worried, again."

Yeah. Worried about her. But not about being seen with her. "I guess work is still on my mind," he lied. It was none of his business, what she did for a living.

But tonight? Tonight *was* his business. Tonight she would enjoy herself.

"Roger said this is a reunion?"

"Football players," Logan said. "We all played football in high school. These are the teams from the various schools."

"An annual reunion?"

"Every September."

"And you have it on a Thursday night? Why not wait for the weekend?"

"It goes all weekend. Thursday is always the kickoff. Tomorrow night is more formal. The wives come. A lot of these guys are from out of town and some of them bring their wives."

He watched her, as she touched the edge of her water goblet, running her finger along the rim.

"The answer is no."

She looked up then, looking him right in the eye.

"I'm not married. That's what you were thinking."

She blushed again. Oh God, this woman blushed. How could that be? Probably a lot of her clientele were married. Why would that make her blush?

"Tell me about your lodge," she said. "Where is it?"

He smiled, feeling at ease, and happy to talk about the project. "Yes. Our lodge." They'd been planning for a long time. "It'll be on Vancouver Island, near Campbell River."

"Not built yet?"

"Not yet. We've just raised the money for the land."

"Near the ocean?"

"Ocean front."

Her gaze softened, and became unfocused, like she was remembering a place like that.

The waiter materialized, this time with the Merlot. He went through the usual routine of presenting the wine. And then the prime rib was there, and the spuds, and the zucchini side dish. Logan hated zucchini. The cast iron pan of sizzling mushrooms was placed between them, next to the candles. Krista asked for everything on her potato. Bacon bits, sour cream, chives. She ate like this was the first meal she'd had all day.

The evening flew by. Quiet piano music in the background. Excellent food. The waiter refilling their water goblets and topping up their wine glasses.

He noticed the bottle was almost empty. When had that happened? It didn't matter. His head felt clear. And it wasn't like he was driving anywhere.

They'd talked about Vancouver Island, and summers there. And fishing. She actually knew how to fish. He'd never known escorts could be so versatile.

And they'd talked about the Lodge. About the building plans. The main lodge, the two private buildings. The dock. The boats.

And then he'd started to talk about his work. The company. His company. About how he and Roger had started it out of university.

She listened like she really cared. She made him feel like he was the first decent man she'd ever come across.

The evening moved on, and the waiter was there again, dividing the last of the wine evenly between their glasses. Strange, Logan thought. She'd probably had as much to drink as him, and yet she seemed so small—

"Can I offer you some dessert? Some coffee?"

"Dessert? I couldn't. That was delicious. The absolutely

best prime rib I've ever had."

"Coffee?"

"I'll have some coffee," Logan answered.

"Decaf, please."

Decaf? For an escort? Didn't they have to stay up all night? Maybe she'd figured out she wouldn't have to do that with him.

"Bring a slice of the chocolate cheesecake," Logan told the waiter. "Two forks." Unable to resist, he winked at her.

"No way."

God, she was cute—

The blare of his cell phone jerked him back to reality. Almost eleven o'clock. Never good to get a call this late.

He checked the readout, and huffed out a breath.

Roger.

Damn. The guy was going to harass him about the auction. About bidding, after all. And about winning. And about—

And then Logan switched focus and concentrated. There could be a problem at one of the sites.

He sighed. "I'd better take this. Sorry." He clicked on. "What?"

"Logan. Good. You still awake?"

"Yes."

"It's the site over at Gavinson. Jim called me. You have the logs at home, don't you?"

"I've got a copy in my office there. I can get them for you in—" He checked his watch. "About forty-five minutes."

"Okay. Great." Roger sounded relieved. He wouldn't have to drive to the office tonight. "Oh, and Logan?"

"Yeah?"

"How'd the night go?"

"Goodbye, Roger. I'll get back to you soon."

Two large white mugs of coffee arrived. And the

cheesecake—presented on a white, gold-rimmed plate. The dessert was drizzled with chocolate and dusted with icing sugar.

"Are you sure this is decaf?" she asked the waiter.

"Positive, miss." He smiled at her as he set the silver cream pitcher beside her. And then he was gone.

She reached for the pitcher. "You have to go to your office? Now?"

"Drilling a well," Logan explained. "Things happen. They need to know what to do next."

"And you tell them," she said, pouring the cream. She liked very white coffee.

"I make suggestions."

"No," she said, setting the pitcher down. "You tell them."

"Why do you say that?"

She gave him that cute little smile. "You like control," she said.

She was right, so what. He picked up his fork and tasted the cheesecake. Smooth and rich. Excellent, as usual. He wanted her to try it. But she hadn't touched the extra fork.

Using his own fork, he cut a piece, for her. Then he motioned with his index finger for her to come closer. She hesitated.

"Don't be afraid."

That gorgeous smile again, and she leaned forward. He touched her chin with one finger and guided the fork to her mouth. She closed her eyes, those beautiful blue eyes, and savored the flavor.

Warmth flooded over him and he felt a lightness in his chest. She made eating cheesecake look like . . . well, the best experience in the world.

Better focus on those well logs, sitting on his desk at home. Still, he thought, it wouldn't hurt to offer her one more bite.

And then, too soon, they'd finished their coffee. The check was paid and they were leaving the restaurant. Logan wanted to take hold of her again, like he had before, when he'd been afraid she'd run away.

He hadn't wanted her to run away.

And now, it didn't feel like he had a right to touch her.

They were outside the hotel, standing on the sidewalk. The wind had died down and it was a beautiful, Indian summer, September night.

"If you have to get to your office, I can walk back to the Palliser."

Right. Like he was going to let her—let any woman— walk the downtown core alone at night.

"Actually," he said, as he started down the sidewalk, "I live around here." Then he stopped walking and turned around.

She wasn't following him. Did he really need to hold on to her?

"You misunderstand," she said. She was about three feet behind him, clutching her little black purse again.

"No. You misunderstand. I know that all I get for ten thousand dollars is dinner with you. But those well logs are at my home office and I need to phone the rig right away."

She hesitated. And, surprisingly, he was glad she hesitated.

"And then I'll call a cab," he said. "Promise."

He seemed to pass the test.

"All right," she said. "Let's go."

Chapter Six

He was walking quickly, like he always did. She was having trouble keeping up. He glanced at his watch. Twenty minutes until midnight. They were waiting for him at the Gavinson site.

Those heels looked great on her, but they weren't particularly functional. He forced himself to slow down. He wished he could take her hand. Except, he wouldn't. After all, technically, he was still going out with Cheryl. So he had no business touching this woman.

He knew she wouldn't try to run away. Not now. Not after they'd spent all that time talking and getting to know each other, but—

Why did she have to be an escort? He wished she wasn't, but there it was.

He shrugged, and once again, he reminded himself that what she did for a living was none of his business.

In ten minutes, they were at his condo. She stumbled as they came up the steps, and he reached out to catch her arm. As he did, he felt icy cold skin. Damn. He should have given her his jacket, but he'd been thinking about the rig.

"You should have told me you were cold," he said, as he unlocked the door.

"It was only a short walk," she answered, shivering.

"In new shoes."

Cold, and her feet were hurting. And she hadn't said anything about it.

"This way." He brought her to the living room, picked up the blanket from the couch and wrapped it around her. Then he guided her toward his favorite chair. "Sit."

She did sit, and then he knelt in front of her, lifted her sandaled foot, and reached for the buckle.

"I can do that," she said, as she squirmed out of the blanket and leaned forward, bringing her face very close to his in the process.

"So can I," he said, with his hands on her ankle.

Her face was right next to his. Their lips, inches apart. And then, she leaned away, dropping back in the chair.

He undid her sandal and tossed it over his shoulder. It landed with a thud somewhere behind him. And then he looked closely at her foot. "I hate to tell you this," he said, still holding her heel, "but you've got a blister."

"Oh no." She had her eyes closed and she was shivering. She hugged the blanket around herself.

He undid the buckle on the other sandal and carefully slipped the shoe off, in case there was a blister there too. There wasn't, but her skin was red, next to her little toe. "You're not putting these back on."

"I'm walking home barefoot?" Her voice was quiet.

Logan glanced at his watch. Almost midnight. He headed back toward the condo entrance, grabbed his gym bag from the floor, and brought it to her chair. They were in here, somewhere. He never wore them, but Cheryl had thought it would be necessary for the shower room at the Y.

There.

He found the blue plastic flip-flops. "These will get you to the cab." He dropped them on the floor next to her chair. She was cocooned in the blanket, looking tired, and she was still shivering.

"Next time, tell me when you're cold." He reached for the switch by the fireplace and flicked it on. The gas flames rippled across the ceramic logs.

As he walked down the hall to his office, he realized what he'd said. *Next time.* Like there'd be a next time.

Yeah. Fat chance.

The chrome and glass clock on the mantle said three minutes to midnight. *Be home by midnight, sweetie.* Oh, Michaela. Wait until you hear about this.

Krista relaxed in the easy chair. All that wine was making her drowsy. That, and the fact that she'd been awake since five this morning. What an amazing day for the first day of her new life.

She could hear Logan's voice, on the phone, down the hall. Reading off numbers. She needed to find the bathroom before he called that cab. Reluctantly, she left the warmth of her blanket and went to look.

Would he simply put her in a cab? Or would he come with her to the hotel? What a silly question. Of course, he'd put her in a cab and send her on her way.

She found the bathroom. A guest bathroom, with a sink and toilet. Modern, and masculine. Black speckled marble fixtures, brass taps, and big thick royal blue towels. Spotlessly clean. The man must have a housekeeper.

But not a wife. He'd said, no wife. And that was true. This whole apartment screamed bachelor. And not just bachelor. Confirmed bachelor.

Pieces of her hair had come loose from the combs. She shrugged. No sense worrying about her hair now.

Stepping back from the large mirror, she took another look at her dress. The tight and very short dress. *What had Michaela been thinking?*

Krista studied herself in the mirror. No wonder she

looked like an escort. She laughed silently. All that wine was making this seem so funny. And maybe it was.

Leaving the bathroom, she could hear him, still talking on the phone in his office. He seemed to be arguing. He probably did that a lot.

She might as well take the tour. There was a hall, straight ahead. His bedroom must be that way. To her right, was the front entrance. His office was down there, off the large foyer. To her left was the living room, where he'd brought her. And taken off her shoes.

The living room connected to a modern-looking kitchen—which seemed to be undergoing renovations. Drop cloths bordered one wall where he was testing colors—shades of yellow, a stark contrast to the current paint scheme which was the color of coffee. The yellow didn't fit. Not with the black appliances.

And there was an ice maker. God, it even made crushed ice. More of the black marble countertops. A large island, with a wine rack on the end of it. Filled with bottles. Part of a newspaper on the counter—the movie reviews. A brochure from the YMCA.

He must work out there. Or swim. Probably work out, considering his body.

No. Do not consider his body. A woman could get to like a body like that. But not her. Never again. She was not ever trusting herself to fall in love again. What a disaster falling in love was.

The tile floor in the kitchen was cold. She was cold. She needed that blanket. Dark brown ceramic tile covered the kitchen and foyer floors, but the living room was plush carpet, and so soft on her poor, aching feet.

Down the hall, the phone conversation-argument continued.

In the living room, two brown leather couches sat at right angles, on either side of the flickering fireplace. Her big chair faced the fire. He probably sat there a lot, to watch the flames dancing patterns on the logs. The couches and chair surrounded a huge coffee table. Heavy dark wood, strewn with magazines. Business Week. Time. Outdoor. Another newspaper—the Financial Post—and three books. Sea Kayaking Canada's West Coast. One of those city books, Campbell River, Salmon Capital of the World. And—that was odd—a poetry book, with a red leather cover.

Collected Poems of Love and Laughter by Maggie Therese.

Krista picked up the book, trailing her fingers over the embossed leather. It didn't seem like something he would own. She fanned through the gold-edged pages, skimming through the verses written in sweeping calligraphy.

Emily Dickinson — Of all the souls that stand create, I have elected one.

William Wordsworth — She was a phantom of delight, when first she gleamed upon my sight.

Elizabeth Barrett Browning — How do I love thee? Let me count the ways.

She gave a short, choked laugh. Love? She'd thought Paul had loved her. But, from this distance, she wondered if he'd felt anything for her at all. She'd been so sure of him. Sure enough that she'd dropped out of university to support him and put him through school.

How could she have done that?

She sighed, and she set the book down. Still standing

next to the coffee table, she let her feet sink into the carpet, savoring the plushness. Then she looked at the black canvas bag beside her chair. His gym bag? And, beside it, the pair of blue plastic flip-flops.

Did he really expect her to wear these things? They were huge. But it was a choice between huge plastic flip-flops, or nothing. Her feet hurt too much to put those sandals back on.

She slipped on the flip-flops, scrunching her nylon-covered toes around the plastic post. They'd do. They'd have to. She kicked them off and, as she picked up the navy blue blanket again, her purse dropped to the floor. She set the blanket down, and picked up the purse.

What if there were actually decent men in the world? Like Logan. How come he was unattached? Was there something in his past that kept him single now? Or was he too busy with his oil well? Was he gay?

No, she smiled, thinking about it. He wasn't gay. He radiated masculine energy. She'd felt it all night. Especially when he'd taken off her sandals.

She opened the purse. The little black beads winked in the firelight. All it contained was her room keycard, a lipstick and a mirror. And there was the check that Roger had given her, for five hundred dollars. She unfolded it.

It was made out to cash. She rubbed her thumb over the heavy paper. This was the piece of paper that declared she was an escort, which she wasn't.

She folded the check again, and reached for the red leather poetry book. It fell open at Elizabeth Barrett Browning and *How do I love thee? Let me count the ways.*

Krista placed the folded check inside, and closed the book. He could find it in the morning. And tonight?

Tonight, she would keep this memory. She would pretend he was her Prince Charming. She dropped her purse beside the flip-flops.

A little black dress, a black beaded purse, and plastic flip-flops. It was all so incredibly ridiculous. She sat down in the chair again, reached for the blanket and tucked her cold feet under it.

He would not accompany her back to the hotel. She knew that. But it would have been nice. Prince Charming delivering her to her door.

Right. Considering how he had started out as . . . less than charming. But then he'd changed. It didn't matter why because, after tonight, she'd never see him again.

He was still talking on the phone. It was past midnight. The fire flickered across the grate, and she started to feel warmer.

Logan tapped the phone, disconnecting from Gavinson, and glanced at the time. A quarter to one. Holding his head in his hands, he thought about the situation at the site. It would improve, soon, and for now there was nothing more to be done. He needed to get some sleep.

And—he leaned back in his chair and slumped—he still needed to bring Krista back to the Palliser. Better call that cab.

He reached for his phone again, and hesitated. He'd kept her waiting a long time. Maybe he'd see if she wanted some coffee first. He headed for the living room.

Right. Coffee. She drank decaf. Well, he'd offer anyway. Maybe some juice. Maybe some milk. Hell, maybe some cookies.

She was still in the chair, wrapped in the blanket, watching the fire. A long piece of her hair had loosened from its comb and was falling over the edge of the chair.

"Sorry that took so—"

She was asleep.

He knelt beside the chair and watched her. With the firelight flickering over her face, she looked so innocent. Not an escort at all. A fairy from a magic night who had somehow come into his life. But where had she come from?

Belatedly, he realized she'd told him very little about herself. She'd talked about her summers on Vancouver Island and fishing with her father, but beyond that, he'd done all the talking. And she'd listened and asked him questions and let him talk about himself. She'd listened like he was the most interesting person in the world.

Cheryl never did that. Not a chance of that happening. Cheryl kept him from getting a big head.

He looked toward the kitchen, where the blotches of yellow paint smeared the wall. He'd get someone to come in and fix that, first thing tomorrow. And he'd get his key back before she tried to do any more decorating.

He tipped his head back, remembering. He was supposed to have lunch with Cheryl tomorrow. Well, technically, today. It was already Friday since it was past midnight. They were supposed to meet at noon for their usual Friday lunch date.

Was that still on?

She'd been pretty mad. He grimaced, and decided. He'd call her, as soon as he got to the office. To confirm their lunch date. Or, un-confirm it. Too late to call now.

And what to do about Sleeping Beauty?

He hated to wake her, but this night had to end. This particular fairy princess didn't belong in his life and the sooner he got her back to her castle, the better. He touched her shoulder and gave her a shake.

She sighed and made a little noise that sounded like a mew. And then she turned her head the other way.

She was definitely cute. Especially like this, all curled up in that blanket, with her hair coming undone.

He drew in a deep breath, straightened his shoulders, and moved to the other side of the chair. Somehow, it made him feel peaceful, watching her sleep. Watching Sleeping Beauty. Without thinking, he kissed her nose.

That didn't wake her either. All she did was wiggle her nose and keep sleeping.

He shook her a little harder. "Come on, Krista," he said. "Time to go."

No response. Her breathing was deep, and regular, and slow. How much had she had to drink?

As much as him, and he was pretty wasted. He sat back on his heels, studying her. She shouldn't be doing this, being an escort. Being with strange men. Drinking too much. Falling asleep.

Defenseless.

He stood up, rubbed his hands over his head, and considered. He could leave her in the chair, but she'd be uncomfortable by morning. Or . . . he could put her in the bed.

Only problem. He slept in that bed. No guest bedroom.

He thought about it, and decided. She was an escort. So what? This was part of the job description. She was used to sleeping in men's beds.

He blew out a breath. Anyway, she'd wake up once he tried to move her, and then he'd call the cab.

He went to fold down the covers.

If anything, she was in a deeper sleep. He'd carried her into the bedroom and set her on the bed. She'd rolled away from him, onto her side, and stretched, like a lazy cat.

The combs holding up her hair were loose. He slipped one out, and a wave of reddish brown hair fanned over the pillow. He picked up some of her hair, sifting the tangles between his fingers.

Better not. He opened his hand, letting the silky strands fall back.

Then, he took out the other comb. The combs were black with shiny bits of glass, and they looked expensive. Someone must have given them to her. A client? A boyfriend?

He set the combs on the bedside table.

The little black dress had shifted high on her legs. The rather tight black dress. Too tight to sleep in. Before he gave it much thought, he took hold of the shiny black zipper on the back of the dress and slipped it off her in a quick motion—leaving her in a skimpy black bra, black bikini underwear, and a silky black garter belt and stockings.

He flipped the blankets over her, and felt like he'd been punched in the gut. She mewed again and tucked her hands under her cheek.

Now what?

He held up the little dress, brushing his hands over the fabric, and he tried to think. The well reports, that was it. He needed to finish the well reports.

Carefully, he laid the dress on the chair next to the bed. Then he took one more look at her, sleeping soundly, and left the room.

Half an hour later, he'd reviewed the well reports, taken three Tylenol and brought a blanket from the linen closet to the couch. Exhausted and uncomfortable, he tried to settle down.

About fifteen minutes passed before he had to admit the couch was not designed for sleeping. At least, not for someone who was six foot one.

This was ridiculous. He needed to be at the office by eight. It was two o'clock in the morning, and Krista was in his bed. His king size bed.

To hell with it. He headed for the bed, tried not to look

at her and crawled in the other side.

He was asleep almost as soon as his head touched the pillow.

She'd been dreaming. Something about the road, about the bus trip from Saskatoon. The long endless road, the long endless hours. Getting to the end of the road, the end of the rainbow.

She hadn't slept this well, not in a long time. As she opened her eyes, she ran her hands through her hair and glanced at the ceiling. Where was she?

Not in her apartment. Not in Saskatoon. Memories flooded back—the rush to pack, to clean the apartment, to leave before Paul showed up again.

She'd come to Calgary. Of course. That was it. And Michaela—her dear friend—she'd met Michaela ... somewhere. Krista sighed and brushed her hands over the soft sheets. Smooth, rich, burgundy sheets. Michaela had such nice things.

No. That wasn't right. This wasn't Michaela's house. No, no, wait. That was it. She was at the Palliser.

Michaela had won a free night at the Palliser from one of her volunteer committees and she'd insisted Krista use the prize.

A big yawn. It must be time to get up. She had to check out of the hotel by noon. Better get out of bed and get ready. Lifting her head, she looked for a clock.

Her stomach fluttered and her chest tightened. This wasn't her room at the Palliser, but that was her dress, the dress Michaela had given her, draped over the chair by the bed.

Biting her lip, she pulled back the sheet, looked down, and saw the black lingerie. She'd fallen asleep in her underwear? But, no. It couldn't be.

Trying not to shake the bed, she turned her head.

Oh. My. God. Logan was sleeping beside her. The man who'd paid ten thousand dollars to buy her at the auction last night. His dark hair fell over his forehead. A shadow of beard stubble outlined his strong jaw. With the blanket folded back, his chest was bare, lightly covered in fine black hair. His shoulders were strong and muscled. On his side like that, his muscles bunched across his chest.

Oh my God. Holding her breath, she slipped out of the bed, snatched her dress off the chair and headed out of the room.

She rushed down the hall toward the guest bathroom she'd used last night. And locked herself inside.

With her heart beating a mile a minute, she studied her reflection in the mirror. Smudged mascara. Her hair was a mess. And her head was starting to pound, a reminder of the wine.

She squirmed into the tiny dress, then took a few seconds to wipe away some of the mascara and shake the tangles out of her hair. She needed a comb.

Where was her purse? Where were her shoes? How cold was it outside? With one last glance at the mirror, she decided she was as presentable as possible. Not that she intended to see him this morning. Certainly not. But she had to walk into the hotel. She had to walk past the reception desk. She had to find her shoes! What time was it?

In the living room, she spied the clock on the mantle. Five minutes to ten. Her mind spun and her head ached. How much wine had she had last night? She was so thirsty. Better take a minute to drink some water. No, better find her shoes first.

A phone rang, a series of loud chimes, a blaring interruption. The sound came from the bedroom. His cell phone. The same sound as last night, like a loud door bell.

She had to hurry. But where were her shoes? The gold strappy sandals?

There. Beside the living room chair, next to a black canvas bag. His gym bag. His cell phone kept ringing. One sandal rested on its side next to the big blue flip-flops he'd offered her last night. On the other side of the chair, she found her purse. The purse Michaela had given her. This was all Michaela's fault!

The hard ringing vibrated through the room. Where was her other shoe? She searched on her hands and knees, looking under the chair.

The phone stopped ringing. "What!!!" Logan shouted.

Krista paused in her search, listening. Better forget about the shoe and get out of this condo. Now.

"Cheryl?"

Cheryl? Her heart froze. Of its own accord, her hand felt inside his open gym bag and pulled out a gray fleece jacket.

"No! Don't come over." Logan's voice was alert, wide awake now.

Krista slipped on the jacket, pushed up the sleeves and reached for the flip-flops. With her purse and the single shoe in one hand, and the flip-flops clutched in the other, she tiptoed across the cold tiles toward the door.

"Did you still want to meet for lunch?" Logan was saying.

She paused. She couldn't have drawn herself away from this conversation if her life had depended on it.

"Are you still angry about last night?" Logan asked, in that familiar, soothing voice of his. "Well, don't be," he said to the phone. "Nothing happened."

Krista put her hand on the door lock. Of course, nothing had happened, but a strange ache echoed deep in her heart. She pushed the feeling away, unlocked the door, and stepped out into a cold September morning.

Chapter Seven

Logan clicked off his cell, dropped it on the table by the bed, and swore. It was after ten. Roger would be waiting, and annoyed. Logan should have been there by now. But at least Cheryl had sounded reasonably civil.

With a deep yawn, he stretched out, letting his hand drop on the pillow—where Krista had slept. He hadn't heard her get out of bed, but the pillow was still warm so she couldn't have been awake long. She was probably in the bathroom, probably looking for Tylenol. He'd give her a few more minutes before he joined her in the kitchen. Then he'd offer her some coffee.

It didn't feel right, putting her in a cab and sending her away. But he didn't exactly have time to go back to the Palliser, and he wasn't sure what the protocol was.

Awkward. He'd never taken an escort to bed before. And, technically, that's not what had happened.

Okay, maybe slipping off her dress had not been the best idea. But he'd wanted her to sleep comfortably. And who cared? She was an escort, *for Chrissake.* She would be used to waking up in a lot less than her underwear. And she—

He sat up in the bed and listened. She was being awfully quiet. He grabbed a robe from the closet and went to look for her. "Krista?"

Not a sound. He surveyed the living room. Her purse

was gone, and her sandals, and—he checked—his flip-flops.

He walked to the front door, and found it unlocked. She'd slipped out, and slipped away. Not a trace of her.

He inhaled deeply, and felt strangely let down.

After setting up the coffee pot, he headed for the shower. Roger would have everything ready for a decision about the Gavinson site and, hopefully, Logan would only need to check a few numbers and sign off. He turned on the water.

And, he had to have lunch with Cheryl. He could get his key back, he thought, as he stepped under the hot spray.

The elevator opened on the twenty-sixth floor of the Sun Valley Tower. Logan turned right, as usual, toward his office. Then he hesitated, absently looking at the glass doors with the sign that said, *Please see Reception in 2600*.

Roger was on the other side, to the left of the elevators, in the office past the reception desk. He needed to talk to Roger. Right away. Except, he didn't feel like facing Roger. Roger, the auctioneer.

Get it over with.

Reluctantly, Logan turned left into the main reception area. It looked messier than usual. Beatrice had outdone herself this time. Stacks of mail tottered on her desk. A magazine was open in front of the small switchboard. She had two cups of coffee on the go, one looked congealed, probably from yesterday. A nail file and polish remover sat next to the phone, which was blinking with calls on hold that had been sent back to reception. Four stick-it notes lined up along the top of the switchboard.

And no Beatrice.

A well supplier sat in one of the chairs, leafing through

a magazine. Other magazines crowded the coffee table, along with a vase filled with droopy pink flowers. The vase perched precariously near the edge of the table.

Beatrice came rushing out of the photocopy room, her gypsy style clothes flowing with her. "Oh, good morning, Mr. Nicholas. When did you get here? Mr. Claymore's been looking for you."

She picked up the phone. "Good morning. Peregrine Oil & Gas."

The well supplier flicked a glance at him, a hopeful expression. No doubt, the guy had been waiting a long time.

Jenny, the newly promoted landman, sauntered in, smiled at Logan, and leaned against the reception desk. She held an empty box in her hand. The label said *roller ball pens*.

"No. He's not here," Beatrice told the caller. "Can you try again later?" As she listened, she brushed some paper clips into a small heap in front of the switchboard.

"Well, how about on Monday?" Beatrice asked.

Who hired this woman? Frank, of course. That's why they had an Office Manager.

Beatrice hung up the phone and noticed Jenny.

"We're all out of the roller ball pens," Jenny said. "Can you order some more please?"

"I'll do that right now. You should have told me earlier this morning. I just sent out an order for staples for Mr. Oliver."

"Is Roger in his office?" Logan asked.

"Yes, he is. Can you tell him that Mr. Oakley from Heart Well Supplies is still waiting for him?"

Logan opened his mouth to respond, couldn't think of an answer and walked around the desk. The salesman probably had a few more perks ready to bribe his drilling engineer. Not that Roger ever accepted them.

When Logan entered the office, Roger was on the

phone, listening. He nodded at Logan and motioned for him to sit.

Beatrice rushed in. For someone who was always rushing she never seemed to get much done. At least, not on time. She handed Logan the morning well reports.

He glanced at them, saw a typo in *September*—that, or she couldn't spell. He bit his lower lip. Roger should get someone in accounting to input his data. He didn't need a lot of clerical work, only the well reports every morning. And Beatrice took forever to get them done.

God, he was in a bad mood. Normally, Beatrice didn't bother him. Not much anyway.

Wishing Roger would hurry up and finish his call, Logan pulled out the check he'd had with him last night. He filled it out for the ten thousand he'd promised.

Roger hung up the phone. "We've got a problem at Gavinson," he said.

"I figured as much." Logan handed the check to Roger. "Let's go over it now."

Roger studied the piece of paper, Logan's donation. "Don't you think you spent a lot of money?"

"It's for a worthy cause."

"The lodge?"

"No, *for Chrissake*, the hooker." Roger had better not make an issue of this. "Of course, the lodge. Is Pro picking this up today? Or should we go upstairs?" Pro's office was on the twenty-seventh floor. One floor up. They could as easily visit him.

"He'll be here at noon. Did you want to meet with him?"

"Yeah, we'd better go over the final numbers before—"

"What?"

Logan briefly closed his eyes, and then, "I've got to meet Cheryl for lunch."

Roger grinned. "Oh," was all he said.

"Will you quit it? Nothing happened. All right? Now fill me in on the Gavinson site."

It had taken Krista almost an hour to walk back to the Palliser, partly because she got lost, which was nothing new. Her sisters always said she'd been born without a compass.

As she crossed the marble-floored lobby, wearing Logan's fleece jacket and his huge flip-flops, her steps made a loud hollow sound. The noise attracted a few glances from the staff at the registration desk.

Was it any wonder? No doubt, she looked strange with the glittery black purse hanging from her wrist, the one gold sandal held in both hands, the fleece jacket as long as her dress, and her hair in a windblown mess.

Yesterday's bellhop recognized her and pushed the elevator button as she approached. "Good morning! Lovely day for a walk!"

"Yes, it's a beautiful day," she agreed, returning his smile. "Sunny and a little . . . crisp." *And a lot cold.*

"That's Calgary for you. It'll warm up later."

The doors dinged open. He gave her a slight bow, and she escaped into the elevator. Seven floors later, she was finally back at her room.

The hotel provided complimentary coffee so she made herself a cup and added four packets of sugar. She drank it standing in the hot shower and started to warm up. Then she shampooed her hair and scrubbed away last night's mascara.

Shower finished, she wrapped in one of the fluffy white towels and took a moment to savor the luxurious softness.

Her thoughts drifted to Logan. She saw him sitting across the table from her at the Pelican's Roost, listening to her talk about summer vacations, laughing along with her. She remembered the view they shared, of the park with the fairy lights decorating the trees. The night had been magical, and unreal. A crazy interlude.

Now it was time to get back to real life, and to get her life on track. Somehow, she would make university work. This time she would pass those courses. She would find a way. Hopefully, she could—

Stop. No use worrying about it until she had to. It was almost checkout time, but . . . cold outside, wet hair. She'd better take a few minutes.

Bending over, she flipped her head down, waving the dryer through her long hair, feathering the hot airflow through the strands. Then she changed into fresh underwear, her jeans and a royal blue turtleneck.

She opened her suitcase, put everything back and added the extra items: Logan's flip-flops, his jogging jacket, the little black dress, the purse, and the lone sandal. But she didn't have Michaela's combs.

A lump formed in her throat. What if they were at Logan's condo? What was she supposed to do? Knock on his door and ask for them? Could she even remember where his condo was? And if she could, what if his girlfriend answered the door?

Krista rubbed her hands over her arms. *Oh please!* Why did she have to be such a klutz?

No, she was not a klutz. Michaela kept telling her not to say that. This had simply happened. Sure, these things happened to her way more than they happened to her sisters, but—

Forget about it. Everything would be all right. Michaela would soon be here. They would find the apartment and Monday, if the fates were kind at all, she would have a job.

Almost noon. Time to go. Krista closed the suitcase and picked up the keycard. A few minutes later, she was signed out.

Pulling her squeaky suitcase across the marble floor, she found an empty couch. A beautiful piece of furniture, gold and black brocade, and elegant. A glass coffee table stretched in front of the couch and a few paces in front of that, a tall round table held a huge floral arrangement of bird of paradise and green foliage and seemingly random twigs. Not random at all.

She parked her suitcase and sat on the couch. And realized she was beside the doors to the Crystal Ballroom. The scene of last night's—

Last night's what?

It didn't matter. She'd never see Logan again. She wasn't sure what she was going to do with his jacket and his flip-flops, but it didn't seem right leaving them in the hotel room. In a way, his things were evidence that the night had really happened, and she had not dreamed it up.

She set her purse on the table in front of the couch and took out her phone. There was a text from her sister Delaney.

> *How could you move without telling us? Are you even in Saskatoon? Paul called this morning with some cockamamy story about losing your new address. Please tell me you're not seeing him again???*
>
> *Let me know where you are.*
>
> *And if you can't afford a phone plan, I'll pay for it. I hate texting.*

Krista winced. He was trying to find her. She'd thought he might. And Delaney, she seemed upset. Of all her sisters, Delaney had been the most understanding, but even she had limits.

Krista texted back.

> *Yes, I've moved and I'm fine. I am not seeing*
> *Paul anymore and I do not want him to have*
> *my address. I'll be in touch soon.*
>
> *Love, Krista*

She put her phone away and slumped on the couch. She wasn't giving anyone her address for this exact reason. Paul was probably contacting her other sisters. And her mother. He wouldn't try to get in touch with her dad.

And no way was she letting Delaney pay for a phone plan. Handouts from her family were the last thing Krista needed. It was bad enough she was relying so much on Michaela.

"Ready to go?" Michaela had arrived. This time she wore a long red coat.

"Yes, but I don't think the landlord will be there yet."

"Not a problem. We're going for lunch first."

"But I can't—"

"I know. You're going to tell me you can't afford lunch. Don't worry about it. I'm buying. You can return the favor once you get a job."

Krista's heart warmed and her stomach growled. "Uh, thank you." What else could she say? She was starving.

"Come on," Michaela said. "We're going to the Black Angus."

Fifteen minutes behind schedule, Logan arrived at the Black Angus to find Cheryl already seated in a quiet corner.

"I ordered for you," she said, glancing at her watch.

"Thanks. Sorry I'm late." He slipped into the chair

opposite her. "We're having a problem with the well site at—"

"I don't like Vesta," Cheryl said. With a sullen expression, she crossed her arms in front of her chest. "I think you should hire someone else."

That was out of the blue. "Vesta?" Now what—

"She wouldn't tell me where you were this morning."

"She didn't know."

"She acts like she can tell me what to do. Me!"

Cheryl might have said more, but the waiter arrived with their meals. A kale and fruit salad for her, and a steak sandwich for him. The waiter refilled their glasses, wished them the standard "Enjoy your meal" and left.

Logan carefully cut a piece of his sandwich. "What is going on?"

"Do something about her." Cheryl picked at her salad. "If you don't want to fire her, tell her I can come into your office whenever I want."

He tried a bite of the steak, but it didn't taste the same as he remembered. "You're not upset about Vesta," he said. "What's bothering you?"

"Besides that stupid auction?" Cheryl leaned toward him. "You were there!"

"I was. And I told you, nothing happened."

"Nothing happened!" She raised her voice. "You spent ten thousand dollars on a hooker!" She quickly looked around, possibly to see if anyone nearby was listening.

"I made a ten thousand dollar donation to the lodge," Logan said, noticing how calm he sounded. He was impressed with himself. He could be calm.

"The lodge." Cheryl pinched her lips. "I am so sick of hearing about that stupid lodge."

"Okay." He set down his cutlery and took a sip of water. "I get you don't like the idea of a fishing lodge. You don't have to spend any time there. And I get the auction wasn't a politically correct event, but it happened. Hayden got a little carried away. If there are any more fundraisers, he won't be on the committee."

Cheryl uttered a quick humph and poked at her salad. "Good. I'm glad we're clear about that." She was quiet for a moment, and then, "Just so you know, I've decided on the color for the kitchen."

He almost choked on his next mouthful. "Pardon?"

"The Lancaster yellow." She speared a grape with her fork.

"Are you talking about my kitchen wall?"

"Of course. And I've decided—"

"No. You haven't." He took a slow steady breath. "Vesta is arranging for a painter to come in this afternoon."

"I have my own painter." Cheryl pushed aside some kale and stabbed a mandarin wedge.

"Cheryl? What is wrong with you?" He spread both palms flat on the table. "You can't paint my condo."

"All right," she said, sitting up straight. "I may have made an assumption when I didn't consult you first. But I'm the interior designer and you're not. And I don't like that brown."

"It's *my* condo."

Pressing her lips together, she stared at him. The muscles tightened in her throat. "It will be my condo too, when I move in. I should have a say in this."

He dropped back in his chair. *Calm.* He could do calm. "You're not moving in."

"It's time," Cheryl said, chasing another grape. "You know it is. We've been going out for a year."

His shoulders slumped and he drew himself in. Almost exactly a year ago, he'd met her at a dinner party his mother had organized. Just before his parents moved to Florida.

Cheryl's parents knew his parents. Her dad was a

geologist. Her mother, a geophysicist. Cheryl had shown up with them that night.

Had it been a chance meeting? Or had his mother arranged it? He still wondered about that.

Setting his elbows on the table, he pressed his fingertips into his forehead. How had this got so out of hand? "Cheryl—"

"Do you ever think about what I'd like?" She dropped her fork and leaned forward again.

"Yes, but—"

"No, you don't." Her voice hissed. "I told you I want to go to The Nutcracker this Christmas. Did you get tickets?"

He looked up. "Yes." Well, actually, Vesta—dependable as ever—Vesta had managed to track down tickets.

"How many tickets?"

He was missing something. "Two?"

"You said my parents would be coming with us."

"I did?"

"Yes, you did. And Logan, I'm getting tired of stalling them."

The steak sat heavy in his stomach. "Stalling them?"

"We've got to set a date." She picked up her fork and sorted through pieces of kale. "Soon. Before Christmas."

"A date," he repeated. His mouth went dry as he replayed the last few weeks, looking for clues. "A date—for a wedding?"

She stared at him as if he were a two-year-old.

"We don't have that kind of relationship," he said.

"We do."

"Cheryl, I like you, but I don't want to get married."

"Of course you do," she said with a mirthless laugh. "I'm thirty. So are you. It's time, Logan."

He sighed wearily. The subtle little hints had been there,

and the not so subtle ones. He'd been ignoring them, hoping their relationship could continue on, the way it had for the past year. But lately they were having more fights, about anything and everything and nothing. He had to admit, they were not on the same trajectory. He might want to get married someday. It might even be to Cheryl, but at this point, it didn't feel right. It especially did not feel right when she was making these demands.

He didn't feel hungry anymore. He was still tired from last night. The Gavinson site had gone from bad to worse. Now they'd lost a section of pipe. He was going to have to fly up there.

And Cheryl was getting to her feet.

"You went to that auction last night, after I specifically told you not to. You owe me."

I don't owe anyone, he thought.

"I'm through with this discussion." She tossed her white linen napkin on top of her unfinished fruit. "Call me when you're ready to set a date." She pushed her chair back, stood up, and marched away.

Multi-tasking, Michaela talked on her cell phone all the way to the car. Her office was sending her to Edmonton for the weekend and she was finalizing details. While she drove, she called her husband on the Bluetooth and talked all the way to the restaurant. Something about making sure the twins followed through on a project while she was away.

She took a moment to introduce Krista to her husband over the Bluetooth. He seemed as charming as Michaela and wished her well at her new job.

Which she didn't have yet, but Michaela seemed optimistic. Michaela was a career counselor and she specialized in helping women who were changing careers. If anyone could find her a job, it would be Michaela.

At one o'clock, they wended their way through the still crowded Black Angus Steakhouse, following the waiter to an empty table in a quiet corner.

"So," Michaela said, as she slipped off her coat, "did you enjoy yourself at Kipling's last night?"

"Yes," Krista answered. She hung her coat on the back of the chair. "Most of it, anyway."

"Most of it?"

The waiter arrived and they each ordered the Grilled Chicken Caesar Salad Combo and iced tea. And they split a basket of sweet potato fries.

When the waiter left, Michaela put her elbows on the table and propped her chin on her hands. "Tell me."

"Oh, Michaela. You will not believe what happened." And then Krista told her friend the whole story.

They were interrupted by the arrival of their food, which was excellent, especially after Krista's morning walk in the cold. Hot garlic chicken, crisp romaine, spicy croutons and the best Caesar dressing ever.

"They auctioned off escorts. I can't believe it." Michaela pressed her palms to her cheeks. "What a strange fundraiser."

"It was for a drink and dinner. Apparently, they were supposed to stay at the hotel."

"But *he* didn't follow the rules."

"I don't think he'd planned to bid. And then when he did, I don't think he wanted his friends to see him with an escort."

Michaela was nodding and smiling. She seemed to think this was funny.

"What did you say his name was?"

"Logan."

"Did you get his last name?"

"I did." Krista bit her lip. "But, I can't remember. There was so much happening."

"It doesn't matter. I just wondered," Michaela said. She was tapping her fingers on the rim of her iced tea to a tune only she could hear. "He didn't talk to you when you saw him at Kipling's?"

"No. He glanced my way, but that was it."

They were silent for a few bites. Then Michaela set down her fork. "Why didn't you explain? That you were *not* an escort?"

"I *was* an escort, wasn't I?"

Michaela tilted her head and smiled again.

"I know. Not really an escort. I was going to explain once he got off the phone. But then I fell asleep."

"Mmm hmm."

"And I didn't keep the check."

"No? What did you do with it?"

"I put it in a book he's reading. He'll have found it by now."

Michaela thought about that. After a moment, she said, "Good for you."

"And one more thing."

"How could there possibly be more?"

"I think I left your combs at his condo, somewhere. I don't remember taking them out of my hair. I suppose I could knock on his door and get them back, but that would be . . ."

"Embarrassing," Michaela finished the thought. "Don't worry about it."

"I'll replace them," Krista added. And she would. As soon as she got a job.

"Will there be anything else," the waiter asked.

"No, thank you." Michaela opened her purse. "You can bring the check."

"And—" Krista got the waiter's attention, indicating the leftovers from her meal, and the leftover sweet potato fries. "Can you please wrap the rest of this to go?"

. . . . .

After lunch, Michaela drove them to the neighborhood called Kensington where they found the apartment Krista had rented online. The landlord met them in the backyard. They followed him up a rickety set of wooden stairs to the backdoor, and then, once inside, down another set of stairs, concrete stairs, to the basement suite.

Probably in his early sixties, the landlord had gray-flecked hair that was balding on top. He wore baggy beige trousers, a red plaid shirt and brown glasses that sat crookedly on his nose. There was a tape measure clipped to his belt.

"Here it is," he announced. "Like the pictures showed you on the Internet site."

The furnished apartment consisted of one room with a linoleum floor, a leather foldout couch, a small table, and two wooden chairs.

There was a large window above the table. On the other side of the table was a counter with a kitchen sink, a microwave and a tea kettle. And at the end of the counter, by the wall, was an old green refrigerator about four feet tall.

Above the counter were two white shelves, mounted on black L-brackets. The shelves displayed a few mismatched dishes, a white basket of utensils, a clear jar holding tea bags and an orange teapot without a lid.

Across the room, a short hallway, with a small closet on one side, led to the bathroom—a toilet, sink and shower. The bathroom floor looked newly tiled. The fixtures looked antique.

The landlord, Mr. Eakles, brushed away some sawdust on the window sill. "I just installed the egress window."

"Egress?"

"Building code. Need to have a window big enough for

you to get out in case of an emergency," he said. And then, "I got your payment for the first month's rent."

"Good."

"But you need to pay the damage deposit."

Krista shuffled back a step. "You didn't say anything about a damage deposit."

"New policy."

"How much is the damage deposit?" Michaela asked in a monotone voice, her features blank.

He told her. It was as much as a whole month's rent.

"Does that cover the cost of the new window?" Michaela crossed her arms.

"Not quite. But the building inspector said I needed it so I put it in."

Michaela nodded. "Thank God for building inspectors." She opened her purse, took out her check book and paid him.

Once the landlord had his check, he gave the key to Krista and he left.

"Thank you," Krista said. "Again. And I'll pay you just as soon as—"

"Not until Christmas, okay? You can pay me on Christmas Eve. Not a day sooner."

"You're a lifesaver."

"I'm in a position to help. You would do the same." Michaela surveyed the room. "It's pretty small."

"It's all I need." Krista opened the old fridge. Spotless, and empty but for a box of baking soda. She deposited her leftover lunch inside and closed the door.

"Well, it's clean," Michaela said, running her hand over one of the shelves. "And it has the little backyard." She peered through the egress window, which let in lots of light.

"And he said it's close to the bus and that little grocery store."

They looked at each other. "Ready for university?"

. . . . .

By four o'clock Krista had enrolled in the Commerce Program at U of C. A month ago, she'd paid the fee for one course—Finance 301, on Monday and Wednesday evenings. The course had started last week, but they would let her start a week late. She had the textbook—from the last time she'd tried it—a year ago, in Saskatoon.

She'd dropped the course after only a few weeks, because it was too much work to study and to support Paul. Besides, the plan was, once he graduated, *he* would support *her*.

Or had that been an excuse? What if it wasn't a question of enough time? What if she simply was not smart enough?

"You're looking scared again," Michaela said. "Don't do that. You'll be fine."

"Right." Krista gripped the registration papers in her hand. *Be positive.* And if that doesn't work, try not to think about it. "When's your flight leave?"

"Not until seven. And I'm already packed."

They made one more stop at a department store. Michaela insisted on supplying Krista with some linen and towels.

"It's an apartment warming gift."

They drove back to Krista's new home. Michaela parked on the street and Krista hopped out, gathering her packages. "Thanks again. This means a lot to me."

"Happy to help," Michaela called out the window. "I'll be back in town Sunday night so I can take you to your interview Monday morning."

Krista nodded, holding tightly to her packages. As she watched her friend drive away, she thought about the old green refrigerator, and she was glad she had saved some of her lunch.

Chapter Eight

Monday morning at five minutes to ten, Krista and Michaela arrived at *Girl Friday Staffing Solutions.* The receptionist told them to have a seat and offered coffee.

"Yes, please," Krista answered. "Extra milk and sugar."

"I'm fine," Michaela said, as she took a seat and opened her purse. She retrieved her Blackberry and started scrolling. "The coat suits you," she said, without looking up.

Michaela had loaned Krista her long blue coat. Much more stylish than Krista's frayed brown one, and warmer. "Thanks again." Krista unbuttoned the coat but, still cold from outside, she kept it on. Someday she would find a way to repay her friend.

This morning was cool, and crisp, like the morning Krista had escaped from Logan's condo. She stared down at her feet and a dullness settled in her chest as her thoughts drifted back to three days ago.

Should she have run away like that? She grimaced. What else could she do? She'd woken up in his bed, and then to have his girlfriend phoning? It was all so embarrassing.

Her phone chirped. A text from Delaney.

You still have not told me where you are.

Krista texted back.

I enrolled in Finance again.

"Is that your sister?"

"Yes. Delaney." Krista turned off the phone and put it in her purse. It would not be good to have her cell phone interrupt this interview.

"Is she the nurse?"

"No, she's the doctor. Jane is the nurse."

"Delaney is the oldest?"

"No, Jane is the oldest. Mom had Jane, then a year later, she had Steph, then a year later, Delaney. Then eight years later, me. I was an afterthought."

"Don't say that."

Why not? It was true.

The receptionist delivered a hot mug of coffee. Krista wrapped her hands around it, inhaled the aroma, and forced herself to sip slowly so she wouldn't burn her tongue. Still, it didn't take her long to finish.

As she set the empty mug on the table in front of her, a woman, about Michaela's age, hustled into the reception area. The woman had light brown permed hair and wore a white silk blouse, a maroon-colored skirt, comfortable-looking low-heeled shoes and a strand of pearls. She also wore a flowing multi-colored jacket, that picked up the maroon of her skirt. Little gold-rimmed glasses perched on the end of her nose.

"There you are!" the woman said.

Michaela stood. "Marge! Good to see you again." The two shook hands.

Krista also got to her feet.

"You must be Krista," Marge said, extending her hand. "I'm Marge Smith. Welcome to Calgary. Now come back here and I'll tell you what I have for you."

They headed down the hall, leaving Michaela to sort through her Blackberry.

Marge's office was a cozy little room with a big window overlooking a winding section of the Bow River. Her desk was covered with stacks of colored file folders and heaps of paper in seemingly random piles.

She was sorting through one of the piles now.

Her desk also held an ergonomic keyboard, a large monitor, a red mouse, a mouse pad with an image of jelly beans, a black and silver multi-line phone with a cell phone beside it, a handheld calculator, a ceramic flower pot full of pens, a snow globe of a winter village, a bottle of Smoky Rose hand lotion, and a gold Starbucks travel mug.

Finally, she chose some pages and placed them in front of her. Peering over the top of her little glasses, she studied Krista.

"You met Michaela in Saskatoon?"

"Yes."

"At one of her seminars?"

"Yes."

"She says you worked as an office clerk there."

"Yes, in a construction company."

"Windows? MS Word? Excel?"

"Yes, yes, and yes."

"Organized? Adaptable? Good people skills?" Marge read from the page in front of her. "Never mind. Michaela says you have all that." Tapping the sheets, Marge lined up the edges and set the papers aside. Then she leafed through another stack.

"This is a receptionist job," she said, skimming. "The pay is good. More than you'd get for a similar position in another company."

Krista wondered why, but didn't ask. She simply nodded.

"It's an oil exploration company with—" Marge tracked her finger down the page. "—forty-three people. Primarily you'll be answering the switchboard. You will also greet any visitors." She turned the page over. "Reception is on one side of the elevators but the executive offices are on the other side. Most of the visitors will be for the executive offices, but they will go to the reception side first." A slight frown. "Don't ask me why they set it up like that."

She took a sip from her travel mug and picked up another piece of paper.

"You will also be dealing with the mail," she went on. "Much of their correspondence is email but there's still a lot of letter mail."

She paused, looking thoughtful. "You'd think it would all be digital by now, but some offices have as much paper as ever. Maybe more." She shrugged. "Oh well. I'm not going to tell anyone how to run their business." She shuffled through her papers and several fluttered to the floor.

"So." She counted on her fingers. "Phone, visitors, mail." A quick tap of her index finger on the desk. "They'll probably want you to make coffee. No, they have those Keurig machines. Just keep them full of water."

A stray piece of blue paper caught her attention. She scanned it, bunched it up, and tossed it in the garbage.

"Let's see." She closed her eyes and placed both palms flat on the desk. "The drilling engineer," she said, opening her eyes again. "You'll take the morning well reports, input the data, and print him a copy. He's a friendly sort. You'll like him."

She looked down at her desk, rubbed two fingers in the space between her brows. "You won't have much contact with the president." She pressed her lips together, pausing. "But don't let him rattle you."

"Pardon?"

"Apparently he's hard to work for." Leaning forward, Marge straightened some papers. "I'm sure he means well but he doesn't realize how intimidating he can be." She set the papers aside. "Okay. What else. Oh yes. The office manager wants a six-week evaluation period before the job is permanent. But don't worry, I'm sure you'll do fine. Any questions?"

Krista's stomach rumbled and she realized she'd been bracing. She planted her feet squarely on the floor and tried to project confidence as she looked back at Marge.

"When can I start?"

It turned out she could start immediately.

Michaela pulled up in front of the Sun Valley Tower. "The C-Train is that way." She pointed. "You can find your way home?"

"No problem." Although it was a problem, because, you know, born without a compass. "I'll call you tomorrow."

Her phone chirped as she entered the building lobby. Delaney, again.

Good luck with your Finance class.

Krista closed her eyes for a second. She was pretty sure her sister expected her to have difficulty with the course. And no wonder, since Krista had failed all those courses when she was still living at home.

Holding the paper with the address on it, she rode all the way to the twenty-sixth floor without a stop. The elevator dinged open, she stepped into the hall, and caught her breath. A large bird sat on a branch near the ceiling—its talons wrapped around the branch, its wings outspread, as if it were ready for flight.

It was brass—the bird and the branch, and the letters that spelled Peregrine Oil & Gas. Obviously the bird was supposed to be a peregrine, and it didn't seem particularly friendly.

"Can I help you?" A young woman approached. She wore a flowing peasant-style dress with a drawstring neckline, bell sleeves and a ruffled hemline that came to her knees. It appeared to be cotton, a tapestry of florals in several shades of red and brown and rust.

"I'm here for—"

"Are you Krista?"

"Yes, I am," Krista said. "Krista MacKenzie. Girl Friday sent me."

"Great. I'm supposed to give you the orientation. Have you had lunch?"

"No." And not breakfast either, unless you counted the coffee at Girl Friday.

"Then first, I'll show you the staffroom. Come with me," the woman said. "Oh!" —as they passed the hall on the other side of the elevator bay— "Bathrooms are that way."

The woman pushed through a set of glass doors with a sign that said *Please see Reception in 2600* and Krista followed her. As they hurried past a computer station on their right, the woman said, "This is Quincy. Quincy Adams. He's one of the admin assistants over here."

"Hi," the young man said, looking up briefly and then returning to his monitor.

"His wife works here too. She's in Accounting." They passed another room. "That's the boardroom." And then, "That's the library." And finally, "Here we are. This is the staffroom. Toast?" The woman held up a white plastic bag of bread.

"Please," Krista answered, feeling a gurgling in her belly, and glad the woman was not in a hurry to do the orientation.

The woman put two slices in the toaster, and then opened a cupboard. "Peanut butter and jam in here," she said. "And there?" She indicated another cupboard. "Get us a couple of plates. I'll put the kettle on. Tea?"

"Yes, please," Krista said, as she stared at the peanut butter and swallowed.

The woman was at the sink, filling the kettle. "We'll eat and then I'll introduce you to everybody."

Eating was a very good idea. And then it would be good to learn a few names. "And you are?"

"Oh! Didn't I say?" The woman plugged the kettle in. "I'm Beatrice. The receptionist. Nice to meet you."

Beatrice spent the noon hour telling Krista about her husband's art supply store. Beatrice would be working with him: selling, ordering, shipping and even teaching some art classes. She seemed excited about her new job.

By the time they got back to reception, it was a quarter past one. The woman manning the switchboard put down the headset and looked at her watch, giving Krista the impression they were late.

Beatrice yawned and checked her cell phone. The switchboard rang, Beatrice picked up, and continued to thumb through messages on her phone.

The stand-in receptionist introduced herself. "I'm Irene Adams. You're the new receptionist?"

"Yes, Krista MacKenzie. Then you're—"

"Yes, I'm Quincy's wife. I handle the switchboard for the first half hour of the day. Did Beatrice tell you?"

"Not yet."

"Of course, she didn't. Okay. Most of the staff arrive at

eight. You come in at eight-thirty and leave at five. Everyone else goes home at four-thirty. I also handle noon hours." A slight pause. "From noon until one," she added, with an emphasis on the *one*.

"Mr. Diamond isn't here," Beatrice told a caller. "I'll transfer you to his admin." That done, she looked at Irene. "Do you know where Mr. Diamond is?"

"He's at lunch. And you can call him Brad."

"Do people go by first names here?" Krista asked.

"Mostly," Irene said. "But Beatrice likes using last names."

Beatrice used last names because that's the way her mail sorting system was set up—alphabetically by surname.

"It's bad enough trying to remember forty-three last names, let alone the first names too. Here." She handed Krista a letter opener and a date stamp. "Open these, stamp the date on the letter, file them here."

They sat beside each other, with Beatrice answering calls, in between sending messages on her cell, and Krista sorting mail into the cubby slots along the front of the reception desk.

"Peregrine Oil & Gas." Beatrice listened, fiddling with her bracelet. "Oberman? I thought I did transfer you to Mr. Oberman. Oh, I see. Mr. Obermeyer." She tapped a button. "I always get those two mixed up." She shrugged. "I should show you how to run the postage meter." And another call came in.

Behind the reception desk, a workroom housed the postage meter, the photocopier, two Keurig coffee machines and everything from pencils and pens to binders and three-hole punches.

By four-thirty, all Krista had done was sort the mail. Meanwhile Beatrice fielded calls and inputted data for a well report that needed to be emailed to the chief drilling engineer, who was not in the office today. He also needed some information about well logs.

Well logs. Krista remembered that night when she'd been at the Pelican's Roost. Someone had called Logan about well logs. He worked in the oil industry, and now so did she. What were the chances they might ever meet?

And how awkward would that be?

Irene stopped by the desk. "Ready?"

Krista surfaced from her thoughts. "For what?"

Irene looked up at the ceiling. "I take the outgoing mail to the post box downstairs. You're supposed to have it ready."

"It's been really busy." Fumbling with some papers, Beatrice dropped several to the floor. "I haven't had time to run it through the postage meter."

"Then I guess it will go out tomorrow," Irene said, with a cold smile. "I hope it's nothing important."

"It's mostly for the Land Department to get signatures." Beatrice focused on pushing back a cuticle with her thumbnail. "If they need it right away, they'll send it by courier."

Irene left, and Beatrice applied some hand lotion. There were only a few more calls to interrupt her as she gave Krista more details about her husband's art store.

At five minutes to five, Beatrice put the switchboard on night service. "Close enough," she said. "I've got to run. Tomorrow, I'll give you the tour of the office. Bye!" And she was gone.

Krista looked around the suddenly quiet reception area.

In front of the reception desk, three comfortable-looking chairs lined up against the wall. At right angles to them, another three lined up in front of the floor-to-ceiling windows. The chairs had black metal frames and burgundy leather upholstery on the seats, backs and arms. Nestled in the corner between the chairs was a round table strewn with magazines and a vase of wilted pink lilies.

On the reception desk, Beatrice had abandoned a brochure about art easels, a drawing pad open at a sketch of tulips, and a ceramic mug half full of coffee. There were several stick-it notes attached to the switchboard, with names and extension numbers scribbled on them.

Krista picked up the coffee mug and got the vase of wilted lilies. She took them to the staffroom, where she emptied the vase, put the mug in the dishwasher and made herself a peanut butter and jam sandwich.

Then she left to find the C-Train to the university.

The next day was Tuesday and Krista was at work by eight o'clock.

"Good morning," Irene said, in a light, relaxed voice. "You're early."

"Not sure of the buses yet."

"Has Beatrice shown you how to use the switchboard?" Irene's brows drew closer together.

"She didn't have time."

"No, of course she didn't." Irene leaned back. "Okay. I'll teach you."

All Krista had to do was memorize forty-three names. Well, forty-two, since she already knew her own, and then memorize the extensions, and transfer the calls. If no one answered, a caller could leave a voice mail.

But, apparently, a lot of people didn't like voice mail and wanted to talk to an actual person. They hit zero to return to the switchboard.

"You could take a message or send them to one of the admins," Irene instructed. "I'm the admin for Accounting. The Land Department and Exploration share an admin— that's Tania. She's here." Irene touched a button on the board. "There are two administrative assistants in the executive suites. The president has one of them—Vesta—here. The other is Quincy—here. He takes care of the comptroller, the office manager, and the two geologists."

"Oberman and Obermeyer?"

"Right. Don't get them mixed up. They hate it when you do that." Irene puffed up her cheeks as she thought. "If any visitors give you a problem, call Frank."

"And Frank is?"

"Frank Keystone. He's the office manager. You'll probably meet him today. Do you know how to work the postage meter?"

"Beatrice didn't have time to—"

"Come on. I'll show you."

Once Beatrice arrived at a quarter to nine, Krista continued to handle the switchboard. Beatrice did the well report again and she made three separate orders for stationery. It might have been more efficient to do them all at once, but Beatrice liked to deal with things as they came up.

At half past eleven, another call lit up the switchboard and Krista answered.

"Krista? Is that you?"

"Michaela! I was going to call you on my lunch break."

"Which is at noon?"

"Yes."

"We're going for lunch, sweetie."

"But I don't have any money yet."

"Not taking no for an answer. I'm buying. Meet me at the Black Angus."

"But—" Michaela was gone, and three other lights lit up the board.

. . . . .

"Order whatever you like," Michaela said. "I mean it. After you've worked for a while, you can take me out for lunch."

With a hollow ache in her stomach, Krista ordered a steak and baked potato with all the fixings. Her mouth was already watering.

Michaela ordered a mixed green salad with pecans and goat cheese. The waiter left and Michaela looked up. "How was your first finance class?"

Krista winced. "I . . . I think it will be doable."

"Don't sell yourself short. You'll figure it out."

Michaela said that as if she believed it. Krista's family didn't. But then, Krista had failed before, so her family would expect her to fail again.

While they waited, Michaela talked about the twins and their courses in economics and calculus. After their meals arrived, Michaela got to the point. "Paul phoned me."

In the process of sipping some water, Krista almost spilled the glass. "How?"

"He wrangled the phone number out of your old landlord."

"Oh." Krista's chest tightened. "When?"

"Last night. Don't worry. He knows you're in Calgary, but that's all."

It was still bad news. "I knew he'd figure it out, but I didn't think he would figure it out so quickly."

Michaela bit her lip and stared at Krista.

"What?"

Huffing out a breath, Michaela straightened her cutlery. "When he realized I would not give him any information about you, he told me he'd taken your money."

Krista closed her eyes and clenched her hands in her lap.

"He said he had a feeling you were going to run. And that if he took your money, you wouldn't leave."

Krista gave a long slow sigh. She'd been so wrong about Paul. So swept away by him.

"Did he actually empty your wallet?"

"Uhhh . . . yes."

"And you had no money at all when you got on that bus?"

"I had my ticket."

"But no money? Why didn't you tell me?"

Krista's shoulders sagged. "Because I felt like an idiot, okay? I let him come in and he must have gone in my purse while I was in the kitchen."

"You let him in your apartment?" Michaela straightened the knife beside her plate again. "You are so trusting." Then she blinked and tilted her head. "And if you don't have any money, what are you eating? How are you staying alive?"

"There's a staffroom at work. I can make peanut butter and jam sandwiches whenever I want."

"I'm bringing you groceries tonight."

"I can't accept—"

"Do not tell me what you can't accept. You can pay me back by babysitting my kids."

"Michaela, they're in university."

"So? They need supervision. And it seems, so do you."

Krista felt a flush creep across her cheeks. "I know." She sat up straight. "I should have said something, but I was embarrassed."

"All right." Michaela picked a pecan out of her salad and nibbled on it. "Moving on. If he does come to Calgary—"

Krista's hand shook and she dropped her fork. "Do you think he will?"

. . . . .

At exactly one o'clock, Krista took the headset from Irene who nodded happily and left to take her own break. Beatrice returned about one-thirty and headed into the workroom.

For the rest of the afternoon, Beatrice dealt with the outgoing mail and did the well report. At four-thirty, when Irene arrived for the mail, Beatrice left with her.

"No use both of us being here."

Five minutes later, a man entered the reception area and approached the desk. He was probably mid-thirties, average height, thinning brown hair, and smiling.

"Krista?"

"Yes, I'm Krista."

He extended his hand. "Frank Keystone. I'm the office manager. Welcome."

The office manager, the person who would need to sign off on her six-week evaluation. "I'm glad to be here," she told him.

"Where's Beatrice?"

"She left at four-thirty."

He frowned, and then he nodded. "Good. Good," he said. "Sorry I didn't get over to meet you yesterday. Dealing with some problems in the field. Let me know if you have any questions or concerns."

"I will. Nice to meet you."

He left, and Krista was left thinking that her only concern was that she pass that evaluation and keep this job.

On Wednesday morning, Krista arrived at eight again. "If you don't mind, I'm going to tidy the workroom until eight-thirty."

"Knock yourself out." Irene adjusted the headset. "It could use some organization."

Once again, Beatrice took care of the well report and

Krista handled the switchboard. And once again, Beatrice promised to do a tour of the office so Krista could personally meet everyone, but that didn't happen because Beatrice dropped a toner cartridge in the workroom and Krista spent most of the afternoon cleaning it up.

Beatrice left at four-thirty again, since she had so much to do at her husband's new store. Krista stayed until five, answering the last few calls of the day, and organizing more of the workroom.

She left in time to get the C-Train to the university, and this time her class was not quite so daunting.

On the way home, she checked her phone and found a text from her mom.

Delaney says you've got a new job. Good for you.

love, Mom XOX

Obviously, Delaney had not mentioned the part about Krista moving, otherwise their mom would be asking. And now, what to say?

Krista tapped her finger against the side of the phone, tried to come up with something, and couldn't, so she decided to text back later.

On Thursday, after another early morning of cleaning, organizing and tossing, the workroom was in better shape. And the photocopier was working again.

Beatrice did the well report and said she would show Krista how to do it later. She also promised to take Krista on a tour of the office right after lunch, and Irene agreed to handle the switchboard. However, when they were about to do that, Beatrice dropped the water reservoir for the Keurig.

While Krista mopped the floor, Beatrice manned the

switchboard and had a loud argument with someone named Mr. Nicholas.

The name whirred in Krista's head, familiar for some reason. *Nicholas. Nicholas.* Then it hit her. Of course. Mr. Nicholas was the president. And, as far as she knew, he was still away from the office.

She closed her eyes and tried to think.

Too many names all at once. On top of learning everyone's name at work, she was learning everyone's name in her finance class. A useful exercise since she'd already found a friend to study with.

"Okay?" Beatrice asked.

"Pardon?"

"I said, tomorrow. First thing. We'll get Irene to take over the switchboard and I'll give you the tour of the office. You'll be able to put faces to names."

Chapter Nine

It was Friday morning, Krista's fifth day on the job. If she made it through the day, it would be one week down and five to go until she got her evaluation. If only that could please happen without anything going wrong. She really wanted to keep this job. The work was reasonably interesting and the pay was good and, so far, everyone was friendly.

Hoping to have more time to put some personal touches to the shelving in the workroom, she stepped out of the elevator even earlier than usual, at fifteen minutes to eight. Unfortunately, the offices were locked, on both sides of the hall. The peregrine falcon stared down at her, as if it were challenging her right to be here.

The other elevator dinged open and Frank Keystone stepped out.

"Krista! Good morning! Um, you know you don't start until eight-thirty, right?"

"Yes, I know, but I've been coming in early to make things easier to find in the workroom."

"I see." He laughed. "And here I thought Beatrice was—well, never mind. I'll open up for you."

Irene arrived right on time at eight. "You've done a great job back here," she said, poking her head into the room. And then she took her station at the switchboard.

Krista relieved her at half past eight and Beatrice

showed up at a quarter to nine. She still had her coat on when Frank came into the reception area holding envelopes.

"Good morning, Beatrice. Your last day. Excited?"

"Yes. I've liked working here but I'm looking forward to my art."

"I'll collect your key." Frank held out his hand, and waited.

Beatrice rummaged in her purse, and finally found a brass key on a ring with a brass decoration—the peregrine falcon. She handed it to Frank.

Weighing the key in his hand, he said, "Why don't you take today off?"

She lifted her brows.

"With pay, of course," he added. "Here's your final check including your salary for today."

"Really? That's great!" Beatrice plucked the envelope from his hand. "Bye, Krista and good luck!"

Frank watched her leave. When the elevator doors dinged closed, he turned around. "And here is your first paycheck."

She must have looked surprised as she took the envelope, and she was.

"Payday is always the second Friday and the last Friday of the month, even though you've only been here a week." He passed her the brass key with the peregrine emblem. "From now on, you'll be locking up this side of the office when you leave at five."

She accepted the key. This had to be a good sign, right? He was trusting her with a key.

The switchboard interrupted them. He waved and left, and Krista dealt with the caller. Then she hit Irene's extension.

"Can you come out here for a moment?"

Irene did.

"Frank gave Beatrice the day off."

"Good," Irene said, with enthusiasm. "She won't be here to break anything."

"She never had time to show me how to do the well reports."

"Of course she didn't. Don't worry about it. I'll do them today, and I'll teach you how on Monday."

Krista continued. "She was going to give me a tour so I could meet everyone face to face."

"No problem. We'll get Tania. Remember? She's in Exploration? She'll cover the switchboard on Monday and we'll do it then."

"Thanks."

The switchboard lit up and Krista went back to work, feeling like she had an ally.

Irene took charge of the switchboard at noon and Krista headed over to the executive suites on the other side of the elevators.

Her side of Peregrine housed Reception, Accounting, Production and Exploration. It was always busy there, like mission control. But it was a different atmosphere over here. Plush, and elegant, and calm.

The executive offices rimmed the large open area where the admins worked. Quincy was already gone. Vesta, the president's admin, was shutting down her computer.

"Going for lunch?" she asked.

"Just to the staffroom," Krista told her.

Frank's office was immediately across from the glass doors. To the left of his office was Brad's office. She'd met him this morning when he'd come over to introduce himself. He was early thirties, short dark brown hair, athletic build, and VP Finance. To the left of Brad's office, in the corner space, was the president's office.

Turning right, Krista passed Frank's office, then the huge boardroom, then the library, and finally she arrived at the staffroom.

She was the only one there. After making herself a cup of tea and a toasted peanut butter and jam sandwich, she settled down to read her finance book.

At one o'clock, she returned to the reception desk and got started on the mail.

A few minutes later, Jenny Reginald showed up with a cup of coffee. She had light brown curly hair, cut short like a pixie, and she had a cute turned-up nose. She'd been an admin in the Land Department and had recently graduated to the Junior Landman position. Leaning on the reception desk, she sipped her drink and watched Krista open envelopes.

"Have you heard? The president and the chief drilling engineer might be in today."

"Where have they been?"

"At a site. North of Fort McMurray. They've been up there for a week," Jenny babbled. "You'll like the drilling engineer," she said. She sipped some coffee. "But maybe not the president."

"No?"

Jenny quirked an eyebrow and smiled. "He's cute," she said. "But he can be a pain."

Krista briefly remembered Marge Smith at Girl Friday saying the same thing. But she'd also said the receptionist would not have much contact with the president.

"Beatrice didn't get along with him," Jenny went on. "But I'm sure you'll be okay. Don't worry about it."

Leaning over the desk, Jenny lowered her voice. "I heard he finally dumped his girlfriend." Jenny paused for a breath. "That woman was such a pain. Do you know what Vesta said?"

Krista looked up, knowing Jenny was going to tell her.

"She said his girlfriend walked into his office whenever she felt like it. Interrupted him, like she owned the place. I don't know how he put up with her. In fact, I don't know how Vesta put up with her."

Jenny stopped talking, took another sip of her coffee. "And if she can upset Vesta, she can upset anybody."

Jenny also told Krista that Frank Keystone was divorced, loved hockey and flirted with most of the female staff. And that he was basically harmless. Although, Krista knew, she would need his approval in order to keep this job.

As long as Jenny was on a roll, Krista thought she might as well ask about the drilling engineer.

"He likes to tease. Watch out for him. Nice looking man. Single, too. You'll be doing his drilling reports, did you know that?"

"Yes. Irene is going to show me how on Monday."

The switchboard rang, Krista held up a finger, set down the letter opener, and tapped a key. After she directed the call, Jenny picked up where she'd left off.

"If they come in, it will be late. I don't know why they're bothering. I mean, why not wait till Monday?"

"Because they run this place, Jenny." Frank had come across from the executive suites.

"You've done a great job organizing things, Krista," Frank said. He was standing up straight, pulling his stomach in, preening for Jenny. "I wanted to let you know our company president and our chief drilling engineer should be arriving this afternoon." He paused, and swept his gaze over Jenny. "But I guess Jenny has already filled you in, right?"

"I heard from Brad," Jenny told him.

Krista sliced open another envelope.

"They're flying in from the Gavinson site," Frank said, absently. "Should be here before we close today."

"I'd better get back to work. Catch you later, Frank." Jenny sent him a smile and left.

The switchboard rang and Krista picked up. Frank glanced at his watch, and went back to his office on the other side of the elevators.

Another broker in New York wanted more annual reports. Krista listened, taking down the broker's address. Then she started typing a label for the package of annual returns.

Logan stepped off the elevator. It was a good thing he'd sent Roger home. The guy was exhausted. Hell. They were both exhausted. And he'd be heading home as soon as he checked with Vesta.

No. He'd check with Vesta and then he'd stop by the hospital. He needed to visit that roughneck. Samuel Burns. Sammie Burns. Just a kid.

It wasn't often they had an injury at the site, and it wasn't pretty. Sammie would be lucky if he kept his leg.

"Mr. Nicholas." Vesta looked up from her computer. "You look tired."

And he probably looked a little rumpled in his jeans and polo shirt. He usually wore a suit to the office, but he'd come straight from the field. "I'll get some sleep tonight. Have you heard anything from the hospital?"

"He's going to be all right," she answered. "Dr. Bainbridge said to tell you."

Logan pressed a palm to his forehead, and quietly exhaled. *Thank God.*

"He also said you're Sammie's emergency contact person?"

"Yes, I am. The kid doesn't have any relatives in the city."

"I see." Vesta nodded.

Mark would keep him informed. Dr. Mark Bainbridge was the chief orthopedic resident at the Nose Hill Hospital, and he was a friend of Logan's.

"Hey, Logan! Welcome back." Frank was coming out of his office, carrying a load of file folders. "How's the site?"

"Everything is back on schedule. For the moment."

"Good. Good." Frank nodded as he shifted the stack of folders. "We've got ourselves a new receptionist," he added, looking pleased with himself.

"What happened to Beatrice?"

"Going to be working at her husband's store. And don't worry. The new one's a temp. If she works out after six weeks, we'll keep her." Frank left them, taking his load of files into the library.

"She seems quite efficient," Vesta said, as she handed Logan two inches of papers. "The Turnstone reports."

No one was as efficient as Vesta. "Thanks, Vesta," he said, taking a step toward his office.

"Oh, and Mr. Nicholas?"

"Yes?"

"Cheryl has been calling."

His heart fell and he swore under his breath. He didn't need this.

Logan hadn't expected to be at the office for this long. Almost four o'clock, and tension radiated in the back of his neck. He'd finish one more report and then he'd call it a day.

Vesta buzzed him. "Mr. Jones is on line one, sir. Do you have time to talk to him?"

"Sure, put him through." Logan picked up the phone and leaned back in his chair. "Pro?"

"Logan. Welcome home."

"I'm not home yet."

"I heard. Had an accident out there?"

"It's all right now."

An audible sigh over the line. "I wanted to meet with you," Pro said. "And Roger too. As soon as possible."

"The lodge?"

"Yes, the lodge. Got some more information. And, I think we should call it Pelican's Cove Lodge."

"Cove?" Funny. It was the Pelican's Roost where he'd had dinner with Krista.

"Yes, Cove. You know, a little indent in the coastline?"

"I know. Why do you want to call it that?"

"Because it's at Pelican's Cove. So call it Pelican's Cove Lodge."

"Sounds cumbersome."

"Leave off the Lodge part?"

Logan let go of a long tired breath. "Is there something that needs to be done right away, Pro? I'm a little busy right now."

"We're ready to put the money on the mortgage. Has Roger got that last check cashed?"

"What last check?"

"His escort's. He handed out twenty checks. Only nineteen have been cashed."

"I'll be seeing him tonight. I'll ask him to get back to you."

"Great," Pro said. "I've got the preliminary drawings for the buildings. There will be three. A main building with six bedrooms and attached baths, in an octagonal shape. Kitchen and storage at the back, living room and fireplace in front for the view, and three bedrooms to either side. Each with a view. The two other buildings are to either side of the main lodge and they're private."

"You've got a copy of the plans?"

"By next week. Need to get the mortgage money off first."

"I'll talk to Roger."

Logan rang off. First, he'd visit Sammie at the Nose Hill Hospital. Vesta had already sent flowers and a smartphone—the newest model of the Samsung Galaxy Sport, complete with credit so the kid could download whatever games he wanted.

After the hospital, Logan would stop by and see Roger, and ask him about that last check. The guy would have slept for a few hours and he'd be ready for something to eat. Some beer and pizza.

Logan wanted to talk to him about the escorts anyway, about where Roger had hired them. Which could be tricky, since he didn't want Roger thinking he was interested. He just needed to find out where Krista had come from, because he had her combs—the shiny black combs with the crystals.

They looked expensive, so she'd want them back. And, he had a feeling she had his jogging jacket. It hadn't been in his gym bag, and it had been cold that morning.

It wasn't that he wanted to see her. And he could buy another jogging jacket. But she would want her combs back.

Another call interrupted his thoughts and he picked up.

Half an hour later, he checked his watch. Almost four-thirty. God, he was tired. He had to leave, and soon.

He should probably say hello to the new receptionist before he left. So far he'd heard from Vesta, Frank, Quincy, Brad and Irene about the new girl.

Correction . . . woman.

They were saying she was excellent at the job. Everything Beatrice wasn't. He'd believe it when he saw it. Thank God Frank had hired her on a temp basis. He'd hate to be stuck with another Beatrice. He'd better take a minute and introduce himself.

Decision made, he filled his briefcase with the reports

he'd need over the weekend, added the lodge file—the Pelican's Cove Lodge—it sounded all right.

"Leaving for the day, sir?" Vesta asked as he walked past.

"In a few minutes," he answered.

He walked across the hall past the elevators and waited. He could hear the receptionist on the phone, so, he might as well listen for a moment.

"Peregrine Oil & Gas. Good afternoon."

Pretty voice. But—he tilted his head, listening closely— something about her voice, something . . . familiar? No, couldn't be. He must be more tired than he thought.

"I'm sorry, Mr. Oliver isn't in at the moment. Can I put you through to Jenny Reginald? She's the Junior Landman."

Still standing outside the reception area, Logan heard her laugh at something the caller said, as if she and the caller were best friends, and then "Certainly, sir." She had a beautiful voice. Well, perfect for a receptionist anyway.

Professional and friendly. That was good. Now if only she could be even halfway organized. He stepped into the reception area and—the world stalled, and the moment stretched.

Wearing a headset, she stuffed envelopes while she talked. Her head was bent slightly as she concentrated on the conversation. That gorgeous reddish brown hair spilled past her shoulders, as wavy and shiny as he remembered it. Today, her face was free of makeup. That, or she wore very little.

With a sudden coldness in his core, Logan stepped back into the hall, leaned against the wall, and took a deep breath.

Right. Friendly and professional. He closed his eyes. She was definitely a professional.

. . . . .

Krista attached the last label for the invitations. In two weeks, the company would complete the preliminary setup for a joint venture project and a celebration was planned. Frank wanted the invitations to go out today, and now they were ready to be mailed. Hopefully this would get her some points with him.

Just as Irene arrived for the mail, Quincy came into the reception area. "How's it going, Krista?"

"All done. The mail's ready for you to drop off." She wrapped an elastic band around the last stack of envelopes.

"Our president's back in town," Quincy said, unnecessarily.

"She knows," Irene told him. "Everyone has been telling her the same thing all afternoon."

"He wants to meet you."

"He does?" Krista tensed. "Why?"

"Maybe he's worried you'll be as bad as Beatrice," Quincy said. "And it would be better to fire you now as later."

"Quincy!" Irene pushed her husband's arm. "Don't listen to him, Krista. He's being a tease."

Krista bit her lip. "Is he coming over here?"

"No. He wondered if you could pop into his office? You know where it is?"

"Sure. When?"

"Right now. We'll handle the switchboard till you get back." He moved around behind the desk. "How do I set this thing on night service?"

"You won't need to," Krista said, "I'll just be a few minutes."

"Well, in case you're not. Maybe he'll want to reminisce about his company."

Feeling a little breathless, Krista stood and smoothed out her skirt. She hadn't expected to meet the president today. Better get this over with.

She left the desk, entered the hall, and took a moment to steady herself.

Marge Smith had said he was hard to work for. Beatrice didn't get along with him. And—*oh no!* In the flurry of new names to memorize, she hadn't bothered to get his name straight. Oh, why did she have to be such a klutz!

She'd seen his name on Beatrice's list—Mr. Nichols, or Nicholson, or something like that. Too many names to remember. She was just getting Oberman and Obermeyer straight.

Calm down, she told herself. She was doing it again. Imagining worst case scenarios. She cleared her throat. Her mouth felt dry. Okay, deep breath. Everything would be fine. The worst that could happen was he didn't like her and she was back to square one.

Just get it over with.

Brad exited the executive suites and held the door for her.

"Bye, Krista. Have a good weekend."

"Bye."

Vesta was shutting down her computer when Krista walked up. "Oh good," Vesta said. "I'll let him know you're here." She picked up her phone. "The new receptionist is here." Then she nodded at Krista. "Go right in."

Bracing herself, Krista entered the huge corner office and saw him standing by the window, with his back to her. He wore a navy knit shirt and jeans. Reflections of the setting sun glinted off the glass of the office tower next door. He seemed to be looking out over the cityscape.

"Close the door," he said, without turning around.

Why did he want the door closed? She clicked it shut, turned back toward his desk and took a couple of steps toward it. It would be best to wait until he invited her to sit. She wished he'd hurry up and do that because her heart was racing and she needed to relax. She needed to say the right things, to come across as competent. She squared her shoulders and stood tall.

Finally, he turned, and faced her.

And her knees wobbled as weakness shot through her body. "You?"

It was Logan. The man who'd bought her at the auction. The man who had taken her to dinner. The man she'd been sleeping with that morning a week ago.

"Sit down."

She did. How embarrassing this was.

At least, it was embarrassing for her. But not for him. He didn't look embarrassed. He looked angry as he stood there, legs planted wide, glaring at her with hard, cold eyes.

He moved closer to his desk. "I don't know why you've taken this job," he said with a careful, controlled tone. "And if I'd been here when Frank interviewed you, you would not have been hired."

"I don't under—"

"Listen." He stood on the other side of the desk, staring directly at her. "So far, Frank has had only good things to say about you," Logan said. "And I haven't told him you're a hooker."

What! "A—a hooker?" She held on tight to the edge of the chair.

"Don't," he said, folding his arms.

She wanted to stand up, so she wouldn't have to be looking up at him. But she felt too shaky.

"Don't even bother, all right? I'm not firing you." He paused, studying her. "Not yet." His voice was deep and his eyes were tight. "But if you think you can drum up business here, you can forget it." He pressed his fingers on his desk with rigid hands as he leaned forward. "Do I make myself perfectly clear?"

"I—" Her throat was tight. The words couldn't get out.

The phone buzzed and she jumped. It was his

intercom. He touched the speaker button. "Sorry to interrupt, sir," Vesta said, "but—"

Vesta's voice stopped and Krista heard the office door bang open behind her. Logan stared over her head and Krista turned around.

A tall blonde woman in a business suit and high heels stepped into the office.

"Logan," she said, smiling. "I'm glad I caught you."

Logan shuffled back a step and his body tensed. "Cheryl," he said, finally. "What are you doing here?"

"We need to talk, darling."

Darling? Yeah, right. He couldn't do this anymore.

He glanced down at Krista, who somehow managed to look like she might faint. How did she do that? Was that something escorts learned to do, so you'd feel compelled to take care of them?

"That will be all," he told her. He watched as she stood up, unsteady on her feet. She was either a really good actress, or—or was she *really* trembling? Odd.

Krista stumbled out the door, looking like he'd hit her, *for Chrissake*. What was that all about? He'd simply told her she couldn't use his company to drum up business. What did she think he'd say?

Cheryl had taken Krista's chair. She hadn't even looked at Krista. "Logan?" Cheryl shook him out of his thoughts.

"I'm too tired for another argument."

She smiled at him. That pouty little smile of hers. He used to think it was sexy.

"There's nothing to argue about, darling. I haven't seen you for a whole week. I miss you." She leaned back in the chair and crossed her legs. Her dress rode up high on her thigh. "Let's forget all that nonsense—whatever it was. I've got a reservation for the Pelican's Roost."

Logan glanced at his watch. "Sorry, I'm running late." He picked up his briefcase. "I've got to get to the hospital."

"The hospital? What are you going to the hospital for?"

"One of the roughnecks was injured."

"So?" Then she changed tack. "Well, I'll come with you. We can talk on the way. And you won't be staying there long, will you?"

Logan walked toward the door. "You're not coming with me, Cheryl."

She got up and put her hand on his arm as he passed her. "All right," she said. "Then I could meet you at your place. I'll pick up takeout and bring it over. I'll have everything ready when you get home."

He shrugged away from her. "No." Taking a deep, slow breath, he held out his hand. "My key."

"What?"

"I would like the key to my condo. Please."

"Don't be silly."

"My key. Please."

"We really need to talk about the wedding."

"There is no wedding." He stepped around her and headed out of his office.

"Logan, don't be so stubborn." She grabbed hold of his arm again. "You're still upset."

He wrestled his arm away from her and continued toward the glass doors. She kept up with him, and as he approached the elevators, she took hold of his arm again. When Cheryl wanted something, she expected to get it.

Irene and Quincy waited there, Quincy with two bundles of mail in his hands. They both glanced at Cheryl and quickly looked away.

The elevator arrived. Logan stepped back and let Irene and Quincy get on first. Then he pulled away from Cheryl and stepped into the elevator. She followed him.

"Krista is back at the switchboard?" Logan asked no one in particular.

"Yes, sir," Quincy said, staring at the numbers as they flashed above the door. "But she looks really wasted."

"I told her she should shut down early," Irene said. "Since it's Friday, I mean. But she wanted to stay till five."

Chapter Ten

Krista gazed out the basement window at the bright September sunshine.

"More coffee, sweetie?"

"Thanks, Michaela," Krista answered, pushing her cup toward her friend. The cup had a slight crack on the rim. "It was nice of you to come over."

"That's what friends are for," Michaela said, as she poured.

Yesterday, the landlord had cut the grass. The old poplar still held most of its bright yellow leaves but the occasional leaf fluttered down to join the gold and yellow leaves dusting the yard. A little gray squirrel worked its way through the leaves, burrowing under them, jumping over them, playing.

"Are you sure she was his girlfriend?"

"Yes, Michaela." With elbows on the table, Krista held her head in her hands. "It was so awful. Even if I had been brave enough to explain—to *try* to explain—I couldn't. Not with her there."

"But you're sure she was his girlfriend? Not one of the admins?"

"Of course, she was his girlfriend. She walked straight into his office. He must have been expecting her. And she called him *darling*, and he called her Cheryl. She must be the same Cheryl who phoned him that morning. Oh, how did I get into this mess?"

"It's only a misunderstanding. Nothing to worry about."

"Nothing to worry about? He actually thinks I'm—a *hooker*. Can you believe that?"

Michaela laughed. "You'll talk to him on Monday. And you'll explain."

"Explain? How? As soon as I realized they were auctioning us off, I should have left."

Michaela took a sip of her coffee. "Why didn't you?"

"I don't know," Krista said, still watching the little squirrel. "I couldn't. It all happened so quickly. And it all seemed sort of . . ."

They were both quiet for a moment.

"Harmless?" Michaela asked.

Not exactly. Krista had been swept into the auction, and she'd been too much of a coward to back out. "Once I was there, it seemed harder to leave, than to go along with it."

"And it seemed harmless too, didn't it?"

"Yes. It did," Krista said. And, she had to admit—to herself at least—it had seemed exciting too. She remembered seeing Logan, standing at the back of the room. She could feel his energy, even now.

"There," Michaela said. "Nothing to worry about." She leaned back in her chair, and checked something on her Blackberry.

"Michaela. I woke up in his bed—in my underwear. And now I'm working for him."

"So?" She dropped her phone into her purse. "He was making sure your dress didn't get wrinkled."

Yes," Krista said, grimacing. "That makes so much sense. And as soon as I get that dress dry cleaned, I'm giving it back to you. You can donate it to someone else."

Michaela tilted her head and studied the ceiling. "It does make sense that he was sleeping in the bed." She pressed her index finger over her lips, tapped twice. "After all, he'd need to get some sleep and there is only one bed in the place."

Reaching for the milk, Krista stopped and turned to her friend. "Pardon?"

"What?"

"How did you know there was only one bed in the condo?"

"Did I say that?" Michaela scratched her head, thinking.

"Yes."

"You said those condos by Eau Claire, didn't you?"

"Yes . . ."

"Well—" Michaela shrugged. "They're all one bedroom units."

"Go away."

"Time to get up, Logan. You've been asleep for twelve hours."

Roger put a mug of coffee in Logan's hand. The mug felt warm and the coffee smelled good. Logan rubbed his other hand over his face and forced himself to sit up. Then he took a sip.

Better.

Roger sat in the chair across from him, wearing a ripped T-shirt and boxers, and holding a white mug with a smiley face on it. Logan wore his clothes from yesterday. His shoulder ached from sleeping on Roger's stupid couch.

"I checked with the hospital," Roger said. "The kid's doing fine. Dr. Bainbridge is hoping to pin the fracture in a couple of days. After that, Sammie will get a walking cast."

Logan had got to know Sammie since the accident. "He already hates being stuck in traction."

"I know." Roger took a long swallow of his coffee.

"He'll be all right, Logan. He's damn lucky."

Yes, he was, Logan thought, inhaling the coffee's aroma. He'd had so much sleep, he felt drugged. "Heard from Jim?"

Roger concentrated on the inside of his mug. He seemed to be studying the coffee grounds at the bottom. "You need to forget about the site for a while. Jim has everything under control."

"I know, I know. Jim's great." Logan stretched his legs out in front of the couch.

"And Logan?"

"What?"

"Cheryl's been calling."

Damn. Logan leaned back, clamping his hand over his forehead. "What did you tell her?"

"I didn't. I let the machine pick up."

"Good." Logan's hand fell to his lap, then he gulped down the rest of his coffee.

"So what's going on with you two?" Roger walked over to his fridge.

"Nothing."

Roger opened the fridge and looked inside. "That's it? You spend the night at my place because you like sleeping on my couch?"

"That's it."

"Wedding bell blues?"

"Will you shut up?"

"You never did actually propose to her?" Roger was staring in the fridge.

"No." Cheryl was the one who had proposed—proposed that it would be a good idea for them to get married. And, at the time, he'd thought *maybe*. Maybe at some future time. When it felt right. But it had never felt right.

Roger studied the insides of the fridge for another

moment. "We need to go out for some breakfast."

"I need a shower first." Logan rubbed a hand over his chin.

"Maybe we could order out for more pizza?" Roger let the fridge door close and stepped away from it.

"I talked to Pro yesterday," Logan said, still sitting on the couch. He rolled his shoulders, trying to loosen the kinks. Maybe he'd go over to the Y. He could do a workout and then shower there.

"About the lodge?" Roger was standing in the middle of the room now, surveying the world outside the window.

"Yeah," Logan answered. "He's ready to send the money in for the mortgage. And he's got the plans. Or he'll have them first thing next week."

Roger frowned.

"What?"

"Nothing," Roger said. "I wanted to get the last check cleared. But it doesn't matter. It'll get cashed sooner or later."

Logan set his empty mug on the floor. "Roger?"

"Yeah?"

"Where'd you get those hookers?"

"Escorts, Logan. Escorts," Roger said, as he gazed out the window. A gust of wind sent a spray of leaves scattering and whirling into the sky.

"Okay, escorts. Where did you get them?"

"Online."

"Online?"

"Yeah, I looked them up on the net, then I phoned several, until I found twenty."

"Which agencies?"

"Agencies?" Roger turned to him.

"Escort agencies."

Eyes narrowed, Roger pressed his fingers along his forehead. "Damn, Logan. It's really over with Cheryl, isn't it? But hey, if you need a date that bad, ask Jenny Reginald."

"Jenny?"

"Yes. Jenny. Your new landman? Logan, don't you notice anything?"

"Which agencies?"

"Ask Jenny out. She—"

"I'm not asking Jenny out. Or anyone I work with. Tell me—"

"My sister has a friend who—"

"*Goddammit*, Roger. I'm not looking for a date!" Logan got off the couch and paced to the window.

"Then, what are you looking for?"

Logan ran his hands through his hair. This was nothing to worry about. This was a simple matter he could deal with. "You know the escort I bought at the auction?"

Roger's face lit up. "Krista? Yeah, sure. She was nice."

"She's working for us."

Roger blinked and his mouth dropped open. "Uh . . . She is?"

"Frank hired her. She's our new receptionist."

"He did?" Roger looked down, figuring it out. "What happened to—"

"Beatrice is working at her husband's store."

"Oh." Suddenly, Roger had a silly smile on his face. He plopped back in his chair.

Couldn't he see the problem? "I want to know where you got her so I can do a background check."

Roger registered a blank. "Why?" He stuck at finger in one of the holes of his T-shirt, tugging on it.

"So I can find out if she's still working as an escort."

Roger's mind seemed to be somewhere else. Then he scratched his head and looked at Logan. "Why would she be working as an escort if she's got a legitimate job?"

"Because, Roger, you thick-headed imbecile, she's only

at Peregrine because she's looking for business, or—and this is bad—she's targeting me. She wants to milk me for more money."

Zoning out, Roger fiddled with a loose thread on his T-shirt. After a minute, he said, "No. Krista wouldn't do that."

"How would you know?"

"Gut feeling." He shrugged. "She wouldn't, that's all. Actually, I don't think she's been an escort for very long."

Logan closed his eyes, and counted. When he got to ten, he opened his eyes and examined the hardwood grain on the living room floor. Was he jumping to illogical conclusions? Was this mental fatigue? If he was paranoid, how would he know?

Didn't matter. "What if she's using our reception job as a front?"

"A front?" Roger laughed. "Come on, Logan. We're not talking the drug trade."

"I don't want her moonlighting from my office."

Pulling at the loose thread, Roger made the hole bigger. "Have you told anyone?"

"What?"

"That you met her at the auction?"

"You mean, that she's a hooker?"

"Escort, Logan—"

"No. Only you. And I want to know if she still—"

"There's no way of knowing. She was probably using a different name with the agency anyway. Is her name Krista now?"

"Yes." *Krista MacKenzie.* That's what she'd told him. He could check Frank's records. If she had a different last name now, then MacKenzie would be what she was called at the agency.

Roger stood up. "Logan?"

"What?"

"Let's get some breakfast."

. . . . .

The elevator doors dinged open and Logan stepped into the hallway. Monday morning, two minutes past eight, and he could hear Krista talking to Irene in the reception area. Beatrice had always come in at eight-thirty, so why was Krista here already? Now, she was laughing at something Irene had said.

Standing in the hallway, he hesitated. On the wall across from the elevators, the brass letters spelled out Peregrine Oil & Gas. The huge brass peregrine falcon perched at the upper right of the name, with wings outspread, as if it were prepared for flight. The falcon had been Roger's idea and Logan had gone along with it.

Like he'd gone along with the auction. Although, Logan had to admit, the auction had been successful. The only unsettling thing that had happened was that his escort had ended up in his bed.

Eyes closed, he rubbed the middle of his forehead and wondered for the hundredth time if she could have known who he was when she took this job. And, once again, the answer was no. She'd had no idea who he was, let alone that he owned this company. Her being here was a wild coincidence. It had to be.

Maybe this really was a legitimate job for her? That would be good. Being an escort was dangerous. She *needed* a legitimate job. But, that little voice persisted, what if she was still working nights?

He shrugged. *Dammit.* It wasn't any of his business what she did with her life. Turning right, he walked toward the executive suites, and stopped at the glass doors.

No. What she did with her life *was* his business because this was *his* company and he wasn't going to have his receptionist soliciting clients here. No way. He pushed open the glass doors.

"Good morning, Mr. Nicholas," Vesta said, as he walked past her desk.

"Morning."

Vesta handed him a message slip. "Cheryl called."

Logan braced, and looked down at the note.

Lunch at noon. Will meet you at your office.

"She's coming here?"

"That's what she said, sir."

Logan crumpled the note in his fist.

But wait. A sense of calm descended over him. This could be an opportunity. "Get me the personnel file on the new receptionist."

"Yes, sir."

"When do you get off for lunch, Krista?" Brad Diamond leaned on the reception desk, toying with the stapler and making small talk. He'd been doing that for the past fifteen minutes.

"Noon. Irene takes over at noon." Krista sliced open another envelope.

"Would you like to go out for lunch?" he asked.

"Can't. Have to study."

He carefully placed the stapler back on the desk. "I could help you study."

Krista set down the letter opener, directed a call, and then turned her attention to Brad. "Are you asking me out? On a date?"

Still leaning on the desk, he said, "I'm trying. How am I doing?"

"Thanks." Krista laughed. "But I've got a lot happening right now. No time for relationships."

Brad was fun, and he was good-looking. He even

bordered on interesting, but she wasn't ready for any more entanglements. In fact, she wasn't quite over her last entanglement because Paul had phoned Michaela again last night.

"I could help you with your university course." Brad picked up the paper clip holder and poked his finger inside, spinning the paper clips.

"I know." Krista nodded. "Everyone should be lucky enough to have a VP of Finance to help them with their Finance 301."

He set the paper clip holder next to the stapler. "Is that a yes?"

"That's a no, on the date. But if I run into a problem with my case study, I'll keep you in mind, okay?"

He grinned at her and stood up straight. Then he dropped his business card on her desk. "I do house calls." He winked and left the reception area to go back to his office.

Krista picked up the business card. An important-looking card, cream-colored with blue and gray embossed lettering. Peregrine Oil & Gas in bold letters stretched across the middle. The logo, the falcon with wings outspread, was in the top right corner. And at the bottom, it said Brad Diamond, then on the next line, VP Finance. Then the address, and the phone and fax numbers, and his email. At the very bottom, he'd written his cell phone number.

Someday, she'd have an impressive little piece of paper like this with her name on it. Someday she would be . . . valuable, like her sisters. She tossed the card in the wastebasket.

. . . . .

Krista directed the last call, quickly gathered a stack of mail and was about to run it through the postage meter when she saw Vesta's intercom flash. Vesta didn't usually call the switchboard.

Krista set down the mail, flexed her fingers and then tapped the button.

"Switchboard."

"Mr. Nicholas would like to see you in his office."

Not again. "When?"

"Soon as Irene relieves you for lunch," Vesta said. "Is that all right?"

"Of course," Krista answered.

Of course, it was all right. It wasn't like she had a choice. And anyway, she'd promised Michaela she'd clear up this escort misunderstanding, and she would do it today. She hadn't known quite how but now, lucky her, here was an opportunity.

But, *oh dear*, why did he want to see her again?

Pressing her fingernails into her palms, she centered herself. What to do next?

The chief drilling engineer was supposed to return sometime today. She'd already inputted the well reports for him. Now, she could finish opening and sorting the mail.

By the time Irene showed up at noon, that was done.

Irene took her place at the switchboard. "I heard Brad asked you out."

Krista touched her fingers to her lips. What a rumor mill this place was. "Yes, he did," she said. "And I declined."

"How come?"

"I'm too busy with—"

"I know, I know. But you can't study all the time, Krista. Live a little."

An incoming call lit up the switchboard and distracted Irene. Krista slipped into the hallway and paused by the bank of elevators to collect her thoughts.

She'd say she'd misunderstood Roger. She'd say that

Roger had made the auction sound like a business meeting. Yes. That's what she'd say, and it was true. She'd say she was new in town, and she'd been expecting a business meeting, and this guy named Roger showed up and—

The elevator doors slid open, and Krista felt her jaw drop as Roger himself stepped out. He wore a dark green polo shirt and khaki-colored slacks. Even without the tux, he was an attractive, impressive-looking man.

"Hi, Krista." He smiled, like they were old friends.

"You work here too?"

"Roger Claymore," he said, holding out his hand. "I'm the chief drilling engineer."

Of course he was. Could this get any weirder?

She held out her own hand and Roger shook it, a solid warm handshake. Then he turned and walked into the reception area, like it wasn't unusual at all for him to meet her here.

He and Logan must have already talked about her. But what had they talked about? She wanted to hide.

Closing her eyes for a second, she swallowed, feeling an ache in the back of her throat. When she opened her eyes, she was staring at the brass falcon—its strong talons wrapped around the branch, its wings outspread ready for flight, its sharp eyes in search of prey.

She took five breaths and walked toward the glass doors of the executive suites.

If he was going to fire her, she might as well get it over with.

"Go right in," Vesta said. "He's expecting you."

With hands trembling, she straightened her shoulders and approached his office. One deep breath, and she knocked lightly, then opened the door and stepped inside.

Logan was working at his desk.

She should probably start thinking of him as Mr. Nicholas. Her employer. Although, he might not be her employer for long.

She closed the door. "You wanted to see me?"

He was tapping numbers into a calculator and making notes on an Excel spreadsheet. "Yes," he said. "Sit down."

She didn't, but she took a few steps closer to his desk. "I need to explain." She held her hands tightly together. "About the auction. I'm not a hooker."

"I know," he said, his voice relaxed. "You're an escort. You can sit down."

"I'm not an escort either." The words rushed out.

Logan's chest rose, and fell. "Don't lie to me, Krista MacKenzie. Tell me you're done with that job and this is the only place you're working."

He sounded so sure of who she was that, right at this moment, she wasn't sure herself. "I—it—this *is* the only place I'm working." Her nervousness disappeared. "And you don't understand—"

Logan glanced at his watch, dropped his pen on the desk and stood up. "But," he said, "you've got one more assignment."

She glanced at his desk, at the spreadsheet and the calculator, and then she looked back at him. "I do?"

He walked around the desk and stopped in front of her.

He was her boss. And he had a completely wrong impression of her.

She looked up at him, felt her eyes widen, heard her heart pounding. He was so tall, his shoulders broad and solid and strong. The expensive cut of his suit emphasized that strength.

She blinked, and took a step back. She had to try again. "I'm not—"

"One more assignment," he repeated, moving closer, leaning toward her.

"What are you talking about?"

His eyes sparkled, and his lips slowly curved up. A playful grin. "Kiss me," he said.

"What?" Her skin tingled and her belly fluttered.

He touched her chin with one finger, and then he slowly drew his thumb across her lower lip.

Her heart raced and her knees wobbled. He was barely touching her and she was frozen, mesmerized by his dark eyes. She felt him reach his other hand behind her, touching the small of her back, gently pulling her toward him.

She touched his chest with both hands, spread her fingers, felt the smooth fabric of his shirt. She could have pushed away but something held her there, captive. She had no will to resist.

Slowly, he bent his head, and lightly kissed her lips. So softly she might have imagined the kiss.

What was happening? Gone was the angry man who had confronted her the last time she was here. Now he was the person she'd had dinner with at the Pelican's Roost. The charming, attentive man who had sat across from her and listened to her.

It didn't make any sense. As she watched his deep brown eyes, they grew darker. She heard him catch his breath, and he kissed her again, this time with more pressure. And now she was responding, melting into him, falling into him. He tightened his arms around her as she clutched the front of his shirt.

Her mind shut down. The world was gone and she was lost in another universe, dizzy and lightheaded. And then, from a distance, a sound that didn't belong there. A buzzing sound, like a trapped bee.

He held her even tighter, in an embrace that was so strong and so safe, a haven she hadn't known she was searching for. Electricity sparked between them, melding them together. And the bee whirred around them, spinning them off kilter, buzzing louder, and—

Was that his intercom?

She thought she heard a door open. She felt Logan stiffen for an instant, but he didn't stop kissing her.

And then the door slammed—loudly. Smashing the magic.

"I . . . what was . . ." She blinked, he let her go, and she stumbled away from him.

He calmly sat on the edge of his desk, his hands resting easily on his thighs. And he smiled at her, like nothing at all had happened between them.

She ran her hands through her hair. "What was that all about?"

"That was Cheryl," he said, with an unfocused smile.

Cheryl? Krista felt a rush of adrenaline and her vision clouded. "Your girlfriend? You're playing some game with your girlfriend?"

"She's not—"

Krista punched his chest, and then clutched her hand. She hadn't hurt him in the least. He sat there, with a blank look. "You ass." She spun around.

He caught her wrist and stopped her. "Hey! Where are you going?"

"Don't touch me!" She glared at him.

He let go of her wrist and held up his hands. "Don't worry," he said, stepping back. "I'll pay for the kiss if that's the problem."

"Pay? You—you—"

"Maybe I should have asked first?" He was laughing at her.

"Maybe? You arrogant, condescending, pompous jerk. You *used* me."

And she'd thought—

Oh, how could she be so stupid? First Paul, and now this! What was *wrong* with her!

She edged away from him. Wanting to throw something, she backed toward the door. "Maybe?" she repeated, impressed with how calm her voice sounded. "Maybe you can have your damn job!"

Then, feeling like her heart was shrinking, and not knowing what else to do, she turned and fled.

Chapter Eleven

Surprised by Krista's reaction, Logan followed her out of his office. He would have caught up with her, but for Cheryl, who was waiting for him.

She stood at attention beside Vesta's desk, looking like the Cheshire Cat. Looking like she'd caught him good this time.

"You're a *sonovabitch*, you know that?"

"Yes, I do." He held out his hand. "Now, you've got a key to my condo?"

She only hesitated a moment, and then she reached in her purse and took out the key. She had it on its own keyring, with a little silver heart attached.

"Cute," he said, looking at the heart. He started to remove the key.

"You can keep it," she sneered. Spinning around, she strolled toward the glass doors. At the entrance, she looked over her shoulder. "It's a cheap bauble," she said. "Like your new girlfriend." Then she stalked out of the office.

Later that night, back at his condo, Logan sat across from the fireplace, watching the flames flicker across the grate. It had been so easy, getting Cheryl to return his key. He should feel good about that, but he didn't. He rubbed his hands over his eyes and looked at the fire again.

"Sammie didn't want the private room."

"What?" Logan watched Roger plop down on the couch on the other side of the coffee table.

"Sammie didn't want the private room," Roger repeated. He took a drink of the beer he was holding and set the bottle on the coffee table on top of a magazine. "He likes talking to everybody in the ward room."

Logan sighed. They'd decided against the surgery for the time being. The compound fracture needed more time to heal, so the kid was stuck in traction.

"Since he's going to be in the hospital for a while, he was wondering if we'd pay for him to do some online courses. He wants to finish his high school."

Good idea. Sammie was a bright kid. He could do a lot more with his life than be a roughneck. "Buy him a laptop and get him signed up," Logan said. "And hire him a tutor."

"A pretty one?"

"Whatever."

Roger leaned back on the couch. "Sure you don't want a beer?"

"I'm fine."

"You don't look fine." Roger picked up his beer again.

"Well, I am."

"I heard you broke up with Cheryl today. Officially." Roger glugged some of his beer.

Naturally Roger would have heard. The whole office would have heard. "Who told you?"

"The grapevine." Roger laughed.

The grapevine. He doubted Vesta would have said anything, but Quincy had been there. Or, it could also have been Frank. It didn't matter.

Roger pushed the Campbell River book to one side and put his feet up on the coffee table. "So, how'd she take it?"

"What do you mean?"

"I mean you've tried to break up with Cheryl before. Even before she was talking wedding bells." Roger picked up Outdoor Magazine.

"I know." And those times had not worked. Having Cheryl see him with another woman was the only way.

Roger flipped through the magazine, absently looking at the pictures. "I remember the last time you broke up with her. I almost had you agreeing to a blind date with my sister's friend."

Logan closed his eyes and sighed. "Your sister is a menace."

Roger tossed the magazine back on the table. "She means well."

"So why doesn't she set *you* up?"

Roger grinned and took another drink. "Because she's busy with you."

Cheryl's poetry book was on the table. *Collected Poems of Love and Laughter by Maggie Therese.* Logan picked up the book and brushed his hands over the red leather cover. He'd have to return it.

She'd told him he needed to think about wedding vows. She'd actually thought he'd read this stuff. Hell, she'd even bookmarked a page with a folded piece of pale blue paper. He flipped the book open, picked up the bookmark and read the beginning words on the page.

> *Elizabeth Barrett Browning — How do I love thee? Let me count the ways.*

Right. Let me count the ways that was not going to happen. Cheryl was one tough woman. He huffed out a breath. At least that was over. Putting the paper back in place, he flipped the book shut and tossed it on the table.

"Cheryl's book?"

Logan glanced over at him. "How can you tell?"

"Leather cover. You're a paperback guy."

Logan didn't say anything. Roger knew him too well.

"So, you'll be seeing her to give it back?"

"I'll mail it."

Roger considered. "That's good, Logan. Maybe it will take."

"Take?"

"Maybe your break-up will last this time." Roger drained the rest of his beer and headed toward the kitchen with the empty. "I'm calling it a night."

When he came back into the living room, Logan was still watching the fire.

"You know, for someone who just got out of a bad relationship, you don't look so happy."

"It's not Cheryl," Logan sighed. "I'm glad that's over. It's—work—on my mind."

"All right," Roger said, sounding unconvinced. "I'll see you tomorrow."

Logan followed his friend to the door, locked it and returned to his chair in front of the fire. This was where Krista had fallen asleep that night.

He picked up the navy blue blanket from the other couch and sat down with it, hugging it in his lap. And he thought about how he'd kissed her.

It had seemed like a good idea, at the time. He'd known Cheryl would come barging in, seconds after Vesta buzzed him. Cheryl never waited to be invited in. Why not let her find him kissing another woman? That would make her realize it was over, and it had worked. For Cheryl.

But Krista had seemed shaken. And she'd said he could have his damn job. But she'd been there after lunch. He'd heard her answering the phone. He'd been afraid to go into the reception area to see her.

Maybe she was simply finishing off the day. Frank hadn't said anything.

Logan let his head drop back and pulled the blanket close. If she quit, Frank would tell him in the morning. And Frank wouldn't be happy. Not after he'd finally found them a decent receptionist.

But, it didn't make any sense. Why was she so upset?

Logan leaned forward again and squeezed the blanket. She was an escort, *for Chrissake*. And he said he'd pay her for the kiss.

Although, somehow that didn't feel right either.

Rubbing his thumb over his lips, he remembered how good she'd tasted. Really good. He steepled his fingers and looked at the fire. It didn't matter. She'd accepted five hundred dollars to go for dinner and a drink. How much was he supposed to pay for a kiss?

"Don't cry, sweetie. It'll be all right."

"But Michaela, I was such a fool. I thought he was kissing *me*. And it was all an act. He was such a jerk."

"Yes, sweetie, a first class jerk."

Krista blew her nose and rubbed her hands over her eyes. She must look terrible.

Michaela sat on the chair across from her, nibbling on popcorn and looking . . . calm.

"You don't seem upset about this?"

"I'm not. I'm proud of you. You went right back in there and kept working. You weren't letting him make you lose your job."

"I couldn't just quit," Krista sniffled. "Not at noon on a Monday. It would look terrible on my record."

"Girl Friday would have understood," Michaela said. "When the boss kisses the receptionist, that's sexual harassment, you know."

Krista laughed to herself, and felt warmth spill over her body as she remembered that kiss. "It wasn't sexual harassment, Michaela. I could have left. But I didn't."

Michaela didn't say anything for a few minutes. "You like him, don't you?"

What? "No! No, I do not. It was a fantasy. Temporary insanity. I am such a poor judge of character."

He came in at seven-thirty, the first one to arrive. After unlocking the executive office doors, he crossed to Vesta's desk, and sat there. This way, he could see Krista, in case she came in early again. Twenty minutes later, he heard the elevator chimes and watched as Tania got off.

Theoretically, Krista was supposed to get here at eight-thirty. But Frank had said she'd been coming in early, to organize things.

It was obvious that someone had been organizing things. The whole reception area looked different. No more magazines spilling off the coffee table. No more half-filled coffee cups littering the reception desk. And the backroom? The supply room? Everything was ordered, labeled, accounted for. It was like someone had set up Inventory Control. She'd done all that in a little over a week. So, maybe she wasn't coming in early anymore.

If she was coming in at all.

Vesta arrived exactly at eight o'clock and Logan disappeared into his office. He looked at the Gavinson reports and tried to concentrate, but he couldn't. The numbers jumbled in his brain and the words swam over the page, meaningless.

Frank would come in at any moment and tell him they'd lost the best receptionist they'd ever had. Logan dropped the report back on the desk.

He could always apologize to her . . .

No. He shrugged. He'd never do that. He didn't apologize to anybody. It would only make him vulnerable to her. She'd use it against him some other time. And besides, what would he say? "I'm sorry I kissed you." He couldn't say that.

Because he wasn't sorry. He was glad he'd kissed her. He'd liked kissing her. He'd liked it a lot. And if he started talking like that—

His buzzer sounded. Vesta, on the intercom. She was going to tell him Frank wanted to talk to him. And naturally, Frank was going to blame Logan for what had happened. He touched the intercom button.

"Krista would like to see you," Vesta announced.

Krista? For a split second, he stopped breathing. "Send her in."

She appeared at the door, hesitated a moment and then closed the door behind her. She looked as beautiful as ever, with her rich brown hair all around her shoulders and her face glowing.

But, now that he thought about it, her clothes didn't suit an escort— not one who made five hundred dollars on a drink and dinner. She was wearing a plain beige skirt and a brown plaid blouse. And no jewelry, none at all.

It didn't matter. She could be wearing rags and she'd still look gorgeous.

"You wanted to see me?" he said, getting to his feet.

"Yes." She approached and stood across from him, touching her fingers to the edge of the desk.

He waited for her to speak. He could feel his heart pounding, thudding in his chest, and he realized he was fisting his hands.

"I'm not quitting," she said, looking right at him. "At least, not yet," she added, quickly. "But if you ever touch me again, I will quit." Then she paused, for maybe two seconds, her eyes directly on his. "Do I make myself perfectly clear?"

"Yes," he said. "You do."

"Fine." She turned around and left his office, pulling the door closed behind her.

Blowing out a breath, he dropped down in his chair, let his head fall back, and smiled.

Later that morning, Junior Landman Jenny stood at the reception desk, flipping through the pages of Krista's finance textbook. Jenny was supposed to be having a coffee break, but mostly she was flirting with Brad.

"How come you're getting a Commerce degree?" Jenny asked.

"Because I've always wanted to finish university."

"Why Commerce?" Brad asked, cradling his coffee mug.

Krista pulled out another bundle of letters. "It's interesting. I like marketing and human resources. And even finance. I'm not sure where I'll specialize but I don't have to decide until fourth year."

The switchboard lit up. She directed three calls and then sliced open an envelope. If she didn't keep at it, she'd still be sorting mail after lunch.

"But that's four years of university," Jenny said. "And you're doing it part-time. It will take forever."

It *had* taken forever, to get as far as she had. "I've already done two years," Krista said.

One year plus three courses at U of T. And then in Saskatoon, she'd slowly completed the last seven courses she needed to finish second year.

Jenny, on the other hand, had taken a few evening courses, and learned most of her work on the job. And that was how she'd graduated to a Landman position.

"If you don't like being a receptionist, you could be an office manager. Right now," Jenny said. "You manage this place great."

"I answer the phone and order supplies. Frank manages this place."

"But you could," Jenny insisted. "I know you could. Why are you going to all the trouble of getting a degree?"

"Because I need the piece of paper that says I can do the job."

If she hadn't met Paul, one year ago, she would be a lot closer to having that piece of paper. She would be in her final year right now.

Instead, she'd let Paul talk her into supporting him while he went to med school. The plan was he would graduate first, and then he would support her while she got her degree.

That plan had failed. Magnificently.

"The piece of paper isn't so important," Brad commented. He flipped open the top of the stapler. He seemed to be counting the staples inside.

"And everybody likes talking to you," Jenny continued, planning Krista's career path.

"She *is* fun to talk to." Brad closed the lid of the stapler. Now he was firing blanks.

Krista took the stapler out of his hands and put it away. The RSVPs for Frank's invitations were already coming in. That would make him happy.

"Would you like me to get you a coffee, Krista?" Brad asked.

"No, thanks." She directed another call. Then she looked up at Brad and Jenny. "Okay. Get back to work. I've got to get this mail done."

"Yes, ma'am." Brad saluted her.

Jenny giggled, and they both left.

What a morning, Krista thought. She'd stood up to Logan. Taking a slow, deep breath, she savored the feeling.

Once again, she replayed what had happened. What he'd said. How he'd looked. He'd actually looked like he was sorry. Was that possible?

It didn't matter. She'd laid the ground rules for their relationship.

A quiet chuckle formed in the back of her throat. *Relationship?* A man she accidentally meets, accidentally sleeps with and accidentally ends up working for. Not exactly a relationship, but it didn't make any difference. The way this office was set up, chances were she'd rarely see him.

And she didn't see him for the rest of the day. Although, when she left at five, she noticed the lights were still on in the executive offices.

The next day, Wednesday, Krista got to work at exactly half past eight, which was when she was supposed to start. The workroom was organized, so no need to come in earlier. She'd spent the extra time at home, working on her case study for tonight's class, and then she'd caught the later bus. On the way, her phone had chirped with a message from her mother.

> *Delaney says you're taking another course for your degree. Finance? Good for you. Just remember, not everyone is good at math, dear. It's okay if it doesn't work out.*
>
> *love, Mom XOX*

So, her mother had her doubts. And why not? Half the time, Krista herself didn't believe she could pass this stuff. She texted back:

> *Course is going well. Midterms soon. I'll let you know. Love to you and Dad.*

Krista pushed open the glass doors and entered the reception area. "Morning, Irene."

Irene nodded to her as she dealt with a caller. Then she took off her headset and set it by the switchboard. "I think this is from Brad," Irene said, handing Krista a small brown paper package.

Krista looked at the brown paper, taped closed, with her name printed in a scrawl on the top. *Oh dear.* Brad was sending her gifts? She thought she'd discouraged him. She'd have to nip this in the bud.

"Well," Irene said, "Aren't you going to open it?" She was pressing her hands together, excited.

Krista felt her shoulders slump. If she didn't open it now, she'd feed the gossip mill, making this into something it wasn't. She had to look unconcerned. Casual. She broke the tape's seal and opened the package.

"It's not from Brad," she said, feeling relieved. And feeling something else. Happy?

"What is it?"

Krista lifted out the two dark glittering combs. Michaela's crystal combs.

"Wow. Those are beautiful," Irene sighed. "So if they're not from Brad . . ."

"They're from my friend Michaela. She's lending them to me."

"Oh." Irene was disappointed. "I was sure it was Brad."

Krista got off the elevator. It was Thursday morning, three minutes before seven. She had all her books with her and the new assignment she'd received last night. She wasn't even sure if the key Frank had given her would work on the executive area's doors. Maybe it only worked on the reception side.

Feeling like she was not supposed to be doing this, she

inserted the heavy brass key into the lock. It nested securely, and it turned easily, sending the tumblers home.

Thank goodness. And thank goodness no one was here yet.

Since she'd started working at Peregrine, the earliest anyone had come in was seven-thirty. But would his office door be unlocked?

She padded silently across the plush carpeting. She didn't think anyone locked the individual offices. And if it was locked, she'd have to think of a different way. But—

No. His door wasn't locked. She set her purse and her book bag by the door, and took the package out of the bag.

Hugging the package to her chest, she cautiously entered his office. His desk was mostly clear. Nothing on it except his computer monitor, a plain blue mouse pad, the phone and a dark blue ceramic mug full of pens, and pencils, and markers. The keyboard slid under his desk on its own tray. There was no desk pad. Just the wood.

The warm brown wood of his desk glowed as the morning sun poured in through the un-curtained windows. Her eyes were drawn to the view outside. The glass towers of the office buildings looked like ships in a sea of early morning light.

She stood in front of the credenza that was behind his desk, standing close to the window, watching. And then she had to look away because it was too bright.

She forced her gaze back to the interior of his office. Photos of drilling sites lined the walls. And there were several framed certificates. A degree from the University of Calgary, a commendation from the Petroleum Club. Something from the Kiwanis Club? Did he volunteer his time?

No. He probably gave them money. She started to read the first certificate and then stopped. She had to get out of here. The last thing she needed was to be caught in his office.

She placed the brown paper package on the center of his desk and left, pulling the door closed behind her. Then she picked up her book bag and her purse and tiptoed to the main door.

Should she lock the main door?

Yes. Because Vesta would be in before he was. And Vesta would wonder why the door was unlocked.

Removing the key, Krista glanced up at the peregrine falcon. It looked as mean as ever. She didn't like that bird.

Quickly, she crossed the hall, unlocked the reception area doors and propped them open like they did. Then she hurried down the hall to Irene's desk. She could work on her case study until eight-thirty.

Pulling out the heavy text, she took a deep, satisfied breath.

She'd done it. She'd returned his jogging jacket and his flip-flops. Now she had nothing of his and he had nothing of hers.

Well, except for the other sandal.

The next morning, Friday, Logan stepped off the elevator and paused before turning to the right. It was eight-thirty-five. Krista should be at the switchboard by now. He listened for her voice.

And he could hear her. Laughing with a caller, commiserating like they were old friends.

"Logan? How come you're late?"

Roger had come out of reception, carrying a stack of files in one hand and a cup of coffee in the other.

"I thought," Roger said, pausing for emphasis, "we were supposed to go over details before Lars got here?"

"Sorry. I slept in."

He hadn't slept in. He'd been up since six, working at home. He'd wanted to show up after eight-thirty, so he could walk into the reception area. So he could thank her for returning his jogging jacket. And, the flip-flops. Though he couldn't care less about either the jacket or the flip-flops. But he needed an excuse to talk to her. He hadn't talked to her since Tuesday and he wanted to talk to her.

"Logan?"

"What?"

"Why are we standing here?"

Poor Roger. He had no idea what was going on. But then, Logan had no idea himself. This was a stretch. He was standing in the hall, hoping to hear her voice.

"Right," Logan said, collecting his thoughts. He turned toward the executive suites and they walked together toward his office.

"Mr. Rodermond's plane has landed and Mr. Diamond met him at the airport." Vesta handed him a stack of messages. "Mr. Rodermond will get settled at the Palliser and then he'll be meeting you here about two this afternoon."

"Thank you, Vesta," Logan said, as he continued to his office.

"Oh, and Mr. Nicholas?"

Logan paused. There was something about the way she was saying that.

"Mr. Keystone needs to see you."

"What's Frank want?"

"Come on, Logan." Roger went ahead of him into the office. "We've got to get this done. Frank can wait."

Logan watched Vesta.

"He said it was important, sir."

It might be about Krista. "Roger, you get started. I'll be right there."

Logan set his briefcase and the stack of messages on Vesta's desk and headed to Frank's office.

Krista finally cleared the switchboard. It was unusually busy for a Friday afternoon, her second Friday at Peregrine. Two weeks down, four to go. In four more weeks, she'd have her evaluation from Frank, and from Girl Friday. If only she could keep this job.

She hadn't seen Logan—Mr. Nicholas—since Tuesday, when she'd talked to him. Well, except for that one time, at her lunch break, yesterday.

He'd been standing by the elevators. As soon as she'd seen him, she'd turned around and headed back to the reception desk. Irene had been answering a call so she hadn't noticed. Krista waited and pretended to look for something in her purse. She didn't go back into the hall until she heard the elevator ding, heard the elevator doors close.

Maybe she should not have run, but she didn't know how to handle this.

If she'd stayed and rode down the elevator with him, he might have acknowledged that he'd received her package. Although, she hadn't expected him to say anything. After all, she hadn't approached him to say anything about the combs.

Or her shoe. The gold sandal. It must still be at his place. Somewhere. Did he even know it was there? It was probably stuck under the coffee table or one of the couches. Eventually his maid would find it. But would he even remember where it had come from?

At any rate, she had run. Again. Like after her second year at U of T, when she had done so poorly. Her parents and her sisters had rallied around her, offering career advice and tutors, and generally treating her like the baby of the family. She felt lost, and worthless. And so, against everyone's wishes, she had moved to Saskatoon to continue university there.

When harsh reality set in, she discovered she could barely afford to support herself, let alone study. And her pride would not let her ask for help.

The switchboard lit up again, and Krista heard the elevator chime. She directed the latest call and watched as a confident-looking gentleman, late forties or early fifties, entered the reception area. He was wearing a taupe-colored trench coat and carrying a briefcase. He approached her desk, set down his business card, and said, "Lars Rodermond," with a slight accent.

Lars Rodermond. Bergren Fisk Exploration.
A Norwegian address.

It was the CEO Vesta had said would be talking to Logan about a joint venture. "Please have a seat, Mr. Rodermond. I'll let Mr. Nicholas know you're here."

Krista pressed the intercom switch to connect her with Vesta and passed on the news. Vesta would be over in a moment to collect their important visitor.

Except, it was Logan who came across. He was wearing a dark navy suit, a crisp white shirt, and a blue tie with gold triangles in it. He glanced at Krista, nodded his head slightly, and then turned his attention to Mr. Rodermond. The two men shook hands, and started talking as they left the reception area. Logan didn't look at her again.

She told herself she didn't care.

Chapter Twelve

Taking a break from the meeting, Logan waited outside the door of the boardroom and checked the messages Vesta had given him.

Roger was returning from his office, another load of files in his hands. You'd think the guy might have worn a suit today, but Roger hated suits. "Guess what?"

"What?" Logan said, absently, as he scanned his messages. *Damn.* Cheryl had phoned again. *What was wrong with her?*

"Lars is talking to Jenny."

"Jenny?"

"Yes, your new Landman—"

"Cut the crap, Roger. Why is he talking to Jenny?"

"Not about the company. Social chit chat. I think he's hitting on her."

Seriously? Lars Rodermond wore a wedding band. Of course, that might not mean anything to Lars, and it shouldn't matter to Logan. All that mattered was the guy had a lot of expertise, and a lot of capital.

Brad interrupted them. "I've got the last of the quotes," he said, tapping a set of sheets together. "And yes, Tripoli's Vice President of Exploration can make it for dinner tonight."

"Good," Logan said. Tripoli would impress Rodermond.

Brad scooted back into the boardroom, headed over to the whiteboard and started erasing it, getting ready for another batch of numbers.

Roger appeared relaxed and confident, as they waited outside the door. "Everything on track for next Friday?"

Right. That. Logan pressed his shoulders back, trying to ease out the strain. They needed to think about the joint venture reception. The big party that would celebrate the completion of this setup.

"Logan?" Roger frowned at him. "The joint venture reception? Next Friday? Everything *is* on track?"

"Hopefully," Logan said. It was Frank's job, but Vesta would have to take over.

"What do you mean, hopefully?" Roger shifted his files to one hand. "Wait a minute. What did Frank want to see you about?"

"The joint venture reception."

Roger wrinkled his brow. "What's wrong?"

"Nothing. Not yet," Logan told him. "Frank has to leave town. His mother's been taken to hospital."

Roger shuffled back a step. "Is it serious?"

"Don't know yet."

"Okay. Let's hope it's not." He looked down at the floor, thought a moment. "But Vesta should be able to manage?"

"Not by herself." Vesta could handle a lot, but not everything.

Roger blew out a sigh. Now he was gripping the files in both hands. "We could ask Jenny to help out."

"No. Not Jenny." Logan rubbed the back of his neck, drew in a breath. "Frank suggested Krista."

"Krista," Roger said, a slow smile forming. "Yeah."

"What do you mean, yeah?"

"I mean, she's organized. She's friendly." Roger stared at a spot on the open boardroom door. "Everybody likes her." He shrugged, then looked down at his stack of files. "She's a natural at PR." A short pause. "Yeah," he repeated. "Krista." Then he squeezed the files together, tapped the air with them and returned to the boardroom table.

As if it was a done deal that Krista would be involved in the reception. That was so reasonable. An *escort* was going to be a PR person for them. *Terrific.*

Logan kept his post by the boardroom, watching the glass doors that led to the outer hall. Lars Rodermond would be back in a minute.

Vesta brought a fresh carafe of coffee. She moved past him into the boardroom, set the carafe down and came out again. "It looks like this is going to run overtime, sir."

"Yes. It will," Logan answered, without thinking. "You'll be staying?" Vesta always stayed.

"I'm sorry. My son's team will be leaving for—"

"Right." Logan remembered. *Damn.* "You told me. But—"

"I can't."

Logan felt his jaw tighten. If it had been anyone but Vesta, he'd have blown a fuse right about now.

"I can ask Krista to stay," Vesta offered.

Logan closed his eyes for a beat. "Do that."

Vesta hurried into the reception area, her coat on her arm, her purse over her shoulder, a thick manila folder in her hands.

"Krista, tell me you know PowerPoint."

"I do."

"Excel?"

"Yes."

"I thought you would." Vesta came around the

reception desk. "I need you to sign this confidentiality agreement."

"I don't know if—"

"Listen. I've got to hurry. I need you to take over for me." She glanced at her watch. "Sign here."

"I . . . Yes." Krista signed her name on the piece of paper.

"Keep the coffee carafes full. They don't want to wait for the Keurig to brew. And switch that thing to night service." Vesta reached across and did it herself. "You'll have to check messages. About every five minutes. See if it's Mr. Mooring or Mr. Sandlewood."

"Mooring and Sandlewood," Krista repeated.

"They may phone before they come over. They're from Tripoli Exploration." Vesta checked her watch again. "Should be here any minute." She set her file on the desk and opened it. "These are the latest figures Mr. Diamond has come up with. You'll need to input them and print out six copies."

"Six." Krista studied the sheets. Standard Excel format. "And the file name is?"

"Tripoli-Bergren. Password is—" Vesta paused, looking slightly flustered. Vesta never got flustered. She leaned her head toward Krista, and whispered, "Logan."

Five minutes later, Krista was working at Vesta's desk. She'd relayed the night service to Vesta's phone and she'd taken a moment to set a fresh carafe of coffee to brew. The office was quiet by the time she'd crossed the hall to the executive offices. Vesta's message light was already blinking.

Krista cleared the messages—a well supplier looking for Roger Claymore, an unidentified male voice asking for Jenny Reginald. Nothing from Mooring or Sandlewood.

Opening Vesta's documents, Krista found the Bergren Tripoli file. And the database. Since most of what she'd done at the Saskatoon office had been Excel, the updates were easy to do.

Ten minutes later, the changes were inputted and the copies were printing. As the last page came off the printer, the elevator chimed.

She hadn't known there was another company involved in the joint venture. All the buzz had been about the great Norwegian firm. The experts from afar.

Krista hurried into the hall to meet the new arrivals. She'd had time to find their bios in Vesta's general info file. Mooring was Doug Mooring, VP of Exploration for Tripoli, ten years at that position, a specialist in seismic.

Tom Sandlewood was the number cruncher. Brad Diamond's alter ego. He'd have the final say on whether or not the project was viable. He'd been with Tripoli for the past seven years, having moved through the ranks of general accountant, to manager of accounting, to the comptroller position.

But which was which?

"Doug Mooring," Doug Mooring said, extending his hand to her.

Krista shook his hand. A solid, firm handshake. He was about five foot seven, her height. But he looked like he weighed at least two hundred pounds. He might have been around forty years old. Flecks of gray appeared in his neatly trimmed beard. Gold-rimmed glasses with round frames accentuated his big smile. He was the kind of guy you'd ask to play Santa Claus at Christmas.

"This is Tom Sandlewood," Mr. Mooring said.

Mr. Sandlewood also shook her hand, or attempted to. He briefly squeezed her fingers, like he was afraid to engage her whole hand. This man was taller, not as tall as Logan. But tall. Maybe an inch under six foot. And lanky.

Wearing a brown suit with a yellow and brown tie, that was not tied well. Whereas Doug Mooring seemed friendly, and even jovial, his partner was somber and unsmiling.

"Mr. Nicholas is expecting you." Krista took them to Logan's office.

She left the two Tripoli officers with copies of the annual report and the prospectus. They would have already read those documents. They would have gone over them with a fine tooth comb. But it seemed like a good thing to do.

Then, using Vesta's phone, Krista called the boardroom to announce their arrival.

Brad answered. "Five minutes," he said.

Krista returned to Logan's office with coffee for the visitors. Wearing a cranky expression, Mr. Sandlewood flipped through the annual report, tapping his foot like he was impatient to get started. Mr. Mooring stood in front of the wall of photographs, with his hands folded behind his back, as he examined the photos of the drilling rigs.

She gave the black coffee to the brooding Mr. Sandlewood, and the black with two sugars to the jolly Mr. Mooring. And then, since he seemed to be interested in pictures, Krista brought the photo album from Vesta's desk.

Krista had organized the photos into an album last week—photos which had been tucked in envelopes and stacked in various piles in the storage room.

"These are of the Gavinson and Turnstone sites," she said, setting the leather binder on Logan's desk. "They're mostly of the crew, but there are some of the rig."

"Who took the pictures?" Mr. Mooring asked, as he walked over to stand by Logan's desk.

"Mr. Nicholas. And Mr. Claymore. They like to go out

to the sites as often as they can."

Mr. Mooring nodded like a pleased Santa and, still standing by the desk, he turned the pages of the album.

They could hear the clamor of several voices as the meeting in the boardroom spilled out into the open area. A few seconds later, Logan strolled into his office. He glanced at Krista for a second, only a second, and then focused on Mr. Mooring who was turning around to meet him.

Mr. Sandlewood quickly stood up, almost sloshing coffee on himself.

Logan extended his hand. "Doug," he said. "Sorry to keep you waiting." Then he shook hands with Mr. Sandlewood.

"Take Doug and Tom to the boardroom," he told Krista, without looking at her. "Introduce them to Lars." Then, to the Tripoli officers, he said, "I'll be right in."

Krista led them to the boardroom where Mr. Rodermond was studying the view, his hands in his pockets. At the moment, he was the only person there.

"Mr. Rodermond? I'd like to introduce Doug Mooring from Tripoli, and Tom Sandlewood."

"A pleasure," Mr. Rodermond said, with that slight accent. He shook hands with both men. And then to Krista, "And by all means call me Lars, my dear."

My dear?

Mr. Mooring spoke with . . . Lars. Something about the seismic he was planning to use for this project, assuming they decided to go ahead with it, and then Brad returned.

"Hey, Tom."

"Afternoon, Brad."

The two accountants moved to the end of the table and Krista left the room. She scooped up the Excel worksheets from the printer. Logan would want to see them. But his door was closed. Did that mean he wasn't supposed to be interrupted?

Well, she thought about it, he'd need to check these changes. Tapping lightly on the door, she opened it.

He had a file open on his desk and he was reading it when she came in. He looked up at her, and it seemed like he was looking at all of her, letting his gaze sweep slowly from her face to her feet and back again.

"I thought you'd want to see these."

"I do," he said without taking his eyes off her.

She set the pages in front of him and turned to leave.

"Wait."

Holding her breath, she turned back to face him. "Something is wrong?"

"No," he said. He studied the printout. "I need you to take this over to Roger. He's in his office. Tell him to check—" He reached for a marker and circled a row of numbers. "This." He handed her the report. "Then bring it back to me."

When she reached his office, Roger was on the phone. Unlike Logan, who wore a navy suit, Roger dressed more casually, a navy striped polo shirt, open at the collar. He was leaning back in his chair, and he looked completely at ease.

But then, Roger Claymore always looked relaxed. Nothing ever seemed to bother him. They were about to commit several million dollars to this joint venture but that was nothing to get excited about.

Krista handed him the printouts and pointed to Logan's note. Roger motioned for her to sit. He reached into a file, consulted a page, and then wrote changes in red ink.

Covering the phone with one hand, he said, "Do you know Excel?"

"Yes."

"Then make these changes and—can you get into Vesta's files?"

"Yes."

"Then print this again and give it back to Logan."

Chapter Thirteen

Krista made the changes. Made one copy this time and brought the new pages into Logan's office. He was also on the phone. She waited by the door, not sure if she should interrupt his call.

"No. I can't tonight. We'll be going to dinner," he said to the phone. He motioned with one finger for her to bring the printouts to him.

Krista set them on the desk, and stepped back, about to leave.

"No. You can't come," he told the phone. "This is business." Covering the phone with one hand, he said, "Sit down."

She hesitated, because she didn't feel like sitting. And she certainly didn't like the way he was ordering her to sit. But, part of her wanted to know who he was talking to. So she sat on the chair in front of his desk.

"I said no. And you can mail it to me."

Folding her hands in her lap and trying to feign disinterest, Krista rubbed a thumb over one fingernail and listened to Logan's side of the conversation. He sounded angry, and frustrated, as if the proceedings for this joint venture weren't going his way.

"No, I'm not—" And then, "Cheryl!" he shouted the name.

She chanced a quick glance at him.

Big mistake. Because he looked away from his conversation and caught her gaze, right at that instant. He seemed to let go of his breath. Then he shook his head slightly and returned his attention to the phone. "I've got to go." He hung up.

It was an argument with his girlfriend. Another argument. Maybe they argued all the time. Maybe he argued with everybody.

"These are Roger's changes." Krista lightly tapped her fingers on the pages between them, and she tried to keep her voice even, and professional.

Oh dear, she'd just said *Roger*. Instead of Mr. Claymore.

Logan didn't seem to notice. He was absorbed by the numbers.

She watched his bent head, his dark eyelashes, the way he tapped his pen while he read. Then the phone started ringing again, annoying and persistent. No doubt, another call from Cheryl. Logan must have given her the code at some point because she obviously knew how to bypass the night service.

He palmed his forehead and squeezed his eyes shut. "Can you deal with that?" he said, without looking up. Still staring at the pages, he added, "I'm in a meeting and I cannot be disturbed."

Krista stood, ready to leave. Of course, she could take a message. But she'd do it at Vesta's desk.

And then Logan did look up. "Krista?"

The phone kept blaring, punching into her concentration. "I'll take it at Vesta's desk."

"No," he said, as the phone continued its assault.

He stood, and then, moving slowly, almost cautiously, he circled to her side of the desk. "Talk here." And then he added, "Please."

Please? She'd never heard him say please before. She wished the phone would stop because she could hardly think.

He stood about a foot from her, sizing her up, as if he were expecting she couldn't handle this. Not like a professional would. Not like his executive assistant would. He was testing her.

Was he expecting her to fail?

He sat on the edge of his desk beside the shrieking phone, folded his arms and studied her, waiting to see what she'd do.

Fine. Krista reached for the phone, careful not to brush against him. If he wanted her to answer it, why did he have to sit so close to it?

"Mr. Nicholas's office," she said, leaning across the desk. "Can I help you?"

"Put Logan on the phone. Now."

It was Cheryl, of course. Krista would never forget the sneer in that voice. "I'm sorry," she said, concentrating on the phone and trying to forget that Logan was sitting a few inches away. "He's in a meeting. Would you like to leave—"

"Who is this?"

Krista paused and slid the phone's base across the desk, so she could stand up straight. She didn't look at Logan, but she felt his closeness.

"I'm Mr. Nicholas's temp."

"Where's Vesta?"

"Vesta couldn't work tonight so I'm filling in for her. Would you like to leave a message?"

"No. I would not like to leave a message. I would like you to put him on the phone. Right now!"

"I'm sorry," Krista said. "But I can't make Mr. Nicholas materialize. Now would you like to leave a message?" And then—feeling a little irritated with Cheryl, and with Logan, and with herself—she added, "Or not."

"I've left enough messages. I want to talk to Logan. Now. And you will either put him on the line or you will be fired on Monday morning."

Great. What do you do when you're caught in the crossfire? What would Michaela do?

She'd feedback what the client had said. "You're going to fire me?"

Logan grabbed her wrist, removed the phone, and slammed it down. He was still sitting on the desk, inches from her, and he kept hold of her wrist, gripping hard. His other hand pressed over top of the phone. Judging by the way he scowled, he might possibly throw it.

Suddenly he noticed her wrist, and he let go.

And then he started to laugh. Frustration and tension seemed to flow out of him. He looked like a boy who'd played a trick on someone.

Rubbing her hand over her wrist, Krista took a step back. Her heart pounded but, forcing calm into her voice, she said, "She didn't want to leave a message."

Krista knew she should move further away from him, but she couldn't make herself do it.

"She was rude," Logan said, still laughing. And then he sobered. "Sorry about that." His shoulders slumped and he watched her. "I—I really am sorry. I shouldn't have put you in that situation."

No. He shouldn't have. But, he seemed . . . well, almost like he really was sorry.

The phone started ringing again.

Logan closed his eyes and he seemed to be holding his breath. Then he opened his eyes, and looked down at her hands. She was still clutching her wrist, easing the sting from when he'd grabbed her. He lifted his hand, as if he might reach out and touch her. But then he stopped the movement, threaded his fingers together and tightly gripped his hands.

He looked at her, at the same time as she looked at him, and she felt the connection, the jolt, as his eyes held hers. She turned away, but the moment remained, echoing between them. And the phone continued to ring, its demanding tones insisting on an answer.

He snapped out of it first. "Do you know how to reset the night service code, so—"

"Yes. I'll do that."

"Good." He took a deep breath, blew it out, and stood. He turned around, and picked up the pages she'd brought in. "These changes are correct. Can you get us—"

"Five more copies."

The phone kept ringing, but Krista could hardly hear it now. She could only hear his voice. His deep, soft voice.

"Right. Five more," he said, watching her mouth. Then he shifted his gaze away from her and walked briskly toward the door. "Bring them into the boardroom."

He was all business again, as if those funny heart-stopping moments had never happened.

She followed him out of the office, leaving the sounds of the phone behind. When she reached Vesta's desk, he was almost at the boardroom door. "Lo—Mr. Nicholas?"

He turned to face her, his hand on the door knob.

"What if—" She wasn't sure how to say it. Or if she even should say it. "What if she comes up here?"

He dropped his business exterior again, and smiled. "She can't get past security," he said. And then he settled into his poker face, turned away, and went into the boardroom.

The spreadsheets needed several sets of changes. Brad kept bringing out the pages. Numbers were crossed out, new ones scribbled in, and then some of those were crossed out again and replaced. Krista delivered the updated pages. Each time she was in the boardroom, she checked that the coffee carafe and water pitchers were full.

And she noticed that Logan didn't seem to be getting what he wanted.

Peregrine and Tripoli and Bergren Fisk continued to disagree. And the message light kept blinking. Krista checked the messages. Most were hang-ups.

One was from a Prometheus Jones, who said to tell Logan that they had the mortgage signed, and the final plans for a building at Pelican's Cove. And that they were still missing the last check. Whatever that meant.

And then Cheryl finally did leave a message, saying, sweetly, that this was all a misunderstanding and they would deal with it.

At ten o'clock, the boardroom door opened.

Brad Diamond and Tom Sandlewood hurried out, each with a set of printouts in hand. Their conversation continued as they walked into Brad's office.

Roger Claymore followed in a moment, carrying a huge stack of files. He nodded to her and then strolled across the hall past the elevators to his own office.

Doug Mooring and Lars Rodermond emerged next, still in a conversation about porosity and field tests. They were walking slowly, shuffling toward Logan's office.

Logan was the last one out. He stood for a moment by the boardroom door, watching her. Then he approached the desk where she was sitting, and set a stack of pages on it.

"Leave these for Vesta. She'll deal with them on Monday."

He seemed like he might say something more, but he was hesitating.

"Your messages," Krista said, holding out the slips.

He looked down at the messages in her hand, as if he was reluctant to accept them. And then he did, and his fingers brushed her hand. On purpose, she knew that. And the look he was giving her now told her he remembered, perfectly, what she'd said last Tuesday. The day after he'd kissed her in his office.

She'd told him never to touch her again. Now, she wasn't sure how she felt about him touching her.

No, she *was* sure. She didn't want to get involved with Logan. She wanted this job. She wanted to keep attending her classes. She wanted to finally be independent. And she didn't want to be a pawn in his current argument with his girlfriend.

He flicked through the messages, skipping over the one from Cheryl, pausing at the one from Prometheus Jones. Then he shoved them in the pocket of his suit jacket and headed toward his office. On his way, he pulled out his cell phone.

Roger pushed open the glass doors to the executive suites and sauntered in. He wore his beige Gor-Tex jacket, carried his briefcase, and had something navy blue draped over his arm.

Her coat? Yes. Well, not exactly hers. The coat she'd borrowed from Michaela.

Doug Mooring and Lars Rodermond exited Logan's office, slipping on their coats. Which meant they would all be leaving soon. And she could leave too. But, at this time of night, how long would she have to wait for a bus?

Roger had reached her desk—Vesta's desk. He set his briefcase next to the computer, and then set her old brown leather purse next to it. "Need anything else from over there?"

"No. This is all I have." She reached to take her coat, but he held it up for her.

"Nice coat," he said, helping her to slip it on. "My sister has one like this."

Of course Roger's sister would have nice clothes. Expensive clothes like Michaela's. And someday, Krista would have money to spend on clothes too. For now though, she had nothing.

She buttoned her coat and then stared at her empty hands. All her savings were gone. A year ago, she'd had enough money for university, enough to complete the final two years of her degree. But then she'd met Paul and everything had changed.

She let go of a weary sigh.

Various conversations continued around her. "I'll review those figures tomorrow," Tom Sandlewood said, speaking to Doug Mooring. "I'll lock the main reception doors," Roger said, to no one in particular. "I'm starved," Brad announced. "Let's get out of here."

Krista was starved too. She hadn't eaten a thing since her sandwich at noon. And, *oh no*, she'd planned to pick up some groceries on her way home. Maybe she'd stop by the Mac's store. That should still be open.

Mr. Rodermond, looking elegant in his dark suit and taupe-colored trench coat, approached Vesta's desk. "Join us for dinner," he said.

"I—" *I need to think of an excuse.* She glanced at Logan, hoping he'd supply one.

"Come with us," Logan said, a little smile playing at his lips. "You must be hungry."

"I insist," Mr. Rodermond added.

And so, a moment later, they paraded into the hall. Roger locked the executive office doors and the elevator arrived.

Lars touched her arm, ushering her into the elevator ahead of him.

October in Calgary could be as warm as summer during the day and as cold as winter in the evenings. Tonight, it was cold.

Brad Diamond and Tom Sandlewood led the way down the quiet street. Roger followed with Doug Mooring, and Krista was behind them, with Mr. Rodermond hovering at her side.

Logan trailed behind her. She didn't turn around to see him, but she knew he was there, listening, as Mr. Rodermond chatted with her.

"What did you say your name was?" His accent was intriguing, and it emphasized how far away his world was from hers.

"Krista MacKenzie." She wasn't sure how many blocks they had to walk. Hopefully it wouldn't be far because the cold seeped into her skin, and into her bones. She should have brought a sweater for under the trench coat.

"And your role here is?"

"I'm the company's receptionist."

"Excellent," Mr. Rodermond commented. "The first person to interface with the public." He moved closer to her, the sleeve of his coat brushing against hers.

Krista stepped away, slightly, not wanting to seem obvious about it.

"Mr. Nicholas made a good choice hiring you."

Lars Rodermond seemed at ease talking with her as they proceeded down the deserted street. "Public relations are important," he went on. "How long have you worked for Peregrine?"

"I only started two weeks ago." *And I hope I get to keep this job.* Then she added, "I just moved to the city."

"You're new to Calgary?" He pronounced it, *Cal Gary.*

Interesting. She now thought of the city as *Cal Gree.* "Yes, I'm from Saskatoon." Krista hugged her borrowed coat around herself, trying to hold on to all the warmth she could.

"Really?" he said, sounding surprised, as if it might be special to be from Saskatoon. But he was from Norway.

Did he even know where Saskatoon was?

"I need someone to show me around," Mr. Rodermond said, facing straight ahead. "We could see the sights together."

It was an idle piece of conversation, so Krista didn't bother to decline. She didn't need or want a tour of Calgary with one of Logan's business associates.

They'd covered a few blocks when she recognized the big glass doors of the Timothy Hotel. They would be going up the curved staircase to the elegant restaurant on the second floor. The Pelican's Roost—where she'd spent her first evening in Calgary—with Logan.

Logan maneuvered himself to the other side of Mr. Rodermond and took over the conversation with him.

Which was a relief. Krista sighed. She didn't feel like being sociable. Not tonight. It had been too long a day. All she wanted was something to eat and to get home to bed.

Logan sat across the table from Krista, who sat next to Lars. She was laughing at something Lars said, and she didn't seem tired anymore. She'd seemed tired when they'd arrived. But now she'd had the Caesar salad and the Pacific salmon—and several glasses of wine—and she'd revived. Of course, these were the hours she was used to.

"He's trying to get her drunk," Roger said.

Logan had noticed, and anger bit into him. "That's what I thought," he said, as Lars topped up her wine glass. Again.

But had she noticed? Maybe not. She absently reached for her glass, took another sip, and set the glass down again.

Doug and Tom had left fifteen minutes ago, saying they needed to get enough sleep for more negotiations in the morning. Lars didn't seem worried about negotiations. And, at this point, he had most of what he wanted. At any rate, he was enjoying Krista's company and he didn't look like he was in a hurry to go anywhere.

Except, maybe, somewhere with her.

"Logan," Roger said, leaning his head toward him, "I've got to get to the airport. My sister's flying in tonight."

Logan listened, keeping his eyes on the events happening on the other side of the table. "Now where's she been?"

"Vancouver."

Roger checked his watch. So did Logan.

Eleven-thirty. Lars had ordered liqueurs for himself and for Krista. The waitress was setting them on the table now. Lars passed the tiny crystal glass to Krista. She waved her hand, no, and when she turned to listen to something Brad was saying, Lars dumped the liqueur into her coffee.

What an ass.

"Look, I've got to go. I promised I'd pick her up tonight," Roger said.

Roger's sister liked to tell Roger what to do. "Where's her husband?"

"He's in Houston. That's why she has this schedule. If she didn't have her work, she'd be bored."

"Doesn't she have kids to worry about?"

"Sure," Roger said. "But they're in university now and they don't appreciate interference."

No, they wouldn't. Not those two. Nice boys with minds of their own. Apparently, Roger's sister didn't interfere with her sons. Instead she interfered with everyone else's life.

Well, maybe not everyone else's life, Logan thought. But she tried to interfere with his.

"I'll see you tomorrow," Roger said.

"Right." Another Saturday at the office. This was getting old.

"And Logan?"

"What?"

"Keep an eye on Krista?"

"Don't worry."

Roger stepped to the other side of the table to shake hands with Lars. Lars staggered a little as he stood up.

Time to put an end to this. Logan got to his feet and joined Roger. "Let's call it a night," he said.

Lars draped his arm over the back of Krista's chair. "But she was just telling me about her other job," he said, with a silly grin on his face. His voice was slurred.

Right. Her other job. *Terrific.* She was propositioning Lars.

"It's late," Logan said. And it was time to take his receptionist home. "Come with me, Krista."

"I'll take her home," Lars offered.

I bet you will. Rodermond was a great petroleum geologist, but right at this moment, Logan wasn't sure he liked the guy.

"I insist," Lars insisted.

"She's coming with me," Logan said, slipping his hand around Krista's and tugging her from the chair. "Brad will drive you back to the hotel, Lars. I'll see you in the morning."

Chapter Fourteen

"**W**here are we going?"

Logan was still holding her hand. He'd helped her into her coat, helped her put the strap of her purse over her shoulder, and then he'd taken her hand again. She hadn't objected so he hadn't let go.

Besides, she was wobbly. She didn't even know she was drunk. But she was doing a good job of keeping up to him tonight. Tonight, she was wearing sensible shoes. Not the flimsy sandals she'd worn on—

The first time.

He caught his breath, remembering that night. Remembering the auction, and dinner with her at the Pelican's Roost, and taking her home to his condo.

Better not think about that. Better focus on the problem at hand. "We're getting my car."

She bumped into his shoulder, and then she squeezed his hand tighter as she tried to keep her balance. "You have a car?"

Not a car. An SUV. But he called it a car. "Krista, everybody has a car."

She was walking on his right side, clutching his hand, and grabbing his arm with her other hand. Totally unaware of what she was doing. Totally forgetting her ultimatum. *If you ever touch me again, I will quit.*

So, as long as she didn't care, he didn't mind the way she was hanging on to him.

"I don't have a car." She staggered again, bumping into him.

"No. I guess you don't." Damn good thing Lars wasn't taking her home. She wouldn't have got there.

He stopped walking and let go of her cold hand. Then he put his arm around her shoulders, and realized she was shivering. "Hey. You're cold," he said, rubbing his hand over her arm. "I told you to tell me when you were cold."

She was lean and slender, and the coat she was wearing was thin. Not warm enough. They continued down the sidewalk. If he'd known she wasn't dressed for the walk, he would have hired a cab to take them the four blocks.

Or, on second thought, maybe he wouldn't have. Not if this was what it took for her to let him touch her.

He liked holding her, liked having her against his side as they walked. And when he turned his head, he liked feeling the top of her head rub against his chin.

He glanced down at her hair, at the moonlight shimmering off the silky strands, at her soft, smooth skin that glowed like porcelain. She seemed surreal, like a fairy princess. A lost fairy princess. Someone who was powerful, and fragile, at the same time. If she hadn't been drunk, he'd have kissed her.

"Oh!"

Now what? "What do you mean, oh?"

"This is where you live. I—I mean—"

Why was she flustered? Half an hour ago, she'd been propositioning Lars.

Or, maybe not. Maybe Lars had been propositioning her? Anyway, right at this moment, the fact that she was— or had been—an escort, didn't seem to matter. He expected she hadn't had a lot of control over her life.

Even now, she didn't seem to have a lot of control, not

the way she tiptoed around him at the office.

Except for last Tuesday, when she'd told him she would not put up with him kissing her.

Since then, she'd been avoiding him. Yesterday, she'd turned on her heel and headed back into the reception area, rather than risk riding down the elevator with him. And today, every time she'd come into his office, she'd been in a hurry to leave.

"I mean," she said, carefully enunciating the words, "we're not going to your place."

"We're not going in," Logan said, and he felt her relax. "We're going down to the garage to get the car."

A few moments later, he settled her in the passenger seat. She leaned her head back on the headrest, exposing her pale white throat. He felt an overwhelming urge to kiss her throat, and—

God. He closed his eyes. What was he doing?

He was tired, that was all. It had been a long, unproductive day. "What's your address?"

She gave it to him. A Kensington address. He knew the area. Lots of expensive in-fills, and falling-down old houses.

She was in one of the falling-down old ones. He parked in front of a small one-story house with faded white siding and a closed-in porch. The lights were out in the house, but the street light illuminated a sign in the window of the porch. It said, *Apartment for Rent.*

He frowned. So the tiny house was divided into apartments? How many?

"Thanks, Logan," she said, as she fumbled out of her seat belt and bent her head to look for her purse. Her hair cascaded over her face.

He got out and walked around to her door. When he reached her side of the car, she was attempting to get out and she stumbled into him. He caught her and held her until she was steady.

"I'm all right."

"You drink too much." He gripped her shoulders.

"I do not," she said, forcing herself to stand up straight. She put her hand on his chest and pushed away from him, indignant. "I had one glass of wine. I'm a little tired, that's all." And then she added, "I was up very early this moring. Morning."

Right.

He slipped his arm around her waist. "I'll walk you to your door."

"You don't need to do that. It's late. You need to get home too."

"Come on." He'd better make sure she'd got the address right.

He had to let go of her when they reached the narrow sidewalk that led to the back of the house. The stones were broken and an overgrown caragana hedge crowded the space. A light was on in the basement, shining a dim glow through windows of opaque glass blocks. At the back of the house, a rickety set of stairs led up to the first story.

He stayed close behind her as she climbed the unsteady steps. A cold breeze blew across the small backyard, swirling dead leaves and whipping her coat against her legs.

On the landing at the top, she leaned her head against the door frame and closed her eyes for a second.

"Give me the key."

"I don't have one," she said, opening her purse and searching inside it.

"What do you mean, you don't have a key?"

"It broke," she said, with a sleepy voice. "In the lock." The wind blew her hair across her face and she pushed it back. "The landlord still needs to replace it." She produced a credit card from her purse. "I use this. See?" She slipped the card into the space between the door and the frame and started to jiggle it.

Good thing he'd walked her to the door.

"Let me." He had the lock open in a second and then they were inside, out of the cold, standing on a four foot square landing. A narrow flight of stairs led to the basement. Soft warm light reached up the stairs.

At the bottom, he could see a small lantern-shaped brass lamp sitting on a tiny wooden table pushed up against the wall. A faint scent of lemon filled the air.

"No one lives upstairs?"

"No. They moved out. Last week. Said they were sick of the place."

"Why?"

"Hard to get the landlord to fix anything," she said, as she staggered toward the staircase.

He caught her arm and stopped her. Bad enough Sammie was in the hospital with a broken leg. He didn't need his receptionist getting hurt too.

He dropped her credit card in his coat pocket and hurried down the stairs ahead of her. When he turned around, she was right behind him. He caught her hands, and she practically fell into him, her face landing on his chest. He spread his hands around her waist. And, once again, he had a sense of fragility. And freshness.

She smelled like roses. Her hair. And her skin. He let his mouth brush over the top of her head, his lips tasting her hair.

She stood up straight, catching her breath. And seemingly unaware of the effect she was having on him. Her purse slipped off her shoulder and landed on the floor by her feet. Then she started unbuttoning her coat.

He had a ridiculous urge to help her with the buttons. Distracting himself, he took her credit card out of his pocket. As he was about to set it on the little table, he took a look at it. A shiny gold card with a spray of lighter gold on the edge.

"Krista," he said, "this card is expired."

"I know." She yawned. She had the coat undone now. "I use it to open the door."

The table was made of natural pine and it had a small red-checked tablecloth placed diagonally over it, so that most of the wood was exposed. The lantern sat on top of the tablecloth. There were two wooden chairs tucked under the table, but not natural wood. One was painted light green, the other, red.

Krista draped her coat over the back of the chair, navy blue on red, and then started to wobble toward the—

Bed? It looked as if it could fold up to become a couch, but now it was opened and covered with a beige sheet, pillows, and a tumbled red floral comforter.

There was only the one small room in this basement apartment, and little furniture: the table, the two chairs, the bed-couch and a coffee table in front of the bed. Not really a coffee table, some kind of hinged wooden box, painted the same light green as that one wooden chair. Books and papers were scattered over the top of it.

Krista was carefully making her way around the green box of a coffee table.

Catching hold of her arm, he helped her toward the bed-couch. She collapsed onto it, in a pitiful little heap, her legs still touching the floor, her hair falling over her face. He'd better remove her shoes.

He bent, took hold of her ankles—cold—and lifted her legs up onto the bed. Her dark brown shoes were low-heeled and laced up. Kneeling, he tugged one lace until it loosened. Then he eased her little foot out of the shoe. Her skin was icy. Unable to stop himself, he wrapped his hands around her foot, and held it for a few seconds.

He quickly removed her other shoe, dropped it on the floor, and stood up.

Folding his arms, he looked down at her—sound

asleep, again. For an escort, she sure couldn't tolerate alcohol.

He couldn't keep from smiling. How many guys had she fallen asleep on? Was that why she was getting out of the escort business?

Part of her blouse had pulled out of the waistband of her skirt. Maybe he should—

No.

He wasn't undressing her this time. No way in hell. He picked up the rose-patterned comforter, shook it out and settled it over her. Then he fluffed up the pillows.

There were two of them, the same pattern as the comforter. He took one, and knelt down again. Lifting her head, he tucked the pillow under her cheek. Then he moved her hair out of her eyes, trying not to touch her skin. A strand of hair wisped over her lips. He carefully brushed it aside.

Closing his eyes, he caught his breath. He needed to get home and get some sleep so he could think. There was still tomorrow's meeting to deal with.

He stood up again and took another look at the room, at the place that was her home.

The wall behind the bed-couch had a little arch over a short hallway, with a closet rod on one side and the door to a bathroom on the other. The wall that bordered the sidewalk with the broken stones had two small windows of opaque glass blocks close to the low ceiling. But the window over the little table was made of glass. It had a thin red-checked curtain that matched the tablecloth and an ornate bar to keep out intruders.

He pulled the flimsy curtains across the window.

To the right of the window were the narrow stairs. To the left was the wall that held a small counter made of dark brown Melamine, chipped. The counter housed a sink, a dented microwave and an old green fridge. Two open shelves stretched over the top of the counter. And, pushed to the back, was a small coffeemaker.

He looked at the lantern on the table and then up the stairs at the door, with the useless lock that anyone with half a brain could open.

He couldn't just leave her here, all alone.

He gave a half-hearted sigh. Then he slipped out of his coat and draped it over the green chair. He shrugged out of his jacket, set it on top of the coat, and loosened his tie.

He was going to have to sleep with her, again.

She was running. Someone was chasing her. She didn't know who it was. It had happened before. This dream. And even though she knew it was a dream, she couldn't quite wake up from it.

This particular dream had a new element. A hammering sound. Like someone was trying to get to her, trying to break down the door, trying to break into her life—

There were voices. But, not dream voices. Real voices. She tried to lift her head, but it hurt. And then, like a tumbler in a lock chunking into place, she remembered—the Pelican's Roost. Dinner with Peregrine and Tripoli, and Lars Rodermond. And Logan.

Mr. Rodermond had been so friendly, and considerate. And Logan had sat across the table from her, frowning.

With a jolt of awareness, she realized who it was—in the dream. It was Logan, trying to break down the doors, trying to break into her life. But she wouldn't let him. She wouldn't let anyone in again. She was such a bad judge of character.

You're too trusting, sweetie.

What she? Was Michaela right?

No, don't think about it. And anyway, Logan was not trying to get into her life. He hadn't wanted her there last night. That much was obvious. Every time he'd looked across the table at her, he'd looked annoyed or irritated or even angry.

But why hadn't he said something before they left the office? Instead of inviting her to go with them? Had he tried to be polite? Since Mr. Rodermond had asked her to come?

Maybe he'd been pretending to be agreeable. Pretending he wanted her there. But she was supposed to decline.

The hammering started up again. What a horrible dream. She needed to wake up, but—

That was *real* hammering. It wasn't a dream.

Her head throbbed. How much wine had she had last night? She hadn't really noticed the waiter. He must have refilled her glass. Maybe more than once.

Oh God. She hadn't been paying attention. Instead, she'd been enjoying herself. For once, she'd stopped working and simply enjoyed herself and this is what happened. Once again, she was living up to her family's expectations and being her usual klutzy self.

She lifted her head, and sunlight dazzled her eyes. She could hear voices. One of them anyway.

"All right. No problem," said a Scottish accent. "I'll check with ye at lunch, sir."

Someone was in the apartment? No. Not in the apartment. At the top of the stairs. Someone was at the top of the stairs.

She brushed back the comforter and sat on the edge of the bed, holding her aching head. She was still dressed in yesterday's clothes. One gigantic wrinkle now.

And then as quickly as a bubble bursting, she remembered. Logan had been here last night. Had he been here when she'd fallen asleep? *Oh God.* Did he think she'd been drunk?

Had she been drunk? Because this pounding inside her head felt like it might be a hangover.

There really was pounding at the door. Hammering. She could feel the cold air from outside flowing down the stairs. Had the landlord finally come to fix that stupid lock?

She hated that lock, and it was about time it got fixed. But why did it have to be Saturday morning? And this Saturday of all mornings. And who was the guy with the Scottish accent?

She ran her fingers through her hair, straightened her skirt as much as was possible and stood up. A wave of nausea washed over her.

She inched around the chest, taking slow steps, until she reached the base of the stairs. Then she looked up.

There was a man working on the lock. He wore a navy blue uniform and his hair was silver. Tools were spread across the landing.

"Good morning," she said.

"Good mornin', miss," he answered, with a Scottish brogue. "I'll have this finished for ye in about twenty minutes."

"Thank you," she said.

The landlord had hired someone to replace the lock, and it looked like he was installing a deadbolt. Which was odd. A deadbolt cost a lot more than the lock that had broken.

She shuffled into the bathroom, found some Tylenol, and washed her face. Then she searched the tiny fridge for some food. But there wasn't any. The proverbial cupboard was bare.

She didn't feel hungry anyway. She'd have some coffee for now and once the locksmith left, she'd have a shower and then she'd get some groceries. And stop at the laundromat too.

She filled the coffeemaker with water and reached for

the box of filters. Almost empty. She settled a filter into the unit, added the coffee and plugged it in. Then she slumped down on the empty chair by the table. Her navy blue trench coat, Michaela's coat, was on the back of the red chair.

A sudden warmth washed over her. He'd brought her home. Walked her to her door. Almost like he cared about her.

She laughed to herself. Silly fantasy. Men like Logan Nicholas did not care about women like her. They wanted sophisticated, self-assured women. Like Cheryl.

A flash of sunlight bounced off the table—off the gold credit card that was propped against the lantern. She picked up the old card, and let her shoulders droop.

She'd kept this card. Mostly to remind herself of what had happened with Paul. Her credit card debt was almost paid off. She was close to being free.

The hammering started again. She tapped the card on the table. At least it had been useful for opening the door.

She squeezed her eyes shut. What about last night? She couldn't get a clear picture. How bad had it been? Had she made a fool of herself? *Please, no.* Why did this have to happen?

The wine. Obviously, the wine had affected her a lot more than she'd thought it would. But what did she expect? She hadn't eaten a thing since noon and then she'd missed dinner and so the wine must have—well—gone straight to her head.

She did remember Mr. Rodermond. Remembered having an enjoyable conversation with him. Mr. Mooring and Mr. Sandlewood had talked mostly with Logan and Roger. But she'd talked with Mr. Rodermond. And Brad too. Mr. Rodermond had wanted to know all about her job in Saskatoon where she'd technically worked as an office clerk, but she'd also answered the phone, inputted data, typed reports and generally acted as a Jill of all trades.

She rubbed her fingers over the edges of the worn gold card. She'd enjoyed her job at the construction company. She would have kept working there, part-time, if she could have stayed in Saskatoon and done her university there. But she'd had to leave. Michaela had been right about that. Michaela had been right about a lot of things.

Smiling at the expired credit card, she dropped it back on the table, and sighed. That part of her life was over. She had to forgive herself and move on. And now?

She blew out her breath. She had to study for a finance test on Monday. If she could get her head to think. She pushed away from the table, walked over to the cupboard and found a mug.

It didn't matter what Logan thought. Not one bit.

She filled her mug with coffee and looked in the fridge for the milk. But, of course, there wasn't any.

True to his word, the locksmith descended the stairs after twenty minutes and handed her two shiny brass keys.

"Ye might want to give the spare to a friend," he said. "That's usually the best way."

He set a piece of paper on the table. "I need ye to sign the work order."

"Where?"

"Right here." He pointed, handing her a slim silver pen that winked in the sunlight coming through the basement window.

Krista signed her name at the bottom of the Coach Locksmiths form. And then, taking another moment, she glanced quickly over the piece of paper. And that was when the name jumped out at her. Not her landlord, after all.

The name printed neatly on the top line of the form was—Logan Nicholas.

. . . . .

"So what if he paid for it? He owed you for overtime." Michaela added sugar to her tea and stirred.

"I'm paying him back. I don't need handouts."

"Maybe he was worried about you." Michaela tapped her spoon on the edge of the cup. "I'd have been worried too, if I'd known you didn't have a proper lock."

Krista took a deep breath and let her head drop back. Then she focused on her friend. "Michaela? Who would break into here? There's nothing to steal."

"There's you."

"It's not that kind of neighborhood." Krista reached for the teapot.

"You're not in Saskatoon anymore, sweetie."

"Logan, my friend. You haven't heard a word I said." Roger tossed his magazine onto the pile on the coffee table. It landed right next to Cheryl's stupid poetry book.

Damn, Logan thought. He still had to mail it to her. He'd get Vesta to do it.

"You don't think Rodermond is the right partner."

"Good." Roger nodded. "At least, I'm not talking to myself."

"The man has a solid reputation." Logan shrugged lower into his chair and watched the cold fireplace.

"In the North Sea, yes, but it's a different expertise here. And—"

"And, I know," Logan held up his hand, stalling Roger. "He wants too big a cut."

Roger stood up, slipped his hands in his pockets and started pacing. He paced into the kitchen and back to the living room twice, and then he said, "Does this have anything to do with your brother?"

Now what? "My brother?"

"Because he's working for that North Sea oil company?"

"Don't be stupid."

"I'm not stupid. I'm your friend, Logan. And you're still trying to prove something. You're good enough on your own. You don't need Rodermond."

"We do need Rodermond. He's the expert."

"Yeah. The expert from afar. What about you, Logan? You're not giving yourself enough credit. And what about Doug Mooring? You don't respect what he's done?"

"I do respect Doug."

"Yeah? Well, Doug is having reservations about Lars too. Especially after the way he was leering at Krista last night."

"That's got nothing to do with oil."

"It's got everything to do with it. He's not a team player. He's not dependable. The guy's a lush, *for Chrissake*."

Logan stretched his arms and then eased his fingers behind his neck, trying to rub out the knot of tension that had settled there. He stood up.

"Let's go see Sammie. We said we'd play cards with the kid."

Chapter Fifteen

She hadn't arrived early enough to go to Logan's office. It was already half past eight and she needed to relieve Irene at the switchboard. Krista entered the reception area, hung up her coat and put away her purse. She still didn't know whether she needed to thank Logan for sending the locksmith or be angry with him for interfering. At any rate, she would pay for the lock herself.

"Vesta sent over the Vacation Requests file," Irene said. "She wants you to work on it."

"Me?"

"Frank's still in London with his sick mother. The new year needs to be plotted out." Irene set down the headset. "Also, I have a dentist appointment at noon. Tania will be taking over for lunch."

The morning flew by with the switchboard extra busy and more mail to open than usual. The RSVPs for the joint venture reception were coming in. No time to work on Vesta's file. But Krista had finished Roger's—Mr. Claymore's—drilling reports. Now she was hungry. Lunch in ten minutes.

Logan's intercom flashed. *Oh dear.*

She tapped the button. "Reception."

"Come to my office when you're relieved for lunch."

That was all he said. He hadn't even bothered to phrase it like a question.

"Certainly," she said, but he'd already switched off. Her legs tingled and her stomach churned. She was going to get a reprimand for being drunk on Friday night. It was her own fault.

Hopefully, Tania would remember she was handling the switchboard at noon. Better remind her.

Right after Tania confirmed, the switchboard lit up again.

"Peregrine Oil & Gas."

"Krista MacKenzie?"

"This is Krista."

"It's Marge Smith from Girl Friday."

"Hi."

"Can you talk freely?"

"Sort of. I might have to put you on hold for incoming calls."

"I'll be quick. How are things going over there?"

"Well, I'm not exactly sure. Mostly good. I guess."

"Except?"

Krista hesitated. Might as well tell Marge. "I'm not sure the boss likes me."

"I know what you mean," Marge answered, almost as if this was what she'd expected to hear. "He's hard to work for. I think that's why the salary is so good."

"Yes, it's good."

"I'll get to the point, Krista. You've got another four weeks before they offer you a permanent contract. And," she paused for a beat, "I've got a different lead for you. You'd start with less salary, but it's as an assistant to the office manager. So there's room for advancement."

Krista braced, holding her breath.

"Krista?"

"When do I have to tell you?"

"They want to know by tomorrow. Noon."

"Noon?"

"Yes," Marge said. "Frank Keystone will have done a

two-week summary of your performance, but he didn't send it to me."

"He's out of town," Krista said.

A long sigh on the other end of the line. "So," Marge said. "I can't read it." She shifted gears. "Okay. If you don't think you can work with Logan Nicholas, then it's best to walk away now. If he's going to let you go anyway in four weeks, this job would be perfect for you."

Perfect? Hardly. Less money. A new office. Another disruption. Midterm exams starting.

And, she smiled to herself, no more Logan. *Damn.* She would actually miss him.

"You wanted to see me, Mr. Nicholas?"

"Logan," he said, setting down his pen. "Close the door."

She did. "I don't think . . ." How should she say it?

"You don't think what?" He got to his feet.

She took a step closer to his desk. "I don't think we have a first-name-basis relationship."

He walked around the desk, sat on the edge of it and folded his arms. "I wish I knew what kind of relationship we did have," he said, with a controlled, anger-tinged voice. "We've slept together twice now."

"Twice?" She inched back toward the door.

"I was at your apartment Friday night. You were three sheets to the wind."

"I'm sorry." She stood up straight, clenching her fists by her sides.

"You should be."

"I—" She put her hands on her hips. "What do you mean?"

He twisted his mouth, a sour expression. "You were propositioning Lars."

Her arms fell to her sides, limp. "What are you talking about?"

Logan sat there, still with his arms folded, drumming the fingers of one hand against his arm. "He said you were telling him about your other job."

"My other— You ass." She stood up straighter and took a step closer to him. "Of course I had another job before I came here. But I have never been an escort. Can't you get that through your thick head?"

He tipped his chin higher, prepared to argue. "You were an escort the night I met you."

She took another step toward him. "That was a mistake. And I didn't take any—"

"So you weren't propositioning Lars?"

"No!"

"Doesn't matter." Logan shrugged. "If I hadn't taken you home on Friday night, Lars would have."

She was standing right in front of him. "No. He wouldn't have."

"You were in no condition to know *what* he would have done."

Why was she trying to explain to him? She spun around and bolted for the door.

But he was there before she reached it, with his back leaning against it, trapping her. "Don't run away, Krista."

"I'm not running."

"You are." His eyes squinted with a hint of mischief.

Was he laughing at her?

She absolutely could not stand anyone laughing at her. She was done with being the cute little sister who bumbled along and got laughed at.

Reaching for his shirt, she bunched the fabric in her hands, trying to pull him away from the door. In the next second, he leaned down, and kissed her.

She hadn't expected that. And she hadn't expected his

kiss to be so soft, and so sweet . . . and so coaxing. And she certainly hadn't expected to be kissing him back.

He wasn't even touching her. Not with his hands, only with his mouth. His mouth and his lips and his tongue. After long, long moments, he lifted his head, watching her with eyes that stared into her soul.

"Don't do this," she said.

He leaned his head, touching his forehead to hers. "Don't do what?"

She could feel her heart racing. Feel her strength slipping, her resolve melting. This wasn't supposed to be happening. She couldn't afford another relationship. She was a bad judge of character. This would never work. "Let me go."

He grinned. "You're holding my shirt," he said.

She released his shirt and took a step back. But he was still there, between her and the door.

"Krista, you've been tiptoeing around me since we met. Why don't you tell me what you're really thinking?"

What I'm really thinking?

She was thinking—no, she knew. She knew there was a spark, an attraction, a connection happening between them. It had started at the Pelican's Roost that night when they'd had dinner and looked out at the trees laced with fairy lights. It might have even started before that, when she'd seen him the very first time at Kipling's, and he'd sat one seat away from her. All they'd done was glance at each other.

She couldn't understand it but something deep inside her *knew* him. It was as if they were two pieces of a puzzle that had finally collided.

And she was afraid to go down that path. Because up until now, everything she'd done in her life had been such a mess, such a disappointment. She was afraid to try again, afraid to see where this might possibly lead. *That* was what she was thinking.

And she was also thinking she was tired of being afraid, and tired of running.

What I'm really thinking?

I'm thinking I don't care anymore.

She reached for his face, pulled his head down to hers and kissed him, feeling an energy flow out of her, and into him, and echo back again.

Then she felt his hands at her waist. Felt his arms slide around her and pull her close. Felt his mouth, no longer soft and tentative, but demanding and hungry.

His hands rubbed over her back and her arms wrapped around him. Then she could feel his fingers threading up into her hair.

She was transported out of that office and into another dimension—as if she were flying, at the top of a kite, ready to be set loose at any second, and not caring.

"Krista," he said, his voice soft, as though he was tasting her name, as well as her skin. He trailed kisses down her throat. His arm was behind her back, holding her close. His other hand massaged her shoulders, gripping, squeezing. Possessing. His mouth was on hers again, sending liquid fire shuddering through her body.

And then she was aware of something else, of a distant sound. An insistent sound.

His intercom?

No! Not again!

Someone was at the door, trying to open it, bumping the door against Logan's back. He ended the kiss, but he still held her, watching her, smiling and looking ... confused?

A second later, Cheryl pushed through the door. Krista felt the kite she'd been riding whirl up, twist, and crash into the ground.

. . . . . .

Logan had a moment of disorientation where his world was spinning like a merry-go-round and then everything jerked to a stop. "Now what!" Krista was running out of his office and Cheryl was pushing her way in.

"You— You—" Cheryl tripped over her words. Then she frowned and gathered herself together. "You're still playing with your receptionist."

"I was kissing her."

Cheryl glared at him. "You've made your point, Logan."

"What point?" He could see Krista pull open the glass doors and slip away.

"You're trying to punish me for insisting we set a date."

"A date?" He ran his hands through his hair. He had to get rid of Cheryl. Now. "You mean—a date to marry?"

"Logan, we've gone out for a year, and we shouldn't throw that away. We are perfect for each other." She paused and gave him a pouty little smile. "Except for these last two weeks—which I can forgive." Raising her chin, she tilted her head. "I realize you're under stress with this job and I understand I may have been pushing you." She touched his arm, and held on. "I'll admit that."

They were standing in the doorway of his office. "Cheryl," he said, taking her hand off his arm, "you are not pushing me. You gave me a wakeup call. And I thank you. I simply do not want you in my life anymore. Now get out of my office and don't come back."

She didn't move so he stepped around her and headed past Vesta's desk, where Vesta sat, looking flustered.

"Sorry, sir, I tried . . ."

He didn't hear the rest, because he was across the hall and in the reception area. Tania was sitting at the desk, reading a magazine. She dropped it when she saw him.

"Where's Krista?"

"She's on her lunch break, sir."

"Where does she go on her lunch break?" He was aware of Cheryl coming into the reception area.

"I—I don't know," Tania said, sounding apologetic.

"Damn it! Cheryl, let go of me!" Logan spun around to face her. "It's over. Can't you see that? I don't love you!"

"Yes. You do," Cheryl told him, as if she was stating a simple fact. But she took a step back. And then she added, "You're upset. I understand."

He stared down at her. Yes, he was upset. Because he needed to talk to Krista. Now.

Roger came out of his office. "Problem, Logan?"

"No problem," Cheryl said, moving close again. "Logan, you must realize you love me. You're going through a stage." She reached out to touch his arm.

He backed away, and studied her.

He'd *liked* her. At least, he'd liked doing things with her. It had seemed as if they were on the same page, in the beginning. But somewhere along the line, she'd turned into a different person. That, or she'd revealed the person she actually was.

At any rate, he knew, with absolute certainty that he had never loved Cheryl.

He didn't know what love felt like. And he sure as hell didn't know what it was he felt for Krista. But he did know that whatever he was feeling for her, it was something he'd never felt for a woman before.

"Sir?"

He'd forgotten Tania was there. "What!"

"It's Mr. Rodermond. He—"

"I'll take it in my office." Logan started to leave the reception area.

"No, it's not that," Tania said quickly. "He doesn't want to talk to you."

Logan swung around. "Then what?" And how come Tania looked so nervous?

"He wants Krista's home address. Am I allowed to give that out?"

What was wrong with these people! "No!"

Logan heard the elevator chime, and saw Brad and Jenny step off.

"Hold that door," Roger called, as he took Cheryl's hand and put it on his arm. He whisked her over to the elevators so fast she was at a loss for words. Her mouth was opening to say something as Roger nudged her inside the elevator and reached around to touch a button.

"Don't call us," Roger said, in a conversational tone. "And we won't call you. That way we won't bother each other."

The doors slid closed.

Chapter Sixteen

At nine o'clock that night, he'd returned to the Y. He'd done a workout, and then he'd run six miles. Now he was standing in the shower, wishing the hot water could beat the tension out of his head. But he couldn't stop thinking.

He grabbed his towel and dried off.

She hadn't come back after lunch. She'd called Tania and told her something that had Tania looking at him funny.

He hadn't set up what happened in his office. But Krista had jumped to the wrong conclusion. It had been his bad luck that Fatal Cheryl Attraction had taken that moment to show up.

In another ten minutes, he was dressed and ready to go. He tossed his towel in the bin and left the building.

After Krista had run away, things had gone from bad to worse. It had been a hell of a Monday.

His mother had called from Florida and said she was sorry to hear he was having problems with Cheryl, but that she was confident they could work things out.

Cheryl must have phoned her. He didn't feel like explaining anything, so he asked about the weather down there. His mother invited them to come for a visit.

Lars Rodermond called and said they should meet again tomorrow. Friday's joint venture celebration was fast approaching and so far they hadn't settled anything.

Then Prometheus Jones had called to say the contractor they'd hired for the Pelican's Cove Lodge had backed out. They needed to find someone else, soon, so they could get the foundation poured before winter hit.

On top of that, Mark Bainbridge had left a report. He said Sammie wasn't ready yet for surgery. So the kid would be stuck in traction for a while longer.

Walking down the dark sidewalk, Logan wondered if he shouldn't go home and try to sleep. He was exhausted and he probably wouldn't make good decisions tonight.

But he was going back to the office to look at the figures one more time. Roger had said he'd meet him at ten. Logan checked his watch. Almost nine-thirty. He had a half hour to look at the file before Roger got there. Not that he expected to find anything different.

Stumbling, he recovered his balance before he fell—a broken piece of sidewalk, where the little chickweed struggled to break through. God, he was unfocused.

He'd wanted to call her. He'd asked Vesta to bring in Krista's personnel file and he'd looked for her phone number. But none was listed.

Now that he thought about it, he couldn't remember seeing a phone at her place. But she must own a cell? Why hadn't she listed a number? He'd even jogged past the house, and gone around to the back. But when he'd knocked, no one had answered.

Because she wasn't home. He would have known if she was there and not answering. Somehow, he knew she wasn't there. Where would she be on a Monday night?

He'd reached the office tower. Now would be a good time to get Krista off his mind. She'd be back in the morning. He was certain of that. She wouldn't simply leave. Not Krista. She'd probably be at his desk first thing, with a letter of resignation.

Pushing through the rotating doors, he blew out a long breath. Time to concentrate on Lars Rodermond, who seemed to have the uncanny ability to know the numbers almost before Logan told him.

Reaching in his pocket, he fumbled for his pass, but he didn't need it. He knew the security guard. The man waved as Logan walked over to the bank of elevators.

Twenty-six floors later, the elevator doors slid open and Logan stepped into the dimly lit hall. The peregrine falcon guarded the entrance to the executive suites. As usual, all the lights were out in there. Except . . . for one.

His office door was closed, but there was light shining under it. Cheryl? Could she have somehow bribed a pass from one of the staff?

After his earlier tiredness, he felt ultra-awake. He slipped out of his coat and piled it on Vesta's desk. Then he edged toward the door, gripped the knob and flung the door open.

Krista stood behind his desk, in front of his credenza. She wore jeans and a long sleeve pink top. At the moment he'd caught her, she'd spun around, spraying papers from a file she was clutching.

A jolt of happiness sent warmth spreading through his whole body. He couldn't help himself. He smiled.

"What are you doing here?" she stammered.

"It's my office."

"I—" She clenched the remaining papers in the file, shuddered a breath, and straightened her shoulders. "I was reading my file," she said, as if she had every right to do that at nine-thirty at night. Then she knelt and started to pick up the scattered pieces of paper.

With a lightness in his chest, he knelt on the floor in front of her. "So?" He watched as she gathered the pages. "Does it sound all right?"

"What?"

"Frank's report." He helped to pick up the sheets. "I've added one too," he said, shuffling through the papers, trying not to let his expectations rise. "Did you see it?"

"No."

She looked frightened, or embarrassed. He couldn't tell which. Maybe both. "Haven't had time to read it?" he asked.

"No. I just got here."

"This one," Logan said, as he found his report. "I've recommended you for advancement. When Frank comes back I want him to start training you as his assistant office manager." He put the report in her hands, careful not to touch her. "That is, if you'll stay."

Up until that point, she'd been relatively calm, considering he'd found her in his office like this. But now she was staring at the piece of paper, and it was shaking in her hands. "I didn't think— This afternoon—"

The memory of this afternoon hit him like a splash of cold water. "This afternoon, when Cheryl barged in, I'm sorry about that. I'm sorry about the first time too. And yes, the first time she found me kissing you, I did set that up. But I didn't set up anything today." He wanted to look into her eyes, but she was looking past him. "Do you believe me?"

Please let her believe me.

Not only were her hands shaking. All of her was shaking. "I can't work for you," she said.

He took the file from her hands and set it on the credenza beside the other one he'd left there. Then, finally, he took hold of her hands, hoping she wouldn't pull away.

She didn't. That was good.

"I can't work for you," she repeated, looking down at their joined hands.

"Please." He had to explain, but he didn't know where to begin, didn't know how to describe this feeling he had.

"You drive me crazy," she said.

His heart sped up and he almost felt dizzy. "That's fair then." He rubbed his thumbs over her hands. "Because you drive *me* crazy." He squeezed her hands. "Stay. Please. I need you here."

Unable to resist, he brought one of her hands to his mouth and kissed her palm. Then he kissed her wrist. And then he stopped. Better not press his luck.

"Sorry," he said. "I can't help myself."

She watched him, warily, he thought, those gorgeous blue eyes of hers widening. She gently untangled her hands from his.

"What are you doing here?" she asked.

"Besides kneeling on the floor behind my desk with you?"

"Besides that."

He shuffled so he was sitting cross-legged and leaning back against the desk. "I'm meeting Roger."

"At this time of night?"

"Only time we had," he said. "What are *you* doing here?"

She maneuvered herself to sit on the floor beside him, their shoulders touching. It felt perfectly natural, perfectly right. Perfect.

"I had to read my file," she said. "I couldn't find it in Frank's office. I had a feeling it might be here."

"I see." He nodded, as if this were a typical discussion during daytime hours, as if they were sitting across from each other at a desk instead of sitting on the floor behind it. "And, you had to read it tonight because?"

"Girl Friday? Marge Smith?"

"I know her. She sent you to us." They sat there, side by side, shoulder to shoulder, staring at the wood grain of the credenza in front of them.

"You insisted on a six-week trial period," Krista said, in a conversational voice.

"I did."

"I told Marge I didn't think you liked me and we both thought you wouldn't keep me after the six weeks, so she has another job for me. They need to know by tomorrow noon."

He sat up straight, shifting, so he could look her in the eye. "I'll pay double what she's offering."

Krista rested her head against the base of the desk. "You already are."

He was? He really needed to consider how he came across to the receptionists. "I'm not going to fire you." He drummed his fingers on the carpet a moment, and then, "Am I really that hard to work for?"

"Yes."

"Okay. Good to know." He watched her for several seconds, watched the way her mass of reddish brown hair flowed over her shoulders and brushed against the dark wood of his desk. "Can I kiss you?"

She blinked and bit her lip.

"Okay. Moving too fast." He gathered his thoughts. "Where were you tonight?"

"Why?"

"I went to your place. You weren't home."

She tilted her head to the side, studying him. "I was at the university. I'm taking a finance class."

"Finance?" *Interesting.*

"I have two years left of a commerce degree."

Even more interesting. "Good for you."

"No. Not good for me. I should have it by now."

"Says who?"

She opened her mouth, about to say something, then pressed her lips together. In the end, she said, "I have three very successful sisters."

He laughed. "I have a very successful brother."

"You're successful too."

"He's *more* successful."

She smiled, a slow curving of her lips. "Says who?"

She understood. His heartbeat was steady and calm now. "My dad," he answered. "And, I know. It shouldn't matter."

"But it does."

Odd, that they both had this family competition going on. "Why aren't you full time at university? If that's what you want?"

"No money."

"Your family?"

"Has offered. But I burned that bridge a long time ago." She grimaced and looked down. "I saved the money. I saved for a long time until I had enough to go back. And then, a year ago . . ."

She moved away from the desk and sat cross-legged, facing him. He put a hand on each of her knees.

"A year ago," he prompted, hoping they could keep talking.

"I met a guy."

Logan felt his stomach harden. "You're still seeing him?"

"Not anymore."

He took a deep, settling breath. And he watched her. The moment stretched. "Don't tell me. He had other plans for your savings."

"He did." A short pause as she looked down. "He does."

Immediately, the tightness in Logan spread. He wished harm on this guy.

"I was going to put him through med school and then he was going to put me through my commerce degree."

She spoke in the past tense. So it had *not* happened. But why? And was she still in love with this jerk?

"You must have liked him, to give up on your own plans."

"I did give up." She closed her eyes as she seemed to go back in time. "And yes, I liked him. A lot. But mostly . . . I think, mostly, I wanted to feel valuable. For a short time I did."

"And then?"

"He met someone else."

What an idiot.

"As soon as I learned about it, I threw him out." She laughed, a tired, sad laugh. "A month later, so did his new girlfriend. He's been trying to get back in my life ever since."

There was a pause while Logan thought about that, wondered if he should ask, knew that he had to. "Are you in love with him?"

"No!"

That was pretty solid. He took a breath, let it out slowly, and tried to get his thoughts in order. Then, it hit him. "He's in Saskatoon?"

"Yes."

"And that's why you left?"

"Yes."

"Does he know where you are?"

"Not yet."

"Do you have a phone? That works?"

"I have a prepaid plan."

Not good enough. "Vesta will get you a company phone. First thing tomorrow."

"I'm not afraid of him," she said.

"I am."

He heard the elevator chime.

Chapter Seventeen

I f he could have done anything to get out of this late night meeting, he would have.

"I should go," Krista said, putting her hands on the floor, ready to get up.

"Not yet." Logan took hold of her hands. She didn't resist.

When Roger found them, they were still sitting on the floor behind the desk. It was a few minutes past ten.

"Uh, hi, Krista," Roger said, with a slight frown.

Krista looked up at him. "Hi, Roger."

Roger rocked on his heels, his hands in the pockets of his coat. "Working late?"

"Going home now." She clamped her lips together, as if she might laugh.

Logan got to his feet, then helped her up. "I'm calling you a cab."

"You don't need to—"

He kissed her, a light quick kiss. It felt good. Then he took out his cell and spoke briefly. "The security guard will arrange it and bill it to Peregrine," he said, putting his phone away.

He took her coat from the rack by the door and helped her into it. They walked to the elevator together. And, for some reason, Roger followed them.

"I . . . we have to work on this. I'm sorry." He pressed

the button for the elevator and the doors immediately opened.

"It's all right," she said, stepping inside.

"You'll be in tomorrow morning?"

She laughed. "Yes." And then the doors closed and she was gone.

When Logan turned around, Roger's mouth was open. Logan shrugged, and glanced up at the brass falcon. It looked foreboding in the dim light. "Let's go to my office."

A moment later, they were there.

Roger was getting out of his coat, ready to hang it on the rack by the door. "Logan? What was she doing here?"

"She was looking at her file."

Roger missed the hook, bent down, and picked up his coat. "Her file?"

"Her personnel file. She thought I was firing her."

Roger turned around, gripping his coat. "She did? Just because Cheryl went ballistic? Logan, what is going on?"

Good question. What *was* going on? He stood in the doorway of his office, trying to figure that out. "I think I'm in love."

Roger stared at him, still holding his coat. "With Krista?"

Yes, with Krista. It was almost too good to be true. Somehow she'd snuck up on him, and eased her way into his heart. Somehow she'd knocked his world off kilter, making him hyper-aware and mentally fuzzy at the same time. Was this the way it felt to be in love?

"Yeah," he said, hardly believing it himself.

Roger lifted his brows, turned to the coat rack and hung up his coat.

Feeling an unfamiliar lightness in his whole body, Logan walked to one of the guest chairs in front of his desk and dropped into it. It had started happening when he'd seen her walk into the Crystal Ballroom, holding onto Roger's arm.

No. It was before that. It had started when he'd seen her at the bar in Kipling's that night, when he'd been waiting for Mark, and Mark had never showed up.

Leaning back in the guest chair, Logan breathed in a sense of contentment, a feeling that all was right with the world.

Roger ambled over to the credenza behind the desk and looked at the files on it. "Uh, Logan?"

"What?"

"Are you sure she was here to read her file?"

Roger was tired, obviously. "Why else would she be here?"

Roger picked up the other file that was on the credenza. The one Logan had left out earlier because he knew he had to look at it tonight.

"To read this?" Roger held it up. The Bergren Tripoli folder.

Logan stared at it, feeling a chill ripple down his spine.

Placing the file on the desk between them, Roger said, "Don't you think it's odd, that she'd be here." He spoke slowly. "This late. Looking at her personnel file. Did she really think she was being fired?"

Yes! She did. She must have.

He had to slow his racing thoughts. Yes. She did think she was being fired. She did.

But, no.

No! It couldn't be—

Except—

Except . . . Rodermond always seemed to be second-guessing them.

Roger came around to Logan's side of the desk and plopped into the chair next to him. "I don't know," he said. "I've wondered . . ."

So had Logan. The chill crept up his neck. "Wondered what?"

"I don't know," Roger said again, thinking. "You met her at the auction. And then—"

"And then she conveniently starts working here the next week." Logan tilted his head, squinted. He felt guilty even considering it. "It's a coincidence. How could she have known Beatrice was going to quit."

"Everybody knew Beatrice was going to quit. I remember talking to my sister about it."

Another picture jumped into his mind. Krista and Lars walking together that night on the way to dinner. Krista and Lars at the Pelican's Roost. Surprisingly chummy. Surprisingly friendly. Lars phoning for her home address this afternoon . . .

"Roger, have you noticed—" It couldn't be. It had to be a coincidence.

"Yeah?"

Say it. Get it out. "Have you noticed how, for all these negotiations, old Lars always seems one step ahead of us?"

"He's got good instincts. I'll give him that." And then Roger caught on. "Or else—"

"He hired her." The words were out and Logan felt his heart stall. Pain hardened over his chest and his lungs tightened.

"To check us out?"

His heart pounded in his ears. "But why? We've been upfront with him. Every step of the way." This could not be true.

"Who knows?" Roger shrugged. "All we really know is she was an escort." And then he added, "Or, she still is."

"It's absurd. I'm not thinking straight. I need some sleep—"

"There is one other thing," Roger said.

Logan didn't want to hear it. He closed his eyes. "What?"

"The night of the auction, I got a call at the last minute. From one of the agencies. I don't remember which one. I didn't care."

"Yeah . . ."

"The woman said that one of the escorts had to cancel. Then I got another call a few minutes later, that said they were sending a replacement and I should meet her in the bar."

Logan tried to swallow but his throat felt dry. "And that was Krista."

"Yeah." Roger stared at a point outside the dark window. "I never gave it another thought."

"Why would you?" Logan felt like someone had kicked him in the stomach.

They were both quiet for several moments, the silence of the late night office echoing around them. And then Roger was the first to say it. "We paid her five hundred dollars that night." Roger turned in his chair, looking him right in the eye. "Who knows how much Lars paid her?" He sagged in the chair. "*Is* paying her."

Logan folded his arms over his chest. There had to be another explanation.

"She has you right where she wants you," Roger said.

And, maybe, there wasn't any other explanation. "Yeah." Logan's chest ached. How could he think someone actually understood him, actually accepted him for who he was, actually *loved* him.

Roger laughed, an unhappy short laugh. "My friend," he said, "I think you have been royally played."

At eight o'clock on Tuesday morning, Logan and Roger set up a conference call with Doug Mooring and Tom Sandlewood.

It didn't make a damn bit of difference. Not in the end.

Without knowing anything about Krista, Doug and Tom had come to the same decision. Lars Rodermond and Bergren Fisk wanted too big a cut and the expertise they could provide for it was overrated. So, the joint venture would go ahead, with Peregrine and Tripoli, but not with Bergren Fisk.

Lars Rodermond had come in at nine o'clock and, almost like he'd been privy to that conference call, he said the same thing. That they didn't need him. He even wished them well on the joint venture, shook their hands, and they parted on good terms. And then Brad drove him to the airport.

"You really wanted Rodermond in on this, didn't you?" Roger said.

"No. Yes." Logan didn't know and he didn't care anymore. He'd been awake half the night thinking about the joint venture. And Lars Rodermond. And Krista. "I thought his reputation . . ."

Roger relaxed back in the chair across from him. "You thought your dad would be proud."

Sometimes, Roger knew him too well. "Yeah," Logan said. "It wouldn't have mattered anyway."

"Maybe you're not giving your dad a chance—"

"So." Logan cut him off. He picked up a stack of papers from his desk, tapped them together. He didn't want to talk about his father. "The reception at the Westin is still on for Friday?"

"Sure." Roger nodded. "We'll have all the staff meet each other. They're going to be working together a lot."

"And if Frank isn't back?" Logan asked.

"We'll get Tania or Jenny to help Vesta," Roger said, then he lifted his eyebrows and looked at the ceiling. "We'll get both of them to help."

Logan wished it could all go off without a hitch. He also wished Roger would quit looking at him like that.

Roger checked his watch. "What are you going to do about Krista?"

Logan gave a half-hearted shrug and retreated further inside himself. "I'm going to fire her," he said.

Almost eleven-thirty. The switchboard had been unusually busy so she was late sorting the mail, but it was done now. She still needed to put together a stationery order, and then she'd be ready for lunch. If the switchboard would calm down. The morning had flown by and she still hadn't come back to earth. Not after last night.

Last night, she'd written her finance midterm, and then she'd rushed for the C-Train and then . . . she'd broken into Logan's office.

Well, not exactly broken in, since she did have a key. Although, she didn't have any right being there, not at that time of night. But, she'd needed to know what was in her personnel file.

She'd needed to know, and she'd dreaded finding out because she hadn't wanted to leave. And now she wouldn't have to. Now she would be training as an assistant office manager *and* she would be seeing more of Logan.

It was like magic, that instant connection she'd felt with him, right from the first time she'd seen him in Kipling's.

In fact, it was as if a determined fairy godmother had pushed them together—that first meeting at Kipling's, and then the auction, and then magically she had ended up working at his office . . . and he'd thought she was an escort.

She bit her thumb. Is that still what he thought?

Touching a strand of her hair, she twirled it around her finger. They hadn't cleared up that misunderstanding. But, no matter, there would be time. Lots of time. Her life was about to change. She could feel it. And she could hardly wait to see him again. She wished she could rush over to his side of the office right now.

Brad came into the reception area. "Got that photocopying done?"

"Right here," she said, handing him the packet.

"You look happy," he commented, as he pulled out the documents and fanned through them. "Want to go out with me tonight?"

"No."

"Just checking," he said, then he ambled back to his side of the office.

She couldn't keep from smiling. She knew Logan was there, on the other side of the office in his corner suite. But she also knew he was busy. Lars Rodermond had come in again this morning for more joint venture talks.

It would have to wrap up soon, one way or the other. And, she'd almost forgotten, she still had to call Marge Smith at Girl Friday.

The switchboard was quiet. No one was around. Better do it now, not that it would matter if anyone heard the call.

"You're sure?" Marge asked. "This job will be gone once we hang up."

"I'm sure."

No sooner had she switched off than Logan's intercom flashed. Krista felt like bouncing on her toes.

"Have Irene relieve you and come into my office. Bring your purse and your coat." He didn't wait for her to answer. As usual.

He'd sounded tired. How late had he worked last night? Had he even gone home? And how come he wanted to see her now? It was only a half hour until lunch.

Maybe he was taking her out to lunch? Maybe they would go to the Pelican's Roost again? Maybe they could sit by that window again, the one overlooking the garden and the trees with all the fairy lights.

She buzzed Irene. Five minutes later, Krista walked into Logan's office.

"Close the door," he said, his head bent over some work on his desk.

She did. Then she approached his desk and stood there, holding her coat and her purse in her hands, as an awareness prickled up her spine. Something was wrong.

He finished what he was writing, dropped the pen on his desk and stood up. He glared at her with dark, narrowed eyes. A vein pulsed in his neck. "Nicely played," he said.

Her ears hummed, and her throat suddenly felt dry. "What—"

"Rodermond hired you to get information on Peregrine," Logan said, his tone low and harsh.

Her heart slowed and her thoughts scrambled. She held up a hand, as if she might stop what he was going to say.

"He didn't need to." Now Logan's voice was level, and controlled. "We gave him everything. It was all up front."

"Logan—"

"As it turns out, we'll be carrying on with the joint venture. But only with Tripoli. So you weren't necessary."

You weren't necessary. You weren't necessary. Bleak and inevitable, the words roared in her ears and crashed through her mind.

He stood there, on the other side of the desk, somehow managing to look terribly in control, and exhausted, at the same time. "You weren't necessary at all."

She should have felt angry, but she didn't. She didn't feel anything, except . . . empty.

"I'm sure he paid you well."

"He didn't pay me."

"No?" Logan stared at her. No emotion showing on his face. "We paid you five hundred dollars."

There was no use arguing. No use defending. He actually believed she would steal information from him. She almost dropped her coat.

If he could think that, after last night, it didn't matter anyway. Nothing she could say would change any of this.

This had been nothing more than a dream, as insubstantial as the fairy lights on the trees in that garden.

"Give me your security pass and your key. And"—he paused, never taking his gaze away from her—"you won't be getting another paycheck from us." A tiny flicker of anger touched his eyes, and was gone again. "Consider yourself lucky I don't press charges."

Time stalled. This is what happened in a life like hers. It was inescapable, and sad, and even funny.

Press charges? She wanted to laugh. "Charges for what?"

"Corporate espionage."

A calmness surrounded her, as if she were standing inside a Plexiglas bubble and safely watching the world from inside it. Nothing could hurt her.

"Corporate espionage?" she repeated, enunciating the two words. "Me?"

"You."

She fisted her hands. "You really think I'd do that."

"You did."

This was what he thought of her, and she had been so sure of him. The same way she had been so sure of Paul. She let go of a long sigh. Then she carefully set her pass and her key on the desk.

In some odd way, from some unknown place, a resolve filled her, a strength she'd never had before. She would survive, she knew that, as well as she knew anything. She would survive, and she would move on.

He glanced down at the surface of his desk, and then,

still showing no emotion—no anger, no regret, no remembering last night—he looked up at her again.

"Goodbye, Krista," he said. "It was fun."

"I didn't bother trying to explain," Krista told her friend. "His mind is made up. No matter what I said, he'd never believe me."

When she'd returned to her basement apartment, Krista had phoned Michaela, and Michaela had come over right away. Now Michaela was pacing from the stairs to the couch and back again, while Krista sat at the table beneath the window. The day had turned cloudy, so little light came inside the dreary room.

"He doesn't want to believe you, sweetie. He's so stubborn," Michaela said, still pacing. Usually Michaela was calm.

"Stubborn? A little, I suppose." Krista scrunched her eyes shut. Why was she defending him?

"He's stubborn," Michaela insisted, convinced of her assessment, and still pacing.

"But, how would you know? You've never met him."

Michaela stopped, stood still, and let go of a deep breath. "I'm guessing," she said.

Krista's phone chirped a message. She swiped the screen. A text from her mom.

Delaney says you're in Calgary. When did you move? You should have told us! Are you still planning on coming home for Christmas? You should move back home, dear.

love, Mom XOX

"Your mom?" Michaela asked.

"Yes."

"She wants you to move home?"

"Yes."

They both looked out the basement window at the tumbled leaves. A ray of late afternoon sunshine peeked out from behind the clouds.

Michaela inhaled, and seemed to gather her thoughts. "Krista," she said, as if she were choosing her words, "something else has happened."

Nothing else mattered. "What?"

"Paul is coming to Calgary."

"Good."

"He's driving in on Saturday and he'll—" Michaela's mouth dropped open. She turned away from the window and stared. "Did you say . . . good?"

"Yes," Krista said, feeling certain. She'd stood up to Logan, after all. Oh, she hadn't been able to explain anything to him but she should not have had to explain. After what she'd been through with Logan, dealing with Paul would be easy.

Michaela straightened her shoulders and continued. "He'll be at my place on Saturday night."

"Then I'll meet him there. It's about time I talked to him."

Michaela rocked on her heels and stared at the old linoleum floor. Finally, she looked up. "Are you sure?"

"Yes. I'm sure."

Logan pushed the stack of files aside and dropped his head in his hands. He'd fired Krista on Tuesday and now it was Thursday. He should be over her by now. He should feel excited about the joint venture with Tripoli, and he should feel excited about the celebration tomorrow night.

But he didn't.

She'd betrayed him. He'd thought she would be different. But she wasn't any different than any of the other women he'd gone out with. Granted, she'd betrayed him with a lot more style than anyone else ever had. Cheryl had only tried to push him into a marriage. Krista had tried to push him into a joint venture.

Hell, it was the same thing.

He laughed at himself. It was hardly the same thing.

And, the worst part was, he still wasn't sure what exactly she'd done. All he knew was she'd been working with Rodermond and she'd been in his office to read the Bergren Tripoli file.

Listless, he let go of a deep, heavy sigh. Then he pushed his chair back, and got to his feet. Turning around, he looked out the window at the jungle of high rises.

Cheryl had finally quit calling last night. He'd picked up the first two times and after that he'd let her leave messages. Until his answering machine had filled up. At least that was—

His intercom flashed. *Terrific.* It had better not be Cheryl.

"Marge Smith from Girl Friday on line one," Vesta said. "She needs Krista's exit evaluation."

"How come Frank isn't doing it?"

"He said you should handle it, sir." A tiny pause. "Since you know the details."

That was Frank's way of telling him he didn't agree with what Logan had done. No one agreed with him about Krista—except for Roger. But Roger was the only other person who knew about Krista's duplicity. Besides Lars Rodermond.

At least Frank was back in the office. That was something. Better get this call over with.

"You weren't happy with her work?" Marge asked.

"Her work was fine. Excellent, in fact. It was—"

It was the fact that she was a spy that was a problem, although he couldn't prove that. "It was a personal issue that had nothing to do with her work. I'm sure she'll make a valuable asset to another firm."

Marge didn't say anything. Probably didn't get that kind of evaluation every day. He couldn't resist asking. "Where are you sending her now?"

There was a long pause on the other end of the line. Logan realized this was none of his business and he doubted Marge would tell him.

But she did, continuing the conversation as if his question were an ordinary one. "I don't have anything appropriate for her at the moment, but she says she needs work, so I'm sending her over to Heart Well Supplies. She'll be doing filing for them. She's overqualified, but she took the job."

How badly did she need a job? Hadn't Rodermond paid her enough? And what if she was a liability at her new job?

On second thought, it wasn't like she could do any damage at a well supplies company. Logan shrugged and looked out the window.

Marge kept talking. "How's the new receptionist we sent you?"

"She's learning," Logan said, and he rang off.

He couldn't help thinking about Krista, working in some dusty file room. She'd probably have their whole filing system revamped by the weekend.

His intercom flashed again. "Yes?"

"Your mother on line three," Vesta said.

Logan scrunched his eyes shut. Not now. Why couldn't Cheryl leave his mother alone? He tapped the line button.

"Logan, dear?"

"Hi, Mom." This would be the lecture about the need for a corporate wife.

"I—" She paused, uncertain for once. "Your father said I shouldn't call, but, I need to say this."

Logan listened.

"Logan? Are you there?"

"I'm here."

"I wanted to tell you, that whatever is happening with you and Cheryl . . . it's all right."

Now what? "What do you mean?"

"I mean—" She stopped, as if she were unsure of how to continue.

His mother? Unsure?

And then her words poured out. "I mean that woman has been phoning me every day. And leaving messages. And telling me what I should tell you, and—I can't believe I encouraged you to go out with her."

His mother didn't usually get this worked up. He didn't know what to say. "Uh, Mom—"

"I mean, I hope—"

Her tone was more tentative now. She never sounded tentative. "I hope this is really over, dear. But if it isn't— well, I shouldn't be interfering. And, I guess I need to mind my own business. I'm sorry, Logan."

He felt like laughing. "It's all right, Mom," he told her. "Cheryl is history."

"Oh." He heard his mother let go of a big breath. "Oh, that's so good to hear," she said. "And don't you worry, dear. I'm sure you'll find someone that's perfect for you. It will happen in its own time. Oh, and Logan?"

"Yes?"

"Your father," she said. "He's very proud of your new venture."

"He is?"

"Of course, he is. You know he never says much, but

he's proud of you. I am too. You've done very well, dear."

"Thanks, Mom."

He rang off. It was a crazy day, a crazy week. And it wasn't over yet.

Chapter Eighteen

The Friday night reception happened and everything went off according to plan. As the celebration wound down, Logan retreated to a quiet corner of the big hall and stood next to some potted ferns. A few minutes later, Doug Mooring found him.

Doug had a glass of beer in his hand. "Good party, Logan," he said, as he surveyed the noisy room. With his round spectacles and his girth, Doug looked like a happy grandfather at a family reunion. "I'm glad the staff are getting to know each other," he said. "And I'm glad you decided against your North Sea expert."

"Me, too," Logan admitted.

They stood side by side on the edge of the room, watching as Peregrine staff mingled with Tripoli staff, and waiters wove through the sea of people carrying drinks and appetizers.

"Where's Krista?" Doug asked. "Is that her name? The assistant that was helping us that night?"

"She's no longer with us."

"No?" Doug frowned for a moment. "Pity."

Logan was saved from further comment by the arrival of Frank Keystone, who staggered a little as he approached. Logan made a mental note to have Vesta keep an eye on him.

"How's your mother doing?" Logan asked.

"She's home now," Frank said, and then he hiccupped. "Got 'er daughters. Don't need me."

Frank seemed relieved to be back in Calgary, and maybe a little sad too, because he wasn't needed at home. Doug Mooring excused himself and left Frank with Logan.

"Sometime yer gonna haf t'explain to me what happen'd," Frank slurred, pointing his empty wine glass at Logan's chest.

"What do you mean, what happened?"

"With Krista." Frank pinged his fingernail on the edge of his glass and tried to stand up straight.

Naturally, Frank would want an explanation. But Logan didn't want to give him one. So he said, "How's the latest receptionist?"

"Marge Smith sent the new temp this morning. We got the electrical repaired last night, 'bout eight o'clock."

"Coffee?" Logan asked. "Was that it?"

"Yeah," Frank grinned. "She spilled a whole mug o' coffee all over the switchboard. I think you made 'er nervous."

Logan shrugged. So, he made people nervous. So what? He was the boss.

"But this one refuses t' do any mail," Frank continued. "Or photocopyin'."

Everyone missed Krista. No one had asked what happened, except for Frank. And Frank wouldn't have asked, except he'd been drinking. The rest of the staff would assume that Logan was hard to work for.

Hell, maybe he *was* hard to work for. He'd have to think about that. Later.

The next person to drop by was Prometheus Jones. "Good to see you, Frank," he said. "How's your mother doing?"

"She's much better, thanks. Had a gall bladder

operation and she's recoverin' nicely. All o' my sisters are takin' care of her."

"Out of the hospital?"

"Dis morning," Frank said. He left Logan with Pro and went to get a refill on his wine.

"He's a little stressed out about his mother," Pro said.

"Yeah. Don't worry. I'll get him a cab."

They watched the crowd ebb and flow around them. And then Pro said, "Ryder found us a new contractor. Construction has started on the main lodge at Pelican's Cove."

Logan nodded. At least something good had come from that auction.

"And Hayden Bonningham is getting a divorce."

"You're kidding? What happened?"

Pro smiled. Pro didn't like Hayden Bonningham either. "His wife caught him with his office manager, in a rather uncompromising position."

Logan laughed and, unbidden, he remembered how he hadn't wanted Hayden Bonningham to win Krista that night. So Logan had won her instead.

Suddenly Roger was there, patting Pro on the back. "Hey, Pro," he said. "I hear we're gonna have a lodge by next summer."

"That's the story." Pro nodded. "And by the way, congratulations on your new venture. You guys will do well. You always have."

Pro wandered off, and Roger moved closer to Logan. "Sammie will be getting his leg pinned on Monday."

"And then a walking cast?"

"That's right. And, he's doing well with his two grade twelve courses."

"Good. Keep paying for the tutor until he graduates."

"He probably doesn't need her."

"Pay for her."

Roger watched the group for a few moments. "Cheryl quit calling you yet?"

"I think so," Logan told him. It was probably something his mother had said.

"Good. That's good." Roger sipped his wine. He seemed to be enjoying the event.

"My brother called last night," Logan said. He wanted Roger to know.

"Really?" Roger smiled and rocked on his heels.

"Yeah. Wanted to congratulate me on the joint venture. I think he was genuine."

"I'm sure he is, Logan. You're too hard on yourself."

Like a chunk of information knocking into place, the realization hit him. He'd never felt accepted by his family before, never felt like he'd done enough. Whatever enough was. Maybe things were changing.

"My sister wants us to come for dinner tomorrow night," Roger said.

And some things never changed, like Roger's sister. "The last time I had dinner at her place, there was a sweet young thing sitting next to me."

"She means well," Roger said. He leaned against the wall, with a casual, relaxed posture.

No doubt, Roger had already told his sister about Logan, and it being over with Cheryl. He turned to Roger. "So?"

"So what?"

"So, she's going to invite some lovely young lady, right?"

"She didn't say."

She didn't have to. Roger's sister liked to plan parties and play matchmaker. She also did some kind of volunteer work, but usually only when her husband was out of town.

"What exactly does your sister do anyway? Besides throw parties?"

"Writes curriculum," Roger said.

"Yes." Logan already knew that. "For career planning."

Roger waved to a passing server, who presented a tray of appetizers. Roger piled some shrimp onto a napkin. "That, and she gives motivational talks."

"She does?"

"Yeah. To women who're changing careers. Want some shrimp?"

"No, thanks. Is that why she was in Vancouver last week?"

"Yeah," Roger said. "Hey look, I think Brad's hitting on Jenny."

"She actually gives motivational talks in Vancouver." Logan shrugged. "Who knew?"

"In Vancouver." Roger absently watched the noisy crowd. "And in Calgary. And Edmonton. A couple of times in Saskatoon. Next month, I think she flies out to Regina."

Imagine that. The woman made herself useful. He'd thought she only planned dinner parties—and tried to hook him up with her eligible friends.

At four o'clock the next afternoon, Logan huddled in his chair, watching the flames flicker across the grate. He'd finished his run, showered and made his decision. He was canceling dinner with Roger and Roger's sister. Instead, he was going to find Krista and he was going to make her explain.

Roger came into the living room. "Maid in today?"

"Yeah. Why?"

"She left something for you. On the kitchen counter."

"What?" Logan twisted around to see Roger.

"A shoe." Roger dangled the strap of a gold sandal. Krista's sandal.

"She left a note." Roger held up the scrap of paper. "It says *from behind couch*."

Krista hadn't said anything. Probably hadn't wanted to talk about her retreat that morning. What was it? Three weeks ago?

"You ready to leave?"

Maybe she'd left because she'd heard him on the phone with Cheryl that morning? And maybe, she'd assumed—

"Logan?"

"What?"

"Let's go."

The fire danced over the grate, swirling patterns of blue and gold and purple. "I can't."

"Why not?"

"I have to return her sandal."

"Cheryl?"

"No. It belongs to Krista."

"Krista?" Roger plopped down on the couch.

"She must have left it here. The night I met her."

"You brought her here?" Roger's eyes widened. He set the sandal on the coffee table. On top of Cheryl's poetry book.

"I took her out to dinner," Logan told him. "After the auction. And then we came here, so I could deal with the Gavinson site. She fell asleep."

Roger was staring, with a funny look on his face.

"She did. She fell asleep."

"Right." Roger snorted.

Logan didn't care. Usually he cared what his friend thought, but not tonight. Closing his eyes, Logan said, "What if I was wrong?"

"Wrong? About what?" Roger picked up the sandal again and tapped it on the poetry book.

Logan kept going over it. That night, he'd been

exhausted, not thinking clearly. What if he'd jumped to the wrong conclusion? "What if she hadn't been feeding him information?"

"Logan—"

"It doesn't make any sense, Roger."

"What doesn't?"

"Krista. Rodermond. Why would Rodermond need anyone to get him information. He could just ask."

"Yeah, I know, but—"

"What if I read something into this that wasn't there?"

Roger dropped the sandal on top of the poetry book again, leaned back on the couch and spread his arms wide along the top of the cushions. "And what if you didn't? You still can't be sure of what she was doing, so you don't want her working for us. We'll find another receptionist."

"I don't care about the receptionist. I want Krista."

"You . . ." Roger didn't finish his thought.

"And," Logan continued, watching the fire, "even if she was working for Rodermond, I don't care. It didn't make any difference to the outcome. He was overpricing himself and we didn't need him."

"That still doesn't excuse what she did."

Logan stared at Roger. "What did she do?"

"She was spying on you."

"I don't know. I don't—" Logan jerked to his feet and paced over to the window. "I can't believe that about her."

"Well," Roger said, from somewhere behind him, "if she wasn't an escort, I'd give her the benefit of the doubt. But it's obvious, isn't it? Think about it, Logan. You don't know a thing about her."

Logan turned to face his friend. "And I knew everything about Cheryl. So what?"

Roger crossed his arms, but didn't say any more.

"I'm going to find her." Logan picked up his jacket from the back of the couch.

Sighing, Roger stood up. "You said you were coming to my sister's tonight."

"I can't," Logan told him. "I've got to find Krista." He slipped into his jacket, then reached across the table and grabbed the sandal. "I've got to return her shoe."

"Yes, I'm sure that's very important," Roger said. And then he added, "I'd better go with you."

Logan was charging down the hall when he stopped. Roger bumped into him. Then Logan headed back to the living room and snatched the red leather poetry book off the table. "And I'm going to drop off Cheryl's book. I'll give it to the concierge at her apartment."

"Good idea," Roger said, following him.

As Logan walked toward the door, he noticed the blue bookmark, and he stopped, and stood still.

Roger bumped into him, again. "Sorry."

With the strap of Krista's sandal dangling from his little finger, Logan held the poetry book in both hands. He rubbed his thumbs over the soft leather cover, thinking, and then he flipped the book open to the pale blue bookmark. Something about it looked familiar, but he couldn't remember what . . .

"Logan? What is it?"

He read the words that had been bookmarked.

How do I love thee? Let me count the ways.

Yes, he thought. Let me count the ways she's got inside my head. Somehow that shy and timid escort had come into his life. And all the while, she'd never asked for anything. Never expected anything. She'd just been there, in the background, slowly working her way into his mind and his heart.

And he'd pushed her away. Had he really done that?

Yes. He had.

He'd not only pushed her away. He'd accused her—of something huge, and he hadn't given her a chance to explain. Had he actually believed her capable of spying on him? His Krista? What was wrong with him?

Now that he'd had a few good days of sleep and he'd had time to think about it, he knew the answer.

He'd fired her because he'd been afraid of her. Not afraid she was a spy. Afraid of what . . . of what he was feeling for her.

He looked at the bookmark again, unfolded it, and felt his chest tighten. "Roger? What is this?"

Roger looked over his shoulder. "That's the missing check," Roger said, as though finding it was no big deal. "How'd it get in Cheryl's book?"

"Krista." Logan's voice sounded hoarse. "She must have put it here. That night."

"Why would she do that?"

Logan felt all his energy flowing out of him, straight into the floor. "Because she didn't want to be paid for her escort services," he said. "Because she's not an escort." He handed the check to Roger and snapped the book shut. Then he gave the book to Roger too. "Tell me where you found her again."

"In the bar."

"That's it? Do you remember anything else about that night?"

Roger tilted his head to one side and gazed into the distance. "I found her in the bar. But . . ." He closed his eyes and rubbed his fingers over his forehead.

"But what?" Logan fidgeted with the sandal. They were still standing by the entrance.

Roger set the book and the check on the floor. "Maybe," Roger said, scratching his head, "maybe she wasn't the right one? She did seem new at this."

"New?" Logan waited, wondering what else Roger remembered. "What do you mean?"

"Like she'd never done this before. I had to practically drag her up on the stage—"

"Let's go."

"There's no one here, Logan. And if we don't quit peeking in her window, someone is going to call the police." Roger's phone rang and he answered it.

Logan stared at the little blue flowers growing beside the basement window. Somehow they had escaped the October frost.

Where was she? On a Saturday night? Was she seeing someone?

No. She would not forget him that quickly. Not her. That night at his office, that strange late night, she'd told him he drove her crazy. She hadn't said she loved him, not in so many words, but he'd felt it.

And he'd pushed her away. What was *wrong* with him?

And where was she? Was she working Saturdays now?

Dammit. Was he going to have to wait until Monday to phone Marge Smith and track her down? He couldn't wait that long. He wanted to see her now. He *needed* to see her now.

"That was my sister," Roger said. "Logan, why don't we eat. You need to eat, right? Let's go for dinner and then come back here."

Logan didn't want to leave. He wanted to sit down on the grass and wait for her. But what if she didn't want to see him?

He hadn't thought of that. It was quite possible she didn't want to see him. In fact, she would not want to see him. Not after—

A heaviness settled over his chest and his body felt cold.

"Come on, Logan." Roger nudged him. "You haven't visited the boys in over a month. We'll eat and then we'll come back here."

Chapter Nineteen

Michaela's husband answered the door when Paul arrived. Now, the two men waited near the entrance. Paul stood with a wide stance, his hands held loosely behind his back, a confident glint in his eyes, a big smile on his face.

Krista felt a sense of disorientation as she walked slowly toward him. Seeing him here, in Michaela's home, it was jarring. It was as if she were seeing a stranger.

As usual, his curly blond hair was tousled. In another time, she'd thought it looked charming, but it didn't look particularly charming now. It simply looked messy. Still smiling, he gazed at her with those light gray eyes that had once seemed enticing, and now seemed shallow.

He wore a brown leather jacket that looked expensive. Probably one of the items he'd put on her credit card. Under the jacket was a crisp white shirt, opened at the collar. He must have recently changed. The shirt wouldn't look that fresh, not after the long drive from Saskatoon. He must have already checked into a hotel.

Krista blinked, trying to bring him into focus. It was as if he wasn't really here. It was as if she were standing outside of herself and watching this meeting on a screen.

"You can talk in here," Michaela said, breaking the spell. She opened the French doors that led to the sitting room off the main entrance. A baby grand sat next to the bay window and high-backed chairs flanked the tall crowded bookcases. The chairs were upholstered in burgundy tweed.

"Can I take your coat, Paul?"

"No, thank you, Michaela. I thought Kristie and I would go out."

"We'll stay here," Krista said, surprised at how strong her voice sounded.

"I'll check on dinner then." Michaela acted as though this were an ordinary visit. "Let us know what you decide." She slipped out of the room, pulling the French doors closed behind her.

No. Not quite closed. One was slightly ajar.

Krista turned away from the doors to study Paul. He didn't seem nearly as imposing as he once had. "You look tired," she said, feeling anything but tired herself. She felt renewed. In fact, she felt like a brand new person. "That was a long drive. Did you come alone?"

"I came with a friend."

Of course he did. An escape hatch.

He watched her a moment and swept his gaze over her. "Yes, darling Kristie," he said, at last, somehow managing to sound like he was talking to a child. "It was a very long—unnecessary—drive. Why did you leave?"

"Because you were stalking me."

Paul rolled his eyes. "Kristie," he said, in his most soothing tone, "don't be so dramatic." He reached out and touched her sleeve. "Come on, darling. Let's get out of here. We need to be alone."

She shrugged off his touch and took a step back.

"Don't do that, Kristie," he said, standing directly in front of her so she had to look up at him. And then, he reached for her again, seizing her elbow.

"Don't touch me," she said, quietly. It sounded like someone else's voice. Strong. And sure.

He hesitated a moment, keeping his hand on her elbow, and then he took it away.

"It's over, Paul," she said. "Whatever we might have had, it's over."

He cleared his throat and put his hands in his pockets. "I didn't stay with Estelle."

"Of course, you didn't. She threw you out."

"That's not what happened."

Krista held up a hand, palm out. "Don't lie."

His lips thinned to a straight line. "I made a mistake, all right? And I told you I was sorry." He turned away from her to face the bookcase. "Can't you put this behind us?"

As if. "No. I can't."

He turned around and crossed his arms. Leaning down to her, invading her space, he said, "Kristie, I love you. You must know that. You're obviously upset, but you can't throw away what we had."

Krista laughed, surprising not only him, but herself. "I'm not upset. I was. But not anymore."

His eyes widened and for a moment, he seemed at a loss for words. He stared at her, as if he were looking hard for some weakness to grasp hold of.

How had she ever thought those pale gray eyes were charming? "When I came to Calgary, I *was* running away from you. But I'm not running anymore."

"Good," he said, glancing over her shoulder, and shifting his weight. He seemed nervous, and uncomfortable.

No doubt, Michaela's husband was standing nearby and Paul would be able to see him through the French doors.

"Come home with me," Paul said, using that charming voice that had once impressed and persuaded her.

"I'm finishing my commerce degree at U of C."

He frowned and his mouth twisted. "You?"

"Me. Funny, isn't it? I decided to put you through med school—"

"And I'll do the same for you, darling."

"I gave up on my own dream, because I was afraid I wasn't smart enough to—"

"Well, maybe you're not. Not everyone can—"

"I was a coward and I was hiding behind you." Inwardly, she laughed at herself. "I thought I was being so generous, supporting you, when really I was afraid to take a chance on myself."

He opened his mouth but no words came out. Maybe he already knew that. Maybe he actually wanted her to think she was stupid. Would he do that?

He glanced over her shoulder again. His posture stiffened and his pale eyes had a flat look. "You really think you can get a degree? Come on, Kristie. Don't be silly."

"I will get my degree. And someday it will get me a good job."

He smirked, latching on to that. "You don't have a good job now, do you?"

She lowered her eyes for a second.

He gave a crisp nod. "That's what I thought." Taking hold of her arm, he said, "Come home, Kristie. We can start over. I have a friend you can work for."

"I'm staying here." She felt his fingers tighten on her elbow, felt the coldness of his hand through the thin material of her shirt. "I'm finishing my degree."

He smiled, as if he were tolerating a child. "Let's face it, sweet little Kristie. You're setting yourself up for failure."

She looked at his fingers pinching into her elbow. "You don't think I can make it."

"Be reasonable."

She jerked her elbow away from him.

He gave a harsh laugh, that sounded like a bark. "I

don't want you to be disappointed, darling. I'm trying to protect you."

It amazed her, now, that she'd put up with this. "I got an A on my finance midterm." She'd had to work hard but she'd done it. And it felt satisfying, and something else. Vindicating, that was the word. She'd needed to prove, to herself, that she could do it. And now she knew she could.

"Finance?" His head cocked to one side. "You're taking finance?"

This seemed more foreign to him than the fact that she didn't want to restart their old relationship. "I am." She tipped her head back to look at the ceiling. He didn't want to understand. In their old relationship, she had been the one who had given and he had been the one who had taken. He wanted that relationship back, and she didn't. "You can leave now."

"No. I can't. We need to talk."

"I'm listening." She crossed her arms and waited. She almost smiled, but she didn't. That would not have been kind. At any rate, she was glad she'd decided to see him. She'd needed to see him for who he really was, to really see him, and not the person she had tried to hope into existence.

He was losing steam. "But Kristie, I love you." He said it as if it were ammunition, as if it gave him some kind of ownership over her.

But, he didn't love her. He didn't know what love was. And she hadn't, either. She'd felt *valuable* to him, while she'd paid for him to go to school. But she knew, now, that she had never felt *love* for him.

"I don't love you," she said, looking him directly in the eye.

"You do." His face reddened and he reached for her, but he stopped. Almost as if he was afraid to touch her. He clenched his hands, and glanced quickly over her shoulder, then focused on her again.

"You can leave now," she repeated. And this time, she did smile.

He moved closer, towering over her. "And what if I don't want to leave?"

"You do," she said, shoulders back, chin high. "There's nothing for you here."

He watched her for several long moments and then he slumped. "That's it?" His eyes were cold and hard.

"That's it."

His nostrils flared as he sucked in a breath. "This isn't you, Kristie. This is your so-called friend Michaela talking. You shouldn't listen to her. You will fail those courses. You're not cut out for that kind of work. Don't say I didn't try to warn you."

"Goodbye, Paul."

"The asshole had better leave. Or he'll wish he had."

"Give her a chance, Logan. She's managing fine."

"Let go of my arm, Roger."

The curly haired pretty boy was coming out of the piano room. He looked right at Logan. Not at Roger.

"Who are you?" Pretty Boy asked.

"I'm a friend of Krista's."

"Are you, now," the intruder said, balancing a chip on his shoulder.

"A very good friend," Logan told him, struggling to stay calm.

Pretty Boy seemed to bite back a reply. And then he grabbed the front door, swung it open, and stomped out.

Roger closed the door behind him. Logan looked back at the piano room.

Krista had noticed him, finally. She'd been standing with her back to him while she'd conducted her interview with Pretty Boy. Now she waited in the piano room, watching him through the glass doors. She wore a long-sleeved white T-shirt and slim fitting navy blue pants. She looked so beautiful and—

Untouchable. And she didn't look fragile at all. She didn't need him.

"You wanted to return this?"

Roger put the sandal back in Logan's hands. He'd given it to Roger when he'd come in the door and seen that joker trying to intimidate his Krista.

Right. *His* Krista.

"Go on in, buddy," Roger said, nudging him forward.

He did, feeling like he'd forgotten how to walk. Feeling, suddenly, quite powerless.

"What— What are you doing here?" Krista stuttered. She'd looked so pleased with herself moments ago. But now, she frowned, and bit her lip.

"I . . ." He wished he knew where to begin. And then it hit him. "What are *you* doing here?"

"Where did you find my sandal?"

He looked down at the sandal in his hands. "It was behind one of the couches," he said, wondering why they were having this stupid conversation. "The maid was cleaning there today."

"I'll give it back to Michaela." Krista took it from him.

"Michaela?" Logan said. "You know Michaela?"

Michaela picked that moment to come into the piano room. Roger followed behind her.

"Logan." Michaela smiled. "So glad you could come."

"You know Michaela?" Krista asked, echoing Logan's question. She looked at Roger and frowned. "Roger? What are you doing here?"

"Michaela is my sister," Roger explained.

"I—" Krista looked from one to the other. "Michaela, did you know that?"

"Yes, of course, sweetie. I know he's my brother. Much

as I hate to admit it sometimes."

"Yes, Micky," Roger said, nodding his head and beaming. "Now I see. It was you, wasn't it?"

Logan turned to Roger.

Roger was grinning. "You canceled the other escort," he told Michaela. "And you had someone phone me, and tell me to look in the bar for the replacement."

Replacement? Logan had missed something but—

"The replacement?" Krista was piecing it together. He watched her move from confusion to understanding, and then she wilted.

In a blink, he realized what had happened. Rubbing the back of his neck, he looked at the floor. "Michaela," he said, and he knew he was raising his voice. "You did this."

"Don't get so worked up, Logan," Michaela said, speaking as loudly as he was. "I wouldn't have had to do it, if you weren't so stubborn."

Roger's mouth dropped open. "You set up your friend? To be in an auction?" He gave a slow, disbelieving shake of his head.

"I didn't know about the auction," Michaela sputtered. "I thought you were hiring escorts to *circulate* the room. And I didn't think Krista would even get as far as the ballroom."

Another piece fell into place. *Mark!* Of all people. *Mark* was in on this! Logan folded his arms and stared at Roger's sister. "You got Mark to phone me. You got Mark to tell me to go to Kipling's."

"You were sitting right beside her! Why didn't you introduce yourself?"

"Because, Michaela, I was still going out with Cheryl. I wasn't going to—"

"You've broken up with Cheryl more times that I can count."

"That's none of your business."

"Umm, uhh." Roger stepped between them. "Let's all calm down a bit before—"

"You decided to take part in the auction." With her hands on her hips, Michaela shouted at Logan. "Out of all those escorts, you bid on Krista. That must mean—"

"Micky. Quit while you're ahead."

"And Krista! For Pete's sake, you ran away that morning. There was absolutely no reason—"

"So, I take it the reception job was a backup plan?" Roger said, in a ridiculously calm voice.

"What?" Michaela derailed for a second. "Yes. Fortunately I had a backup plan."

"Of course you did," Roger agreed. "Any matchmaker worth her salt has a backup plan."

"You *told* me you needed a receptionist." Now, Michaela was going after Roger. "You're the one that said Beatrice was driving everybody crazy."

Roger pursed his lips and blew out a sigh. "Right. I forgot you know Marge Smith at Girl Friday."

"Michaela!" Logan knew he should calm down but he couldn't. "Why the hell didn't you just introduce us?"

"I tried to. You wouldn't come over to meet her." Michaela glared at him. "And I couldn't get her to stay with me. And she didn't want to meet anyone either, so—"

"That does not excuse—"

"Enough!"

They all stopped talking and turned to Krista. She stood there with her arms crossed, her chin high, her eyes tight. Definitely angry. Maybe even more angry than when she'd confronted him in his office. He was afraid to speak, and, it seemed, so was Michaela.

Krista opened her mouth, closed it again, and then finally found her voice. "Michaela," she said, with a careful, controlled tone. "I appreciate everything you've done for me, but I don't need you managing my personal life."

"Don't be upset, sweetie. I was only—where are you going?"

Krista bumped against his arm as she pushed her way out of the room. "Home," she said.

Three seconds later, she was out the front door, slamming it behind her.

"Krista. Wait. Please." Logan chased after her.

She stopped on the sidewalk, thank God, and she turned to face him. Her whole expression was tight and she seemed to vibrate with frustration.

"I want to explain," he said. Yeah, right. Explain. As if he could explain being such a jerk.

"You thought I was spying on you!" Her gorgeous blue eyes drilled into him.

"I had to."

"You thought I—" She'd been ready to speak her mind again. And then she cocked her head and her eyes widened. She clutched the forgotten sandal. "What?"

"I had to come up with something like that," he said. She was talking to him. That was good. "Because I couldn't believe I was falling in love with you."

Her mouth opened, but no words came out. Then she closed her eyes and bent her head.

"From the moment I first saw you. It started then. Do you remember?"

"Kipling's," she said, staring at a spot on the sidewalk.

"Yes. I sat one seat away from you."

"I know."

"And then you walked into the Crystal Ballroom." He clenched and unclenched his hands, wanting to touch her. "I've never felt someone take over my life the way you have."

She was trembling, gripping that gold sandal in both hands.

"Michaela gave you the shoes?" He touched the sandal strap, letting his finger brush against hers.

She lifted her head, looked at him. "Yes. The shoes and the dress." Then she looked away, and laughed, a tired little laugh. "I wondered why she was so insistent that I wear that dress—"

"It's a gorgeous dress," he said.

"I looked like a hooker in it." She grimaced.

"Escort," he clarified.

"Whatever." She slumped, watching her sandal swing from her finger. "I didn't take any money for it. I left the check—"

"In the poetry book. I know. I just found it."

"Oh." Still looking at her sandal, she stood up straight. "Then I'm glad that's cleared up." She turned to go.

He reached for her hand. She didn't pull away, but she wasn't looking at him. She was looking at the sidewalk again.

"I don't care whether you're an escort or a spy," he said, holding her hand, holding it lightly so she could pull away if she wanted to. "Or a receptionist or . . . a file clerk." *Please let her look at me.*

She did. Her beautiful deep blue eyes were full of tears. "How did you know—"

"I asked Marge Smith. I thought I was going to have to beg her to tell me where you were."

"You did?"

He brought her palm to his lips and kissed her palm. "I love you, Krista. I've never had that happen before."

She looked uncomfortable. She didn't want to hear what he had to say. He'd waited too long to let her know how he felt. She would not meet his eyes.

"Krista?" He kept hold of her hand, and with his other hand, he touched her arm, hoping he could get her to look at him. She did. "Can I kiss you?"

"No." She looked over his shoulder.

"I understand," he said. "I know I was a fool and—"

"No. It's not that. It's . . ." She looked down at their hands.

"What?" He bit his lip.

She smiled then, and her cheeks were pink. "There are five people watching us," she said, lifting her head to look at him. "In the bay window."

Logan turned back to look at the Andrews' house. Sure enough, Roger and Michaela and her husband and the two teenagers were all watching. Logan waved, and they all waved back. Roger gave him a thumbs-up.

"I don't care if I have an audience," Logan said, hugging her hand to his chest.

"I do."

He laughed, and caught her other hand. The shoe dangled between them. "How did you ever get up on that stage?"

"It was difficult," she said, blushing.

Pure joy flowed into his heart. "Do you want to stay for dinner?" he asked, bending his head down to hers. "Or would you like to go somewhere else?"

"I suppose I shouldn't have run like that, I mean, we can't just leave." She looked up at him. "Can we?"

"Yes," he said, taking the sandal from her and setting it on the sidewalk. "We can. They'll understand."

"Oh. Okay." Her eyes lit up and her lips curved in a slow smile. "Then how about—"

"—the Pelican's Roost? That's what I was thinking too."

"Yes," Krista said. "I'd like that."

If you enjoyed spending time with Logan and Krista
in WEDDING BELL BLUES,
would you please consider leaving a short review at
your favorite online retailer site?

~ Read all the books in the series! ~

A Wedding and a White Christmas

On the Way to a Wedding

Wedding Bell Blues

About the Author

I've been telling stories since I was a child. Then, it was stories about fairies and mermaids, told to my sisters when we were supposed to be sleeping. As a teenager, I wrote long diary entries and I wrote short pieces of fiction—that no one but me ever read.

Don't get me wrong, I was not a total recluse. I did lots of "real world" things too. I became a nurse, I spent time with friends, I traveled a lot. And I always wrote.

Sometimes after a difficult day at work, I would re-create the day in a story that had a better ending. That's still what I do—I create stories with happy, hopeful endings.

"Suzanne Stengl has a lovely voice with a subtle hint of humor."
—*A.M. Westerling, author of A Knight for Love*

"Suzanne Stengl's descriptions and characters are really memorable."
—*Amy Jo Fleming, author of Death at Bandit Creek*

Find more books by Suzanne Stengl at
www.SuzanneStengl.com

www.ingramcontent.com/pod-product-compliance
Lightning Source LLC
Chambersburg PA
CBHW061613100726

47898CB00002B/643